The Last Prophet

by

Jeff W. Horton

World Castle Publishing
http://www.worldcastlepublishing.com

This is a work of fiction. Names, characters, places, and incidents are products of the author's imagination or are used fictitiously and are not to be construed as real. Any resemblance to actual events, locations, organizations, or person, living or dead, is entirely coincidental.

World Castle Publishing
Pensacola, Florida

Copyright © Jeff W. Horton 2011
ISBN: 9781937085032
Library of Congress Catalogue Number 2011928104

First Edition World Castle Publishing August 1, 2011
http://www.worldcastlepublishing.com

Cover Artist: Spittyfish Designs
Editor: Marissa Dobson

Dedication

For my family...

The Last Prophet

Prologue

I sat there on the sofa waiting, staring intermittently at the clock, the one with the minute hand that seemed to be racing around its circular course faster than any timepiece should. I looked out the living room window, where I could see nothing but gray skies and stillness. I knew he was coming for me, and that he would arrive within the hour. He would come and this time, kill me. Addon and his followers would undoubtedly rejoice once I was gone. I was the one that they feared and despised, the one they held responsible for the many plagues they had endured.

Having long ago said our goodbyes to our families and the believers we had met since arriving in Jerusalem––the wonderful, glorious, holy city-- Moe and I were ready. We had done all that we could to comfort our brothers and sisters, to assure them that we would see them again very soon. While all of them rejoiced with us that we were about to go be with the Father, some had left only when we told them that it would be easier for us if they did so. Even then, they left in tears for our sakes.

We knew that our waiting was almost over when far off in the distance we heard a low, faint, rumbling noise that seemed to be getting closer. The reverberating sound grew louder and more distinct as the source of the roar drew near. It soon became apparent that the noise was coming from the rolling tracks of a column of tanks. The house began vibrating with an ever-increasing intensity as the tanks drew closer to our home. Several paintings hanging on the walls in the living room began to rattle. They leapt from the walls and crashed onto the hardwood floor, shattering and sending shards of glass in all directions. Judging by the considerable contingent Addon had sent for us, we assumed that he knew what happened to our would-be executioners the last time someone had attempted to silence us before our time had come.

Moe and I looked at one another before rising unsteadily from our seats. We both nodded in unspoken agreement as we began walking towards the door. We were scared, but we refused to stay and cower inside, just waiting for our enemy to arrive. We would meet him outside and face him as the faithful soldiers we were. Each of us took comfort from the words, "greater is he that is in you than he that is in the world." We would not give the enemy the satisfaction of finding fear in our eyes when he arrived.

Our work was finally finished after traveling a long and difficult road wrought with many trials and tribulations. We had dutifully accomplished our mission by delivering the message that the Lord had sent us to bring, and we had warned the peoples of the Earth about the coming destruction. Our work was over; it was time for us to go home...

Chapter 1-The Beginning

"There are more things in heaven and Earth, Horatio, than are dreamt of in your philosophy"
Hamlet, by William Shakespeare

Life is only a brief stop on the road to eternity. Our loved ones, acquaintances, and strangers pass away before our very eyes on a daily basis. Yet each of us carries on with our lives as if *we* will live forever. This is merely an illusion; of course, as it is an inevitable consequence of life that each of us must die. Nevertheless, we blindly follow the music of the piper of this world, progressing steadily on our journey toward the end. We go about life in a dreamlike stupor, living only for the day and for the dollar. We live so entranced and enamored with worldly pleasures and concerns that we become completely oblivious of what awaits us all. We ignore the truth of our mortality at our own peril, however, when we choose to focus on this brief and temporary existence called life, while continuing steadily on our journey toward the eternal existence that awaits us all. It was when humanity lost sight of these truths that it became so susceptible to the deception that was to come, despite having already been warned of the coming apocalypse.

Of the billions of men and women that have lived and died on planet Earth across the millennia, I was one of only two men chosen for a unique and honorable undertaking. A rare gift bestowed upon us from above, though we did nothing to merit it...the unique *privilege* of being the last prophets of the Lord, sent on a mission to carry a most urgent message to a lost and dying world. The message: That the world would soon end and that every individual should turn to the Lord while there was still time; that they should beware the power and the deception of the beast; and for them to prepare for the imminent return of the Lord Jesus Christ. My life, which had started out like any other, would soon end up taking a very different path.

Perhaps I should start from the beginning.

I was born Jonathan Elijah March, on a cold January morning in High Point, NC. My father, William March, was a firefighter and my mother, Elizabeth, worked as a nurse at a local hospital. We never had much money, but then again we never really needed it. We had each other, and somehow that always seemed to be enough. My father was a strong yet humble man who always taught us that financial wealth represented just one of many different kinds of prosperity. He said that while money may be the most sought after kind of wealth, it is also the least rewarding, and certainly the most fleeting. Both parents would often remind us that the gift of *love* was the greatest gift of all.

One Christmas Eve, when I was just five years old, money was especially tight at our house. As we all sat together in the living room that evening my father, who had been frustrated with our financial circumstances, suddenly looked at me and smiled broadly. He then rose and walked into the kitchen, before returning a few minutes later with a blank sheet of paper in his hand. After writing something down on it, he smiled at me once more, wrapped the small strip up in some plain brown paper, and placed it under the tree. "I am giving you something very special this year Johnny, one of the most precious gifts that one person can ever give another," he said.

I still remember sitting there quietly with my parents next to the fireplace, the flames glowing and crackling in the silence. I kept trying to imagine what he could possibly have written down on that small piece of paper that was *so* special.

In my mind, I imagined a map to an ancient treasure, buried by some pirate long ago. I then saw myself standing alone on a small deserted island in the middle of a vast ocean, with nothing but a shovel to keep me company. I began digging away on the white sandy beach, where a large "X" marked the spot. After just a few moments of digging, the shovel struck something hard. I reached down and jerked a big wooden chest out of the ground. When I flipped the latch and opened the lid, my eyes opened wide as I looked upon the beautiful gold coins that filled the chest.

Filled with excitement, I jumped into my father's lap and hugged him before telling him good night. After repeating the same ritual with my mother, I raced up the stairs and after saying a prayer, I jumped into bed. Eventually I fell asleep, dreaming of everything I would buy for my parents and myself of course, with all of the wonderful treasure.

When I awoke the next morning, I immediately leapt out of bed, and ran straight for the Christmas tree. It was the first present that I looked for and the last one I found. When I finally located the small present from my father at the bottom of the pile, I looked back at him and smiled big. With his nod of approval, I tore the small package open, nearly ripping apart the piece of paper inside in the process. Because I was still too young to read, I handed it to my mother, pleading with her to read it to me. She smiled as I climbed into her lap, never taking my eyes off the white piece of paper.

"Your father never shared with me what he wrote, Johnny," she informed me, "so this is every bit as exciting for me as it is for you."

I still remember being quite surprised to see tears welling up and streaming down her cheeks as she read the words from that special piece of paper.

"My precious son, Johnny,

I want you to know that I love you dearly, my son, more than you will ever know. Today, I am giving you one of the most valuable presents that I can possibly give to you… my time. This note, worth one-hundred hours of playtime with Dad, is redeemable as of today. I hope that you will enjoy this gift half as much as I will!

I love you Son, and I always will,

Dad"

I still recall the initial disappointment I felt that Christmas morning over the fact that there was no map and no chest full of treasure. After thinking about it for a moment however, I looked up at my mother and asked, "Does this mean that I get to spend more time with Daddy?"

My mother wiped the tears away from her eyes and answered, "You bet it does, Johnny."

I looked over at my father, smiled, and yelled, "Yeah!", as I jumped out of my mother's lap and into my father's waiting arms. Yes, our family may not have had a lot of money, but we did have a lot of love. Our home was filled with it.

Because my parents loved us so much, they made it a point for us to be in church each and every Sunday. I didn't mind, because I always enjoyed going out on Sunday mornings. They were always a magical time for me as a boy. For some reason, the weather always seemed to be perfect. There could be rain, snow, and sleet for six days out of the week, but *never* on Sunday. It seemed as if every Sunday morning the sky would be bright blue and sunny, the air clear and crisp. My father said it was not the weather that made them special, it was being in the presence of the Holy Spirit. I came to think it was both.

As devout Christians, both of my parents made certain that we were always in church. We read the Bible frequently and we prayed often, because they believed that these served as vital nourishment for the spirit. "People need to feed their spirits, children, just like they feed their bodies," my father often said.

While growing up I always knew that my mother was one of the finest cooks on the planet, and every Sunday she made it a point to remind us. I would frequently wake up to the smell of bacon or pancakes in the frying pan. After returning from church in the afternoons, my mother would always go right to work in the kitchen preparing elaborate lunches of fried chicken, pot roast, or turkey and dressing.

On occasion, an hour or two after lunch, my father would take me out fishing, just the two of us, at one of the many lakes near our home. We usually fished from the bank, but every once in a while, he would take me out in a boat. When I was still very young, he would bait the hook for me so that all I had to do was to sling the hook out into the water. As I grew older however, he began allowing me to put the worm on the hook myself. Most of the time I did okay, but on occasion I would hook my finger instead of the worm, which taught me a painful lesson about the value of patience and a discerning eye, especially when the hook went in past the barb.

I spent most of my father's gift of time on these fishing trips with him. They would prove to be special memories that I would cherish for the rest of my life.

I suppose that my life during that time was about as perfect as a child could possibly hope for while he walks the Earth. They were full of love, joy, and happiness. I wanted nothing more than to be doted upon by my mother, and to grow up to be just like my father.

Like so many other people, I took it all for granted, never realizing that just as all things have a beginning, they must also have an ending.

Chapter 2-The Visitor

"*Faith*, we use that word frequently these days, but do we *really* know what it means? Do we really understand it? Is faith the same as trust?"

The silver-haired man standing in the pulpit took a moment to collect his thoughts. It was warm in the sanctuary and he was beginning to sweat profusely. He knew it was not the temperature inside because the air conditioning maintained an even seventy-two degrees. He was not hot on the outside, he was hot on the *inside*. He had a message that burned inside of him like a raging forest fire, and it was becoming very clear.

"Perhaps the apostle Paul best defined faith in the first chapter of Hebrews when he said, '*Now faith is the substance of things hoped for, the evidence of things not seen… But without faith it is impossible to please him: for he that comes to God must believe that He is, and that He is a rewarder of them that diligently seek him…*'

"If we accept *Paul's* definition of the word *faith*, then the number of *faithful* men and women in our sinful world *must* be shrinking daily. Just turn on your television and what do you see? I will tell you what you'll see; you'll see lust, and plenty of it. You will see the lust for glory, sex, riches, and the lust for power.

"Now I'll tell you the one thing that you *won't* see, *faith in God*. Man simply does not put his trust in God anymore. People today have more trust in other human beings than they do in *God*. Consider for a moment how much faith you place in the men that pilot the aircraft you fly in every day, the engineers and inspectors that design and maintain the elevators that you use day in and day out, and the faith you place in the manufacturers and mechanics that installed the brakes in your family car. We place not only our own lives, but also the lives of our precious families into the hands of complete strangers each and every day. Brothers and sisters, if we can have such great faith in mere men and our fallible machines, why is it that we cannot have just a little faith in the Lord God Almighty, who created the universe?"

The clergyman paused for a moment, hoping that some of what he had said to those in attendance had sunk in. The only explanation he had for the intensity he felt coursing through his being was the powerful presence of the Holy Spirit. He doubted he would be able to restrain himself from proclaiming the message even if he wanted to.

"The world is a very transient place, dear brothers and sisters," he continued. "Though some have started to fall away in the faith, *we* know that one day perhaps sooner than later, our Lord *will* come again to rule over his people. Remember the words of our Lord,

'Watch therefore: for you know not what hour your Lord will come... Therefore, you should also be ready: for in such an hour as you think not the Son of man comes.'

Brothers and sisters, our Lord has instructed us to be ready for his return. We must start preparing ourselves today, by turning our hearts and our minds back toward our God. We must trust that the Lord will do exactly as he said he would, but in *his* time. In the book of the apostle Matthew, the Lord says,

'Who then is a faithful and wise servant, whom his master has made ruler over his household, to give them meat in due season? Blessed is that servant, whom his lord when he comes shall find so doing...But and if that evil servant shall say in his heart, my master delays his coming; and shall begin to strike his fellow servants, and to eat and drink with the drunken; the lord of that servant shall come in a day when he does not look for him, and in an hour that he is not aware of, and shall cut him asunder, and appoint him his portion with the hypocrites: there shall be weeping and gnashing of teeth.'"

I was still only a boy of eleven years when the Reverend James Weathersby, pastor of His Sovereign Glory Lutheran Church, gave his fiery sermon on faith. It had been a very difficult time for the country as it struggled in the grips of the greatest economic downturn since the Great Depression. Pastor Weathersby felt an obligation to offer the members of his congregation a sense of perspective and hope, and a reminder that God was still in control. He also took the opportunity to chastise a world that he felt had become increasingly vile, as humanity strayed further and further away from God.

Though he could preach quite a fire and brimstone sermon when he was moved to do so, Pastor Weathersby was generally a very warm and friendly man. He cared deeply for his flock, even for the more mean-spirited and apathetic members of the congregation. He understood that hard times tend to bring out the best and the worst in people. The kindly pastor often went out of his way to encourage church members to soften their hearts towards their brothers and sisters rather than hardening them. My parents always told us that if everyone were as warm, kind, and genuine as Pastor Weathersby was, then the world would certainly be a better place for it.

The sermon he gave that particular Sunday morning truly *did* seem to spread hope throughout the congregants gathered there, at least for a time. For a year or so following his fervent plea for people to turn back to God before it was too late, other Christian leaders across the country and then around the globe began doing the same, and it seemed that a new revival might sweep the planet.

While godly men like Pastor Weathersby were trying to lead people *to* Christ, another much darker and sinister force was working overtime to lead them *away* from Christ. That same year the mainstream press mysteriously began a bizarre campaign against the Christian Church. Whether the stories were about celebrity clergy caught in adulterous relationships, or new allegations of abuse by, of it served to undermine the momentum of the new "Great Awakening" that was beginning to blossom, causing the movement to suddenly dry up and wither. My parents had been quite disappointed with this development, having held great hope that men and women would begin turning back to the Lord in great numbers. What we did not know at the time was that it was all part of God's plan. That it all fit perfectly into the prophecies of the Lord for the last days. The Lord had been long-suffering, giving humanity numerous opportunities to repent. Soon, however, it would all be over. Unbeknownst to the people of the world, the time of the judgment would soon be upon them. The final fulfillment of the prophecies regarding the end times was already fast approaching.

The week that Pastor Weathersby gave that sermon was also the same week it all started, when everything began to unravel for me, and my world was unexpectedly turned upside down. It was the week that I had my first vision. I was only eleven years old when the dream came to me, but I would remember it for the rest of my life. In the dream, I stood in a hospital room, my unconscious and motionless father lying on the bed in front of me, attached to a ventilator. The machine worked away steadily at its assigned task, removing the carbon dioxide from his body while helping oxygen get into his lungs. The electrocardiogram machine beeped weakly, the sound growing steadily weaker, as the electrical activity in his heart slowly diminished. While I stood watching, the sound slowed to a trickle before stopping altogether. The beep suddenly changed to the dreaded yet familiar flat and steady tone, proclaiming to the world that another great man's life in this world had ended.

My eyes began to tear up as I looked around, scared and confused by what was happening. I was so young and the experience seemed so real, so unlike anything I had ever experienced before. I had just started walking toward his bedside when he unexpectedly sat straight up in bed and opened his eyes, as if suddenly waking from a deep sleep. At first, I thought he was looking at me, until I realized that his gaze was fixed on something *behind* me. I turned around to see what he was staring at and found myself back peddling, nearly tripping over the edge of the bed, while my heart froze in my chest. I stared in fear and wonder at the object of his attention, for we were not alone. A large, imposing figure stood against the wall opposite my father. It appeared to be a tall, fair-skinned man, though it was not really a man at all, but *something else.* With wings protruding nearly four feet from each side of his body when fully outstretched, it stood looking at me for several seconds before turning to look down upon my father, still sitting up in his bed.

"Come, William March, good and faithful servant of the Lord. It is time for us to go," the angel said, extending his hand to my father, who then grabbed hold. It was then that I discerned that it was not my father's physical form, *but his spirit,* that moved. His physical body lay motionless on the bed, the sound of the EKG continuing its morbid announcement. I saw a nurse abruptly fling the door open as the room began to fill with doctors and nurses. Then suddenly, the room, the doctors, and the bed, all began fading away, until only the angel, my father, and I remained.

We were standing together in the back of a large auditorium, facing a vast and empty stage. As we stood gazing at the front of the vacant theater, a large curtain slowly and steadily began to descend towards the stage. The entire time the angel said nothing, yet I somehow perceived that the curtain was representative of my father's life. Just after it reached the bottom, we were transported to the edge of a strange and extraordinary doorway, a passageway that opened into a seemingly endless expanse of beautiful, soft blue space. I sensed that it was some type of passageway, a doorway that opened to eternity, from which no man returned save those few returned thus by the Lord.

My father, who up to that point had in no way acknowledged my presence, suddenly turned to face me, and smiled. "I'll see you again soon, son. Always remember that I love you very, very much." He then turned and walked through the doorway, his face aglow with joy as he did so.

Standing alone with me outside of the doorway, the angel, who had said nothing to me up to this point, then turned to face me.

"As for you John March, know this and remember; the Lord has chosen you from among all men to serve as one of his messengers. You will pass through a time of uncertainty and darkness, as you grow into the man that you will become, after which you *will* be strengthened. Prepare for your service to the Almighty, John March!"

We then entered the doorway into a field of extremely bright white and orange light, and I suddenly awoke to find myself alone once more in my bed. I immediately jumped out onto the floor, opened the door, and ran out of my bedroom and into the hallway. I made my way to my parent's room where I carefully opened the door, and taking a deep breath, peeked inside. Upon finding my mother *and* my father still fast asleep in bed, my heart once more began to beat, and I let out a great sigh of relief. I walked back to my room so exhausted from the ordeal that once back in the comfort and security of my bed, I immediately fell asleep.

I was playing a game of chess with my brother William the following week when the phone suddenly rang. My mother, who had been smiling as she watched us engaged in a battle of wits at the kitchen table, answered the phone. The cheerful, beautiful smile on her face suddenly evaporated, replaced by a look of dread, before morphing one last time into an expression of profound sadness.

"Who was it, Mommy?" asked William, frightened by the change in our mother.

"That was Bob Alexander, the fire commissioner, a man that works with your father. There was a big fire over at a warehouse on the south side of town this evening, and your father was badly hurt." She reached for us and we raced into her arms, crying and scared.

My father died that same night in his hospital room bed, exactly as I had seen in my dream, having never regained consciousness. My grandfather took all of us to the funeral just two days later. I had resolved to be strong, to be brave for my mother. I was now the "man" of the house. A torrent of emotion swept across me however as my mind was flooded with memories of all the wonderful times my father and I had shared. Despite my best efforts, I broke down, unable to hold back the tears, and cried silently as the minister gave the sermon. My feelings alternated between a tremendous sense of loss over the passing of the father I loved so much, and the anger I felt at God for taking him so soon.

At the reception following the funeral, a girl named Lara who lived next door and was nearly the same age as I was at the time, came over and put her arm around me to comfort me.

"I'm really sorry about your dad Johnny, really. He was a very nice man. Are you okay?" she asked.

I looked over at her, unsure of what to say and how to act. I ended up doing what most kids my age would have done… I ended up saying the first thing that came into my pre-teen mind.

"Oh, it's not that bad," I answered, as tears once more began streaming down my face. It was a strange and inappropriate thing to say, I know, but I was after all, only eleven.

She sat there for several minutes, feeling sorry for me I guess, looking at me with sad eyes as she tried to find the right words, until at last she surrendered and abandoned the effort.

"Well, I guess I better get back inside with my parents. I'll see you later, okay?"

After I nodded my head, she got up and walked over to be with her family. As I watched her walk away, I thought about what a nice girl she was. It was the first time that I ever really noticed Lara, despite the fact that we had grown up living next door to one another. It was the first time, but it would certainly not be the last.

"You okay, Johnny?" My friend Bryce walked over to where I was sitting, with a soda in his hand. "I thought you might want something to drink," he said, looking down at the floor sheepishly.

"Thanks," I answered, popping the top on the can. The drink felt soothing inside of my throat, which was still quite hoarse after talking with so many family members and friends. I sat there, wondering what I was going to do without my father around.

"He's gone, Bryce. My dad is–gone," I said, more to myself than to him, fighting to hold back the tears.

"I'm sorry about what happened to your dad, Johnny. My mother said that he was a good man and is with the Lord now. So that's good, right?" he asked,

"Yeah, I guess so," I answered, looking out the window and up at the beautiful blue sky, dotted with soft clouds that floated along like lily pads on a sea of blue, "but I wish he was here with me instead."

Bryce looked around the room, searching for something to say that would comfort me. My thoughts soon turned back to memories of all the time I had spent with my dad, and how much I was going to miss him. Despite my best efforts, the flood of tears soon returned.

Chapter 3-Turbulence

One of the guards came to my cell and took me to where my mother was waiting. The expression on her face as I walked into the waiting room said it all. *I was in trouble*. I guess she wasn't very excited about having to pick me up from the police station, again. It didn't seem like such a big deal to me at the time. After all, from my point of view back then, I had only stolen some clothes from a store at the local mall. It wasn't exactly a major crime worthy of the six o'clock news. I guess the police were getting tired of seeing my pretty face however, so they were starting to toughen up on me.

We were starting to walk out the front door when a man named Daniels, the arresting officer, caught up with us.

"Ms. March, my name is Sergeant Jeffrey Daniels, may I speak to you both for just a few minutes before you leave, please?"

"Why of course, officer."

The man escorted us to a small, plain interrogation room, not far from where my mother had been waiting for me. She and I went in first followed by Daniels, who gently closed the door before joining us at the table.

"Ms. March, Johnny here is now fifteen… he turns sixteen next month, isn't that correct?"

"Yes Officer, that is correct, but I don't see what that has to do with any–," the police officer's hand rose motioning for my mother to pause.

"Please, bear with me a moment. As you know, Ms. March, this is now the third time that we've had a run-in with your boy here in the last six months. The first time we let him go with just a warning. The second time we brought him down here and held him until you arrived to take him home. Today however we had intended to arrest your son, which could easily have led to a conviction and possibly even some jail time. It was only because the store owner knew your husband, God rest his soul, and sympathized with the impact his death has had on you and your son that he decided to drop the charges against Johnny." At this, my mother sighed with relief and sank back into her chair. The look she gave me made me feel so guilty that I just wanted to slink out of my seat and crawl under the table.

"Your son got off *very* easy this time Ms. March, and just barely at that. I guarantee you that the next time we have another run-in with little Johnny here, he will not be so lucky. Do you understand what I'm saying here, Ms. March? The next time, your son will be spending some quality time behind bars, possibly for quite a long time; this was his last free pass. I'm only telling you this because I knew your husband well, and I respected him. This is it for Johnny, Mrs. March, there is nothing else I can do for him, do you understand?" My mother looked up at Daniels and nodded her head. The officer then looked at me with a stern look on his face.

"This is it, Johnny. The next time we see you down here you're going in front of a judge. You have one last chance to turn your life around before it's too late. It's something that most people never get. Don't pass up this opportunity to straighten out your life young man, it's the last one you'll ever get, I promise you."

"Yeah, whatever," I answered roughly, with a bit of a sharp, wise-guy/tough-guy tone to my reply. I thought he was just another stupid cop being a jerk. Why couldn't he just let us leave and be done with it, instead of giving us the lecture? I really didn't care about anything he had to say. I was ready to get home and crash for a few days. What I didn't realize at the time, until my mother told me later, was that Daniels and my father had once been close friends.

He just sighed and threw up his hands. He then turned back to my mother, got up, and made a beeline for the door. Looking at her once last time he added, "Good luck with little Johnny here, Ms. March... I believe you're gonna need it. Just let me know if there is anything I can do to help. You're free to go." With that, we got up and left the station.

As we walked out of the building and made our way to the car, I could tell by her silence that I was in serious trouble. It was at times like this when she said nothing that I knew she was really upset, and worried about me.

"Mom, I..." she threw her hand up and stopped my standard apology in its tracks. She had heard the same speech many times before. How I had 'learned my lesson', how 'sorry I was' for causing her so much trouble, and so forth. I guessed that she had heard it enough, and probably didn't see any point in listening to it again.

We drove the rest of the way home in silence, neither of us speaking another word for the remainder of the fifteen-minute trip. When we finally arrived back at the house, I was ready to go straight in and crash on my bed. I had been at the station most of the day and all that night, until my mother finally got off work at eleven o'clock. She had come home after a very long day only to find a message waiting for her on the answering machine, a message stating that the police had taken me into custody. We were both exhausted. Tired and in desperate need of some sleep, we said good night and went to our rooms. Despite the lack of discussion after getting home, I knew that I would get the lecture of a lifetime the following morning, so I jumped into bed and fell quickly to sleep.

That night I had my second dream. I found myself sitting in a large pontoon boat called *The Wave Cutter,* with the girl next door, Lara, and her parents. As before, I was not actually in the boat with them, yet *I was there*.

I sat and looked at Lara in her bathing suit, sitting in the back of the boat, soaking up some sunshine and enjoying the cool breeze coming off the water. She looked amazing, the white nylon of the two-piece suit contrasted with her dark, tanned skin and her flowing, sandy blonde hair that nearly ran the length of her back. She was the most beautiful creature I had ever seen.

There we were, sitting in a boat in the middle of Lake Norman, an hour's drive from High Point. Lara was in the back of the boat, now busily looking for skis and a life jacket so that she could enjoy some water skiing on the relatively calm water. Just then, her father turned back to say something to Lara, pointing to a compartment in the stern of the boat. As he tried to describe to Lara where he had put the lifejacket and the skis, he briefly turned his attention away from the other boats on the water. That is when it happened. A much larger boat, which had slowly been making its way in our general direction, suddenly shifted speed and direction *and* was now moving very quickly through the water, on a path that was on a collision course with our own. Her father had taken his eyes off the massive boat just long enough to miss it accelerating, apparently in a misguided attempt to cross in front of us. Instead, the larger boat was suddenly on top of ours. Lara's father turned back around just in time to see the yacht smash into the side of his much smaller boat. Lara and her parents were flung high into the air and into the water, yelling and screaming. I awoke to find myself covered in a cold sweat. It was my first such dream since my father's passing four years earlier.

While any dream can seem real, it is difficult to describe exactly what it was that made these two dreams unique, but they were considerably different from anything I had ever experienced before. They were extraordinarily vivid, both sensually and emotionally. I could smell the air, feel the water splashing on my face and the sun bearing down on my back, and hear the boats motor purr as we bounced up and down through the water. Somehow, I *knew* the events in this dream *would happen* just as they had in the first one. Both dreams began with the same misty light, like a foggy morning just as the sun rises. Incredibly, I was somehow able to recall every detail of the dreams, no matter how minute. Looking back on it now, I am surprised it took so long for me to understand what was happening to me.

I sat up in bed for some time, debating what I should do next. I was fifteen, and clueless about how I should handle something as big and as serious as this. What was I supposed to do? Walk over to Lara's house, knock on the front door, and announce that they were all about to die? They would either laugh at me or call the police. Besides, maybe it *was* just a dream like any other. Even if it were true, I was not sure that telling them would make any difference anyway. I remember feeling as if I was in one of those horror flicks where a teenager has a premonition about a disaster that is going to happen, and somehow finds a way to cheat death. Death, however, insists on having its way and, of course, everyone dies in the end.

Finally, I decided to say nothing. After all, it was probably nothing more than a dream. Besides, what business was it of mine, anyway? I was just another delinquent teenager after all, one who had just had yet another run in with the police. The last thing I needed was to be accused of harassing or even threatening my neighbors, causing me to get in even more trouble with High Point's finest. I grabbed my MP3 player, cranked up the volume, and tried desperately to go back to sleep. I laid in bed listening to music in a fruitless attempt to drown out my guilt with song after song. For two long hours, my ego and my super ego engaged in a struggle for the mastery over my soul. In the end, my concern for Lara's family emerged victorious as my conscience got the better of me. I resolved that regardless of the risk involved and the price I would likely pay, I would go next door in the morning and say something to Lara. If she laughed at me, or if her father called the police, I would look like an idiot and might go to jail. However, if I said nothing to her and there really was an accident that I could have prevented, I would never be able to look at myself in the mirror the same way again. With my guilty conscience now relieved, I soon fell quickly back to sleep.

The following morning, I grabbed some cereal and orange juice for breakfast, before heading out the front door to find Lara. A great sense of dread fell over me as I neared the driveway. Their truck was already gone, *along with their boat*. I was starting to panic so I walked back to our house and sat down on the porch, trying to calm myself and deciding what to do next. I kept bouncing back and forth between telling my mother and just calling the police. Given my recent encounters with local law enforcement, I decided it would be best if I woke my mother and told her what was happening. Maybe she would know what to do. If she did not believe me, *then* I would call the police. I was heading for the door when I suddenly saw the familiar truck driven by Lara's father coming down the road and back towards their house, with the boat in tow. *Had they already been to the lake and back?* Looking down at my watch, I saw that it was only 8:30 in the morning. There was no way that they could have made it to Lake Norman and back already. After pulling into their driveway and parking, Lara hopped out and ran towards the back of the house. *She must have forgotten something.*

"Good morning, Johnny," she said, stopping to talk with me for a moment.

"Oh, hi Lara. Are you and your family on the way to the lake now?"

"Yeah. We took off and left the skis in the garage." She looked at me with a curious look on her face, as if she was trying to determine whether she liked what she saw. Apparently she did, because after several moments she smiled and asked me, "Would you like to come with us? There is plenty of room in our boat for another person."

While we had lived next door to one another for most of our lives, Lara and I had never been very close. I often suspected by the way she looked at me that she had a thing for me. The last few years had been a bit turbulent for me, however, and I had serious doubts that her parents would have approved of me anyway. Either way, I was surprised to find myself pleased that she had asked me to go with her; it was a very promising sign.

"No, I don't think so, but thanks for the offer, Lara. Maybe next time?" I asked, displaying the most flirtatious smile I could without overdoing it.

"Sure," she responded, returning the smile.

"Listen, can I talk with you for a second?" I asked, getting closer and looking her squarely in the eyes.

Lara's face took on a puzzled expression as she turned and looked back at her parents. Her father glared at me, then at her, with a disapproving look on his face. It seemed he did not like seeing his daughter associating with the delinquent boy from next door. At that point in my life, however, I could not have cared less. Lara ignored her father's disapproving look, turned back to me, and smiled.

"Um, sure Johnny. What's up?"

"I had a dream last night, like the one I had the week before my father died. Do you remember me telling you about that?"

"What are you talking about, Johnny?" She looked back at her father.

"Do you remember that dream, the one I told you about, the one I had the week before my father died?"

"You mean the one with the angel?" She laughed. "Yeah, I remember. You were only eleven then, Johnny."

"Well I had another one just like it last night."

"About your father?"

"No, this one was about you, and your family."

"About me? Johnny, I'm flattered!" she said, blushing.

"I'm afraid that it wasn't such a good dream, Lara."

"What do you mean?"

"I dreamt that you and your folks were in a pretty serious boating accident."

After looking confused and uncertain, she began shaking her head. "It was just a dream, Johnny, nothing but a dream. You have nothing to worry about, trust me. We've been boating and water-skiing since I was a baby. We've been on the water more times than I can remember, and we've never had an accident. My father is very serious about boating safety."

I suddenly noticed her bathing suit. *It's the same one from the dream.*

"But you *will* have one today, Lara, I know it."

"I never realized you were so superstitious, Johnny. It was just a dream, that's all. It was a sick dream maybe, but *only* a dream." She was starting to get a little irritated. Her father honked the horn.

"Look Johnny, I appreciate your concern, really, but I've got to go. We have to be back early tonight, my grandparents are coming over for dinner and well, you know what that's like."

"Lara…" She ran back to their garage, retrieved the skis, and ran back to where I stood waiting.

"Listen, I'll see you later Johnny, okay? We should be back by late this afternoon. Would you like to get together sometime after we get back? We can talk more then if you like."

"Sure. You bet, Lara, I'd like that."

"Me too!" she said, backing away and waving her hand, before turning and jogging towards where her parents were waiting.

I stood there watching as Lara tossed the skis into the boat and climbed back into the truck. She looked back one more time, looking more concerned about me than she was about herself. She clearly did not believe me in the least. I was filled with a disturbing and pervasive sense of dread as I watched them drive away. I shook my head, threw up my hands, and walked back to the house and into my room. I plopped down on the bed as my hand mindlessly reached for and found the MP3 player that was still in my shirt pocket. I flipped the switch and lay in bed for several minutes, hoping some old-time rock-and-roll would drown out the screams from my dream about Lara and her family, which kept playing repeatedly in my head. Eventually I gave up, jumped out of bed, grabbed a towel, and stepped into the shower. Fifteen minutes later, I was out the door and on my way to Bryce's house.

Chapter 4 – The Question

"That's crazy, Johnny! You don't really believe that, do you?" Bryce sat back down in the beanbag chair and picked up the controller from the coffee table. He began pressing buttons on the controller and soldiers on the TV screen carrying MP-5 9mm submachine guns, began running from building to building, firing at enemy combatants as they did so.

"Yeah, sounds kind of freaky, doesn't it? It seemed pretty real though, Bryce, I'm telling you."

"I didn't think you believed in that kind of stuff anymore, Johnny."

"What kind of stuff?"

"You know, stuff from the Bible."

"Well, I don't know. I used to," I answered.

"So what happened yesterday," Bryce asked, changing the subject. "I lost track of you at the mall, and then you just disappeared."

"I got caught at the store lifting a cool Panthers' jersey. They called the cops."

"Aw, man, tough break. I was afraid something like that had happened." He stopped playing the game for a moment and turned to look at me. "You'll have to be more careful next time, dude," he said, before getting back to the game, just in time to avoid being cut down by a pair of Huey Cobras.

It was late when I finally made it back home. My mother was still in the kitchen cooking when I walked in. The smell of hamburgers cooking on the stove filled the house. I kissed my mother on the cheek and sat down at the table. William lay sprawled out on the sofa in the living room watching television.

"Hi Will. Anything good on?"

"No, not really. I'm just watching some dumb old movie."

"Hi, Mom."

"Hi, Honey." She glanced into the living room to see if Will was still on the sofa. "Come on Will, dinner's ready."

I noticed she was biting on her lower lip, something she often did when she was worried about something. She glanced up at me with a troubled expression on her face as she scooped up the patties and placed them on a plate, before bringing it over to the table where we were sitting.

"Johnny, listen honey, I just heard something on the six o'clock news that I thought you should know. It's about Lara and her parents, our neighbors from next door. They were in some kind of a bad boating accident earlier this afternoon. I believe they were taken to Concord Memorial Hospital, down near Charlotte."

"They're still alive?" I asked, with more than a little surprise. My mother looked at me with a shocked expression.

"Yes, Johnny, *of course* they are alive," she answered, "why wouldn't they be?"

"Oh, yeah, of course they are…I mean, that's great!"

"Are you okay, Johnny? You sure are acting peculiar about the whole thing."

I wanted to answer her. I wanted to tell her that I was definitely *not* okay. I wanted to tell her about the dreams. She deserved to know what was happening, especially after everything I had put her through since my father died, but I was uncertain how she would react. I already felt guilty about all of the trouble I had caused her. She was worried enough about me without my adding to it. I decided to remain silent, at least for the time being. She had enough to worry about working two jobs and paying the bills. Besides, I figured I would have to tell her eventually anyway.

"I'm fine, Mom. I'm just relieved to hear everyone is okay, that's all." She looked at me with a curious expression. I wondered whether she suspected anything.

"Would you like to visit Lara in the hospital tonight? I was thinking about driving down to the hospital to see her and her parents."

The question caught me off guard. I had never considered that Lara might actually survive the accident, much less whether I should go and see her afterward in the hospital.

"Yeah—sure, Mom, that would be great. It's in Concord though, do we have time?"

"I think so. If we leave as soon as we finish dinner, there should still be time for you to visit with Lara."

We left for the hospital as soon as we finished eating. It was already getting late and my mother was concerned that visiting hours might end soon, making for a wasted trip.

We arrived at Cabarrus Memorial Hospital in Concord around seven-thirty. My mother soon found a space in the huge hospital parking deck and we hurried to the entrance. An elderly woman sitting at the information desk greeted us as we walked in and after giving us directions, told us that visiting hours would end at eight o'clock, we would have only thirty minutes to visit. We rushed to the elevators and five minutes later, we arrived at Lara's room.

"William and I are going to check on her parents, Johnny. We'll be back for you in about thirty minutes or so, okay?"

"Yeah, sure Mom, thanks." She put her hand on my head and smiled, before walking towards the nursing station. I knocked gently on the door in case Lara was asleep, *and* because I was unsure of what I was going to say to her.

"Come in," she answered weakly.

I pushed on the door and walked inside. "Hi, Lara, how are you holding up?"

"Oh, Johnny, is that you?" she asked, frantically running her fingers through her hair in a vain attempt to freshen up. I began to question whether coming down was such a good idea. She had enough to worry about without being concerned about me.

"Yeah, it's me." As I drew closer to her bed, I could see she was a wreck. She had a cast on her left arm from her bicep to the tips of her fingers. I could not tell for sure because she was under several blankets, but it looked as if she had a cast on her left leg as well. Most of her face was black and blue; it looked like one big bruise.

"Wow, Lara, you look like hell." I rolled my eyes, cursing under my breath for my own stupidity. "Sorry."

Lara tried to smile but she whimpered in pain instead.

"Gee thanks, Johnny. You should look so good when *you* get run over by a yacht."

"Yeah, you've got me there," I said, smiling back at her as I walked over to stand beside her bed.

"Hey, listen, I'm real sorry about what happened to you and your folks. I feel awful… I should have done more to try and stop you."

"How, Johnny, what could you have done? You warned me, you tried to keep us from going. I'm the bonehead that wouldn't listen. I

29

didn't even say anything to my parents about what you told me. If I had said something to my Dad, I wouldn't be *here now*! What an epic failure!"

I just shrugged my shoulders and chuckled. I tried making some small talk, talking about the weather, then about school. I even tried talking about world politics. I would have done just about anything to avoid the question that I had known was coming ever since my mother first told me what had happened. I dreaded the question because I had no answer. I had actually tried my best to forget about it, and I desperately wanted for *her* to forget about it too. Despite my silent pleading, however, the question came anyway.

"Johnny, tell me something, and *please,* tell me the *truth.* How did you know? How did you know what was going to happen?"

There it was, out on the table, sitting there like the elephant in the corner, forcing me to acknowledge its existence. I began pacing about the room, hoping that she would fall asleep or move onto something else, but she did not.

"Johnny?"

I stopped pacing, shrugged my shoulders, and sounding a bit exasperated, I looked into her eyes and said, "I don't know Lara, I just don't know."

"How could you have possibly have known ahead of time what was going to happen to us today, and to your father four years ago, for that matter? How could you see into the future?"

"I have no idea, Lara. The first time, when I dreamed about Dad, the angel in my dream said something to me, something I've been trying to remember. But it was just so long ago…"

"What's it like, Johnny, when you have one of these, dreams?"

"I don't know!" I answered, a little harsher than I had intended.

"I'm sorry, Johnny. I didn't mean to pry. It's just that…"

"What?" I wanted to move on, to talk about something else.

"Well, these dreams, they could mean something important, Johnny."

"I thought you weren't superstitious, Lara."

"I'm not; at least I don't think I am." She looked up at me and hesitated for a moment. I suspected I knew what was coming next. I knew, because I had been asking myself the same question. "Do you think you'll have any more dreams like it, Johnny?" I just looked at her and sighed.

"I…"

"Yeah, yeah, 'I told you, Lara, *I don't know,'*" she answered for me, smiling. We both laughed for a moment, until she once again winced in pain.

Despite the fact that visiting hours were almost over when we first arrived at the hospital, I was able to spend another hour or so with Lara, talking about the accident, my brushes with the police, her family, my family, even about school. I never was much of a conversationalist, but for some reason, talking with Lara seemed to come easy for me.

"Johnny, I was wondering something. There's a movie that I've wanted to see for a while now that's playing down at the South Lake Cinema. I was wondering if, well, maybe you would like to go see it with me, if it's okay with my dad of course."

"Are you asking me out on a date?"

"No–well, yes, I guess I am," she answered, smiling again.

"Um, yeah, sure Lara, that would be great. I don't know that your dad is going to let you go with me though, especially after the trouble I've been in."

"You just let me handle my father. The doctor said I won't be out of here for a week, so I have plenty of time to work on him. If the movie's *not* still playing when I get out, how would you like to go with me to the school dance next month?" She laughed as she pulled the sheet off of her leg enough to reveal the cast that ran from just below her hip down to her big toe.

"Well, I think that would be fun to watch!" I answered.

Lara and I laughed and told stories for another fifteen minutes, until the nurses finally came by and ran me out of her room. We never did make it to that movie because of her father, who stubbornly refused to let her go out with me, telling her that she was still too young to date. Despite the setback however, Lara and I began spending more and more time with each other at school, and on occasion, around the house on the weekends as well. We even began dating for a short time during our senior year in high school. I give credit to Lara for helping me through some of my more difficult teen years. She had a tremendous calming influence over me. Fortunately, for whatever reason, I had no further conflicts with High Point's finest.

Thankfully, the angel had been correct, and I *did* make it through those dark times, though given the dangerous lifestyle I led, I often doubted I would live long enough to see my eighteenth birthday. I later came to believe that the Lord *had* sent Lara to me at just the right time.

The Last Prophet

Chapter 5- Back Home

Having made it through my troubled teenage years relatively unscathed, I was able to avoid getting into any more trouble long enough to get into college. I even graduated from North Carolina State University four years later with a bachelors' degree in computer science, making me the first in my family for generations to graduate from college, though my brother William would soon join me. My only regret was that my father did not live long enough to see it. I know he would have been extremely proud.

When I finally made it back home after graduation, it was as if the future opened up and blossomed before my eyes, the possibilities seemed endless. I planned to move to Silicon Valley in California, the Mecca for computer geeks from all over the world and the birthplace of some of the most innovative technologies ever invented, to find a job working for one of the large computer giants.

Life was determined to have its own way however, and it had something else in mind for Lara and me. The same night I arrived back home after graduating from N.C.S.U., I had my third dream, or "vision" of the future, one that was considerably different from the first two.

In the vision, Lara and I were walking together hand-in-hand, taking a pleasant stroll around a small lake on a cool autumn morning. Two adult mallard ducks led a troop of ducklings along the shoreline on the other side of the lake, their distinctive green heads and orange beaks leading the way. A fish splashed in the water nearby, where a light misty fog still floated just above the water along the end of the lake where we were standing.

We walked together along a path near the water, each of us with our arms wrapped around the other. We talked and we laughed, enjoying each other's company immensely. While there were other people walking around the lake, we never noticed them. We were in our own world made just for two.

Feeling that the moment and setting were perfect, I reached into my coat pocket and brought out a small black jewelry box trimmed in gold. I then turned to Lara, opened the lid, and showed the engagement ring to her. Lara's eyes opened wide at the site of the diamond.

I then knelt down on one knee, and presented it to the beautiful woman standing before me.

"You are such a wonderful and amazing woman, Lara! I must admit the day I fell in love with you. I adore you more than words can convey. I want you in my life; I *need* you in my life, Lara, permanently. Will you please become my wife? Will you marry me?"

I could see Lara's eyes open wide, until she buried her face in her hands and began crying. She then looked down at me kneeling on the ground, and began nodding her head.

"Yes...yes...absolutely yes! What took you so long, Johnny March?"

We embraced and kissed, before continuing our walk. The conversation, which up to that point had been ordinary and casual in nature, suddenly took a very serious turn, as we began discussing wedding plans, dates, and invitations. We had walked only a short distance when she abruptly turned to me with a troubled look on her face.

"Oh, no, I just realized something, Johnny! It never came up, we never talked about them!"

"Talked about, whom?" I asked.

"Johnny, do you...want...children?" she asked, rather distressed.

"Well, I don't know...wow... children," I answered, feigning uncertainty. I was joking, of course, but her furrowed brow and painful expression convinced me that it was time to change course.

"Of course I want children, sweetheart, are you kidding?"

Lara jumped into my arms, just as everything began to change.

The scene in the vision shifted. This time, Lara and I were sitting together in the audience of a crowded auditorium, dressed somewhat differently, a little older, and clearly more comfortable together. On the stage stood a plethora of tiny little actors and actresses, each one playing his or her part in an abridged version of *A Christmas Carol*. We smiled proudly as a tiny little boy, *our son*, played the part of the crippled Tiny Tim. We sat in the second row and listened to the precious boy recite the famous and most often quoted line from Dickens's story, "God bless us everyone!"

The scene then shifted several more times, each one taking place at various stages in our son's life. In one scene, we were all sitting in church together, much as I had been with my parents when I was a child. In another scene, we were attending a football game together, and in yet another, a Boy Scout trip. The three of us were very happy together. The boy grew before my eyes, even while Lara and I grew older.

The visions ended and I suddenly sensed the presence of a dark, malevolent, and featureless force that began to envelop our son, threatening to take him away from us. It tried to separate us from one another, coming between the boy and his parents, then the parents. I tried desperately to get a look at the face of the sinister and evil man that had suddenly intruded into our private paradise, but the vision was cloudy and the face unclear. I was able to make out just enough during that brief moment that it occurred to me that I recognized the face, vaguely recalling that I had seen it somewhere before. No matter how hard I tried, however, I could not place where. I continued watching in vain, as the darkness enveloped and overtook our son. Then I awoke.

I laid in bed for two hours grappling with what I had seen in the vision. It was a very uncomfortable feeling to get such a view of my own future, and a bit frightening at that, especially given my track record of such visions coming true. All things considered, it seemed inevitable that what I had seen in my dream, all of it, would most certainly come to pass. I had also to come to terms with the fact that there was absolutely nothing I could do to stop it.

It was time at last for me to face the question Lara had asked me years earlier. How *did* I know what was going to happen? And why was I having such visions? I had to try to find out what was going on, to understand what was happening to me. I had to discover how it was that I seemed to be able to see the future, and the significance, if any, of my dreams. Perhaps once I learned the answer to these bewildering questions that I had been asking myself for so many years, everything else would start to make sense.

I desperately wanted to talk with someone about what was happening to me, but I was unsure where to start. It occurred to me that Lara would soon be coming home following *her* graduation from Georgetown University, and that it made sense to talk with her about it, given that she was such an integral and *personal* part of my dream. We had kept in touch during our time in college, even getting together for dinner on occasion during breaks and holidays. With me in North Carolina, and her in D.C., however, we had inevitably drifted apart, though we remained close friends. I wanted to talk with her, tell her about my vision, and tell her we were meant to be together. I wondered how she would react when I told her that we were destined to marry, and to have a child together. After all, she had been dating some guy from Georgetown, and I had gone out with several different girls during the course of my time at N.C. State.

I decided to wait and watch for her to return home, before asking her to dinner under the guise of "*catching up.*" I would lay everything out on the table and let the chips fall where they may. I knew if anyone could understand what I was going through, it would be Lara. She might believe me, she might not; either way I had no choice but to try.

While I waited for her return, I began doing some research into dreams and visions, hoping to find out what was happening to me. I also decided to tell my mother, whom I had kept in the dark for so long about my visions. The burden on her was somewhat lessened, now that William and I were grown.

While I feared upsetting her, I also felt she might be able to help me. A very pious Christian, she had walked with the Lord for a long time. If God had something to do with these dreams, perhaps she would know something that would help.

After my father died, I had only gone to church on the rare Sunday morning that my mother was able to coerce me into going. I had harbored resentment against God for years, resentment that he had taken my father from me so soon. My walk on the dark side following my father's premature death meant that even when I did attend church, I was anything but devout. Still, whatever *was* happening to me, I was starting to believe it must have something to do with God. Maybe, if I told my mother everything… what I had seen, about the strange visions and how they had come true, about the angel and my father…maybe *she* could advise me.

I climbed out of bed, got dressed, and went downstairs, where I found her in the living room reading the Bible. She smiled when she saw me come in. I walked over to the sofa and kissed her on the cheek before sitting down beside her.

"Good morning, Honey," she said.

"Good morning, Mom, did you sleep well?"

"I slept just fine, Johnny; but I doubt that *you* did! I heard you yell out several times during the night. Were you having a nightmare?"

"Yeah, I guess so-- sort of. Hey, if you have a minute, I was hoping that we could talk about that. I need to talk about it with *someone.*" My mother's face took on a familiar expression, that peculiar maternal expression of compassion and concern that only a mother can have for her child. She had always been one of the most intelligent and caring people I had ever known, and one of the strongest. It occurred to me what a dunce I had been for not confiding in her sooner.

"Of course, Johnny, is something wrong?"

"Yes and no. It's complicated."

"Well, okay, why don't you just start at the beginning?"

"Okay." I struggled to try to find a way to tell her about the visions without mentioning the first dream; the one about my father's passing. I considered skipping over it entirely in an effort to try to spare her the pain, but I realized that doing so would leave out some important details; and besides, talking about that dream in particular might actually provide her with some comfort.

"Something's happening to me. I've been having these strange dreams, visions really, about events *before* they happen. They do happen later however, just as they happened in the dream."

I paused to see how she would react.

"When did these dreams start, Johnny?"

It all started about a week before Dad died," I began. A sad, distant look fell over her face. I stopped, uncertain whether I should proceed.

"Mom, we don't have to…"

"Please, go on, Honey."

"Are you okay?" I asked.

"Oh, yes, Johnny. It's just been such a long time since you and I talked about your father."

I smiled and hugged her before continuing.

"I had the first dream a week or so before the accident. I dreamed that Dad was in a hospital room, hooked up to a ventilator and an EKG, *exactly* the way it later happened. In the dream I saw him die, Mom, *and* I saw an angel escorting him to Heaven–all this a week *before* his accident ever even happened!" Tears began to trickle and then stream down my mother's face. I felt terribly guilty about re-opening the wounds, the old pain.

"Mom, I'm so sorry. I should never have said anything."

"No honey, it's alright, really. I loved your father dearly, and I will never love another the way I loved him. I know where he is now, However that he is with God. It is a fact that has long brought me comfort. But, I'm not crying because of your father's death."

"You're not? Then why *are* you crying?"

"We were told to never tell you Johnny, at least not until you were old enough to understand, so we didn't. You were so young then that you wouldn't have understood anyway. After the accident, well, you took your father's death so hard; I just did not want to burden you with it. With everything you went through later on, well...to be honest I was beginning to have my doubts, to question it all myself anyway."

"Doubts about what, Mom? What do you mean you weren't supposed to tell me? What are you talking about? Please, tell me."

"One evening, before you were born, a most unusual man, a stranger, appeared in our living room. He didn't come in through the front door, mind you, or the back door for that matter. He just materialized out of thin air! At first, we thought he was an intruder, who had somehow crept in unnoticed. Your father was going to call the police until the man looked at us with that haunting, piercing look! There was something about our visitor, Johnny, something about his appearance, the look in his eyes, I'm not sure...which caused us to instantly trust him. He told us that he was a messenger sent by God. He said he was sent to tell us that we were going to have a baby, despite the fact that the doctors had told us for many years that I wasn't able to bear children. The man told us there was going to be something very special, something unique about you, Johnny, and that you were meant for something very important."

"Mom, what are you talking about?"

"He said he was an angel, Johnny. He told us that you were part of God's plan for the world."

I sat staring at her for several moments in dismay. *How ironic.* I thought that my news was going to leave her dumbfounded, not the other way around.

"Me? Mom, how do you..."

"...know he was an angel?" she said, finishing my question for me. "Because when he was finished, he disappeared in front of our very eyes. Furthermore, you were born exactly ten months later, just as the angel predicted."

"Wow." I sat back in my chair and considered what I had just heard. How odd, I thought. Could God, *if he exists*, really have some grand purpose for *my* life, for *me*?

"Honey, did you have something else that you wanted to tell me? I didn't mean to interrupt you."

While I sat there, staring at her as I tried to absorb what she had just shared with me, I noticed for the first time how relieved she looked after telling me. It was as if a great burden had finally been lifted off her shoulders.

"Well, I'm not sure that I can top *that one* Mom! Well, let's see, I had two more dreams…"

I went on to tell her about my dream about Lara's boating accident the night before it happened, and my most recent dream about Lara and me, and our *son*.

"Oh, Johnny, I'm very happy to hear about Lara. I always thought you two would make a wonderful couple! That darkness you described, however, and what happened to your son… I don't know what to tell you or how to advise you. I can only encourage you to place your heart and your trust in the Lord, Son, just as I have always tried to do."

"That's okay, Mom. I mean after all, we don't even know if any of it is actually going to happen anyway."

"But didn't your first two dreams come true?"

"Yes, but…"

"Then why do you doubt that this one is any different? Isn't it just like the other two?"

"Yes, for the most part, but this one…"

"Then we should assume that this one will come true as well, *all of it*." She sat there for a moment, trying to determine what the next course of action should be.

"I know something we could try, John. How about talking with Pastor Weathersby, I'm sure he can advise you."

"Pastor Weathersby? Isn't he retired now?"

"Yes, he's retired, but it seems like he did quite a bit of research into prophecy both before and after retired. Please go and see him, Johnny. I know he would be able to help."

"I don't know, Mom. I haven't seen Pastor Weathersby for years now. I wouldn't know where to begin."

"Well I do. You just leave that to me." She walked over and picked up her rolodex, thumbed through it until she found what she was looking for, and picked up the phone and started dialing.

"Pastor Weathersby? Emma March, how are you? It *has* been a long time… How are you and Suzette? Oh, I am so glad to hear that… Please tell her that I said hello! Thank you… Listen, Pastor, I have a bit of a unique situation here that I was hoping that you might help me with. It's about my son Johnny, you remember him? I'll tell him, thank you… Well he…" She proceeded to tell him most of what I had relayed to her. After a long pause, she had her answer, and hung up the phone and smiled at me.

"He said hello, and that he would be happy to help in any way he could. He said that if he wasn't able to help, he might know someone that can. He's expecting you this afternoon, Johnny."

"Aren't you coming, Mom?"

"No, I think not. I feel like this is something that you should probably talk about privately with him."

"Thanks Mom, you're the best." I got up and walked towards the door.

"Where are you going Johnny, you haven't even had any breakfast yet?" she asked as I opened the door.

"I'm going to the library; I have some research to do. I'll just grab something to eat on the way."

Chapter 6- The Congressman

Supporters and opponents alike all over the United States hailed Congressman Abe Addon as the new rising star for the fledgling Socialist Party of America. Already known to be a very charismatic and eloquent speaker, he was also proving to be a very persuasive figure. A man that many found to have an irresistible persona, he attracted larger and larger gatherings at each speaking engagement he attended. While still in his first term, just a freshman in the halls of Congress, he had already established himself as a powerful presence, a real mover and shaker both inside and outside the beltway. By the time he was elected to his second term, he was already busy winning the hearts and minds of the people. Ever the consummate politician, he made grandiose promises to the people, offering to deliver to each person their heart's desire for the price of their vote. It soon became clear that his was a message the public was eager to buy. Few ever questioned *how* he was able to deliver on his promises, but deliver is exactly what he did. He promised them a better economy, and the stock market inexplicably soared. He promised them peace, and warring parties immediately sat down to peace talks. He promised them jobs, and unemployment fell to historic lows.

Congressman Abe Addon, believed to be the latest great leader reminiscent of King Arthur of Camelot, was in actuality more like Merlin the wizard than Arthur the king. And like the magician of legend, Addon seemed capable of accomplishing many incredible feats. When reporters questioned what made him so successful, he said it was merely the trust and faith of the people. Politicians soon adopted the herd mentality in following Addon, wanting to ride the coattails of his success. To further deepen the mystery, the very few that ever openly challenged the shining knight, did so only once. Rumors quietly circulated among Washington's elite about the fate of the challengers, ranging from fear and intimidation, to unfortunate accidents, or worse.

Rising from obscurity, the background of the junior congressman from California had been something of a mystery from the very beginning, and it had remained so. It troubled me that such a man, a politician so popular with the people, hailed as "Abe the Reformer" by many of his supporters, was able to spend so much of his time in the public spotlight, while so much of his background and past remained hidden in the murky shadows.

I had never spent much of my time thinking about politicians, or politics in general for that matter. It was an oversight that I would later come to regret. Like so many others, I suppose I was living in my own little world, too busy with my own problems to look outward at the world at large, at everything happening around me. Because of my dereliction of duty as a citizen of such a great democracy, I missed much of Congressman Addon's meteoric rise to power. By the time he came to my attention, he was already being talked about as a candidate for any number of elected positions beyond the House of Representatives. Sources close to Addon spoke of a possible run at several elected offices ranging from Governor of California, to the Senate, and even a possible presidential bid in the next election. Even then, it struck me as odd that a lowly congressman with only a few years of public service and virtually no record whatsoever was already being considered, however remotely, as a presidential candidate.

Not surprisingly, Addon soon began making numerous public appearances, rarely passing up any opportunity that would get him exposure to the voters. Everywhere he went he repeated the same message; the troubles of the people were over because he, Abe Addon, would ensure they received everything they deserved. It was a powerful message that resonated with the many men and women who had suffered during the severe economic downturn, and were looking for hope.

There was a dark side of the congressman that I found profoundly disturbing, however. It began subtly at first, a comment here and a look there, but eventually he began openly discussing his utter contempt for Christians. As he gave more speeches and interviews, it soon became apparent what the congressional representative from the state of California thought about the so-called religious right, especially the more pious members of the group. Addon cared little for anyone or anything having to do with the God of the Christians.

"Most of these fanatics are uneducated and easily manipulated by leaders of their movements," he said in a speech before the ACLU.

"These Christian zealots care only for some ancient desert deity, an obscure figure manufactured from their own imagination, or from that of religious fanatics much like themselves in the forgotten past. Their outdated, obsolete ideas of morality and values simply have no place in our modern society, where our enlightened minds long ago discarded such primitive beliefs. These so-called "Christians" no longer have any place in our modern world, and neither does their prehistoric, trumped up morality, which does nothing to address the pressing, contemporary problems and challenges of our day."

Even after declaring his candidacy for the United States Senate, Addon continued his relentless assault against Christians throughout the course of his campaign. Whatever the motivation for his tirades against Christianity, on the rare moments when he let down his guard, the careful observer could clearly see his deep-seeded contempt for it.

On one occasion, however, during a nationally televised interview by INC News, Addon seemed to contradict himself when he said that he respected some religious groups that call themselves Christian.

"Some in the media have suggested that I despise religion and that's patently untrue. Of course, I'm not against religion. I'm not even against all Christians for that matter. I only dislike the extremists in the Christian Right who seek to *live out* their faith. I have many supporters among those that call themselves 'Christians' because many of them, like me, believe others should keep their religion to themselves. These folks are some of my most energetic and productive supporters, even working against the radicals in the Christian Right who want to spread their poison, hoping to 'reach the world for Christ.' These wonderful people of the 'Religious Left' care nothing for spreading the Gospel; many don't believe that God even exists. They just want to feel 'good' inside, and of course, there is nothing wrong with that. I know that when I win this campaign, it will be because of men and women like these. After the election, we will address the question of what to do with these 'Christians' by finding an acceptable solution to the problem, and we will change the world, together."

To any rational human being, it should have been apparent that Addon was making promises that no man could possibly deliver. Worse yet, he was even suggesting policies eerily similar to what the Nazis referred to as *The Final Solution*. It was alarming that so many people listened to what he had to say. I found it profoundly disturbing that so many people followed him.

"Just as many have learned over these past few years, I am all about giving people what they want, what they deserve to have, to help them unlock the potential inside of each of them. All I ask is that people do everything in their power to support me in my efforts to rid the world of these dangerous Christians who constantly push their beliefs on others. All we need to do is to 'reeducate' them, to teach them the virtues of post-modern relativism, that what is right and good for *me* may not be right and good for *you*. Of course, anyone with a high school diploma is smart enough to realize that there are no absolutes in the universe.

I also want to protect the rights of every American. I want to ensure that every man, woman, and child can grow up believing whatever they want, living however they want, and acting however they want, as long as they follow me. I ask Americans to join me, and together we will change the D.C. in Washington, D.C. from the District of Columbia, to the 'District of Caring'."

Much to the consternation of my devout mother, and despite her fervent prayers on my account, I had never been one of the "Christian zealots" that Addon had been railing against in his rants. Still, I could not believe what I heard coming out of his mouth. Never in the history of the United States of America had any elected official made such statements in public and remained in office for very long, much less grow exponentially in popularity the way that Addon had. Unbelievably, people were actually buying into Addon's escalating persecution of Christians, which grew in correlation with his popularity.

Maybe believers had become too numb to notice what was happening, or perhaps they were just like me; too self-absorbed and caught up in their own problems to discern the growing threat. With the guards asleep, the time was ripe for Addon to sneak onto the world stage. He was indeed a magician, a great deceiver, a master of the art of distraction and misdirection. His lies and empty promises were poison that filled the veins of the people, and they were quickly becoming addicts. While they gorged themselves on his promises of ease and plenty, they failed to notice that they were sinking ever deeper into the quicksand.

Knowing what I know now, I wonder whether it would have made any difference had the public known from the beginning who he was, what was really happening, and what was coming. Most people had made their choice *before* Addon appeared on the world stage. I suppose that while they would not have been able to change the course of events had they known the truth, perhaps they would have chosen differently.

But they would have an opportunity to hear the truth once more before the end however, God would make certain of it.

Chapter 7- Pastor Weathersby

I arrived on time around two o'clock that afternoon, at the address given to me by my mother. Pastor Weathersby lived in a small, unassuming house in an older, quieter neighborhood. His wife was planting beautiful red tulips in a small flowerbed in front of the house. As I approached, she saw me and stood to greet me.

"My heavens! Johnny March, is that you?"

"It's been a long time, Mrs. Weathersby."

"Indeed it has young man, indeed it has. Look at you! You've grown into such a handsome young man, the splitting image of your father."

"Thank you, ma'am."

"Well, I expect you're not here to see me. I believe Jim is expecting you inside whenever you're ready." I started towards the house and as I stepped onto the porch she added, "And by the way Johnny, it's so good to have you back." Her broad smile and penetrating eyes suggested that her comment held more than one meaning.

I knocked on the door and soon Pastor Weathersby answered. He wore a perplexed and worried expression on his face, which soon vanished as we exchanged pleasantries. That same troubled look would reappear a number of times throughout the course of our conversation.

He escorted me inside and into the living room, a small but neat and attractive corner of the house, where we sat and made ourselves comfortable.

"So Johnny… do you still go by Johnny?"

"John would be fine Pastor, thanks." Pastor Weathersby chuckled.

"Okay *John*, tell me about why you're here."

"You mean the dreams?"

"Yes, the dreams."

"Well, the first two events seem to have happened exactly as I saw them in my dreams, or visions, or whatever you want to call them. The third, well, I don't know yet. It seems that one was a little further down the road..."

"Hmmm. Your mother told me that she and your father had a visitor just before you were born. Did you know anything about that before today?"

"No sir, I did not. Today was the first time I heard about it."

"I've known your parents since well before you were born John, and they always were as honest and pious Christians as I have ever met. However unusual the circumstances may be, I certainly have no reason to doubt that what your mother told me on the phone actually happened. I assume you believe her as well?"

"Of course," I answered promptly. "Pastor, I was there when my mother told you about what's been happening to me. What do you think about these dreams? Are they visions from God, or something else?"

"Well, based on what your mother told me, God certainly *could* be at work here. As I'm sure your mother probably told you, I did a considerable amount of research into prophecy before I retired. In fact, I picked some of it up again after I retired from active ministry. Although I haven't published any of my research, I still consider myself something of an authority on Bible prophecy."

"That's great. Did you learn anything that can help me?"

"That's just it John, I don't know if I did or not. My research always centered more on Bible prophecies that have already been fulfilled, rather than prophecies that have yet to be accomplished. To be completely forthcoming, in many ways my research generated at least as many questions as it did answers."

"Such as?" I asked.

"Well, take the Book of Revelation. I once firmly believed that without a doubt, Revelation was almost entirely symbolic. I was convinced that the few prophecies in the book that were not entirely symbolic in nature had already been fulfilled by the time Saint John wrote them. Over the course of my research however, I began to question my beliefs. Now, I am of the opinion that while there is still some symbolism in the Book of Revelation, much of the book contains literal prophecy that has yet to be fulfilled."

"Pastor Weathersby, I'm not sure what any of this has to do with me. As you know, I haven't been much of a churchgoer since my father died over eleven years ago. I don't know why God, if he does exist, would choose someone like *me* as His messenger."

"God often works in mysterious ways, John. He chose Abraham from the land of Ur to be father of the children of Israel. He picked David, a poor shepherd boy, to be king, and he chose Jeremiah, still a boy himself, to prophesy to the people of Israel, warning them of the Lord's wrath, and the coming threat from Babylon. As He said about David, '...man looks on the outward appearance of a man, but God looks in the heart.' No man is perfect...even David sinned against God by having Uriah the Hittite murdered to hide the sin of adultery. David suffered terribly for his sin, and yet he never turned away from God."

"Still..." I began before being cut off by Pastor Weathersby.

"Dreams, visions, and prophesies, they always have to be treated with some measure of skepticism and scrutiny, John. How does one know when a dream is just that, a dream, and when it is a revelation from God?"

"But these were so real, Pastor, and unbelievably vivid!" I countered.

"I'm sure they were John, and believe me, I'm not discounting the possibility that these dreams or visions *were* from God. I'm only saying that you have to be very careful."

"Then what should I do about them? If they *are* from God, there must be a reason he is showing them to me!"

"Keep in mind that in most cases, the visions that God gave had to do with Israel, or something to do with the end of days. Furthermore, there have been many men and women over the millennia that have claimed to have the gift of prophesy but were proven to be nothing but frauds. Be patient, John. If these visions *are* from God, I believe he will make his will known to you."

"I feel like my head's spinning, Pastor. If God is going to send me these visions, I sure wish he'd tell me what I'm supposed to do with them."

"I know it must be frustrating. I believe the best advice, the only advice, that I can give you is this; open your heart, and your will, to God. Trust him, seek him, and he will find *you*. If he has a plan for you, and I believe that he does, he will make it known to you, at the proper time."

"Thanks Pastor," I said as I rose to leave. "I really appreciate your taking time to talk with me about this."

"I know I wasn't much help John, and I'm sorry. I will add this one thought to what I have already said however; whenever God chose to send prophets to carry His message to his people, it was always for something important. He chose Moses to deliver the Israelites from the

Egyptians. Many of the prophets were sent to warn Israel of the coming judgment and of the coming captivity in Assyria for the Northern Kingdom, or Babylon for the Southern Kingdom. Other prophets, including Isaiah, Malachi, and John the Baptist, heralded the single most important event since God created the world; the coming of the long awaited Messiah, Jesus Christ, to Earth."

"What are you trying to tell me, Pastor?"

"Only this... that if God *has* appointed you as some kind of modern prophet, it likely means that he is preparing to do something extraordinary, and he wants to warn his people about it." Pastor Weathersby put his arm on my shoulder, before adding, "You must be strong, you must prepare yourself for whatever is coming. I would like to pray for you, John, would that be okay?"

"Yes, sir. In fact, I would appreciate it."

Pastor Weathersby cleared his throat and began.

"Lord God, you see into the hearts and minds of all of your creatures, and only you know what you have in store for each of us. We pray now that if you have indeed chosen this young man for your purpose as a prophet, please bless him, guide him, and strengthen him for whatever is coming. Lead him, bless him, and open his heart to your will. Lord Jesus, you died a terrible and painful death on the cross, in order that we might be free from the power of sin, death, and the devil. Please fill the heart of this young man with your power and with your Holy Spirit. We ask these things in the precious name of Jesus Christ our Lord, who lives, and reigns, with you and the Holy Spirit, one God, now and forevermore. Amen."

When he had concluded the prayer, Pastor Weathersby looked at me, and once more placed his hand on my shoulder. I guess I must have had tears flowing down my face, because several dropped and landed on the top of my foot. I felt all of the pain and bitterness that had built up in the years since my father's death just melt away, replaced by a new and powerful sense of belonging and purpose. I raised my head and looked directly into the eyes of the kindly old pastor.

"Thank you, Pastor Weathersby. I don't yet know what he wants me to do, but whatever his will for me is, I am ready to serve the Lord."

Chapter 8- The Date

It was twelve o'clock on a sunny, Monday afternoon, when I rushed out of the office and to my car on my way to meet Lara for lunch. It had been only one year since the dream, but it might as well have been a hundred. Ever since the vision, every moment that passed without her near, without her familiar scent filling my nostrils and her soft and delicate hands in mine, grew increasingly difficult for me to bear. Unfortunately, it turned out that learning that Lara was my soul mate had come at a cost; I lived with an agonizing fear that at any moment, my future wife might be embracing another man; maybe the man she had dated at Georgetown. It made the wait seem interminable and the longing for her unbearable. There was no longer any doubt in my mind that the beautiful young woman I had grown up with *would* one day be my wife. Why I had not recognized my feelings for her before the dream was a mystery, especially given what she and I had shared together during high school. Why had I reacted so coolly to her repeated overtures toward me? The question left me confounded, leading me to the only flimsy excuse I could come up with; bad timing.

Over the past few years while we were in college, the only effort I had made to see her was for an occasional lunch date while she was home during breaks, or whenever I was near Washington. As I now made my way to the restaurant to meet her, I was kicking myself for my own cluelessness.

Surprisingly, as had I continued to reflect on my predicament over the past year, I realized that the glimpses of our future relationship had not created some spontaneous flame of desire for Lara; rather it had only shed light on the longing that had always been there.

An unanticipated consequence of my last dream had surfaced over the course of the past year, which created a conundrum for me; I suddenly realized that that I no longer thought of Lara as anything other than my wife, which wasn't fair to her or to me for that matter. I had no idea what would happen if I pursued the relationship too aggressively. Despite understanding intellectually that the course of events must play themselves out over time, the inexplicable and irresistible draw I now felt towards Lara had become all-consuming for me. The attraction I felt was not unlike the overwhelming lure that a moth might feel toward a flame, well aware of the fiery embrace that awaits it, but powerless to prevent its own demise.

As I worked through the puzzle, it became clear to me that treating the present as if it was the future was unwise, especially since as far as she was concerned, the future was still unwritten. In her mind, she was just as likely to marry a movie star, a doctor, or even the President of the United States, as she was to marry her longtime neighbor and onetime boyfriend, yours truly.

Given my circumstances, I was understandably excited at the thought of seeing her again. Before learning that Lara would become my wife I had always envisioned marrying a stranger, someone exotic and unfamiliar. The idea had started to grow on me over time; however, as I contemplated marriage to a woman I had known almost my entire life, a woman that had also been my closest friend.

All I could hope for now was that our time together would arrive soon. I wasn't sleeping soundly, I wasn't eating well, and I was miserable. I had tried dating other women, just as Lara had been seeing other men, but I always ended up feeling as if I was cheating on her. Frustrated with my predicament, and weary of the self-inflicted wounds and failed relationships, I eventually decided that I would just wait for Lara, regardless of how long it took.

On a more positive note, despite my languishing personal life, my career had been progressing nicely over the year since my return from college. I had found a good job as a computer systems engineer and had thrown myself into my work. This served to distract me somewhat from my growing impatience as waited for Lara. I began working late nights and weekends as a result, hoping that someone would notice my work. Eventually, near the end of my first year with the company, my efforts were finally rewarded with a promotion, along with the substantial pay raise that came with it. The hours were long and the position had proven to be more challenging than I had anticipated, but I was content. More importantly though, I felt it would put me in a good position to settle down, get married, and start a family.

Lara had sent me a letter the week before we were to have lunch, telling me that she had landed an opportunity as a paralegal at a large law firm in Washington. The position would begin soon after she graduated from Georgetown, which would make it extremely difficult for us to spend any quality time together. I became apprehensive after finishing the letter, wondering what her decision to remain in the Georgetown area would mean for *us*. She was still coming home; she just wasn't planning to stay very long.

I was, however, still exuberant at the prospect of seeing her again, even as the dream of our life together continued to haunt me. We were to be married and have at least one child, a son; maybe even more. I had not yet told her about the dream, though at times I felt that I should have. Once more, I found myself questioning whether it had been a vision or a dream, thinking that maybe it was something my mind had conjured up.

After speeding across town, I finally arrived at our designated rendezvous, Paradise Barbecue, a restaurant that we had frequented while dating as teenagers. I was running a few minutes late, so I already had an apology in-hand by the time I pulled into an empty parking space. I jumped out of the car and ran through the front door of the restaurant, which was already packed with the regular weekday lunch crowd. As I walked around inside, scanning the restaurant for Lara, I was astonished to discover that she was nowhere to be found. After making a second round to be certain that I had not somehow missed seeing her, I grabbed a table and ordered a cup of coffee while I waited. Thirty minutes later with Lara still a no-show; I gave up waiting and ordered my lunch. I ate in silence, wondering what had happened; it was so unlike her to stand anyone up, *especially* me. I tried calling her cell phone several times but each time the call went into voicemail. Flustered and confused, I finished my barbeque sandwich, downed my coffee, and paid the bill. As I walked out to my car, I vacillated between feelings of anger and confusion; anger at having raced across town, risking my life *and* a speeding ticket to have lunch with Lara only to be stood up; and confusion because the behavior was so out of character for her. I began to worry that she had been in some sort of accident. Little did I know as I drove home from the restaurant that I would soon have the answer to my many questions around Lara's absence.

It was seven o'clock that night before I made it home from work. I went inside my apartment, laid my coat and keys down on the table, and glanced over at the answering machine. I noticed the new message indicator light flashing. Fearful of what I might hear, I reluctantly pushed the play button. The sound of Lara's voice filled my apartment.

"Hi John, its Lara. Listen...I'm so sorry I didn't meet you for lunch today as we had planned. I know I should have come to see you, or at least called you to let you know I wasn't coming. To be honest with you, I chickened out on both counts. I couldn't face you, in person or on the phone, at least not yet. You see, John, I've met someone. We ran into each other last year at Georgetown and, well, we have been going out off and on ever since. It's not serious yet, but I still didn't feel right about meeting you for lunch today. I guess I felt guilty for some reason. I'm sorry, John...please don't be angry with me. Please try to understand! Listen, I will try to call you again sometime next week to apologize. I just need to figure out what it is that I want John, I'm sorry. Take care of yourself."

Great. Here I was on the verge of proposing to Lara, my future wife, and she dumps me before we ever get started dating again for someone she barely knows. Not only was I angry, disappointed, and disillusioned, I was also perplexed. How could the dream have been so wrong, and who was this man that had stolen the heart of my would-be wife anyway? It was a severe blow and I took it hard. For the first time since the night of the third dream, I began to wonder whether the dreams were truly visions from God, or just some sort of bizarre coincidences.

I began praying about it. It was Lara's decision, not mine. Perhaps the dream had been only a dream after all. My father, my mother, the supposed angel, how could I possibly have been so blind? Lara didn't love me, she was in love with some guy from Georgetown. Maybe the dream had just been a wakeup call. I walked into the kitchen and fixed my dinner, thinking about what I would do next. I had pinned all of my plans on that one dream, and the assumption that Lara and I would end up together. I could not have been more surprised that Lara had written me off just to ease her guilt. Who *was* this man she was seeing and what power did he hold over her that she would cancel a lunch date with *me*, her lifelong friend and future husband?

After eating a TV dinner, I cleaned up and walked into the living room, wallowing in self-pity as I turned on the television. The nightly news streamed into my living room.

"Thank you, Ed. I am standing outside of the Grande Hotel here in Washington, DC, where this evening presidential hopeful Congressman Abe Addon attended a fundraiser, which was intended to help with the final push to get out the vote, and to garner additional support for his agenda going into the Senate. Here is a clip of Congressman Addon as he arrived for the private fundraiser earlier this evening."

The network then ran a clip featuring the Congressman from California arriving at the fundraiser in a *limousine. What a pretentious jerk.* I had not cared for him before and I liked him even less after I saw him emerge from the limo. At his side stood a beautiful young woman, still in her early-twenties, one of the most beautiful women I had ever seen. As the camera zoomed in on his date, there was a flash of recognition and I suddenly realized the horror of it. *The woman's face on my television* belonged to *Lara,* my future wife. Her appearance was so different that I had not recognized her at first, but it was unquestionably her. *Unbelievable.* Not only was she with someone else, she was with *him.*

I sat dumbfounded for the rest of the evening. I had seen my future with Lara, and had made so many plans that up until that day, I had not considered, even for a moment, that we might not end up together. The revelation had tempted me to question my faith in God. After all, if the Lord had never intended to use me, why would he have sent me a vision of something that was never going to happen? Was everything that I had come to believe in recent years real, or just some fabrication?

I found myself longing for my teen years, when my life had been so much easier, when I had only myself to worry about, when life was simpler.

Getting down on my knees, I began praying as fervently as I knew how, asking the Lord to provide evidence that he had chosen me for something, selected me as his witness. I asked him for faith, for direction, and for strength. I knew that whatever lay ahead of me, I could do nothing without the Lord. After thirty minutes, I finally rose back to my feet, purged of my anxiety and doubt. As I sat down in my easy chair I felt renewed, refreshed, and my faith strengthened. I picked up a copy of *The Case for Christ* that was laying on the end table. After reading straight through for *a* couple of hours, I soon grew tired and prepared for bed.

It was around one o'clock in the morning when the phone rang, sounding more like a fire alarm. I leapt out of bed, expecting an emergency. No one had ever called me so late, so I figured whatever prompted the call, it had to be important.

"Hello?" There was a short pause, which lasted for several moments; I nearly hung up the phone.

"John, is that you?"

"Lara?" I answered simply, too stunned to say much else.

"Yeah, it's me, John. Listen, I'm really sorry for calling you so late."

"Oh, hi Lara. I um...saw you on television this evening...with Congressman Addon, wow. You looked, well, you looked great Lara, really. You were dressed to kill, I liked it."

"Thanks, Johnny. Listen, I'm soooo... sorry about standing you up for lunch. There is no excuse for it, I know. I'm also sorry about the lame way I let you know, and for not telling you about Abe sooner."

"Hey, no worries. Is that why you're calling now, to apologize?" I asked, with a nasty edge to my voice. "That's not necessary Lara, really. After all, how could I ever compete with the future president of the United States?"

"Compete? What do you mean? Oh, it's not like that Johnny, I promise, it never was. Besides, it's not like you and I still had a thing going on... or did we?"

"I thought I knew you better than that. But, well, no...I guess we weren't dating anymore so sure, whatever you say, Lara."

"Johnny, I know you're upset, but you don't need to be. It is over with Abe and me."

"Over? But today you said..."

"I know what I said, John, but things have changed, I mean seriously changed. I can't talk about it now, but I desperately need your help. Will you come to D.C, please? I need you to come and get me as soon as possible. I will answer all of your questions, and tell you everything I know *after* you get here."

"Come and get you? Why? When?"

"It's complicated; and like I said, I can't talk now. Please John, please, if you are still my friend, if you ever cared anything about me, *please* come, and get me, *now!*" Her shrill voice sounded desperate, her request a frantic plea for help.

"Are you okay?" I asked. "Are you in trouble? Tell me *something!*"

"Can you just come pick me up, now John, please?"

"Now? You mean, right this minute? Are you kidding?"

"Yes, I mean right now, John, please! I need your help!" I shrugged off the rest of the grogginess that lingered. It was a five-hour drive to Washington, and it would be another five-hour drive back to High Point. Fortunately, it was Saturday now, so I would have the weekend to sort things out with Lara.

"Sure, yeah, okay, of course. Just give me a few minutes to get dressed and I'll be on my way. Where are you?"

"I'm at a hotel. Here is the address." She rattled off the address and I scribbled it down on a piece of paper that was on the nightstand.

"Hurry Johnny, please hurry!"

"Alright Lara, don't worry, I'll be there as quickly as I can. But you know it will take at least five hours for me to get there."

"I know. Thanks, John. Hey, do you want to know something?"

"Sure, what," I answered.

"I had a crush on you when I was growing up, and I can't tell you how much it means to me that you are the one coming to my rescue now. I *am* sorry about everything that has happened lately, John. I guess I was never sure how you felt about me, until now. I hope that somehow, you can forgive me, and give me...and us...a chance. If you do, I promise you, nothing like this will ever happen again."

"Okay Lara, we'll talk once I get there. Well, like I said before, I'll be there as quickly as I can."

"I'll see you soon."

I hung up the phone and splashed water on my face several times just to be sure I was awake. I was beginning to wonder whether I had been dreaming until I looked down at the paper and saw the address written on the piece of paper. I called the phone number that Lara had given me and a desk clerk at the hotel answered. I had not been dreaming after all, the phone call had been real. What could possibly be going on? Lara had said that it was over between her and Abe...what was that about?

I dressed, found my GPS, grabbed my cell phone, and walked into the kitchen. After fixing a pot of coffee, I took out my thermos and filled it to the brim, before sitting down for a moment to plug the address into the GPS. When I finished, the GPS came up with an estimated drive time...five hours and fifteen minutes. I would hit the road and grab a biscuit on the way.

For a moment, only for a moment, I asked myself whether she was worth all of the trouble. Even before I reached the door, I smiled to myself and nodded. Who was I trying to kid? Of *course she was.*

Chapter 9- No Consequence

The sun was rising as I approached the outskirts of Arlington, VA. I had never been to Washington, D.C. before, but I had heard the traffic around the capital was horrendous. I guess one of the benefits of driving to D.C. in the early morning hours on a weekend was the relative lack of traffic. Given the lack of sleep and the long drive, it was something for which I was exceedingly grateful.

After exiting the interstate, it took me another fifteen minutes to find the hotel where Lara was staying. It was a plush hotel, at least a four-star, and most definitely expensive. A shot of adrenalin unexpectedly hit me as I pulled into the hotel parking lot. I still had no idea what was going on with Lara, what danger she might be in, or what danger I was walking into. Whatever it was, it didn't matter; Lara was in trouble, *my Lara*.

I parked the car and rushed inside, finding myself somewhat surprised at my lack of fear. Based on the sound of Lara's voice on the call earlier, I should have been nervous, but I wasn't. I guess I was too caught up in trying to determine whether she was safe, since I still had no idea what was happening, or why Lara had asked me to drive five hours to get her. I decided to slow down and try to keep a low profile. The last thing I needed was to attract unneeded attention given the sense of urgency in Lara's phone call.

I rode the elevator to the fifth floor and walked towards Lara's room. I glanced at my watch to check the time. It was six-thirty in the morning by the time I reached her room and knocked on the door. Lara cautiously opened the door, saw it was me, and leapt into my arms, holding me so tightly that for a moment I felt as if I was suffocating. She then looked up at me with a curious little smile on her face, and kissed me passionately. *Wow.* She had caught me off guard, but finding it enjoyable, I did nothing to resist her.

"You're my knight in shining armor John, and you always have been. Thank you so much for coming through like this!"

She had changed into some casual clothes, but from what I could tell, it looked as if she had been up all night. Her hair and makeup were still much as they were from the night before, though she had tried to make it look otherwise. Whatever was going on, one thing I knew for certain... she was scared. I was amazed at how beautiful she looked, despite the curious circumstances surrounding our reunion.

"Lara, what's going on, are you okay?" She shoved her packed suitcase in my chest, grabbed the rest of her things, and pushed me out the door.

"I'll tell you all about it on the way, Johnny. We need to go, *now!*"

We climbed into my dark blue Honda Accord, and made our way onto the 495 beltway. I kept looking over at her, watching as she constantly looked out the back window, clearly afraid we might be followed. I wanted to ask her what had happened, but she needed some time to decompress. I decided to let her open up on her own, to wait until she was ready to talk about it, or at least until we had put some distance between us and whatever it was in D.C. that had scared her out of her wits. We were driving down I-95, halfway between D.C. and Richmond, when I finally built up the nerve to try to find out what was going on.

"Okay, Lara. Now can you tell me what happened that scared you so much that you called me in the middle of the night?"

For a fraction of a second, Lara looked at me with a strange, frightened look in her eyes. After some hesitation, she grimaced for a moment, and nodded her head.

"Sure, I guess you deserve to know, Johnny. Besides, I have to tell someone." She paused for a moment, gathering her courage. "It's Abe, John. He is not who he appears to be; for that matter, he is not *what* he appears to be, either." I laughed for a moment before catching myself. Lara just gave me a cold, hard look.

"That's it? Few politicians are ever what they appear to be, Lara, it's part of the job description." I smiled, trying to bring some levity to the conversation.

"That's not what I am talking about. He's *something else,* John." For the first time I noticed that she was not just scared, she was *terrified.*

"What are you talking about, Lara, what are you trying to say?"

"I mean he's not human, Johnny, he's...*something else.*" I looked at her, trying to determine whether she could possibly be on drugs, or maybe even delusional. She seemed lucid enough however; shaken up badly, but still in her right mind.

"Lara, are you sure you're feeling alright? Have you taken something?"

"Stop it, John, I'm serious! No, I'm not on drugs and I'm not crazy. I saw…something…last night, something I wasn't supposed to see."

"Maybe it was just the light playing tricks on you."

"John, you of all people should know that sometimes things happen that we don't understand, things we cannot explain."

She had made a good point. *I* had seen an angel and had visions of the future. Now that *she* had experienced something unusual, here I was accusing her of being psychotic or on drugs. I felt like a hypocrite, a real *schmuck*.

"Touché. All right, all right, point made, I'm sorry. Now tell me what you saw, Lara."

"Well, when we first met, he was giving a lecture at Georgetown, something about the cost of freedom. I could tell even then that there was something different about him, something…unusual. I thought it was just his dark personality; you know the kind of man that just has a different sort of look or feel about him. He also seemed to have a lot of money, which didn't hurt, so we went out a few times, mostly on expensive trips out of town, once even out of the country. I had never been around anyone like him before, John. I guess I just got carried away with the glamour…"

"Did you…"

"No! Thank God, no! I never even considered it; you should know me better than that, John."

"Of course I do," I replied, inwardly breathing a deep sigh of relief. "So what happened last night?" I asked again.

"Well, it was just after yesterday's fundraiser. We went back to his house for a nightcap, something I had initially refused, but after his insistence, I finally agreed to. Soon after we got there, some man I had never seen before showed up unexpectedly at the door. I know that because Abe said he wasn't expecting anyone."

"Oh."

"Anyway, his demeanor changed immediately after he answered the door. He apologized to me, and said that we had better call it a night. He kissed me goodnight and as I left, a second strange man I had never seen before arrived. All three of them went into his study just as I was leaving. Before I got to the door, however, I realized I had left my purse behind, so I went back to where we had been sitting in the living room and found it sitting on the floor next to the sofa. When I picked it up, I spilled the contents onto the floor, and spent the next five or ten minutes picking them up. On the way back to the door I passed by the study. The door was slightly ajar, and I heard a strange voice coming from inside the room. It was more like a dark, guttural sound really, the likes of which I have never heard in my entire life. I looked inside and..." She burst into tears as she broke off her account of the prior night's events.

"It's okay, Lara, you don't have to do this now, we can talk later."

"No John, I'm okay. I need to tell you now, or I may lose my nerve and never tell anyone. Let's see, I looked inside and ...I saw those two men standing there, and in front of them was this... *thing*. I can only describe it as some black *thing*, hovering a few feet above the floor in front of them. It wasn't black so much as it was the complete absence of light."

"Like some sort of ghost?" I asked, trying to seem serious but also wanting to chuckle. It was just so bizarre. *Just like my dreams,* I reminded myself.

"Something like that," she continued, "only, it was something else. It was terrifying, John, I mean *really* terrifying... whatever it was, it was *unearthly*. The strange voice I had heard coming from that...*thing*...I recognized it. Johnny, I think that thing was *Abe!*" She burst into tears for a second time. This time I said nothing, opting instead to let her get it out of her system. I knew she would feel better afterwards; not good perhaps, but better. After another five or ten miles down the road the tears began to subside and she gradually fell asleep on my shoulder, where she stayed all the way to High Point. She would stay with me, at least for a while, until this thing, whatever it was, blew over.

***

Abe Addon opened the door and invited the three well-dressed men, all of them wearing earpieces, into his home. "Please, come in gentlemen." He then turned toward the older of the two men, the one that was just starting to turn gray. "So did you find her, Mr. West?"

"No sir, we did not. We found the hotel where she was staying. It looked like she just checked out and disappeared. Her rental car was still sitting in the parking lot outside of the hotel, which seems somewhat strange, since all of her things were gone from her room. She must have called a cab, or maybe someone may have picked her up. We think she may have gone back to North Carolina. It looks like she left in a hurry, sir."

"She must have ditched the car because she knew we could track her rental car," the other agent offered.

"Thank you, Agent Harris, I appreciate the update." Addon gestured toward the door. "Now, if you gentlemen would wait outside for a few minutes I would certainly appreciate it."

"Yes, sir."

As he closed the door his aide, Raul Raymond came up from behind him.

"What are you going to do? *She saw you,* sir."

"I know that, you fool!" he replied. After a few moments of deliberation, he turned back to Raul. "Tell them not to bother with her. Even if she were to tell anyone what she saw, who would believe her? They are all coming under my power now. It is unlikely she will find anyone who will listen to any wild stories she tells them about me."

"But not *everyone* is under your power, sir!"

"Careful, Raul," Addon snarled, walking over and taking a seat behind a large, wooden desk. "Yes, the cursed Christians, the ones that truly worship *him*, they seem to be completely immune to my influence. It's because *he* protects them." He walked back inside and sat on the sofa. "This is nothing for us to concern ourselves with at this point, Raul. She is of no consequence. The stage is set; no one can do anything to stop us now. There are thousands, hundreds of thousands of women just like her, all over the world, and any of them could be my first lady."

"But not all of them have such a pure spirit, my lord."

Addon looked at Raul, who then felt a sudden urge to flee the room before he once more felt his master's rage. He was relieved when he saw Addon simply turn back into the living room and sit down.

"That is why I chose her to begin with Raul. It was a splendid opportunity to take my time corrupting one such as her!" Addon shook his head and took a sip of the martini sitting on the table next to him. He then looked back up at Raul and asked, "Have you contacted him yet?"

"No, sir."

"Go ahead and do it now. Tell Faust he needs to prepare, and that I will be contacting him very soon."

"Yes, Master."

The Last Prophet

Chapter 10-Family Matters

Lara and I spent a great deal of time together over the months following our trip back from Washington. We spent time catching up on each other's lives, filling in the gaps of time since we both left for college, rekindling the old flames. She never said anything else about what she had seen in Washington. As time passed after our return to High Point, I believe she began to doubt her own story, her own recollection, of that night's events. Perhaps she convinced herself that the drink had gone to her head, and that she had never really seen anything as fantastic as what she had described to me. In any event, we moved on with our lives.

The two of us became practically inseparable during that time, spending most of our free time together. We went out to dinner, watched movies, and took trips to the beach and the mountains. Our time together removed the barriers that separated us before, enabling us to grow closer than we had ever been before. One Saturday afternoon, just as I had seen in the vision, I proposed to Lara, asking her to become my wife, and just as she did in the dream, she enthusiastically accepted. We were married a few short months later. Of course, everything happened *exactly* as it had in my dream, not one detail was incorrect or missing.

We spent our honeymoon on a romantic beach in Hawaii, courtesy of her father. The two weeks we spent on the island were the most incredible, memorable, and fulfilling I had ever experienced. Time came to a standstill as I began my new life with Lara on the white sandy beaches of Hawaii, where we would often sit and relax day after day, each of us completely absorbed in the other, talking about anything, and everything. We sat and watched the sunset every night as Sol gradually followed its appointed route before descending and being swallowed up by the massive ocean.

The island was a paradise, arrayed with palm trees, coconuts, beautiful beaches, magnificent sunsets, and perfect weather. It was truly a storybook honeymoon, complete with exotic Polynesian dishes, island hopping, and quiet walks together on moonlit beaches. It was a time we would always cherish, a time to get to know one another in a way few couples ever do, a time when all of our troubles, all of our cares, just melted away. It was a time for us to recharge, a time to prepare for what was to come.

Three months after we returned from Hawaii, Lara discovered she was pregnant. That was when I finally told her about the dream, the one I had about us, and about our son. "Well then," she said, smiling as she did so, "I will be sure to buy only boy's clothes, since I have it on the *highest authority* that it will be a healthy baby boy!"

Seven months later, true to my dream, Lara gave birth to our son, Samuel Joshua March. He was perfect, the most beautiful baby either of us had ever seen. Like so many new fathers, I was overjoyed just to see that all of his fingers and toes were there, and that his mother was doing well. We rejoiced together, and thanked God for blessing us with a healthy, wonderful, baby boy.

After our son's birth, we gradually found equilibrium in our new home together, adjusting little by little to our new roles as husband and wife, and as parents. Lara took a break from working as a paralegal for the first few years in order to devote all of her time and energy to raising our son. She embraced her new role as a mother, often doting on Samuel, and constantly reminding each of us how much she loved her two boys.

While Lara took care of things at home, I went back to work with an even greater vigor than before, determined to be successful in my career so I could provide well for my new family.

Those first few years together were some of the best years of my life. We spent them together as a family, often doing little more than just enjoying each other's company. Sam was baptized at Sovereign Glory Lutheran, the Lutheran Church Missouri Synod (LCMS)church where we attended services every Sunday, two weeks after he was born. When he turned five, we enrolled him in the kindergarten there, while Lara went back to work part time at a law firm, though she never returned full-time to her career.

Throughout those warm and tender years, I never forgot about the dreams, or visions, but we moved on with our lives doing what families do. We celebrated birthdays and holidays, took vacations together, went to church, all while gradually growing closer to the Lord as individuals, and as a family. Our lives remained mostly calm and peaceful, until the time Sam entered elementary school; and I had my next vision.

I had only been in bed for an hour or so when the vision came to me as I slept. In it, I saw the White House and inside, Abe Addon sitting on a throne.

Then everything changed, and I saw him kneeling in obeisance on the floor before someone, or something; a black *shape* hovering above the floor. I wondered who, or what, it was if it wasn't Addon. As if someone whispered quietly in my ear, I heard the words, '*his master*'. Addon knelt before the other creature as he himself transformed into a similar, though somehow lesser, being.

The vision jumped ahead into the future, where Abe Addon was hard at work, fulfilling his master's will. He ordered the assassination of three conservative Supreme Court justices, so that he could replace them with men and women with a more flexible morality, justices that *he* would appoint, and that Congress would invariably approve. The vision then fast-forwarded again to a time even farther into the future. Acting as one, Addon and Congress began passing *waves* of unprecedented laws one after the other, starting with a constitutional amendment that abolished the two-term presidential term limit. They passed another law giving Addon *emergency powers*, enabling him to deal more *effectively* with the looming economic and political crisis that was threatening to destabilize the world's economic and political structure. Addon then led the charge for yet another constitutional amendment, one that limited the Freedom of Religion for Christians, soon followed by a ruling that abolished the tax-free status of the Christian Church.

Next, Addon orchestrated and set in motion one of the greatest religious persecutions since Hitler. He began labeling the Christians as *terrorists*, ordering the arrest of pro-life and pro-family leaders, having them thrown into prison or in some cases, executed. Predictably, he successfully intimidated all but the staunchest, and the most faithful Christians into silence and inaction.

Then, having nullified the Christian threat, he set to work on his other assigned tasks. He began a campaign of mass corruption, in which he deceived the masses, convincing the godless to follow him, while he inflicted upon them greater and greater pain and suffering.

I then saw myself, standing next to a man I had never seen before. In the vision, I seemed well acquainted with the man, as if we were close friends. We stood as one, denouncing Addon, while carrying an urgent and powerful message that we had been instructed to carry to the masses; news of the imminent return of the Lord Jesus Christ to Earth, also known as the Second Coming. My companion was an older man with long grayish-white hair that reached down past his shoulders. He was taller than I was, at least six feet in height, with a tough, leathery exterior, formed through a combination of hard times and exposure to the elements.

I watched on as Abe Addon and his followers, along with the old world, were swept away in a moment's time. In its place, I saw an incredibly beautiful city, where the streets were made of gold, and walls were adorned with beautiful jewels, endowed with a power and beauty like nothing I had ever seen. In the distance, I saw a large throne, where God himself sat.

I awoke from my dream to find that I had been sweating profusely, and as I looked at my hands, I realized they were shaking. I did not understand everything I had seen in my vision, but it was becoming obvious to me that God was showing me something of great significance; that the prophecies in the book of Revelation were about to be fulfilled.

I turned over in bed to see whether I had disturbed Lara. I was shocked to find her wide-awake, sitting up in bed, her eyes opened wide.

"John, are you okay? You just had another dream, or vision, didn't you?"

I looked at her for a moment, one foot still in the ether of my dream, another in this world.

"Yes," I answered, "and it was the most powerful, the most vivid one of all."

"What was it about this time, can you tell me?"

"It was about something big Lara, something really big. This vision contained events that will affect the country, the entire planet, all of *humanity*. My dream was about the end of the world, at least as we have known it." I sighed, caught my breath, steadied myself, and continued. "I'm not certain, but I believe I know why this has been happening to me."

"Why?" she asked, a worried look in her eyes.

"I think that the three dreams I had before... the ones about my father, about your accident, and the one about us... all had one thing in common; they have all been about events around me, events that I could clearly see would later come true. Maybe God gave them to me to help strengthen my faith in them, in him, in order to prepare me for something much, much bigger. Whatever the reason, I believe God wants me to do something, something important, something amazing." I looked at her and I could tell she was trying to take everything in.

"Listen, Lara, I don't know exactly what is happening, at least not yet, or what will happen to me, to us. I…" Lara put her hand over my mouth.

"Jonathan March, now you listen to me. I have loved you for as long as I can remember, even when we were apart, and even more so now that I'm your wife. Whatever happens I promise that I will support you, that I will be with you, come what may. If these *dreams* of yours, these *visions, are* from God, then who am I to stand in your way? Remember, I have been a follower of Jesus Christ since long before we were married. If God has a plan for you, for us, I am not just okay with it; I am thrilled, and deeply honored, to be a part of it. And I am grateful that He has chosen *you* to accomplish His will. Now that you're my husband, now that we have little Samuel, I *know* that we will all have our own part to play in God's plan. This is now a family affair."

As I looked adoringly into my wife's beautiful blue eyes, it occurred to me how much I admired her tremendous courage, her deep conviction, and her unwavering faithfulness.

"Do you have any idea what a wise woman you are, Mrs. March? Do you know how blessed I have been ever since the Lord saw fit to bring you into my life, and how grateful I am that he did so? Do you have any idea how much I adore you?"

"I consider myself lucky to have you as well, Mr. March, I always have. Give me a little credit too, by the way! After all, you don't *really* think that proposing to me was your idea, do you?"

Chapter 11- A New Age

"America is all about freedom. The word *freedom* itself resonates with every red-blooded American on the planet. We thirst for freedom, we hunger for it. As Americans, we cherish our freedom above all else. We cherish many various and sundry freedoms in this country, such as the freedom to have an abortion, the freedom to stay home on Sunday, and the freedom to marry anyone or any *thing* that we want to. This is a new Age for America, an age in which every man, woman, and child will be freed from the bonds of the past. I promise you, that if you vote for me, I will make certain you get *everything* that you deserve, a life where *you* decide what is right for you."

Addon's speech was interrupted by thunderous applause, which echoed throughout the now-empty manufacturing plant. The facility, abandoned when the company was forced to move its manufacturing overseas, offered what he knew would be a great the perfect background for the evening news. He glanced around at the many cameras now pointed towards him, and smiled. Had someone known the truth about him, they would undoubtedly have been quite surprised to learn that the smile was actually quite sincere. It was the motivation that hid behind the smile of course, which was so sinister.

"It is a new age of enlightenment my friends," he continued, "a time for a new way of living, a life in which you will no longer be discriminated against because you have the intelligence, the insight, and the enlightenment to know for yourself what is best for you. You don't need anyone to tell *you* what is right, and what is wrong, especially those that claim that they represent God, not when you have *me*! After all, what tangible proof can anyone offer that there is now or ever has been for that matter a God, a supreme being, who can dictate right from wrong because he created the universe? If then there is no God, who do these 'Christians' worship? What right do they have, and whose authority do they carry, that they go about dictating their "so-called morality" to everyone else? Entrust me with the authority to rid the world of these irritants, and they will trouble you no more. I will remove the obstacles that bar your way, enabling you to reject the authority of their God. Together we will venture forth into a brave new world, void of all of their sickening, endless nagging trying to convince you to follow their God. Give me your support, stand with me, and I will give you what you want, the freedom to choose what you will. Vote for me, 'Honest' Abe Addon for President, and I promise you, the world will never be the same. Thank you."

The picture on the television set switched from the floor of the manufacturing plant in Tupelo, Mississippi to the GNN studio headquarters in Los Angeles, California. Four commentators sat at a table arranged in a semi-circle, which provided an optimum profile shot of each man or woman.

"Presidential Candidate Abe Addon's campaign launched his new 'All you need is Abe' Bus Tour yesterday, with stops in major markets all across America. Now for some analysis, here is Larry Adams, with GNN, News. Larry?"

"Thank you, Dick. On our panel this evening, we have Brock Banter, Frank Hifler, and Marty Goldman. Frank, let's start with you, what did you think of Senator Addon's speech yesterday in Tupelo?"

"Well, to be honest, I thought it was far and above the best speech I've ever heard. It makes all others pale by comparison. I believe that speeches like this one will undoubtedly cinch the presidency for candidate Abe Addon."

"Brock, what do you think?" asked Adams.

"I have to agree with Frank on this one Larry. Abe Addon has taken the nation by storm. He is offering Americans everything they want to hear, and he's offering a positive, uplifting message to everyone."

"Which is?"

"That America has grown up. We no longer need religion as a crutch to lean on. We live in a new and enlightened America. We are the world's most educated and affluent society. Everyone *should* be able to choose for themselves what is right and what is wrong."

"Marty, do you agree with Frank and Brock?"

"Somewhat Larry, except I must add something. Not only was this the most articulate, gracious speech ever given, it was also the best *message* ever given. It was the gospel according to Abe Addon. 'I will take from others and give to you. I will remove the difficult burdens and pressures of life. I will make all decisions for you.' Who can top a message like that? It's what everyone wants to hear!" exclaimed Goldman enthusiastically.

"Well, for the first time it appears as if our panel is unanimous in their conclusions," Adams announced. "Abe Addon seems to have touched on a nerve, something that is not only vitally important to Americans, but for everyone. I have been speaking with my colleagues from all over the world; from Great Britain, France, Germany, Russia, China, even Iran. To a person they all report the extremely positive reception that presidential candidate Abe Addon has elicited from the peoples of the world. Without a doubt, he is the most popular U.S. presidential candidate both at home and abroad, that the world has ever seen."

"You know Larry," began Hifler, I saw several newly released polls today that showed that if the election was held today, Abe Addon would win in the largest landslide in U.S. presidential election history, with well over eighty-percent of the vote, more than twice what the Republican and the third party candidates would have combined."

"I saw the same polls, Frank, absolutely astonishing!" Adams replied. "It seems there is nothing that anyone can do to stop the Abe Addon juggernaut at this point. With only a few months remaining until the election, it seems that it's all over but the ceremony."

"I have to agree, Larry," Goldman interjected, "I have been talking with my sources at the State Department and it appears that world leaders have already started conferring with President Addon, err…excuse me, my mistake…Senator Addon."

"What do your sources say about how the congressman is viewed by other world leaders, Marty?"

"Almost everyone seems to have the highest regard for Addon," replied Goldman, "and from what I am told, they have each pledged their full support and fidelity to him both now *and* after he is elected president."

"You said *almost* everyone, Marty. Is it possible that there is still a world leader out there somewhere who does not have the highest regard for the beloved senator from California?" asked Adams.

"Well, there is one holdout I am afraid," Goldman answered, "but it really will not come as a shock to anyone. The Pope in Rome has refused to meet with or pledge any support for Senator Addon either now or after he is elected. Of course, other radical religious zealots of the so-called Religious Right have also been protesting the inevitable election of Abe Addon as president. Some of them have even gone as far as to take out ads, warning against some 'dire' ramifications if he is elected president. Can you believe it? These people are nothing but a bunch of close-minded hypocrites. Why can't they just abandon their ridiculous beliefs and get onboard with Addon's message? Most world leaders have already aligned themselves with Senator Addon and his movement, because they share his vision of freedom from religion, and prosperity."

"But the Pope is, of course, also a head of state."

"The Pope, a head of state? You must be joking! He's nothing more than the *mayor* of Vatican City, Larry!"

"That's right, Brock, there are heads of state and then, there are heads of sta…<click>"

I turned off the television and lay down on the sofa. I had my fill of the gushing media coverage of Abe Addon for the evening. Images from my recent dream, or vision, flooded my mind. I continued to be astonished at the number of people that seemed to sit on the edge of their seats when Addon spoke, hanging on every word that came out of his mouth. The entire world seemed to be clamoring after the enigmatic Addon. As a rule, I had never given a lot of thought to politics. Other than exercising my civic responsibility to get out and vote on Election Day, I tended to avoid listening to all of the talking heads on television. Everything about Abe Addon troubled me, though. Whatever else he was I knew one thing for certain; he was trouble. I was one of the few people I knew that had not been completely swept away by the man. My vision and Lara's experience notwithstanding, there was an air about him, something that I could not quite put my finger on. Were it not for my vision, I might have dismissed what Lara had told me as excessive alcohol, or just an overactive imagination. Had she really *seen what she had described to me that day, several years earlier*?

Addon was without a doubt a most extraordinary and charismatic creature. He possessed some quality, some attribute that attracted non-Christians to him like moths to the flame. His capacity for mesmerizing and controlling the swarms of people that followed him was beyond anything I had ever seen or heard of before. The enigmatic influence, which drew people to him in droves, along with the mystery that surrounded Abe Addon, revealed a puzzle that I felt increasingly compelled to solve. Little did I know that I would soon learn the full extent of both who, and what, Abe Addon was.

Chapter 12-The Street Preacher

"The Revelation of Jesus Christ, which God gave him to show to his servants, even the things which must shortly come to pass: and he sent and signified it by his angel to his servant John, who bare witness of the word of God and the testimony of Jesus Christ, even of all things that he saw. Blessed is he that reads, and they that hear the words of the prophecy, and keep the things that are written therein: for the time is at hand." Revelation Chapter 1:1-3

It was a brisk, cool, autumn morning. The sun struggled to break through the thin layer of clouds that formed a canopy over the city of High Point, and covered it like a blanket. I rushed out of the house, splashing coffee all over the driveway along the way, before climbing into the car. I quickly turned the key in the ignition, pulled out of the driveway, and sped down the street on my way to the office.

That fateful Monday morning when I first met Moe Princeton began like any other. I had stayed up late with Lara and Sam the night before, playing yet another game of Monopoly, after watching one of the NFL playoff games on television. As a result, I was running late and trying to get to work through the morning rush hour traffic. In my haste, I failed to notice when the gas light came on, beckoning furiously with a bright orange glow. I ran out of gas within only a few miles from my office. Fortunately, I was able to pull off the side of the road and in behind another car that just as the engine cut out completely. Since I was so close to the office, I decided to continue on foot. I would return after work with enough gasoline to get the car started so I could get it to a gas station before heading home for dinner.

As I walked down Main Street on my way to the office, I noticed an odd-looking fellow standing on a street corner, talking to anyone and everyone within earshot. Despite my anxiety over running so late, something compelled me to stop, just for a moment, to listen to what he was saying.

"…and what I say to you, I say to one and all, the Lord Jesus Christ will soon return in majesty and great power. He will reign forever, and will cast the wicked into the place reserved for all who despise him." Then, ignoring a number of other people standing all around us, he unexpectedly fixed his gaze upon me and said, "and to you God has given a great gift, the privilege of becoming his messenger, his faithful witness. He has called you to carry his word to everyone, to share with others what he tells you, and he has called you to do battle with the messengers of evil until at last, you have completed what he has called you to do. What I say to you now I say to you all, as it is written in the Book of Proverbs, 'Trust in the Lord with all your heart, and lean not upon your own understanding. In all your ways acknowledge him, and he will direct your paths.'"

I shook off the sensation that he seemed strangely familiar, the feeling that I had seen the street preacher somewhere before as I walked by him and continued on my way to the office. I looked back at the preacher only to find him watching me, staring at me with his dark piercing eyes. As I continued on my way, I could tell even without looking that his gaze followed me as I made my way down the street. Had he been talking to me? Was it possible that he knew something about me, about my dreams? *The dreams.* The realization struck me like a slap on the face. *That* was where I had seen the odd man before, in my dream. The preacher was the older man that had been my companion in the dream. Perhaps talking with him would shed some light on what lay behind my dreams, my visions. Ignoring the consequences of showing up late for work, I felt compelled to go back and talk with him. It was to be one of the most pivotal decisions of my entire life.

As I turned and walked towards him, I found that indeed, he had never taken his eyes off me. Curiously, he seemed to be as interested in me as I was in him.

"Good morning, I…"

"Good morning, John March. It's good to finally meet you!" The street preacher extended his hand, along with a warm smile. He sounded different somehow, more approachable.

"You… know my name? How is that possible? I don't remember ever meeting you before."

He just smiled again and asked, "Oh, you are quite correct, we have never met. But why, John, do you of all people, ask me that question?"

"You know about my…"

"About your visions? Why yes, of course I do! The Lord told me about you, and about what he has shown you in your dreams. To be honest with you, I was beginning to grow concerned that you were not coming. I have been waiting for quite some time, you know."

"Waiting for *me*? But why?"

"Because John, you are the last one."

"The last what?" I asked, already knowing the answer but unwilling to admit it.

"The last *prophet*, of course. You already know the answers, but you have been unwilling to accept their logical conclusions."

"What are you talking about? What is this about a last prophet?"

"You *are* the last prophet, John. Together, you and I are the Lord's two witnesses, the last two prophets to appear on the Earth before the second coming of the Lord Jesus Christ.

'And I will give power to my two witnesses, and they will prophesy for 1,260 days, clothed in sackcloth. These are the two olive trees and the two lamp stands that stand before the Lord of the Earth. If anyone tries to harm them, fire comes from their mouths and devours their enemies. This is how anyone who wants to harm them must die. These men have power to shut up the sky so that it will not rain during the time they are prophesying; and they have power to turn the waters into blood and to strike the Earth with every kind of plague as often as they want.

'Now when they have finished their testimony, the beast that comes up from the Abyss will attack them, and overpower and kill them. Their bodies will lie in the street of the great city, which is figuratively called Sodom and Egypt, where also their 'Lord was crucified. For three and a half days, men from every people, tribe, language, and nation will gaze on their bodies and refuse them burial. The inhabitants of the Earth will gloat over them and will celebrate by sending each other gifts, because these two prophets had tormented those who live on the Earth.

'But after the three and a half days, a breath of life from God entered them, and they stood on their feet, and terror struck those who saw them. Then they heard a loud voice from heaven saying to them, Come up here. And they went up to heaven in a cloud, while their enemies looked on.'

"Look it up. It's from the book of Revelation, Chapter 11, verses three through twelve."

"Who are you, anyway?" I asked, still reeling from the revelation.

"You can call me Moe."

"Well, 'Moe', it's been really nice meeting you this morning, but I have to get to work now. Have a nice day." I started walking on, waiting for Moe to say something. I looked back to find him silently watching me with a grimace on his face.

"Well, aren't you going to try to stop me or something?" I asked him, with a touch of surprise and disappointment.

"I can't, John. Serving God is, and must always be, your choice."

"What do you mean, 'my choice'?"

"Just that, you always gets to choose."

"What if I choose not to be this 'last prophet'? Will the Lord be okay with that?"

"If you reject his plan for you, John March, then the Lord *will* choose another. Nevertheless, I caution you not to make such a decision lightly, for you would do so only at your own peril."

I walked back to where Moe was standing. He was starting to annoy me. I could already tell that he seemed particularly good at that.

"Alright then, Mr. Moe, tell me, what is it exactly that I am supposed to do?"

"You must witness to the world that the Lord's Second Coming is already upon us. Warn humanity not to follow after the words of the beast from the Abyss. Tell everyone that they must stand against him, his minions, and his master."

"The beast? What beast?"

"You have already encountered him, or rather, your wife has," answered Moe. "*You* have seen him only in your visions, and on television of course."

"You don't mean..."

Moe nodded.

"Abe Addon?"

"The same," said Moe.

"Are you telling me that the President of the United States is the beast from the Abyss?"

"I am indeed. His true name is Abaddon, the Destroyer."

"So his Master is..."

"Satan, yes. But take heart, John March, for 'greater is he that is in you than he that is in the world.'"

"Great."

"You have read the book of Revelation?" he asked me.

"I have," I answered.

"Then you know how the story ends?"

"The dragon, the beast, and the false prophet are cast into the lake of fire, where they will be tormented forever and ever," I recounted.

"Why yes, take comfort in that fact," Moe said, attempting to comfort me.

"Let me ask you Moe, how am I supposed to stand up against the devil?"

"Remember John, as it says in the book of Revelation, no harm can come to you until the end of your testimony, which will last three and a half years."

"But after that we will both be killed," I stated flatly.

"Yes, we will be killed, but after three and a half days we will be called up into Heaven to be with the Lord."

"Moe, one of us has to be out of his mind… more likely than not it is me."

"We are both quite sane, John, let me assure you." I sat on the curb for a moment to rest and to think. Moe sat next to me. The crowd had dispersed, and the others walking around us cast us only casual glances.

"Okay, say for a moment that I believe you, and that *I have* been called by God to be his 'messenger'. Look, I live in the real world. If I do this, how am I suppose to support my family? The Lord still wants me to take care of my family doesn't he? I mean, this doesn't exactly sound like a part-time gig."

"But the Lord has already provided for you. You don't know it yet, but a wealthy uncle on your father's side recently passed away. He had no children of his own, so he left everything to his closest living relative; you."

"An uncle? I hope that I'm not responsible for his death!"

"No, no, of course not. On the contrary, you were the cause of his *life*! The Lord blessed him mightily ahead of time on your account. You will find later that your mother has already left you a message at your home to call her. She only found out herself a short while ago."

I looked off into the distance and pondered everything that had happened. I thought about my parent's visitation when I was still young, about the dreams, and how they all came true. It was the overall gravity and shock of the situation that weighed most heavily. It was a lot for me to absorb.

"John, the Lord knew that this would be a difficult time for you, and so did I. I went through much of what you are experiencing right now, not so long ago."

I must have looked at him with more than a little surprise on my face.

"Or did you think that I have prophesied since the womb?" he asked smiling.

"I guess I didn't even think about it," I answered.

"Of course you didn't, nor did I expect you to. Listen, you have just been told that you are a prophet of the Most High; you have had confirmation that God truly does exist; that he has selected you to stand against evil and proclaim his message to the world, and that you will die when you are finished. It is a lot to take in, I understand. Some men, most men perhaps, would not be able to deal with such an overwhelming reality."

"But you think that I can?" I asked him.

"No, John, I *know* that you can. The Lord has prepared you for this role. You are uniquely qualified, as am I, to fulfill that part of the vision that the Lord shared with St. John the Apostle so many years ago."

I put my head in my hands, questioning how someone like me could ever accomplish the task that had been set before me. Moe patted me on the back.

"Go home John, ponder what you have learned, and share this wonderful news with your wife! Take care to offer her plenty of comfort and support, as the news will likely come as a shock, and the adjustment will not be easy. Remember, you both must keep in mind that this is from God himself, the one that created the universe, and all that is in it. If you can't trust him, who can you trust?" He placed his hand on my shoulder, just as Pastor Weathersby had done. Only with Moe, power, faith, and peace, seemed to flow from him and into me. It was something I had never before experienced.

"Oh, and one more thing, John. The Lord Jesus will send a messenger to you tonight, one who will confirm all that I have told you, and instruct you on what to do next."

"Okay. Will I see you again?" Moe just laughed.

"My dear boy, I will be around so much over the next few years that you will be sick of seeing me, of that I can assure you! Now go, and go in peace."

I left Moe feeling bewildered and perplexed, with many more questions than answers bouncing around in my head.

Chapter 13-News

"And to the angel of the church in Thyatira write: These things says the Son of God, who has his eyes like a flame of fire, and his feet are like burnished brass:

I know your works, and your love and faith and ministry and patience, and that your last works are more than the first. But I have this against you, that you suffer the woman Jezebel, who calls herself a prophetess; and she teaches and seduces my servants to commit fornication, and to eat things sacrificed to idols. And I gave her time that she should repent; and she will not repent of her fornication. Behold, I cast her into a bed, and them that commit adultery with her into great tribulation, except they repent of her works. And I will kill her children with death; and all the churches shall know that I am he that searches the reins and hearts: and I will give unto each one of you according to your works. But to you I say, to the rest that are in Thyatira, as many as have not this teaching, who know not the deep things of Satan, as they are wont to say; I cast upon you none other burden. Nevertheless that which you have, hold fast till I come. And he that overcomes, and he that keeps my works unto the end, to him will I give authority over the nations: and he shall rule them with a rod of iron, as the vessels of the potter are broken to shivers; as I also have received of my Father: and I will give him the morning star. He that has an ear, let him hear what the Spirit says to the churches." Revelation 2: 18-29

When I got home from work that evening, Lara told me that my mother had indeed called and left me a message to call her as soon as I got in. I called her immediately and found that it was exactly as Moe had told me that morning. Unbeknownst to us my uncle, Joe March, had passed away only a week earlier, peacefully and in his sleep. We only learned of it when his attorney called to share with us what was in the will. He had left us a significant sum of money, far more than enough to enable me to quit my job.

It had been several years since we had last heard from my uncle. He had moved to Seattle a year or so after my father, who was also his brother, had died. Uncle Joe had been a computer programmer when he left. Soon after moving to Seattle, he had started up his own software company, March Software, Incorporated. He had designed a new predictive modeling software tool that had quickly become a runaway success. After running the company for over ten years, during which time it grew to become a Fortune 500 company, Uncle Joe sold the company for an enormous sum of money and retired an extremely wealthy man. Soon after his retirement however, he learned he had a particularly aggressive form of cancer. As his only family, he had secretly named my mother and me as the sole beneficiaries of his entire estate, a fact that my uncle had never shared with us. I was saddened by the news and disappointed that we had missed the funeral. Uncle Joe had been the closest thing I had to a father for a long time, and I would miss him very much.

After my mother and I finished our conversation and I had hung up the phone, I decided to sit Lara down and fill her in on the day's events. I began sharing details of my encounter with Moe that had taken place earlier that morning, the details of our subsequent conversation, about Moe's declaration of who and what was behind my inexplicable dreams, about God's plan for me, and about what it would mean to our family.

"But John, this is all so…"

"Unbelievable? Fantastic? Insane?" I asked.

"Well, yeah, I suppose that pretty well sums it up."

"Tell me about it," I replied.

Lara walked into the living room, picked up our family Bible, and turned to the eleventh chapter in the book of Revelation, the chapter that mentions the two witnesses. After a few minutes she looked up at me, her face pale, and her eyes beginning to water.

"Johnny, I don't want to lose you, I haven't had you with me long enough. I couldn't bear it!" She broke into tears as she laid her head on my chest. I wrapped my arms around her shoulders and squeezed her gently.

"We are going to be in for a tumultuous four years, Lara," I told her, "but then, so is every other human being on the entire planet." She sat there for some time saying nothing, just staring off through the window and into the darkness. Finally, she turned to look at me.

"Must you do this thing, Johnny?"

"I believe I should, Lara. I have been given a great honor. The Lord has chosen me to do a great work, who am I to deny him?"

"Then I will take great comfort in the knowledge that we will be reunited soon after you are taken from me; once the remaining prophecies in the book of Revelation are fulfilled."

I held her head in my hands, looked into her beautiful eyes, and said, "You are an incredibly special lady, Mrs. March, and I thank God for you."

We then embraced with a warm, pure, and sincere kiss that far exceeded anything associated with passion. What we had was extraordinary, and the sudden realization of the intense feelings I had for my wife nearly brought me to tears as well. We had just finished our embrace when the phone rang. Lara answered the phone.

"Hello?" "Oh, hi! I'm doing just fine thanks, how have you been? We haven't seen much of you the last few months, what have you two been up to? Well don't be strangers! Yes, he's here, hold on for a minute." Lara handed me the phone, wearing a surprised look on her face. "John, it's Bryce!" she whispered.

I took the phone from Lara, raising my eyebrows and repeating the word *Bryce* in surprise as I did so. It was quite a shock given that we had not seen Bryce or Lisa for over six months, and all of our phone calls to them during that time had gone unanswered. I could not help but wonder what had prompted the unexpected phone call.

"Hello?"

"Hi, Johnny, it's Bryce."

"Bryce, how have you been doing? It's been a while, are you and Lisa okay?"

"Yeah, sure Johnny, we're doing just fine. What about you and Lara?"

"We're fine too," I replied, still trying to discern the reason for the unexpected call.

"And Sammy?"

"Sam's great."

"Good."

It was small talk, something Bryce despised. His voice was also strained and something less than sincere. Given our argument six months earlier and my encounter with Moe, I couldn't help but be a little suspicious of Bryce's motives for calling me now.

"Listen Johnny, we were wondering whether the two of you would like to join us for dinner this Saturday; you know, get together and maybe have a cookout. As you said, it's been a while."

"A cookout? Um, sure, Bryce, that sounds like a great idea. Your place or ours?"

"Why don't you and Lara come over and bring nothing but yourselves, it's our treat. How does six o'clock sound?"

"Okay, see you then," I said, before hanging up.

"What was that all about?" asked Lara. "We haven't heard anything from Bryce or Lisa in over six months and now, out of the blue, they invite us to a cookout. What's going on, Johnny?"

"I don't know but don't forget, Bryce and I have been friends for a long time, Lara."

"I know, John," she said, looking confused, "but that was a heated argument you two had a while back. I never knew he felt so strongly about politics."

"Neither did I and we've been friends for fifteen years. Anyway, I think the invitation is just his way of saying he's sorry."

"Maybe," she said with the same inauspicious tone, "it's just odd, that's all," she said, before walking into the kitchen to prepare dinner.

Pushing aside our suspicions about Bryce, I made it a point to spend some extra time with little Samuel that night before putting him to bed. I read him various stories from the Bible, and played several rounds of tic-tac-toe with him, most of which I lost, of course. As I took a few moments to reflect, I realized how truly amazing life had turned out for me. Never in a thousand years could I, as a rash, rebellious, troubled teenager, have imagined how my life would unfold only a decade or so later.

After putting Sam to bed, I turned on the television. Once more, I found myself watching yet another talking head singing praises and adulation for President Addon. As I watched and listened, I found myself looking at Addon in a completely new light. The day's events had shown me the gravity of whom, and what, he really was, and the diabolical plan he had for corrupting humanity. I watched and listened to the news commentator as he continued exalting Addon. *Like goats blindly following their master.*

"And we thank you, President Addon, for everything that you have done for us, and for everything that you have done for America, and for everything that you will do for the entire world. We love you, Mr. President!" It was sickening, the only thing missing was an "amen" at the end. As I reflected on it, I realized that one of the obvious issues with the media's coverage of Addon was that none of them seemed to question anything that he had been doing. Not even the more moderate and conservative new channels were voicing any objections, concerns, or negative opinions whatsoever about Addon, outside of the occasional commentator or Christian guest. Everyone seemed to adore the man, *the thing*, whatever he was. It seemed that only those that worshipped the Lord appeared to be immune to Addon's power.

The world was in dire need of someone to sound the alarm and to awaken Christians everywhere to what was happening around them. Many Christian leaders had already been imprisoned on trumped up charges, though not all. More than anything, it had been an attempt by Addon to use fear, uncertainty, and doubt to terrify Christians into inaction and silence, and to some extent, it *was* working.

"What are you thinking about honey?" Lara asked me, as she walked up from behind and wrapped her arms around me.

"Oh, I've been thinking about Addon, about everything that's been going on in the world lately, and about what Moe and I could possibly do to put a stop to it."

Lara leaned in so she could look me in the face.

"Now remember, John, the way I understand it, you and Moe aren't supposed to stop it, you are only supposed to be witnesses, prophets, sharing God's message with the people. Stopping Addon will be the job of someone of much greater importance, and power, I believe." I looked up at her and smiled.

"You're right of course. I guess I'm just trying to figure out what I'm supposed to do here."

"Be patient," she said reassuringly, "and I'm sure he will let you know what he expects from you." I just smiled and nodded.

Lara walked over to the television and put in a DVD. She then glanced at me with a mischievous grin, before holding up the DVD case with the words *The Ten Commandments* printed on the outside.

It must have been sometime after midnight when the vision came to me. It was an incredibly vivid and realistic dream. I was sitting on the front pew inside a large and magnificent church. Hanging on the wall of the church in front of the altar was a large wooden cross. Images taken from the many stories in the Bible covered the interior of the sanctuary, including the ceiling. It vaguely reminded me of photographs I had seen of the Sistine Chapel. As I sat admiring the beauty inside the church, an angel, aglow in light, with wings outstretched on either side, suddenly appeared in front of the altar. It was the first time an angel had spoken to me since before my father's death.

"Greetings, John March, chosen prophet to the Most High God! I have come to you now in the name of Dominus, the Lord. I am here to confirm for you the words that you heard this morning, to prepare you for what is to come, and to encourage you in your mission!"

Stunned and scared almost out of my mind, I knelt down at the altar before the angel.

"No, you must not do so! Rise, John March, for I am your fellow servant in Jesus Christ."

The angel touched me and I felt strength and courage flowing through me. "Tell me please, why was I chosen to be the Lord's witness?"

"Why has anyone ever chosen by God to do His work? Why was Moses chosen, or Samson, David, Elijah, John the Baptist, or Peter? The Lord chooses whom he will to do His work."

"What exactly am I supposed to do? I have no idea what I am supposed to do next."

"Do not be anxious or afraid, John March, for the Lord himself will guide you and strengthen you, he will place his words in your mouth. You will be His mouthpiece to the people, and you will warn them to turn away from following the ways of the beast. They must turn their hearts to the Lord now, while there is still time, for the Lord will soon return! The beast from the Abyss however, will deceive the nations and through his deception, he will lead those that follow him to their demise and eternal punishment. Only the Lord's anointed, those with the Lord's seal on their forehead, will not be deceived. On Monday morning of next week, you will find Moe at the same time and place where you first met him. You will meet with him there, where you both will be filled with the Holy Spirit, and you will begin to prophecy before all men. Do you understand what I have told you?"

"I understand," I replied.

"Good. Now choose a sign that you might know with certainty that the Lord is with you. Shall the bow appear in the sky when there has been no rain, or shall rain fall from the sky on a clear day?"

"How about rain on a clear day?"

"Then tomorrow, when the sun is highest in the sky, you will see rain fall on a clear and cloudless day. Have courage, John March, and do not worry about what you are to say, for the Lord will surely put his words into your mouth. Have no fear and trust in the Lord, for it is the Lord himself that calls you to do this, and he will always be with you."

The angel gave me a nod before vanishing, and I awoke from the vision, pondering its meaning for several minutes before drifting back to sleep.

I awoke the next day to the smell of fresh bacon and eggs in the kitchen. It was Saturday morning, and Lara had risen early and prepared a wonderful breakfast, which also included corned beef hash, sausage, gravy biscuits, and waffles. As we sat together at the table enjoying our breakfast, I told Lara of the incredible vision from the night before. After removing a few slices of toast and spreading butter on them followed by apple jelly, she placed the toast on Sam's plate, and looked at me.

"Listen, John, despite the other dreams, visions, whatever you want to call them coming true, I am still having a difficult time accepting all of this. I mean, does this kind of thing actually happen anymore?"

"Well, let me see." I looked down at my watch before adding, "We will both know in about three hours." Lara looked at me with an adorable, puzzled expression. "You've really been a rock throughout all of the unusual happenings in my life, Lara, and I just want to say thank you."

"What in the world do you mean by that John? And what happens in three hours?"

"Yeah, I guess I left that part out. The angel promised me a sign today at twelve o'clock. He said it will rain."

"That's supposed to be a sign, John, really? That must have been an ordinary dream this time, since it rains frequently this time of year."

"True enough, but how many times have you seen it rain on a clear day?" Her jaw dropped.

"You're kidding." I just shook my head and smiled. "Well then Mr. March, why don't you sit down and enjoy your breakfast while we wait?"

It was 11:55 AM when Lara and I walked through the living room and out onto our patio. We looked up and saw nothing but bright blue, unable to find a cloud anywhere in the sky. A sign like this from God would confirm for both of us whether what had been happening was real, and show us where everything was headed.

I said nothing to Lara about my fears and concerns but inside, I was still struggling. I very much wanted to see the sign, but I questioned why I needed one. After all, how many Christians come to faith each day without the need for a sign from the Almighty? I had not asked for the sign, but I had jumped at the opportunity when offered one. I realized that without one, I would still have had trouble swallowing everything Moe had told me. I smiled when I realized that's why the angel had come to me; the Lord had known it too. As we stood there together, waiting to see what would happen, I resolved that if the Lord did give me a sign, I would require no other. I would be faithful to the Almighty, and thankful that he had chosen me, until the end.

I looked down at my watch. It was twelve o'clock, the sun was shining brightly, and there was still no rain.

"Is it time, yet?" she asked. "Did we miss it?"

Lara and I looked at each other and shrugged our shoulders, preparing to step back inside. Maybe it had been only an ordinary dream after all. Suddenly the heavens suddenly opened up and rain began falling from the clear blue sky, in a manner unlike anything I had ever seen. It rained so hard and so fast that puddles quickly formed all around us, and water poured off the rooftops as gutters backed up from the onslaught of rain. We looked up at the sun shining brightly in the blue and cloudless sky, at the rain falling in sheets all around us, as far as the eye could see, and at the streams of water now flowing down the street in front of our house. I then looked at Lara, who stood there grinning from ear to ear. We were both already completely drenched, soaked to the bone, but we stood there laughing, filled with an indescribable joy at the miraculous rain. The visions were true, and God had indeed called me for his purpose. At last, my life was beginning to make sense. Lara tapped me on the shoulder and pointed to the east. In the distance was one of the grandest, brightest, and most beautiful rainbows I had ever seen, also under a beautiful clear blue sky, without a single cloud in sight.

LORDChapter 14-Prophecy

"And to the angel of the church in Laodicea write: These things says the Amen, the faithful and true witness, the beginning of the creation of God:

I know your works, that you are neither cold nor hot: I would you were cold or hot. So because you are lukewarm, and neither hot nor cold, I will spew you out of my mouth. Because you say, I am rich, and have obtained riches, and have need of nothing; and know not that you are the wretched one and miserable and poor and blind and naked: I counsel you to buy from me gold refined by fire, that you may become rich; and white garments, that you may clothe yourself, and that the shame of your nakedness be not made manifest; and eye salve to anoint your eyes, that you may see. As many as I love, I reprove and chasten: be zealous therefore, and repent. Behold, I stand at the door and knock: if any man hear my voice and open the door, I will come in to him, and will sup with him, and he with me. He that overcomes, I will give to him to sit down with me in my throne, as I also overcame, and sat down with my Father in his throne. He that has an ear, let him hear what the Spirit says to the churches." Revelation 3:14-22

The following Monday I went to the spot where I first met Moe. As promised, he was there, his gaze once more fixed on me, but this time, he was smiling at me, grinning from ear to ear. He seemed more content now, thankful perhaps, that he was no longer alone in his work. He now had a companion, a friend, a fellow servant in his unique service to the Lord.

"Moe, it's good to see you again," I said, unsure where to begin.

"It is good to see you again as well, John March," he answered. "So… how are you holding up?"

"Much better, thanks. I believe it is all beginning to make sense to me now, all of it."

"Good, I am relieved to hear that John, I truly am."

After shaking hands with Moe, I took a moment to take in my surroundings. "Okay, so what do we do now Moe?"

"Now, we wait. As always, we wait for the Lord, and for him to reveal his will to us. It is what I've done for years and from now on, it is what we will *both* do, my friend."

We stood there together talking for an hour or so before a television crew appeared across the street from us. A reporter got out of the truck, preparing to do a story on a building that was about to be recognized as a historic landmark, when it happened. A strong wind suddenly came from nowhere and nearly knocked us both to the ground. Flames of fire sat upon our heads, and we began prophesying. The entire event lasted for several minutes, long enough for the television crew to turn their cameras on us and film most of the event. When the prophesying ended, I heard a voice whisper to me.

"John. The television crew will come over here. Tell them...."

A few minutes later, the television crew walked over to where we were standing. The reporter was an attractive woman, who appeared to be in her mid thirties. She had the look of a female reporter waiting to catch her big break, before her age made certain that she never would.

Looking over at the cameraman she said, "Mike, keep the camera rolling." She walked up to me first and smiled. "Um, excuse me, can you gentlemen please tell me what just happened here? Are you street preachers, illusionists, what? I mean, that was pretty extraordinary."

There comes a time when a man reaches a pivotal point in his life, a fork in the road, when he has to make a decision which road to take. While he may never understand it, the decision he makes at that moment will determine the direction his life takes until the day he dies. Sometimes, it determines the course that the lives of others take as well. I was at such a point in my life; I had a choice, and I knew it. I could fabricate a story and then just disappear, or I could do what I had been called to do. I could go on with my life as I had been, or allow it to take an entirely new and different path that while difficult, would be the correct path to take. I thought it rather strange really that when the time came for me to decide, it was not nearly as difficult a decision as I thought it would be.

"Excuse me, what..."

"Good morning, Vicki Reynolds and Mike Tanner. Are you still recording now?"

"How did you know our names?" the woman asked.

"Never mind that, are you still recording now?" I asked again.

"Um, I don't know...Mike, are we still recording?"

"Um, no. I stopped recording when we ran over here."

"Listen, I would like to ask you about what we just saw. What were...?"

"Please, turn your camera back on, Mr. Tanner, and we will explain everything.

"Mike, please, do as he says."

The cameraman then picked the camera up, sat it on his shoulder, and began recording.

"We are servants of the Lord, his messengers, the witnesses or prophets that were to appear to the world just before the end. We have come with a message that we have been given to share with you, with *all of* humanity. You are living in the end of days, and the time of the Second Coming of the Holy One, the Lamb of God, our Lord and Savior, Jesus Christ. Soon, very soon, the Lord will come, and he will bring with him righteousness, judgment, and for his people, eternal peace.

Know also that there is a wicked creature walking among you now, one of the fallen ones, who knows that his time grows short. Freed for a time from his prison, he sets himself and his master up as gods, as the ones deserving worship, rather than the Lord. He is the beast from the abyss. His words are false, and his promises are empty, yet he will deceive many. Already he works to turn the people away from worshipping the Lord, and to worshipping his master. The power of the beast and his power in this world are transient, but the Lord is omnipotent, and eternal. Those who would seek the Lord should turn to him with their whole hearts, and worship him. Turn to the Lord now, while you still can, for your time grows short."

The words issued out of my mouth on their own accord, I was only the conduit through which they passed. All I had to do was sit back and let them flow. It was surreal, and very, very cool.

Vicki Reynolds stood there silent and motionless, her mouth open, and stared at us for several moments. Eventually, she shook off the astonishment and asked, "Excuse me but did you just say that you are some kind of *prophets*, and that the *end of the world* is coming soon?"

Once more, the words materialized in my mind and quickly found their way to my mouth.

"We are prophets of the most high and yes, the world will soon end. As a sign to the world that the Lord has sent us, and so that you can know with certainty that these words are true, there will be no rain anywhere on the Earth for three weeks. No nation, no man, woman, or child, will see rain of any sort fall from the sky until this same time exactly three weeks from now. Once the time has passed, the rains will be released."

Moe and I began walking away, and Vicki Reynolds came running after us. "Wait a minute, tell us more, please. What is it that you want?"

"Our message is not our own, Ms, Reynolds, but the Lord's," I answered. "In three weeks we will return to this place. Until then, look to the skies, for there will be no rain. Watch and see that the Lord *is* God."

"Hold on a minute, what about this 'beast' that you mentioned?"

"His name is Abaddon, the destroyer. You know him as Abe Addon." Her jaw dropped again.

"You mean, *President Addon?*"

"Of course. Thank you Ms. Reynolds, we will return in three weeks. Until then, may God go with you."

As we left, Vicki Reynolds took her position before the camera.

"Well, there you have it; you've seen it for yourselves. Two men made some remarkable claims today, in front of our camera. They assert that they are modern day prophets, sent to us by God himself. They also made a fantastic claim that President Abe Addon is some type of beast, or demon, seeking to wreak havoc on unbelievers and believers alike. Perhaps the most incredible claim of all is that there will be no rain anywhere on the planet for three weeks, as a sign from God that what they say is true. As if taken from some page out of the Bible, this has truly been an extraordinary day. If what these men claim is true, it will turn out to be a day with many more questions than answers. Could the end of the world truly be just around the corner, as they have proclaimed? Is there more to President Addon than meets the eye? Will there truly be no rain anywhere on the planet for three weeks, something that will be easily verifiable given today's technology? Well, I can only tell you one thing... this reporter will be here at this same spot exactly three weeks from today, to once again meet with these modern day prophets, to learn more about them, about their mission, and if possible, to confront them with evidence of rain. If that is not possible, we should all pay very close attention indeed, to what these two men have to say. This is Vicki Reynolds, with INC Channel 9, in downtown High Point, North Carolina."

With the global news cycle in a bit of a slump that week and with no major crisis happening around the world, it was the perfect time for a fantastic news story from a local news station in a small town to begin circulating around the world. The story, which stated that two men, probably suffering from delusions of grandeur, had claimed that the world was about to end, was picked up by one network after another. Soon, clips of Moe and I were being broadcast all over the world, along with the message we proclaimed and with it, the declaration that there would be no rain for three weeks.

By the time it came to the attention of most people around the world, two days had passed. Climatologists from the NOAA - National Oceanic and Atmospheric Administration- as well as scientists from universities all over the world, had already observed and reported an inexplicable lack of rainfall anywhere in the world. While two days was not a long enough period to be of intense concern to scientists, after two weeks, real concern began setting in. At three weeks, scientists were beginning to panic, as a world without rain is a world doomed to perish.

The news of the two witnesses spread like a raging forest fire after that. It became the lead story every night during the third week. Our proclamation that the end of the world and the Second Coming of Christ were eminent sparked considerable discussion in homes all over the world. Nowhere were the discussions more intense than in the homes of our families and friends, some of whom actually disowned us. Outside of the church, only our closest family members, and strangely enough, Bryce and Lisa, stood with us. Most of our former friends only laughed at us in scorn.

***

Someone found the news particularly disturbing, however. In the White House, Abaddon shed his Earthly guise and knelt before his master.

"Do not worry, master," said Addon. "I will find these two so-called prophets, and I will have them executed immediately."

"You will do no such thing," his master replied, "at least not yet. We must proceed cautiously, for we have not been given permission by the Eternal to attack them openly, not until their time is over, in three and-a-half years. At that moment, rest assured that you *will* reach out your hand and crush the lives from these two troublemakers. Until then however, we will be patient, we will wait. You will trouble them, antagonize them, and slow them down in their effort to turn the hearts of the people toward the Eternal. You will work through others, not to kill them, but to make them suffer. We must be extremely careful that we do not cross the line by attacking them directly."

"Yes, my lord."

"Besides, we still have our spy in place, do we not?"

"Yes, my lord."

After returning to his human form, Abe Addon summoned Raul Raymond into the oval office.

"What were his instructions, my lord?"

"We are to wait three and-a-half years. At the end of that time, we will take these two, and we will extinguish their pathetic little lives. Until then however, we will work through others to trouble these men. We want to minimize the impact of their effort to turn the hearts of the people back to the Eternal." He turned and looked at Raul Raymond. "Pass the word; tell everyone that they are absolutely forbidden to trouble these men without my express permission. No harm may fall on them until the three and-a-half years have expired. Until then, we must tolerate their miserable existence."

"Yes, sir. I will take care of it immediately." Raul Raymond left the oval office, walked into his office, and sat down. As he began making phone calls, he could not help but wonder whether he had chosen the wrong side in the coming conflict.

Chapter 15-The Home Front

"After these things I saw, and behold, a door opened in heaven, and the first voice that I heard, a voice as of a trumpet speaking with me, one saying, Come up here, and I will show you the things which must come to pass hereafter. Straightway I was in the Spirit: and behold, there was a throne set in heaven, and one sitting upon the throne; and he that sat was to look upon like a jasper stone and a sardius: and there was a rainbow round about the throne, like an emerald to look upon. And round about the throne were four and twenty thrones: and upon the thrones I saw four and twenty elders sitting, arrayed in white garments; and on their heads crowns of gold." Revelation 4:1-4

Two weeks after we gave the prophecies and the warnings, Moe and I agreed to gather our families together at my house. It was a time for us to get better acquainted, a time to fellowship, and a time to discuss the future.

While Lara and Moe's wife Doris sat talking in the dining room, Moe and I relaxed in the living room, discussing the past, the present, and the future.

"So what do you think the Lord will have us do, John, after the three weeks has ended?" Moe asked me, as he looked thoughtfully through a Bible.

"I don't know; you have more experience at doing this than I do."

"That may be, John, but the Lord spoke with you when we were standing in front of that camera," Moe replied.

"You know, this all seems so surreal, that the Lord would choose someone like *me* for a time like this. I feel so…unworthy," I told him.

"Well, you are in good company, then. After all, who *can* ever feel worthy for such a high calling? I suppose that all of the Lord's chosen that came before us must have felt much the same way as we do now. They were mere men, just as we are, with faults, problems, and insecurities. Surely, they also had doubts, fears, and questions. Besides, if not us, then who? Who *is* qualified?" asked Moe.

"I suppose you're right about that, Moe. I just don't know what I'm supposed to do, or how I'm supposed to behave."

"May I share with you how *I* handle it, John?"

"Please do, I would really appreciate that," I said.

"Well, I just try my best to remain open to the Lord's will, whatever it is. From my seminary days, I learned that the Lord is always the one who does the heavy lifting. It is our responsibility to seek him with our whole hearts and to trust where he leads us."

I laughed. "You make it all sound so simple, Moe."

"Because it is! It is not the Lord that makes it hard on us; we do that all by ourselves. Consider Moses, David, Elijah. Did Moses part the waters of the Red Sea? Of course, not, the Lord did. Did David win so many battles because he was an invincible warrior? No, of course not… the Lord fought for him. Was it Elijah that brought down the fire from Heaven? Of course not; again, it was the Lord!" Moe said fervently.

"So what am I supposed to do, just wait for the Lord to tell me something and then do what he says?" I asked.

"That's about it, yes. Leave all of the heavy lifting to the Lord, John. You wouldn't be able to get very far on your own anyway."

"Thanks, Moe." He just nodded in reply. "Excuse me just a moment," I said. I got up from the sofa and made my way into the dining room where Lara and Doris were still talking.

"So how are you holding up, Lara?" Doris was asking. "All of this must be quite difficult for you to deal with, especially with little Samuel."

"Yes, to be honest, it has been a bit much. I mean, John had his first dream when we were still kids, but we had no idea what it meant at the time."

"How old was John then?"

"Oh, I guess he was around eleven."

"Wow. Moe was already well into his forties when he was called to be a prophet. He was serving as a pastor at a church in Charlotte when it happened."

"Pastor, really? He is a minister?"

"Well, yes and no. After his call to be a prophet, he took an early retirement as a pastor."

Lara saw me coming and allowed me to interrupt their conversation.

"Pardon my interruption, ladies. Lara, would you like for me to go ahead and put Samuel to bed?" Our son had fallen asleep in his mother's lap as she sat and talked with Doris.

"Sure, honey, that would be great, thank you."

I scooped up our precious child and carried him up the stairs and into his bedroom. He was already snoring as I laid him down in bed and pulled up his covers. I kissed him goodnight on his forehead and turned on his nightlight. As I stood there and looked at him, I was so grateful to the Lord for my son; being his father was one of the highest points of my life. I knelt down next to his bed, and thanked God for my wonderful little boy, Samuel, and for the wonderful privilege of being his father.

When I returned to the living room, Moe wore a furrowed brow on his face. He looked up at me once he noticed I had returned.

"John, I think you need to take a look at this." He seemed engrossed with something on television.

"What is it Moe?" He never answered; he did not have to.

"Thanks Fred. Yes, we just learned today that President Addon is holding a special news conference that was scheduled to start ten minutes ago. Hold on a minute, I think he may be coming. Addon appeared on the screen, making his way to the podium.

"Good Evening. I would like to begin by saying how thankful I am for everyone's support since the election. I appreciate all of the outpouring of affection and veneration from so many." He paused, looking to reconcile his notes with the teleprompter. "As you may know, two weeks ago, a pair of religious fanatics in North Carolina threatened our great country, no...I'm sorry, the entire *world*, by saying that there would be no rain for three weeks. Well, we're two weeks into this and people around the world are growing increasingly alarmed. Water supplies in many large cities are already running low. Panic is something that we do not need and that we must avoid at all costs. As you have heard me say before, right-wing Christian fanatics like these are nothing but trouble. It is for this reason that I am invoking my emergency powers and taking these two troublemakers into custody immediately. Thank you." Moe flicked the control and the television set went blank. He turned his head, looked at me, and said nothing. We sat there in silence for several moments before Moe eventually spoke.

"Well, it certainly didn't take long him long to hear about us, did it? It looks like we must be doing something right!" Moe said, chuckling. No sooner had he finished then we heard someone pounding at the door.

"Lara, were you expecting anyone?" I asked.

"No, were you?" she answered.

"No. Well… I wasn't up until a moment ago," I said, raising my eyebrows and looking back at Moe.

I opened the door to find several men in dark suits standing at the door. Behind them was another pair of men with FBI printed in large letters on the front of their navy blue jackets. Behind them were a half-dozen local police cars with their lights on, with police officers pointing there Glock 9MMs at us. The men in suits held up their ID badges, complete with *FBI* stamped below their pictures.

"Mr. March?" asked the older of the two agents.

"Good evening, how can I help you?" I asked them.

"Are you John March?" they asked me.

"Yes, I'm John March."

"You need to come with us Mr. March, you're under arrest."

"What for?"

"For inciting a riot, disturbing the peace, for being a threat to national security, take your pick."

"Now hold on there. If you take him, you take me!"

"Are you Moe Princeton?"

"Yes, I am," he affirmed.

"Then you are also under arrest on the same charges as Mr. March. Let's go."

While Lara and Doris began screaming behind us, held back by two other FBI agents, Moe and I were shoved into one of several unmarked SUVs that were parked outside, which immediately whisked us away. Our wives stood there crying, watching helplessly as we disappeared into the night.

Chapter 16-Imprisoned

We travelled for hours, handcuffed in the back seat of the SUV. The personalities of the two FBI agents sitting in the front seat were dry and no-nonsense. After listening to them talk for an hour or so however, it soon became obvious that they were divided as to whether we should ever have been taken into custody. The agent in the passenger seat argued that we had done nothing wrong.

"It's wrong Hank, I'm telling you. I don't know what he's thinking. When was the last time a president had someone arrested for practicing freedom of speech or religion?"

"Times have changed Jimmy, that's just how it goes. We're just doing our jobs, doing what we're told, because that's what we are paid to do. When *you're* elected President of the United States, Jimmy, maybe *you* can make things better."

"Something is wrong with this, Hank. The President is overstepping his bounds on this one."

"Alright look, what do you want me to do about it, Jimmy?"

"Let's cut them loose."

"What? Are you kidding? I'm only a few years from retiring and drawing a pension. I'm not about to jeopardize my retirement just because I disagree with a decision made by my superiors!"

"So you *do* agree that the President was wrong?"

"It doesn't matter whether I agree with the decision or not Jimmy. I'm going to do my job because like I said, that's what they pay me to do."

Jimmy turned and looked back at Moe and I. Moe had drifted off to sleep.

"I'm sorry about this, Mr. March," said Jimmy. "I wish we didn't have to take you in."

"So do I," I replied, feeling a little sorry for myself. "So where are you taking us?"

"We have been ordered to take you back to Washington. It seems someone there would like to interrogate you."

"Great." Was the only reply I could muster.

"John." I looked around just to be certain and, as I expected, no one in the SUV was talking.

"Yes, Lord." I answered as quietly as I could.

"Tell these men there will be a plague on the waters for your sakes. The rivers and the lakes will be turned to blood until you are released unharmed. This will start tomorrow, as the sun rises in the east."

"Yes, Lord. I will tell them."

Jimmy turned around. "I'm sorry Mr. March, did you say something?"

"Agent Harris, is it?"

"Yes, that's right. Special Agent Jimmy Harris."

"The Lord just told me there will be a plague on the waters starting tomorrow morning. The rivers and the lakes will be turned to blood, and will remain so until we are safely released."

"You're kidding right? I mean, I never pictured you as a nut job," quipped the older agent.

"I assure you both that I am quite serious. It will happen in the morning just as I have said."

Jimmy's face took on a hint of fear, as he considered what I said. I could tell by the way he was looking at me that he was trying to read my face, assessing whether I believed what I was saying.

"Ignore him, Jimmy. He's just trying to get to you."

"I don't know, Hank. I think he believes what he's saying."

"Well then, I guess that means tomorrow should be an interesting day," Hank said dryly.

As we continued driving onwards towards Washington, DC, I drifted off to sleep.

When I awoke, I found that we had left the highway and were sitting still at a traffic light. I looked over at Moe and saw that he was still sleeping. A few minutes later, we arrived at the FBI office in downtown D.C. We pulled into the parking garage, parked, and Special Agents Harris and Brown escorted us into the FBI building. We were quickly processed and taken to a cell, where we remained for the remainder of the evening, with no further communication with anyone. I noticed that we were alone; there were no other prisoners in the detention area where we were being held. Exhausted, Moe and I lay down to get some rest, saying little to one another until the next morning.

The following morning, we had only been awake for a short time when Agent Harris paid us another visit at nine o'clock. His face was pale, white as a sheet.

"Who are you guys...*what* are you guys?"

"We are prophets of the Most High, the Almighty God."

"You mean, like in the Bible?"

"Yes," I answered.

"It's all over the news man, just as you said. The rivers and lakes all over the world are red, like blood! It's unbelievable. They are still running tests to determine what the red stuff is, and what caused it to happen."

"Listen to me young man," said Moe, "they will most assuredly find that it *is* blood."

The young agent turned away, agitated and confused, pacing the floor like an expectant father. After staring out a window for several moments, he turned back to face us.

"Tell me, please, what's going on?" he asked us.

"You seem like a good man, Jimmy. Let me ask you a question, are you a Christian? Do you love the Lord?"

"Well, um, I go to church sometimes on Sunday."

"You need to listen to us, Jimmy; this world, at least as we have known it, will soon end. We are the last of the Lord's prophets, the two witnesses said to appear before the Second Coming of the Lord Jesus Christ."

"Are you really so certain he *is* coming?" The voice came from around the corner of the wall that blocked our view. Someone had somehow walked in without making any noise whatsoever.

"Quite certain," I replied, recognizing the voice's owner.

Addon walked around the corner and stood glaring at us through the bars of our cell.

"Mr. President!" exclaimed Agent Jimmy Harris, star-struck in the presence of Abe Addon. He had never before been so close to a President of the United States. Unsure how to act; he fumbled as if he were in the presence of an emperor. For a moment, it appeared that he might even kneel or bow to Addon.

"Agent Harris, would you please leave us?" said Addon dismissively.

"Of course, sir," Jimmy answered, looking back and forth at Addon and us, unsure whether he should say anything. He decided against it, and closed the door behind him.

Smiling, Abe Addon walked over to where we were standing in our cell.

"Well, well, well. So whom do we have here? Mr. John March, and Mr. Moe Princeton, supposed prophets of the Eternal. I have been looking forward to meeting both of you for quite some time."

"Abe Addon," I responded, "or should I call you President Addon? Perhaps I should just call you by your *true name*, Abaddon the Destroyer?"

"President Addon would do nicely for now, thank you Mr. March."

"You should let us go now Addon, while you still can," I warned him. "You know that you are forbidden to trouble us until after our time is over."

Addon flashed red with anger.

"Who do you think you are, little man?" he retorted. "You are nothing more than a glorified, hairless monkey compared to us! What makes you think that *you* are worthy to be witnesses for the Eternal?"

"Call us what you will, the waters will remain as blood until you let us go unharmed."

Addon said nothing for several moments as he paced in front of our cell door.

"Now, now, listen, I apologize. I'm prone to sometimes losing my temper. I am afraid I got things started off on the wrong foot. I did not come here to argue, I only came here to offer you a proposal."

"We are not interested, demon" Moe shot back. "Go back to your master and tell him that his place in the Lake of Fire awaits him."

"Listen, he has instructed me to offer you a deal. If you stop talking and prophesying publicly, we will let you go, and we will let you and your families live in peace, unharmed. We will even give you great wealth and honor, so that you may live out your days in leisure and comfort, with no worries about anything. Perhaps you would even like to rule a city or two as well? That could also easily be arranged, much sooner than later. So what do you say?"

"Go back to your master and tell him that we are the Lord's servants. We do *his* bidding, not yours," I answered.

"I urge you to think carefully before rejecting our offer because if you do reject it, you will most certainly die at my hand. You know this to be true."

"Yes, we know, and we are delighted and deeply honored that we have been counted worthy to serve the Lord. You will only be doing us a great service, speeding us on our journey to be with him in Paradise, forever. We will gladly continue doing his will until our time here is over."

Addon paced back and forth, staring at us with a gaze that seemed to vacillate between hatred and false empathy. After a few moments, recognizing that our faith was unwavering, he said, "Very well, last prophets of the Eternal, have it your way."

Addon left with no further discussion.

Chapter 17-The Interview

Agent Harris showed up in the detention block again later that evening, where he found us sitting in our cell, praying and meditating on the Word of God. He waited until we were finished to speak.

"Mr. March, Mr. Princeton, you have been released, you are free to go."

"Thank you, Agent Harris."

"Listen, would you mind answering a question before you go?"

"Certainly, if I can. What is your question?"

"I believe that you are who you say you are. I didn't believe you at first, I mean... how could anyone? I believe you now, though. Please, tell me what I must do to become a Christian. I have a wife and baby at home."

I tightened my lips, trying to decide how I might best answer his question. I decided to punt.

"Moe, would you like to answer his question? You were a pastor, after all."

"Fair enough, John, but the man asked you." He passed it back to me, probably trying to help me settle into my new role. After some contemplation, I offered him the best answer I could muster.

"Well, Jimmy, you must be willing to give your life to God, because if you stand for God's will, you directly oppose the beast. These are the end times; there can be no more sitting on a fence. Everyone, every man, woman, and child on the planet will be forced to decide. Call on the name of Jesus Christ; believe in your heart that he is the Son of God, that he died for your sins, and that he rose from the dead. Do this and be baptized in the name of the Father, and of the Son, and of the Holy Spirit."

"Seek the Lord Jimmy, and he will be found by you. Reject the evil and hold to the good," Moe added.

"Thank you Mr. March, Mr. Princeton. I will, I promise." With that he unlocked our cell, helped us collect our things. Agent Harris offered to give us a ride back to our home in North Carolina. Moe and I were still exhausted from the late night drive and subsequent stay in an uncomfortable cell however, so we took a plane instead.

On our flight, we picked up where we had left off the night before, on our discussions about the future. We were considering relocating to the Holy City, Jerusalem, where we would spend the remainder of our days prophesying to the world. When we landed, we took a taxi back to my house, discussing along the way how we would tell our wives what we were considering.

After spending time with our families and catching up on some rest, we broke the news to them separately, deeming it most appropriate to discuss the matter in the privacy of our respective homes. As expected, neither Doris nor Lara was thrilled about the idea of relocating to one of the most volatile regions on the planet. They would not relent until we convinced them of the importance of Jerusalem in the conflict.

We then brought our wives together to discuss the move, and each of us began praying fervently about it for another couple of weeks before making a final decision. We would get started on the visas and passports immediately afterward, *if* we all agreed the move was the right thing to do. Meanwhile, it would soon be time to return to where we made the original prophecy.

Lara came to me crying after Moe and Doris left.

"Is this what it's going to be like for the next few years, John? FBI showing up at the front door, you getting arrested in the middle of the night, not knowing when or even *if* I am ever going to see you again?"

"Yes, Lara, to be brutally frank, I'm afraid that is a definite possibility and at times, it will likely be even worse."

"Why does it have to be *you* John, why can't it be someone else?"

"I suppose that it *could* be someone else Lara, but for whatever reason; the Lord has chosen me for this particular task. How could I ever walk away from that?"

"Shouldn't it be a single man, someone that doesn't have a family to leave behind?"

"Lara, I'm sorry. I know that this has been so hard on you. Is there anything I can do that will make it any easier?"

"Sure, get a desk job?" She managed a weak smile. I took her in my arms and held her close.

"I love you, Lara March, so very much." I said.

"Why couldn't I have married a plumber?" she asked playfully, poking me in the shoulder after doing so.

The following Monday morning Moe and I met back at the same spot where we had first met several weeks earlier. The reporter, Vicki Reynolds, and the cameraman, Mike Tanner, were already there waiting, but they were not alone this time. The entire area was buzzing with excitement. Police had cordoned off the block, which was standing room only with news crews, cameras, and vehicles filling the area like a sea of marabuntu ants.

Moe and I exchanged glances as we walked towards Vicki Reynolds, uncertain what to expect.

The instant she saw us she ran over to Mike Reynolds, the cameraman. "Mike, they're here! Are we ready?"

"We're good to go, Vicki."

"Gentlemen, good morning," she said, clearly concerned that she could lose the interview at any moment to any or all of the throng of press that surrounded her. She spoke relatively quietly, trying not to draw the attention of her competition.

"Good morning, Ms. Reynolds," we said, almost in unison.

"Well, it looks like you gentlemen were right; there has been no rainfall anywhere in the world for three weeks. From what we have been able to determine, it is the first time in recorded history that something like this has happened."

Suddenly, as if on cue, the other film crews realized almost simultaneously that we had arrived and came rushing over. They started asking a barrage of questions, pushing for better positions and shoving microphones in our direction. The result was pandemonium. We could not make out what anyone was asking.

"Ms. Reynolds, perhaps we could do this back at your studio?"

"Of course! Please, come with me," she said smiling, ecstatic about the opportunity to scoop her competition.

We rode in their van with them back to their studio, where she promised us a first-rate interview, assuring both of us that the network would air it immediately, or would even do a live broadcast if we preferred it. I told her that it didn't matter whether it was taped or live, as long as they aired the interview in its entirety that same day. After checking with the network, they agreed.

It took them a few minutes to get everything prepared but soon they had everything ready to go. Vicki Reynolds had hoped we might agree to an exclusive, but now that we were now worldwide celebrities, she had not allowed herself to get her hopes up. It was obvious that she was beside herself as she walked over to where we were sitting.

"Okay gentlemen, we are ready whenever you are."

"We are ready."

"Is there anything we should stay away from, anything you want to make certain we address?"

"There is no need to plan anything, Ms. Reynolds," replied Moe. "The Lord will give us the words to say."

"Okay, great then, let's get started." She motioned to Mike Tanner to start the camera.

"Good morning. I am here this morning with the two prophets of God, who made a remarkable prediction three weeks ago today that there would be no rain anywhere in the world until this morning. Expecting to prove them wrong, we contacted twenty-five governments scattered around the world twice a week, with the last round of calls made late yesterday. As of four o'clock yesterday afternoon, not a single government had any rainfall to report since the day that the prediction was made. After checking with other sources, including a number of scientists and meteorologists, they all said the same thing; there has been no rain anywhere on Earth. We were able to follow-up with the same twenty-five governments, which by the way includes the United States, again this morning. Every single government we contacted reported having rainfall this morning, which is incredible. How did you do it gentlemen?"

"We did *nothing*, Ms. Reynolds," I answered. "We have no power to do anything. It was not us, but *God* that held back the rain."

"Right. That of course leads me to my next question, who exactly are you two anyway? No one even knew who you were a month ago, now the whole world knows about both of you!"

"My name is John March, and this is my brother, Moe Princeton."

"You two are brothers?"

"We are brothers in Christ, Ms. Reynolds," answered Moe.

"So how did you learn that God had chosen you to be his prophets?"

"Simple," I answered, "he told us. God also gave us dreams and signs that he was with us."

"You mean like the lack of rainfall?"

"Well, in my case, it rained a downpour on a clear day without a cloud in the sky. There was even a rainbow."

"Incredible."

"President Addon said in a brief news conference that he was going to have you arrested. He made good on that threat and arrested both of you last week didn't he?"

"He did," I answered.

"But he released you shortly after freshwater supplies all over the world started turning red, some say the color of blood. Is that also true?"

"It is, and it *was* blood."

"Did you have anything to do with that?" she asked.

"We did not do anything, Ms. Reynolds, God did it all," I answered.

"What is this all about, Mr. March," she asked. "If indeed God is causing all of this to happen, what *is* his purpose, what does he want to accomplish?"

"It's simple, Ms. Reynolds. The Lord is fulfilling the prophecy that he gave to the apostle John on the island of Patmos many years ago. We are his witnesses, and we have come to say this, that the Lord Jesus Christ *will* be coming again soon with great glory! The ungodly will be punished, and the beast and his master will be cast into the lake of fire, along with death and Hades." Vicki felt a cold chill go down her spine as he finished.

"When, exactly when will this take place?" she asked.

"That we cannot say, as we do not know ourselves. As he said, he will come as a thief in the night. We can only say that it will be soon, very soon."

"I did some research on the prophecies of the book of Revelation. According to what I read, if you *are* the two witnesses mentioned in Revelation, you and Mr. Princeton here are going to be murdered by the beast in three and a half years, is that also correct?"

"That is correct. I assure you, however, that we are both prepared to die."

"Do you have any other message that you would like to share with the rest of the world?"

"Yes. The Lord loves his people and wants everyone to be saved, and to come to the knowledge of the truth. Your time is running out to decide whom you will serve, however. The evil one has already begun deceiving the people, working to convince them that religion is only the "opiate of the masses," that God is not real, and that Christians are evil. Those that follow the beast are doomed to share in his fate, namely, eternal torment in the Lake of Fire. The sins of the nations are great, Ms. Reynolds; the stench of them reaches up into Heaven itself. Abortion, homosexuality, greed, lasciviousness, evil of every sort, limited only by the imagination of man's evil heart, runs rampant throughout the Earth, covering it like a great flood.

"God however, is holy; so too must his people be holy. The only way for a man to be holy is through the saving faith in Jesus Christ, the Son of the Living God. Those that turn to the Lord with all their heart will have eternal life with him."

"Mr. March, Mr. Princeton, what is in store for you now? What does the next three years or so hold for you?"

"We will continue to do as we have done, Ms. Reynolds," Moe answered. "We will prophesy as the Lord leads us. We will call down plagues as the Lord leads us. Then we will die, as the Lord leads us, and go to be with him."

"What exactly will happen after that?"

"The seals will be opened, the plagues will strike the Earth, and when the Lord Jesus Christ returns, the world, as we have known it for thousands and thousands of years will end. There will be no more crying, no more fear, no more suffering, and God will dwell with man."

"Wow. We are living in the end time, which means we have three-and-a-half years to decide whether to serve the Lord, or the beast."

"That about sums it up, Ms. Reynolds," Moe answered, "though I would recommend against waiting that long to decide."

"Well, Mr. March, Mr. Princeton, thank you again so very much for consenting to do this interview. I hope that we are able to do it again soon."

"We *will*, Ms. Reynolds," I said. The reporter looked at me with a mixed and confused expression.

"Once again this is Vicki Reynolds, with INC News."

Chapter 18- Headlines

Iran Attacks Israel, Launching Missiles Against Tel Aviv. Israel Retaliates by Destroying Secret Iranian Nuclear Facilities with Bunker Busters.

Tel Aviv, Israel

The country of Iran launched an unprovoked attack against the state of Israel at approximately 6:30 AM this morning. The attack, apparently intended for a local military installation, struck a local hospital and elementary school instead. Initial casualty estimates range from three hundred to four hundred dead, nearly all of them children.

The Israeli government military launched an immediate retaliatory strike against Iran's key nuclear sites, including an Iranian Uranium enrichment plant in Qom, just to the southwest of Tehran, the capital of Iran. The facility was located deep inside a mountain, on a former Iranian Revolutionary Guards' missile site, just to the northeast of Qom on the Qom-Aliabad highway. According to a source inside the Pentagon, who wished to remain anonymous because the information has not yet been cleared to be released to the public, the Israeli Defense Forces, or IDF, used American-made BLU-113 penetrating munitions, which were able to successfully penetrate the reinforced concrete structures at each of the sites, and obliterate the facilities. Other key nuclear sites destroyed included a nuclear power station in Bushehr, in the southernmost part of Iran, on the Persian Gulf; a uranium conversion plant in Isfahan, located between Bushehr and Qom, in central Iran; a second uranium enrichment plant in Natanz, just south of Tehran; and a heavy water plant located in Arak, in western Iran. The Israeli counterattack is reported to have completely destroyed the facilities. In addition to the nuclear sites, Israel also destroyed all known missile launch sites in Iran.

The Israeli counter attack was widely seen as a comprehensive effort by the Israelis to eliminate Iran's nuclear and missile launch capability. Israel has long been expected to launch a pre-emptive strike against Iran given the many threats against Israel made by the Iranian President and high-ranking members of the

Revolutionary Guard. Israel has been unsuccessful at persuading the Addon Administration to give it a green light for a pre-emptive attack, so they have therefore been unwilling to act unilaterally, until today.

The Prime Minister of Israel warned late this morning that any further aggression against any Israeli city would not be tolerated, and would result in full-scale war…

I finished reading the article in the paper even as Lara continued flipping channels, looking for coverage on various national news networks. It was curious that almost all media coverage was overwhelmingly against the Israelis and in support of Iran, the rationale being that Israel's retaliation was not proportionate to the Iranian attack. *How ridiculous.*

"John, I'm scared." I looked up at Lara. A terrified look had settled on her delicate features, and I could tell that news of the attack had greatly upset her.

"It's going to be okay, Honey." It *was* going to be okay, but not in the sense that our lives would ever be normal again.

"Okay? John, are you blind? China is on the verge of invading Taiwan, North Korea launched the missile strike against South Korea last week, and now Israel, which will soon be our new home, was just attacked by Iran, *today*, John. They are on the verge of an all-out war, and you want to move our family there, to take our *child* there?" The floodgates opened up as Lara began crying uncontrollably. I walked over to the sofa where she was sitting, trying to comfort her. The strain was getting to her and I could tell she needed a break.

"Hey, I have an idea honey; let's get away for a little while, just the three of us. Let's take a week or two and get away, go on a short vacation somewhere. We can finish preparations for moving to Jerusalem as soon as we get back. It will take some time for us to get our visas and papers back anyway."

She sat there for a few moments in silence, until the tears began to slow before stopping altogether. She got up and went to the bathroom for a few minutes before returning, having regained her composure.

"I'm sorry, John. I guess that's been building for a while."

"I understand, honey, believe me. It's all a lot to take in and you've been a real trooper."

She looked at me for a moment before smiling. "Yeah, right," she answered with a furrowed brow. "I don't know John, what about Moe, and Doris?"

"I'm sure they will understand, Lara. I believe we could all do with a break, and I'm sure they feel the same way. What do you say?"

Lara thought about it for a few moments until a smile came over her face.

"Could we go to Emerald Isle, maybe spend some time on the beach, and at the pool?"

"Sure, if that's what you want to do. We could rent the same oceanfront condominium we rented last time, the one that you like so much."

"As long as we don't have to drink the water from the tap," she said, managing a weak laugh.

"Agreed," I answered. "Now then, would you like to do something special while we are there this time? After all, it will likely be the last time we will have an opportunity to vacation there again."

"There is just one thing I want to do while we are there, John, and I'm quite serious about this. I want us to spend some *real*, quality time together, just the three of us. Which means I want you to leave the television turned off, and I forbid any newspapers from being brought into the condominium for the entire time we're there. Deal?"

"Deal, I answered."

We spent all evening arranging for the trip and the packing, before going to bed early.

We left for Emerald Isle the following morning, watching the sunrise pass in front of us, as we drove east along on I-40 on our way to the coast. The weather was perfect the entire morning, with clear skies and sunshine the entire trip. After a four-hour drive, we finally arrived at Emerald Isle, located at the southern-most tip of North Carolina's Outer Banks, around lunchtime. We stopped for lunch at a pizza restaurant on the island, next to the local movie theater and grocery store. Later, we made it to the condominium and unpacked everything. We then grabbed our chairs, suntan lotion, and some toys, along with the football and Frisbee, and made for the beach. Just a few minutes later, we were in the sand setting up our chairs. Samuel went right to work building a sand castle and playing in the sand. Lara and I relaxed in our chairs, taking in the sunshine and the peaceful sound of the waves lapping on the beach. It was to be our best, and last, vacation there together. There was barely a cloud in the sky our entire time there.

The following week we made our way back home. As I drove on Highway 24 to pick up I-40 west, I took a moment to look over at Lara. The week of sun and relaxation had made a big difference; she looked rejuvenated, peaceful, happy, and well rested. I could easily see the difference that the week had made to her as I watched her smile, listened to her joke around, and noticed how she looked at Samuel and me. Lara wasn't the only one that benefited from the impromptu vacation, however. All of us were re-energized now, ready to confront the challenges that we all knew lay ahead.

The day after arriving back home, we began completing our final preparations for our move to Jerusalem, where we would live for the next few years. I found our passports in the mailbox, which meant we had everything we needed for the trip and the move to our new home; it was now just a matter of booking our flights and taking the plunge. As I looked out the living room window in a moment of nostalgia, it dawned on me that I was going to miss the old neighborhood, and my old life for that matter, though I was looking forward to my new life even more. I was preparing to close the blinds when a familiar face suddenly appeared on the walkway leading to our front door. I opened the door before I heard the knock.

"John, what's going on? I hear that you're moving to *Israel*, of all places!"

"That's right, Bryce. Hey, please, come inside." Bryce walked inside, brushing past me as he did so. It was evident that he was worked up about something.

"What's the matter, Bryce? Is everything okay?"

"You can't just pick up and move to Israel, John. I thought we were friends!"

"We *are* friends, Bryce. But I have no choice; I have to go so I can fulfill my mission."

"Because the *Lord* told you to?" he said disparagingly.

"Well, not exactly, but yes, because I have been called to serve the Lord."

"What's going on?" Bryce asked again. "Since when are *you* a prophet? I know you John; I've known you for a long time, so believe me when I say that this is not you!"

"People change, Bryce," I said dryly, "especially when they've seen what I've seen."

"So when do you leave?" he asked, raising an eyebrow.

"Friday," I told him, still baffled by his reaction.

He sat there across from me in the living room, just looking at me and saying nothing for several minutes. Finally, he let out a heavy sigh.

"Okay, John, okay. It's just so hard to believe... my best friend, some kind of prophet. Wow! I want you to know that I'm going to miss you, man." I was stunned to see tears begin to well up in his eyes. I had never realized that our friendship meant so much to him.

"I tell you what, Bryce, why don't you and Lisa come over and see us once we settle in?"

"You mean, to Israel?"

"Yes! Lara and I will take you both around and show you the sights. What do you say?"

"Count on it John, count on it." As he rose to leave he added, "You and Lara take good care of yourselves, okay? If you need anything, just call us."

"You bet," I answered, walking him to the door."

"See you around, Johnny."

"I hope so, Bryce, take care."

I watched him from the living room as he walked down the walkway away from our house. We had been lifelong friends and at times, we had even been close, but that had been a long time ago. I shook my head in amazement. I had been oblivious to how much Bryce had valued our friendship.

I turned away from the window and picked up a copy of *The Case for Christ that was* sitting on one of the end tables, failing to notice the Crown Victoria parked just down the street, as it silently pulled away from the curb and drove off.

Chapter 19- Israel

The sky was a beautiful blue that darkened as the atmosphere met the blackness of space, and there was not a cloud in sight. We rose early that morning, around five o'clock, in order to make it to the airport and get through the long security lines in time to catch our flight. Our plane left JFK International Airport as scheduled at eight o'clock in the morning. We had been flying for four hours, the average flight time for a direct flight from the east coast of the United States to the west coast, yet we were still not even halfway to Israel. The flight time from New York to Israel was around twelve hours but with the time difference there, it would be eight o'clock the following morning before we would arrive at Ben Gurion International Airport in Tel Aviv. After the forty-five minute drive from the airport, we would arrive at last in Jerusalem, our new home.

There had been considerable anxiety for our two families over making such a big change by picking up and moving to Israel, especially in light of everything else that was happening in the region. Packing up and moving to the other side of the world was going to be a difficult adjustment even under the best of circumstances, much less with the storm clouds of war approaching, nevertheless we all knew in our hearts that it was the right thing to do. Jerusalem, the Holy City, the most revered city on the planet, *was* the proper place for us to spend the rest of our lives, as the old world began to fade making way for the new. The Lord, in his wonderful and tender mercy, had continued to draw me closer to himself as I read and reread the Bible, gradually causing me to develop a deep and genuine love for His people, both Jews and Gentiles alike. I could think of no better place to take my last breaths on Earth, than the Lord's city.

I looked past my sleeping wife and child and peered out of the window, staring out into the darkness. I struggled to recall a passage in Scripture, something about Jews and Gentiles. I reached into my carry-on bag and pulled out my Bible. As I thumbed through it, I found a passage in Book of Romans, which reminded me of the special relationship between God and the nation of Israel, and the opportunity that unbelieving Jews still had to be reconciled to him through Jesus Christ. While warning the Gentiles not to boast because the Jews that had fallen because of their unbelief, and the Gentiles shown kindness because of *their* belief, Paul wrote:

"If some of the branches have been broken off, and you, though a wild olive shoot, have been grafted in among the others and now share in the nourishing sap from the olive root, do not boast over those branches. If you do, consider this: You do not support the root, but the root supports you. You will say then, "Branches were broken off so that I could be grafted in." Granted. But they were broken off because of unbelief, and you stand by faith. Do not be arrogant, but be afraid. For if God did not spare the natural branches, he will not spare you either.

"Consider therefore the kindness and sternness of God: sternness to those who fell, but kindness to you, provided that you continue in his kindness. Otherwise, you also will be cut off. And if they do not persist in unbelief, they will be grafted in, for God is able to graft them in again. After all, if you were cut out of an olive tree that is wild by nature, and contrary to nature were grafted into a cultivated olive tree, how much more readily will these, the natural branches, be grafted into their own olive tree!

Romans 11 v17-24

Israel. There has never been another country like it anywhere in the world. It has been the crossroads of the world for millennia. Modern-day Israel is a unique mixture of the ancient world and the modern, yet remains best known for the many great stories from the Bible. Extraordinary men from Israel's ancient past including Abraham, Moses, Samson, King David, Solomon, and of course the Lord Jesus Christ, continue to be revered all around the world today as they have been for thousands of years. All of these men had once lived, and died, in the land where we would now call home.

"John, where are we?" Lara was awake, looking out of the window in a futile attempt to get a fix on our location.

"We're not even halfway there yet Lara, why don't you go back to sleep?"

"John, tell me about Israel," she said, still half asleep. "Do most people live in the cities or in rural areas?"

I took a brochure out of my carry-on bag and began reading.

"Well, let's see...'many of Israel's inhabitants live in urban centers, on or near ancient sites, which still bear their original names, cities that include Jerusalem, Be'er Sheva, Nazareth, Ashkelon, Akko, Safed and Tiberias, whose old towns now form part of spreading new cities.

The four main cities in Israel are Jerusalem the capital; Tel Aviv, where most of the country's industrial, commercial, financial and cultural life is located; Haifa, a major Mediterranean port and the industrial center of northern Israel; and Be'er Sheva, the largest population center in the south.'"

"What about Jerusalem?" she asked sleepily.

"Okay, where did I see that? Oh, yes, here it is. *'Jerusalem.* It has stood at the center of the Jewish people's national and spiritual life since King David made it the capital of his kingdom over three-thousand years ago. From the siege and eventual destruction of Jerusalem and its Temple by Titus and the Roman Empire in 70 B.C., to the restoration of Jewish sovereignty in the land with the establishment of the State of Israel in 1948, the city was under the control of successive foreign powers.

"Until the latter half of the 19th century, Jerusalem consisted of a walled city made up of four distinct quarters: Jewish, Muslim, Armenian and Christian. The growing Jewish population, which had maintained a continuous presence in the city through the ages, became a majority and began to build new neighborhoods outside the wall, forming the nucleus of modern Jerusalem.

"In the first half of the twentieth century, and under British Control, Jerusalem was transformed from a neglected, poverty-ridden provincial town of the Ottoman Empire into a flourishing city. During this period, many new neighborhoods, with unique ethnic characteristics, were built.

"Israel's largest city, Jerusalem flourishes with a population of almost seven-hundred thousand inhabitants. As modern as it is ancient, Jerusalem is the location of the President's residence, the Knesset (Israel's parliament), the Supreme Court, and government ministries. It is also a city of diverse populations - Jews and Arabs, religiously observant and secular, Eastern and Western.

"Many places sacred to the three major world religions are located in Jerusalem. The Western Wall, also called the Wailing Wall, is the last remnant of the Second Temple and a focus of prayer and a source of inspiration for Jews in Israel and all over the world. The Dome of the Rock is the traditional site where Muhammad was said to have ascended to heaven. The Garden of Gethsemane, the Church of the Holy Sepulcher, the Via Dolorosa and other Christian sites associated with the life and death of our Lord and Savior Jesus Christ are there...'"

I looked down at Lara, her head now resting on my shoulder. I could tell by her breathing that she had fallen back to blissful sleep. I put the brochure away as I looked out the window.

As I watched the clouds that dotted the sky outside of my window gradually pass by, I contemplated how, since the days of Abraham, a myriad of empires have ruled the land of Israel. The Assyrians, the Babylonians, the Medes and Persians, the Greeks, the Romans, and the British, all had at one time either conquered or governed the land. During the twentieth and twenty-first centuries, the land had once more been fraught with violence as neighboring states sought to destroy the tiny nation.

Israel was once again about to become the center of attention, but this time for an entirely different reason. Men, women, and children from all over the world would soon focus their attention on the nation of Israel once more, and on the great signs and wonders that the Lord had prepared for the days immediately preceding the Second Coming of the Lord Jesus Christ.

I picked up my Bible, which was still sitting on my tray, tucked it into my travel bag next to the brochure, and gradually drifted off to the blackness of sleep.

I awoke hours later to a flight attendant's announcement that we were on the final approach into Ben Gurion International Airport in Tel Aviv. Lara and Samuel were both awake and apparently had been for some time. We all looked out the windows, straining to view the incredible majesty of the Holy Land from the air. As we passed over the Mediterranean Sea, I was able to see what I thought was Jerusalem off in the distance.

We landed without incident and disembarked the aircraft, excited that we had landed and anxious to explore our new surroundings, and our new home. An hour later, we cleared customs, and with our bags in tow, walked over to the rental car counter where we found a large line of people ahead of us. Lara asked that I watch Samuel while she looked for a place to freshen up. Sam and I crept closer and closer to the counter, as one by one, weary travelers walked away from the counter with rental car keys in hand. I was almost to the counter when someone suddenly bumped into me, causing me to fall on top of our luggage. Flustered and angry, I rose to my feet, looking for the cause of the awkward and embarrassing moment. It took a few moments for me to notice that something was terribly wrong. My sudden embarrassment turned to shame and fear. My heart began pounding in my chest like a jackhammer, beating uncontrollably fast as I raced around the airport in a state of panic. My blood chilled when I came to the realization that my mishap with the luggage had been no accident. Samuel was gone; he had been *taken*.

Chapter 20- Abducted

"Calm down, Ms. March, we will find your son, I promise," the Israeli police officer said in English but with a thick Hebrew accent. He is young, and in a strange place. When your husband had his *accident*, your son probably became frightened and disoriented. Don't worry, we'll find him."

Lara's eyes widened as she leaned over the desk and glared at the man. She was scared and angry, and I could tell she wanted to demand that he send every man and woman at his disposal out to find Sam. She was also fearful of doing or saying anything, however, that could possibly hinder or delay the authorities efforts to find our son.

As the police officer made additional notes about everything we had told him, I looked over at Moe, who was sitting at a vacant desk across the aisle from us. We were both thinking the same thing and we both knew it.

"Officer Begin, please excuse me for just a moment," I said.

"Of course, Mr. March," Begin replied. Lara shot me a confused and angry look, letting me know in no uncertain terms that she was frustrated with me for not giving the situation the attention it warranted. Ignoring her silent plea, I walked over to Moe and asked him to take a walk with me.

"We'll be right back, Lara. Tell him everything about Samuel."

"Where are *you* going?" she demanded hotly, flustered in anger and surprise.

"Honey, I promise I'll be right back. Moe and I are going to grab some coffee. We'll be right back."

Moe and I walked out of the room where we had been sitting for the past thirty minutes and found a small vending area with some tables and chairs. With the exception of an old man sitting in a corner reading a newspaper written in Hebrew, the vending area was completely deserted. We bought a couple of cups of coffee and sat down at one of the tables."

"Moe, has the Lord said anything to you?"

"No, for some reason he has hidden this thing from me. You?"

"Same here. I have a feeling however, that the Lord doesn't need to tell me who has Sam."

"Addon?" he asked me.

"Addon." I repeated.

"But why?" asked Moe. "How? He can't do anything to Sam, can he?"

"We know that he isn't permitted to kill *us*, but our families? I'm not so sure," I answered.

"This is hard on you, John, I know, but we must have faith. We have to trust that the Lord will protect your son."

"It's not that easy, Moe."

"I know John, I know." Moe came over and put his arm around my shoulder. "I tell you what, let's pray together, pray that the Lord will protect Sam bring him back to us unharmed." We prayed together for several minutes. About the time we finished, someone poked me in the shoulder. I turned to find the old man who had been sitting in the corner reading the newspaper, standing behind me.

"He will call you shortly; have your cell phone turned on," the man said coldly.

"Who are you and what are you talking about?" I asked him. "*Who* will call me?"

"Oh, I think you know exactly who I am talking about, March. Be ready, or you might regret it. He is not known for his patience. Who knows what he might do in a fit of rage?"

I started to reach out and grab the man by the shoulder. I would force him to tell me where my son was. Just as my hand touched his garment however, several police officers walked casually into the room, interrupting our conversation and allowing the old man to creep away and out of our sight. Just then, my phone rang.

"Hello?"

"Hello again, Mr. March. I'm so glad that we have this little opportunity to talk again. So tell me, how was your flight? Is your family doing well?" he asked, chuckling as he did so." My blood froze as my worst fears were realized. *He had Sam.* Abe Addon continued laughing. "Well, I guess I should ask how the *rest* of your family is doing, isn't that right, Samuel? Here, why don't you say hello to your father."

124

"Hello, Daddy." I heard Addon ask for the phone back before I could reply.

"What do you think you are doing, Abaddon? You know we have only begun our mission. What do you want?"

"Let's just say that I'm curious. Curious whether you will now reconsider my offer and if not, whether you have enough faith in *him* that you are willing to risk your son's life."

"What do you mean?"

"Oh, I think you're about to discover that for yourself, Mr. March. Well, I've enjoyed our little chat. Say bye to Daddy now, Sam."

"Daddy, help m…" My heart sank and my blood froze. All I could do was collapse into my chair, and look up at Moe, who stood beside me.

"I have to tell Lara, she deserves to know the truth." I was preparing to stand up when Moe placed his hand on my shoulder.

"Perhaps you should wait, John. See what the Lord will do. He will have compassion on you and your son, and protect him from the beast, I know it." His words were of little comfort as I shrugged off his arm. I rose from my chair and started back to tell Lara what had happened.

I was just approaching the interview room where Lara sat with the Tel Aviv detective, when I noticed a beautiful painting hanging on the wall. The image caught my attention and caused me to stop in my tracks, frozen in place as I carefully studied the work. It was a beautiful work of art, though it was not the aesthetic beauty of the painting itself that captivated me, but the subject matter. An older man stood over a younger man who lay bound on top of a large flat rock. In the hand of the older man was a large knife, raised high above the younger, poised to strike. It was a painting of Abraham and Isaac, depicting the scene when God tested Abraham by commanding him to sacrifice his son, Isaac. On the other side of Isaac facing Abraham, there stood an angel, his hand raised towards him, stopping him from taking the life of his son. In the Genesis story, God tested Abraham in order to see whether Abraham would choose him over his own son.

I walked back to where Lara was sitting and handed her a coffee. As she continued asking and answering questions, I sat beside her feeling numb, and pondered what it all meant. Would I have the courage and strength to do what the Lord called me to do and let my son die, or would I instead fold under the pressure and take Addon up on his offer to spare my son.

We were at the precinct for another two hours before leaving to find a hotel. The police recommended that we stay close to the precinct so they could easily contact us once Sam was found. We found a hotel in Tel Aviv that was close by, checked in for the night, and made our way to our room, all while the police searched diligently for our son.

We stayed up late that night, waiting by the phone into the early morning hours. Finally, after tossing and turning for hours, exhaustion took its toll and we both fell off to sleep. That night an angel came to me in a dream. He reached out his hand to me and took me away in the spirit. Suddenly, we were in Washington, DC, where Addon dedicated a statue of himself. It was tall as most statues go, topping out almost twenty-five feet in height. People fell down to kneel and worship before the statue of Addon.

The angel then looked at me and said, "The beast now makes men to fall down and worship him and his master. Such is the objective of the beast, to cause as many as he can to turn from the Lord and to worship him and the dragon, which he serves. You must turn the people back to God, John March, and away from following the ways of the beast."

I awoke more confused and more desperate than ever. I thought back to the picture of Abraham and his son Isaac. While I knew I would never be able to demonstrate the kind of faith that Abraham had, I had to do what I could to stop Addon. I had to carry the message that I had been called to bring to the world, whatever the cost, and I had to *trust God*. Even if I *had* agreed to Addon's terms, there was no way I could trust him to return Sam to us unharmed, and there was no chance that I could recover my son on my own. No, I came to the conclusion that the best course of action, indeed the *only* one I could safely follow, was to *trust the Lord*, and pray that he would return Samuel safely to me unharmed, so that we could share the few remaining years we had together on Earth as father and son.

I would place a call the next day, a call that I hoped would provide me the venue I would need to fulfill my mission.

I rolled over and put my arm around my wife, who was still soundly asleep, being careful not to wake her. The Lord had been kind to her, mercifully allowing sleep to overcome her overwhelming need to spend each moment of every day looking for him. *Tomorrow.* I would let Lara know that I knew who had our son. I suspected that she already knew, and that she had tried everything she could to prevent that thought from making the leap from her subconscious to her conscious mind. After all, what could she possibly do to find her son and bring him home, if *he* had Sam?

Soon after, the overwhelming need for sleep overcame my own fears and concerns about what would happen to our precious boy. The Lord had been faithful thus far, and I would trust him to the end. No matter what happened to Sam, or any of the rest of us, I was prepared to go all the way, and I had been ever since I first became aware of the plan God had for my life. I now knew how and where I was going. Sleep soon found my eyes and I drifted off.

Chapter 21- Friends of Addon

I opened my eyes early the next morning to the blinding white light of the sun, as it rose in the east. The sunlight peered in through the bedroom window of our hotel room, sneaking in between the venetian blinds and bathing us in its glow. I climbed out of bed to get into the shower, since we planned to go ahead and settle into our new homes instead of trying to live out of a hotel. We would contact the detective assigned to our case, the same one that had been interviewing us the day before, and provide him with the contact information that he would need to reach us. Our new home outside of Jerusalem was only forty-five minutes from the police station, so we could easily travel back to the precinct in the unlikely event there was ever anything they could do to help us. The only one that could do anything to return my son to me now was the Lord. What happened to Sam would be as it always had been, in *his* hands.

After a quick shower and shave, I walked out into the hotel hallway and down to Moe and Doris' room. I knocked gently, hoping that Moe would hear and come to the door, allowing Doris to get some much needed and well-deserved rest. Just as I was about to knock for a third time the door opened and Moe stood in the doorway. He also looked as if he had very little sleep the night before.

"John? Is everything okay?" he asked, still half asleep.

"We need to go, Moe, as soon as you're able to get ready."

"Huh? Oh." Moe nodded. He understood. "Okay, sure. Give me a few minutes and I will be out."

"Okay, Moe," I replied. "I'll meet you in the restaurant whenever you're ready."

"That sounds good," he answered. The door closed and I made my way to the elevator, stopping to pick up the newspaper, written in English, which the hotel had left outside of our door as a courtesy.

As the elevator dropped down a floor at a time, picking up passengers as it did so, I glanced at the paper. The headlines jumped out at me, printed in bold letters over a picture of Addon.

"Friends of Addon Sets up Statues of President Abe Addon in Major Metropolitan Centers All Over the World.

Washington, D.C.

The group calling itself 'The Friends of Addon," led by a man named Simon Faust, announced today that it was placing statues of the most popular president in American history, the celebrated President Abe Addon, in key metropolitan centers around the world. Locations where the statues will be erected include: Washington, London, Moscow, Paris, Beijing, and most other large cities around the globe. Of all the world's nations, only a few declined the honor of having a statue of Abe Addon placed there, most notably Vatican City. In all the nations where they were erected, the statues were welcomed with great fanfare. Followers of the host countries immediately gathered around the statues, making petitions of Abe Addon ranging from good health, to great riches, and everything in between. Many also asked for the destruction of their hated enemies, the Christians. Others hailed the statues as a sign that humanity is now entering a new age of prosperity, peace, and hope, with Abe Addon leading the way. The primitive notion of some ancient desert deity being the only way to happiness has now been made obsolete, because a new savior of the world has arrived, and his name is Abe Addon.'

I shook my head in utter disbelief. How could so many people be so devoid of discernment, how could they be so *blind*? I wondered whether *I too* would have been deceived, had the Lord not chosen me, or had I rejected the role to which he had appointed me. I wanted to believe that I would never have bought into the lies, yet so complete was the deception, so powerful was Addon's hold over the people, that I knew it was likely that without the gift of discernment, which the Lord gives to those who follow him, I *would certainly have* been just as deceived as everyone else. Addon was attracting more and more followers each day, leading them astray so that they might accompany him when he was cast into his new home in the Lake of Fire.

How sad it was that they rejected the Lord, the one that had sent his own beloved son to die so that they might have eternal life. So powerful was the desire to reject God's authority, to have their fill of sin and rebellion, that they chose *eternal* suffering over the eternal happiness. *How ironic, and how sad.*

The waitress in the hotel's restaurant escorted me over to a table and brought me some menus, orange juice and a cup of coffee. A few minutes later, Moe arrived and joined me at the table. We walked over to the elaborate buffet, complete with everything from bacon, sausage, eggs, Belgian waffles, and French toast, to cereal, bagels, and oatmeal.

After giving thanks to God for our meal, we began discussing the current state of affairs.

"I made a decision last night Moe." A frown cropped up on Moe's face.

"You mean regarding what to do about Samuel?"

"Yes."

"John, I …" Moe started to say something, which I knew would be to encourage me to not abandon our mission and by so doing, play right into the hands of Addon. I interrupted him.

"Moe, I want to continue on our mission, I want to stay the course."

"What about Samuel?" he asked, surprised by my decision.

"I have given it a lot of thought. If I were to take him up on his offer, it is still doubtful that he would ever let Samuel go; he would probably hold onto him as insurance. No, the right thing to do, for Samuel, Lara, and me, is to trust in the Lord. Only *he* can deliver Samuel from the hand of the evil one." Moe looked at me, seemingly uncertain at first as to how to take the news. After spending a few moments considering the matter, he offered me a warm and thoughtful smile.

"I honestly cannot say for certain how I would have reacted had I been in your place; you are a remarkable man, John March. I am beginning to see why the Lord chose you."

I just looked back at Moe in disbelief. I didn't agree with his assessment of me at all. "Listen Moe, I am simply following the course of action that I believe will save the life of my son."

"That's called faith, John, and it's the reason I am so impressed with your decision."

I took out the newspaper and showed it to Moe. "It's getting worse, Moe. More and more people are starting to worship the beast. We need to do something, soon."

"Do you have something in mind, John?" he asked, already knowing the answer to his own question.

"I do. I think we should see if Vicki Reynolds would be interested in another interview." Moe just raised his eyebrows and tilted his head.

We finished breakfast and got to work on finalizing plans for moving into our new homes in Jerusalem. We contacted the moving company and arranged to have them meet us at our respective houses that afternoon. We then began moving our luggage down to the rental car while our wives went down to the restaurant to grab some breakfast.

Once they had finished eating, we checked out of the hotel and made our way to the police station. We left our contact information with the police there, asking them to call us as soon as they had any new information. The detective apologized for their lack of progress and after instructing us to check with him daily, promised us that he would let us know as soon as he had any new information to share.

I waited until we were well on our way to Jerusalem before I broke the news to Lara. She was still feeling distraught and uncomfortable. We both felt it, the cold, sick, empty feeling inside, that we were starting our new lives without our precious son. When I finally told her about my initial suspicions, and the subsequent phone call from Addon, she was understandably angry with me for withholding the information about our son, and the fact that Addon was using Sam as leverage in trying to discourage me from my mission. After venting some of her pent-up emotion, she apologized, before again breaking into tears.

"Oh, John, what are we going to do? He *has* our *son!*"

"We will continue to do what we have been doing to this point, Lara. We will pray for his safety and his safe return."

"Do you think he'll let little Samuel go?" she asked me.

"I don't know for sure, Lara, but I think he will. I don't believe the Lord will allow harm to come to Sam."

We completed the trip from Tel Aviv to Jerusalem in just under an hour. After driving around Jerusalem for another thirty minutes, we finally found the realtor's office, and after signing some additional paperwork and picking up the keys, we left to find our new house, our new home in the Holy Land. We pulled into the driveway for the first time around noon that same day. We were pleasantly surprised to find the electricity already on and the phone service already active upon our arrival. We spent the remainder of the afternoon unpacking. The most difficult task for either of us fell to Lara; unpacking the boxes meant for Sam's room. She had barely opened the first box when she burst into tears. I silently chided myself for being so thoughtless and inconsiderate. The painful process of unpacking his things was something she should not have to do alone.

"I'm so sorry, Lara. I don't know what I was thinking. Just moving into our new home for the first time, the excitement of being here, in Israel... I just wasn't thinking," I said shamefully. I knelt down on the floor beside her, and held her close. "I'm so sorry, sweetheart. Listen, maybe we should wait and unpack his things later."

"No!" she screamed. "I will not! He's coming home, Johnny, do you hear me!" I wanted to beat my head into the wall. I asked myself if God could have made a mistake in choosing me.

"Honey, I didn't mean to imply that he wasn't. I just thought it might be better for you to rest for a while, and that we both could finish his room later, together." I watched as the mixture of intense anger and fear on her face slowly began to fade, before disappearing altogether.

Lara let out a heavy sigh. "Will God do anything, John? Will he return our child to us, so we can spend time with him for the few years remaining?"

"Lara, life will not be ending, for any of us... it will go on. All of us, including Sam, will be with the Lord for all eternity!"

"I know, John, I know. It's just, well, I feel like such a failure for not protecting him, our child, from that...*thing*."

"I know, Lara, me too. Remember, I was the one watching him when he vanished. It really doesn't matter, however. There's nothing either of us could have done, he's too powerful. There is something *God* can do, however, and I have been praying that he will do just that ever since Sam disappeared. We have to trust him, Lara; we have to trust God no matter what happens."

We sat there in silence for several minutes, looking at Sam's things, looking around the room, and finding comfort in our embrace.

"You know something?" Lara asked, breaking the silent vigil, "I find it comforting to know that Addon has Sam."

"What?" I asked, dumbfounded by the strange and completely unexpected remark.

"For two reasons," she answered. "First, at least I know where he is."

"Okay, I guess that makes sense, sort of. And the second?" I asked, still befuddled.

"Because I know that you're right, God is in control, and we have to trust him, no matter what. Besides, somehow, I just know that everything is going to be okay."

It was nine o'clock that evening when Moe and I tried calling Vicki Reynolds. We had surprisingly little trouble getting through to her.

"Hello, Ms. Reynolds. We were wondering whether you would be interested in doing another interview with us?"

Two days later, we met Vicki Reynolds at the Western Wall in Old Jerusalem. The same cameraman, Mike Tanner, was with her.

"Good morning, gentlemen. It's good to see both of you again. Thank you for flying all the way to Israel, just to meet with us."

"Believe me, it's my pleasure! You're going to make my career as a journalist, Mr. March!" She then turned to face Moe. "Hello, Mr. Princeton."

"Good morning, Ms. Reynolds."

"The networks have promised that I can stay on the story and continue the interviews for as long as we keep bringing in the ratings," she said, smiling through tight lips.

"I'm afraid that this 'story' is much more important than your career or the network's ratings, Ms. Reynolds," Moe told her sternly.

"Of course, I didn't mean to ..."

"Don't worry, Ms. Reynolds, we understand. We just want to make sure that you understand how significant this really is."

She nodded, before looking around where we were standing. "Okay, this looks like a great location. Are you ready?"

"We are," I answered.

"Then let's get started, shall we?"

Mike Tanner held up his hand toward Vicki Reynolds and began counting. "Okay, we're on in 3-2-1."

"Good morning. We are here live today in Old Jerusalem, Israel, at the famous Western Wall, with the now-famous last two prophets, John March and Moe Princeton. They are with us today with a new message." She then held the microphone up to me.

"Mr. March, would you like to share this new message with us?"

"Yes," I answered, before clearing my throat. "The message we are about to share with you is intended for every man, woman, and child, in every nation, all over the world, that follows the beast rather than God. Why is it that you sin against the Lord by disobeying him? Do you believe you can strive against the Almighty and win? The only reason he has not already destroyed us is that he is longsuffering, and desires for all of us to be saved, and to come to the knowledge of the truth. He wants you to *accept* his greatest gift, Jesus Christ. Moreover, because he loves you so, he has given you another, most precious gift, free will. Because he wants those that worship him to be free, he has granted you the power to either accept or reject him.

"Your time to choose is quickly running out, however. The window of opportunity in which you can turn from your sin and seek the Lord is now closing. These *are* the last days before the return of our Savior. Just as he said over two thousand years ago, 'lift up your eyes and look for behold, the fields are ripe for the harvest'.

"Now, in these last days before his return, the beast, Abaddon the destroyer, whom you know as Abe Addon, has come up from the pit. He now sets up statues of himself all over the world, images that many of you now fall down and worship, instead of worshipping the Lord! Remember, the Lord created every man, woman, and child, the evil and the good. Did he not create you also, who now fall down before the image of a demon? Why seek after demons, after wood, stone, money, pleasure, power, fame, fortune, and wickedness, instead of after the Lord?

"From the very beginning, humanity has sought to find an alternative explanation to explain man's origin; how we got here, and where we are going. Because man *knows* that if God *is* responsible for his creation, he must therefore exist. If God exists, then the Bible must be true. If the Bible is true, then man must obey the Lord, and keep his commandments.

"Now, the Lord is a jealous God. So that you may know that the Lord is God, and that he reigns over the whole world, you should prepare yourselves. For the Lord will send great signs and wonders, all of the plagues listed in the book of Revelation. You will see the handiwork of the Lord, before the return of the Son of God.

Do not be deceived by the rage and the power of the beast, for he knows the time approaches, when he will be cast into the Lake of Fire, where he will be tormented forever."

Once I had finished speaking, Vicki Reynolds motioned to Mike Tanner, who turned the camera towards her.

"This morning, John March and Moe Princeton, prophets of the Lord, have said that we should expect to see some rather remarkable signs and wonders over the next few years, until, they say, the end of the world arrives. In addition, they have also warned against following the President of the United States, Abe Addon, whom they refer to as 'the beast', saying that that he will be punished for his rebellion against God in the Lake of Fire. If the past prophecies of these men are any prediction of what is to come, please pardon the pun, then Mr. Faust and the others that set these statues up might want to give some serious thought to tearing them right back down again, and I mean fast. Reporting from Jerusalem, I am Vicki Reynolds, with INC news."

After arriving back home, I sat down on the front porch with Moe for a few moments before going inside.

"Any regrets?" he asked me.

"No, not really. That doesn't mean that I'm not worried, only that I believe I made the right decision. I just don't think the Lord will allow Addon to harm Sam." With the decision and the test past me now, I slipped into a moment of self-pity and despair.

"What have I done, Moe? I'm not cut out for this! I'm no prophet! I'm just an average guy!"

"You want to hear my opinion, John? I don't think there is anything average about you. Furthermore, I believe that you have a tremendous faith." I must have looked surprised by his comment because he continued. "But John, don't you see? You have demonstrated tremendous faith and trust in the Lord, by entrusting the life of your only son to him! And I'll tell you something else," he continued. "I think that somewhere, a little boy is sitting in a room, possibly even watching the interview we gave just a short while ago. Wherever that little boy is, my guess is that he is extremely proud of his father right now." I managed a weak smile, but sat there wondering what was going to happen to that little boy. Just then, my cell phone, which I had absent-mindedly placed inside my shirt before the interview, began to vibrate. When I answered, I heard a familiar voice on the other end of the line.

"Well, well, John March, that was impressive, very impressive indeed. You sacrificed your son rather than disobey the Lord. I guess I underestimated you, and believe me when I tell you that is something that I never do."

"What do you want, Addon?"

"I want a meeting with you John, a face to face."

"Why should I…"

"I'll give you your son back, alive and unharmed, if you agree to meet with me."

"Okay, just tell me when and where."

Chapter 22- Meeting in Washington

I was walking into the dragon's lair and I was afraid, not for myself, but for my only son, Samuel. Everything that man had ever known since the Garden of Eden was going to change, and I desperately wanted to spend at least *some* of my remaining years on Earth with my beautiful wife and son.

As I passed the time on the long plane trip back to the states, I found myself once more reflecting on my new role, and wondering what life was like for the prophets that had come before me. Had *they* experienced any of the same doubts I had experienced since learning the Lord had chosen me? Were they ever as unsure of themselves as I had been? Had *they* ever endangered their children the way I had endangered Sam? My tortured mind drifted from prophet to prophet, causing me to imagine them sharing in some of the challenges I was having. In my mind's eye, I could see them sitting in their homes next to the fire, trying to console their distraught wives, just as I had tried to offer comfort to Lara. Were they scared for themselves and for their families? Did *they* often doubt their own flimsy courage? Were *they* afraid that when the time came, they would run and hide, rather than face certain death? How did *they* handle the unbelievers, the scoffers, the danger, and the evil that *they* encountered? Did *they* have to contend with someone like Addon?

As I flipped through the various biblical figures in my mind that parade throughout the pages of the Bible, it became clear to me that most of the great heroes chronicled in scripture failed miserably at one time or another. Abraham lied about his wife, Sara, because he feared for his own safety. Moses struck the rock at the waters of strife out of anger, disobeying the Lord. David killed Uriah the Hittite so that he could have the man's wife without being stoned to death for adultery. Even Simon Peter, when confronted with the possibility of his own death panicked, denying three times that he knew the Lord. It seems all men share some of the same moral deficiencies, the same character flaws descended from original sin. Either way, my own doubts now weighed heavily upon me. I had always believed prophets were larger-than-life figures, always certain of themselves, always confident, while here I was, an average, ordinary man, caught up in extraordinary circumstances. I didn't have the kind of faith, *or* credentials, to be a *prophet*; or did I?

Doubts or not, I would soon face Addon once more, and God willing, see my son again. I squirmed yet again in my seat. The military plane Addon had sent to pick me up in Tel Aviv was obviously built for speed and not for comfort. The flight back to D.C. would take considerably less time however, than our flight *to* Israel aboard the more comfortable, civilian aircraft. The estimated flight time for the trip was around three hours, instead of the original twelve it had taken me to get from New York to Tel Aviv.

I had never expected to see Washington, DC again, except perhaps on television, nor had I ever planned to be back in the *United States* for that matter. Nevertheless, Addon had said if I wanted Samuel back I would have to meet with him in Washington, and that I would have to meet him alone.

Lara had done her best to dissuade me from going to meet with Addon, warning me that it was an obvious trap, and worried that she would end up losing us both. I reassured her by reminding her that the one that had called me was faithful, and that I believed he would protect me *and* my family until my work was complete.

I was on my own this time. Addon would not allow me to bring anyone, not even Moe, to the meeting. Though I trusted in the Lord for deliverance, fear sat in my chest like a lump of coal as I flew to meet with the beast. I knew who, and *what,* he was. I reminded myself that I also knew who and what the *lLord* was, the one who is sovereign over the entire universe, the one who formed everything. I found great comfort in the words in 1 John 4:4, "greater is he that is in you, than he that is in the world..."

As I looked out of the small window and into the deep dark-blue of near space, it struck me how cold and lonely it looked, and I was reminded how lonely Sam must have been at that particular moment, held captive by a creature like *Addon.* My thoughts turned toward Addon as I struggled to ascertain what he wanted from me. He was certain to threaten Samuels life, probably Lara's as well, but I did not care. I was going to face him again and no matter what he threw at me, I *would* stand my ground, resting firmly in the arm and protection of the Lord.

Thirty minutes later the pilot's voice came over the intercom, announcing that we would soon be landing at Ronald Reagan Washington National Airport. The announcement stirred me from MY contemplations, and caused me to forget about Addon for a time. There were just under a dozen military men and women on the flight with me, all of them returning from the Middle East. One of the tougher-looking soldiers in the group was an Army Ranger; the others were in the 82nd Airborne out of Ft. Bragg, NC. Following the announcement, the soldiers continued chatting amongst themselves, just as they had been since the plane left Tel Aviv. The discussion spanned a wide-range of topics, mostly centered on what they would do when they got home, until the conversation gradually shifted to politics. Several talked on and on about Addon, and about how he was changing things for the better. One of the men read a newspaper that had Addon's picture splashed all over the front page. The pitch in their voices rose as they talked about Addon, revealing the sincere, if misguided, affection and high regard they held for him.

As I listened to them talk, I began to understand what we were up against. So many people had been seduced by Addon and his sacrilegious railings against the Lord and his people that trying to refute him sometimes seemed pointless.

I was thinking about what I would do when Sam and I arrived back in Jerusalem when one of the soldiers, the one reading the newspaper, suddenly looked up at me with a flash of recognition. He called to his friends and began pointing at me, and then to a picture in the newspaper… *my* picture. The attitude and the demeanor of the soldiers then took a turn for the worse as they began talking about me, pointing and staring at me with great displeasure and furrowed brows. Two of them unfastened their seatbelts and started walking towards me.

"Hey, I know who you are," one of them said, poking me in the shoulder with his index finger. "You're that nutcase that keeps popping up in the news. You're one of those creeps threatening all of the plagues and stuff if we don't take down the statues of President Addon. Don't you know that he's the greatest man to ever walk this planet! What do you think you're doing anyway? You're scaring people with that kind of talk. *I* say you're just a *punk*." He grabbed my shirt around the shoulder, jerking me around a bit before throwing me back into my seat. Another soldier came over and sat next to me before pulling out his K-BAR and holding it close to my throat. I was beginning to wonder whether I would survive the trip, much less my meeting with Addon, when another soldier, the lone Army Ranger, came over from where he had been sitting alone. He grabbed the man closest to me and shoved him back towards his seat.

"Alright Rodriguez, Shipton, that's enough, knock it off, and I mean *now*." Rodriguez stepped away from me, leaving only Shipton, the one with the knife. The ranger looked squarely at Shipton, who continued pressing his K-Bar against my larynx until blood began trickled down my neck.

"Do you have any idea what will happen to you Shipton, if you mess this up? We are under direct orders from the President himself that under *no circumstances* is this man to be injured or harassed in any way. From what I am told, the President was quite adamant about this. Disobey his orders at your own risk." Shipton looked down at me, then at the ranger.

"Oh, come on Miller, lighten up a little. Maybe I'll just leave him a little scar, a souvenir to remember me by," he said, snarling and smiling as he did so. The ranger, recognizing that the situation was now under control, simply shook his head.

"That's a negative, Shipton. This man is to be left alone at all costs," Miller responded. He was a little more forceful this time around. Shipton looked at me again, still weighing his options. "If you harm that man, you will answer to me for it, you got that?"

Shipton studied Miller for a moment before smiling and nodding his head. As a seasoned combat veteran himself, he knew that Miller meant what he said. While he did not seem to know Miller personally, he was clearly familiar enough with the ranger's reputation as an extremely dangerous fighter, and one not one to be trifled with. Undoubtedly, Shipton could not stand the sight of me, but he was not prepared to die yet either, not just yet anyway.

"Hey, no harm done," he said smiling, carefully taking his knife away from my throat, so as not to cut me by accident. "Just relax, Miller," Shipton told the ranger, as he walked back over to his seat. He looked over his shoulder and back at me several times, smiling at me, almost as if to say, "Next time, March…"

After catching my breath and regaining some measure of composure, I walked over to where Miller now sat in his seat, reading, "The Sum of All Fears."

"Hey, listen, I really appreciate that, thanks," I said to Miller. He looked up at me for several moments. I had difficulty reading his expression, so I could not tell whether he had helped me because he was just following orders, or because he was sympathetic to my plight.

"Don't worry about it, Mr. March, I was just following orders." He paused for a moment, contemplating whether he should continue or just stop there. He decided on the former. "Listen sir, I have a lot of respect for you, and what you represent. You see, I too am a believer. There seems to be very few of us around these days however, at least few that are willing to stand up for what they believe. I admit that I don't understand everything that's going on right now, but I *do* know that you really need to be careful. People that follow President Addon *really* follow him, if you get my drift. Most of the soldiers I come across these days are just like those men up there. Whatever this strange attraction to Addon is, it is so powerful and fervent that you must be extremely careful, Mr. March. They will kill you if they can." He looked down for several moments, before looking up thoughtfully to add, "These are some pretty scary times, Mr. March, would you, err…please pray for me and my family?"

I must have been taken aback by Miller's response, because it was a while before I finally answered, "Of course, it would be my pleasure."

We landed at Reagan International Airport about fifteen minutes later, without any further incidents of threats or intimidation. I made my way to Ground Transportation, where a driver holding up a sign with my name was waiting for me. I grabbed my bags and followed the driver to the car that was waiting for me outside. He placed my luggage in the trunk of the car and opened my door. I climbed inside and we sped away from the airport, and towards downtown D.C.

"Peace be with you John."

Startled, I turned my head to see an angel sitting next to me in the limousine. "Who are you, and why are you here?" I asked. The limousine driver must have heard me talking because he looked at me with a puzzled expression through his rear view mirror. It seemed I could see the angel but he could not.

"I have only a few minutes John, before I must go. I am here to provide encouragement and to comfort you, and to confirm that your suffering is on account of the Lord, whom you have proven yourself faithful to serve."

"Will anything happen to my son? Will he kill my son?"

"No, your son will not be harmed by the beast. He has been restrained from harming you or those close to you, until your witnessing has been completed."

"Then why does he seek this meeting with me? What does he have to gain?"

"Because he knows that he can do nothing to stop you, so he seeks instead to instill fear into your heart, to do anything he can to slow you down. Nevertheless, the beast will not be successful in this, because the Lord *will* prosper your way. Do not be afraid, John March, and remember, it is the Lord that fights for you. He *will* protect you in all that you do." I was starting to say something else, when he suddenly vanished, just as we pulled up to the White House grounds. We had arrived.

The security screening went quickly and was surprisingly smooth, and I was inside the Oval Office within ten minutes after our arrival. It was another fifteen minutes before Addon finally made his appearance. He walked into the office, looking at me as he did so, with an uncanny, intense, cold, hard stare, and a disarmingly warm smile, wearing both at the same time. Despite what I knew about him, I found myself *wanting* to believe it was sincere, even though I knew it was only a lie. Addon's charisma *was* as powerful as it was supernatural.

"John March, hello again. Please, don't get up," he said, walking towards the desk, not even looking in my direction." *That smile and stare again.* "Please pardon my fashionably late appearance. It really is a lot of fun playing the part of a human being, especially the role of the president. Think about it, I could push 'the button' at any moment, and turn this zoo of hairless apes into a pile of nuclear ash. How *cool* is that, to use the vernacular of the young humans of this age." He sat down and focused his gaze on me once more. *The smile and stare again.*

"John March, oh, John March, what *am* I supposed to do with you? I can't kill you, yet, as much as I would like to, and believe me, I truly *would* like to." *The smile.* "Your *son*, however, well, he is an entirely different story. I…"

I interrupted him. "No, he isn't *demon*." He looked at me again.

"What do you mean by that?"

"My son isn't a different story at all. An angel of the Lord appeared to me on the way over here. He told me that you cannot harm me or anyone close to me until my work here is finished." Addon was furious and he did not bother to hide it.

"*An angel*? One of *his* angels?"

"Of course." I answered. Addon stood and began walking around. "In fact, I believe that you've already pushed the limits by just kidnapping my son." He wheeled and got down within inches of my face. It was meant to be an intimidating gesture and to be honest; I teetered on the brink of panic. The feeling soon passed, however, and I returned his gaze, remembering 1 John 4:4, '*greater is he that is in you, than he that is in the world.*' Once he realized that the intimidation tactic was not working, he grunted, and walked back over to the desk and sat down.

"Humans. I never understood why the Eternal ever bothered creating you pathetic, hairless apes." He leaned over the desk a little, looking as if he might come over it to get at me. "Mark my words human, we *will* see each other again, soon, I promise. I can be patient. To one as old as I, three hundred years is but a blink of an eye, how much less three years? Remember that, you pathetic ape. You may be one of his favorites today, but that can change at any moment."

"And *you* remember…" I retorted, "…the ending to this little drama has already been written, by him, with *you* ending up in the lake of fire."

Enraged this time, he momentarily shifted back to his true form. It was the first time I had ever seen it with my own eyes. Suddenly, I felt the Holy Spirit fill me. The words left my mouth of their own volition.

"*But the beast was captured, and with him the false prophet who had performed the miraculous signs on his behalf. With these signs, he had deluded those who had received the mark of the beast and worshiped his image. The two of them were thrown alive into the fiery lake of burning sulfur.*"

At this Addon wailed loudly in anger, completely changing back to his true form. The unearthly noise echoed so loudly throughout the Oval Office that for a moment, I fully expected the Secret Service to come storming through the door, guns blazing. Apparently, however, those outside the door were oblivious to what was happening inside. After a few minutes, his rage subsided, and he resumed his human shape once more. He took a deep breath before staring at me once more, his eyes focused like lasers but cold as ice.

"I too, know how this little drama ends," he retorted. "I especially like the part that goes, '*now when they have finished their testimony; the beast that comes up from the Abyss will attack them, and overpower and kill them.*'"

"Oh, but you didn't finish it," I interjected. "*But after the three and a half days a breath of life from God entered them, and they stood on their feet, and terror struck those who saw them. Then they heard a loud voice from heaven saying to them, Come up here. And they went up to heaven in a cloud, while their enemies looked on...*"

Addon gritted his teeth and pushed a button. "Bring our *guest* to my office."

"Yes, Mr. President."

A beautiful woman opened the door. Someone came up from behind her.

"Daddy!" Samuel came running into my arms.

"Sam! Oh, Sam. My son, my sweet, sweet son, I've missed you so!"

"Ms. Fairchild, please see to it that these two are provided with transportation to the airport."

We hugged for what seemed like the longest time. As we were walking out of the Oval Office, Addon yelled after me.

"I'll see you again, Mr. March, *real soon.*"

"I look forward to it!" I yelled back.

Chapter 23- The Seals

"And I saw in the right hand of him that sat on the throne a book written within and on the back, sealed with seven seals. And I saw a strong angel proclaiming with a great voice, Who is worthy to open the book, and to loose the seals of it? And no one in the heaven, or on the Earth, or under the Earth, was able to open the book, or to look thereon. And I wept much, because no one was found worthy to open the book, or to look on it: and one of the elders said to me, Weep not; behold, the Lion that is of the tribe of Judah, the Root of David, has overcome to open the book and the seven seals of it...

"...And when he had taken the book, the four living creatures and the four and twenty elders fell down before the Lamb, having each one a harp, and golden bowls full of incense, which are the prayers of the saints. And they sang a new song, saying, You are worthy to take the book, and to open the seals of it: for you were slain, and did purchase for God with your blood men of every tribe, and tongue, and people, and nation, and made them to be to our God a kingdom and priests; and they reign upon Earth..." Revelation Chapter 5

A White House car took Sam and I to Reagan International Airport, where we purchased a couple of tickets for our trip back to our new home in Jerusalem; a new home that Sam had so far had no opportunity to enjoy. It was on the flight back to Tel Aviv, while Sam slept on my shoulder, that another vision came to me from the Lord. The angel appeared to me to encourage me, and to offer a word of warning.

"John March, you and Moe Princeton are to carry the Lord's message to his people. Warn them that the plagues of the prophecy he gave to his servant John, the ones written in the book of Revelation, will soon come upon the Earth. It is time for all men to repent of the great evil that they have done by turning away from the Lord, and clinging instead to demons and falsehoods, and their own foolish pride. Behold, he has put his words in your mouth. Take care to warn his people, for if you withhold the Lord's warnings from them, then their blood will be upon your head. As he told his servant Ezekiel long ago, 'But if the watchman see the sword come, and blow not the trumpet, and the people be not

warned, and the sword come, and take any person from among them; he is taken away in his iniquity, but his blood will I require at the watchman's hand.' As he sent Ezekiel, so he now sends you. You must warn them, or their blood will be upon *your* head."

The return of our son to us was a time of joyous celebration in our home in Jerusalem. Our son, Sam, was back home now and the March family was whole once more, at least for a time. We spent the rest of that evening celebrating Sam's return, enjoying some of our precious time together, immensely grateful to have Sam back with us. The celebration was short-lived however. After several days of spending time together as a family, I told Moe about the visitation, and the warning. We had work to do, for the words the Lord had placed in my mouth were like a consuming fire, bursting to get out.

The following morning Moe and I made for one of the more bustling areas of Jerusalem, Machane Yehuda, and the central market in Jerusalem, where tourists and residents alike could find great deals on vegetables, fresh chickens, and so forth. A noisy, bustling, and often-crowded market, people gathered in search of food that was fresh and inexpensive. We arrived early on a particularly busy Saturday.

My heart began to race and pound in my chest, as I prepared to do the work I had been called for. As before, the words came forth of their own accord.

"People of Israel," I began, "worshippers of YAHWEH and unbelievers alike, hear my words. The time has come for *all* to repent, and to come to the knowledge of the Truth. Turn your hearts, and the hearts of your people, back to the one true God. It is the fulfillment of the *Hisgalus,* the revelation that our Lord gave to his servant John over two thousand years ago. The *divrei hanevu'ah*, the words of this prophecy, are about to take place. Behold, a time of war, of famine, of pestilence, a time of great suffering and death, is at hand. Do not turn away from the Lord, but turn back to Him with all of your heart, for by so doing you will save your souls!"

"Behold!" Moe cried out, "some of the seals have already been broken, and the great and terrible Day of the Lord is now upon you. Has the Lord your God not warned you time and time again? Has he not repeatedly called out to you across the ages, pleading with you to repent? As it is written in the book of Isaiah, the prophet,

'Come now, and let us reason together, says the LORD: though your sins be as scarlet, they shall be as white as snow; though they be red like crimson, they shall be as wool.'

Or as it is written in he book of Micah the prophet,

"He has shown you, O man, what is good; and what does the LORD require of you, but to do justly, and to love mercy, and to walk humbly with your God?'

Has the Lord not given you plenty of opportunities to turn away from the sinful ways in which you walk, and to turn back to follow your creator, the God of your fathers? Why have you turned your backs to him, denying his very existence to the peril of your eternal souls? You must turn back to him now, before it is too late."

Crowds started to gather around us as we continued to prophesy. Most of the men and women in the crowd seemed stunned by what we were saying, unsure how to react. One man, dressed as an orthodox Jew, asked us, "Who are you men, and what exactly do you want?"

"We are witnesses of the Lord, the last of the prophets, sent to warn you to repent in these last days, before it is too late," I answered.

"Are you the two Americans that caused the waters to turn to blood, and withheld the rains from us?"

"We have not done this thing by our own power, but the Lord's. It is *he* who warns you now, and gives you these signs and wonders."

Another man in the crowd, dressed in an expensive suit and acting as if he owned the world, looked at us with contempt and said, "This is the twenty-first century. Do you honestly believe that anyone believes in prophets anymore? Most of us here are secular Jews anyway, many don't even believe in God, so go and peddle your God-stuff somewhere else, and leave us alone."

I looked at the man, and at those standing all around him, nodding their heads with him in agreement with what he had said. "Very well then," I said to them, "behold, the plagues of the Lord begin which are written in the book of Revelation. You will now witness the wrath of the Lord, and you will know that he *is* God. Repent, and seek the Lord, or perish in your sin and suffer the eternal consequence of your rebellion! Behold the plagues!"

I pointed toward the sun, which would soon be darkened by a sudden and unexpected eclipse, even as the Earth beneath our feet began to tremble. As the earthquake intensified, glass began to shatter and fall from the buildings. The structures themselves began to rumble and shake, before collapsing into heaps of rubble. The crowd, led by the arrogant businessman, began running through the streets in terror as the eclipse and Earthquake threw the city into a state of panic. As we calmly walked back toward our homes, a young mother with two small children in tow ran up and grabbed me by my arm.

"Tell me, man of God, what must I do so that my children and I are spared from God's wrath?" I looked upon the woman as she stood there clutching her small son and daughter, neither of which could have been more than eight years old. She had tears streaming down her face. "Please sir, tell me!"

"The Lord loves you *and* your children, dear lady. I will tell you what the apostles Paul and Silas told the prison guard, when there was a great Earthquake and the walls of the prison were shaken,

'And they said, Believe on the Lord Jesus Christ, and you shall be saved, and your house. And they spoke to him the word of the Lord, and to all that were in his house.'

So I now tell you, believe on the Lord Jesus Christ, and you shall be saved."

The young woman looked up at the sky, where the light of the sun remained obscured by the moon. She looked around her as the buildings continued to crumble under the relentless shaking and rumbling of the Earth.

"I believe, sir, I do believe that Yehoshua, Jesus, *is* the son of God. I believe that he died for my sins, and the sins of my family."

"Then go in peace, dear lady, and may the peace of our Lord Jesus Christ be with you, and with your family." She nodded and after thanking me once more, ran off towards her home with her children beside her.

While the crowds scattered in all directions, struggling to find their way in the unexpected darkness, I pondered what other wonders I would see over the next few years, as the will of God was manifest to the world. One thing I knew; it was going to become increasingly difficult for those who despised the Lord, spurning the forgiveness and mercy he had freely offered them. These Godless men and women would soon learn the frightening cost associated with mocking the creator of the universe.

Chapter 24-Reassurance

Like everyone else, we spent the first few days immediately following the earthquake without power, though we still had water. Streams of visitors made their way through our small home during that time. Many were Christians, either asking questions or expressing support for our mission. Some were Orthodox Jews, seeking to understand what our message was in light of their faith.

Others, however, were enemies of God, seeking to disrupt or put a stop to our mission through intimidation, throwing rocks at our home as they drove by, yelling obscenities, or making threatening phone calls. Throughout the growing threat to our lives, the Lord gave us a tremendous peace, covering each of us in a soothing blanket of serenity. Despite this great gift from God, however, Lara was unable to forget how Addon had snatched away our son in the blink of an eye, and how he might have done unspeakable things to Sam in order to get to me. One evening, while we waited on word from the Lord, Lara finally let out some of the pent-up emotion.

"What are we going to do, John, if someone breaks into our home and tries to burn it to the ground one evening while we are in bed?" "What if someone injures or even kills our son?" she asked in tears. "It seems like more and more people hate us anymore, John," she added. "Are you sure you know what you're doing?"

I walked over to Lara and sat down next to her on the sofa, hoping to console her. She snuggled up next to me, sobbing, as I put my arm around her.

"You know something, sweetheart?" I asked her, pulling her close to me as I did so.

"What?"

"The Lord brought us together, Lara. You want to know *why* I believe that?"

"Why?" she asked, as the sobbing began to subside.

"Because I know for certain that there are few women on the face of this Earth that would be able to go through what you are going through, and still keep it together. In fact, I know of only two women that could, and one of them is named Doris."

"And the other?" she asked me, a hint of a smile on her face, that curled up slightly on either side of her mouth.

"Well, let's see…" I started. She grabbed one of the sofa pillows and hit the side of my head with it.

"You are a real piece of work Jonathan Elijah March!" she said with a smirk. It was good to see her smile.

"You have been such a trooper through all of this," I continued, "and I want you to know that whatever we face, we will never face it alone. God chose us for this work, and I believe he will be there with us until the end, and beyond." I paused for a moment, watching her countenance change from despair to contemplation. "Listen, Lara, I know it's been hard for you lately, especially with what happened with Sam. I know that I've said this before, but I think it bears repeating, we must have faith that the Lord will see us through all of this. That is what faith is after all, isn't it? We must trust him to strengthen and support us, and to be with us through our times of tribulation. As it says in Proverbs, 'Trust in the Lord with all your heart; and lean not upon your own understanding. In all your ways acknowledge him, and he shall direct your paths.' It will all be over soon, sweetheart, and we will have a much greater home than this waiting for us on the other side."

"I just get so scared sometimes, John. I *know* that what you are saying is true, and I know that God *is* faithful, and that He will perform all that He has said he would do. It's just that…"

"…that it's not so easy to do?" I finished for her. "I know Lara, I know." I looked at her and I could see the lingering fear in her eyes, the uncertainty. I dreaded asking the question forming in my mind. "Lara, any regrets?"

"About what, John?"

"About marrying me? I know this is probably more than you bargained for, when you married me that is."

She looked at me with her beautiful, piercing eyes, and said, "Absolutely not." "None," she added for emphasis.

I realized that I had stopped breathing as I waited for her answer, so I took in a deep breath.

After a few moments, Lara turned to me again and asked, "What do you suppose it will be like John, after Jesus returns?"

I just shook my head, stared out the window at the clouds for a moment, before turning back to face her. "I'm not sure, Lara, but I do believe that it's going to be *wonderful*. Remember, he has offered us some descriptions in the book of Revelation. Remember how it says, *'Then I saw a new heaven and a new Earth, for the first heaven and the first Earth had passed away, and there was no longer any sea. I saw the Holy City, the New Jerusalem, coming down out of heaven from God, prepared as a bride beautifully dressed for her husband. And I heard a loud voice from the throne saying, "Now the dwelling of God is with men, and he will live with them. They will be his people, and God himself will be with them and be their God. He will wipe every tear from their eyes. There will be no more death or mourning or crying or pain, for the old order of things has passed away."'*

"Those are reassuring words, John, I must admit." She looked off for a moment, as if she were reflecting on something and wanted to gather her thoughts. "You know, Johnny," she said, "the world often seems so cruel and so unkind. So many people go about their lives each day, living in such suffering and misery! How will we ever be able to adjust to an eternity of bliss and happiness with the Lord?"

"Well, I suppose that we will have all of eternity to make that adjustment. I would say that ought to be time enough," I answered, smiling. She hit me with the pillow again.

Samuel came over to the sofa and sat next to me. He leaned his head on my shoulder and said to me, "Dad, I'm tired. Can I go to bed now?"

"Of course you can, Son. Why don't you go and get me the Bible so we can read before you turn in, okay?"

"Sure, Dad."

Samuel walked over to the table where we kept our family Bible. We read a chapter out of it every night, a habit that dated back several years.

"Thanks, Sam," I said to him, taking a moment to give him a hug.

"Okay, let's see, where are we tonight?" I asked, looking for the bookmark. The Bible opened to the Book of Matthew, the fourth chapter, and I began reading. When I arrived at verse twenty-nine, I looked up at Lara for a moment before continuing, "'... Immediately after the tribulation of those days shall the sun be darkened, and the moon shall not give her light, and the stars shall fall from heaven, and the powers of the heavens shall be shaken: And then shall appear the sign of the Son of man in heaven: and then shall all the tribes of the Earth mourn, and they shall see the Son of man coming in the clouds of heaven with power and great glory. And he shall send his angels with a great sound of a trumpet, and they shall gather together his elect from the four winds, from one end of heaven to the other.'"

After we finished reading, Sam gave us both a hug and went off to bed. Lara and I sat back down. She lay down on the sofa and put her head in my lap.

"You want to know something, John?"

"What, honey?" I asked.

"You certainly have changed from that little boy I met so many years ago, the one I was so worried about. Those years following your father's death, when you started getting into trouble…well I wasn't sure what was going to happen to you."

"Neither was I, Lara, for the longest time. I guess the Lord had plans for me."

"I want you to know how very proud I am of you, for having the courage to do what you're doing. I could never have asked for a better man to call husband."

"Thank you, Lara."

"And you want to know something else?"

"What?"

"I think your father would be proud of you too." I sat there and as my thoughts turned back for a moment to my father, I smiled broadly, beaming at the thought of him being proud of me.

"Thanks honey, that means a lot to me."

She yawned before glancing at the clock on the mantle. "Ready to go to bed yet, Johnny?" she asked me.

"You bet I am."

That night, I dreamed of a scene from the book or Revelation, in which a group of angels poured out plagues on the land and on the sea. I heard a voice saying,

'…After this I saw four angels standing at the four corners of the Earth, holding back the four winds of the Earth to prevent any wind from blowing on the land or on the sea or on any tree. Then I saw another angel coming up from the east, having the seal of the living God. He called out in a loud voice to the four angels who had been given power to harm the land and the sea: "Do not harm the land or the sea or the trees until we put a seal on the foreheads of the servants of our God." Then I heard the number of those who were sealed: 144,000 from all the tribes of Israel…'

I awoke in a cold sweat, climbed out of bed, and walked quietly out of our bedroom so as not to awake Lara, who was still sound asleep in our bed. I walked into the living room, picked up the family Bible, and sat down on the sofa. I thumbed through the book of Revelation until I found the chapter containing the imagery I had seen in the vision. I then looked up from the Bible, stared blankly across the room, and whispered quietly to myself, *The Seven Trumpets*.

Chapter 25-The False Prophet

I watched on television as the man known as Simon Faust arrived at the White House dedication in a long black limousine. He had a large entourage with him, all of whom wore a shirt or a badge with a picture of Abe Addon, wearing an insultingly fake smile, and the words "Friends of Addon" printed in large red, white, and blue letters underneath. One of the press cameras suddenly zoomed in for a close-up of Faust, and I felt a chill run down my spine. As he walked toward the platform, Faust stared into the camera and smiled. Somehow, it felt as if he were looking directly at me, *through the lens of the camera.* As he paused for the photo op, it was easy enough to see that the man had the same unsettling look, the same intense cold stare, and the same disarmingly warm smile that Abe Addon had. I began to understand the connection between the two men. Faust had been the driving force behind the Friends of Addon movement that had swept the globe. It was simply too much of a coincidence that a man that shared the same unnatural qualities as Addon, would also be the leader of a movement that had gained him an international following. Tirelessly traveling the globe, Faust had relentlessly peddled the suggestion to the masses of humanity that they should look at Addon not only as the President of the United States, but as the world's spiritual leader as well. Furthermore, he frequently suggested that Addon was something *more* than a man. I wondered what secrets he shared with Addon.

As Faust approached the lectern, I turned up the volume, wanting to listen to what he had to say.

"Friends, Americans, countrymen, lend me your ears!" he said. "Oops, how impolitic of me! That speech has already been given, by Marc Antony about Julius Caesar!"

That smile again. That chilling smile, even as he tried to elicit laughter. It made my skin crawl. Predictably, the crowd erupted with laughter and applause as excitement rippled throughout the gathering.

"Pardon me; I am afraid I am getting ahead of myself. Let me ask you, why are *we* here today? Why are *you* here today? I will tell you why. We are here to dedicate this effigy, this *statue*, as a monument to a very remarkable man, the man who most of us gathered here today believe to be our savior. This man, if I dare call him that is the best, brightest, most intelligent, most caring, wisest, bravest, most spiritual, and most discerning man on the planet! He is indisputably most worthy to be praised, worthy to be followed, and worthy to be worshipped! I am referring of course, to President Abe Addon!"

The crowd burst into yet another fervent round of applause as Faust paused for a moment. By this time I could clearly see that the man, the *creature*, possessed the same supernatural charisma, the same unearthly influence over the masses, as Addon. There could no longer be any doubt; Simon Faust *was* one of *them*.

"This magnificent statue of our wonderful and gracious leader is but a small token indeed, a most modest gesture, of the deep and boundless affection and adulation that we have for the magnanimous Abe Addon."

I began feeling as if I would vomit. The crowd at the ceremony, however, was eating it up, eagerly buying into everything Faust was selling.

"For the first time in human history, we have a leader that can and will make certain that all of you get what you deserve," Faust continued. "He is a leader that cares about you and me. We at the *Friends of Addon* believe that everyone should love and worship Addon as much as we do, because he truly deserves it." He turned to look down and behind where he was standing. I could now make out a stairway that approached the platform from behind where Faust was standing.

"And now, I present to you, our benevolent spiritual leader, our President, and our *lord*, Abe Addon."

Addon appeared from behind the platform and ascended to the lectern. He waved and smiled before shaking hands with Faust. The audience once more erupted with an ear-bursting roar of applause that lasted over five minutes, ending only when Addon motioned to everyone to stop. Seeing the two of them up on stage together was unbearable. I felt my nausea coming back.

"Thank you, thank you, everyone." The crowd exploded with applause, which continued until Addon finally motioned for the crowd to quiet down. You know, when Simon Faust first called my office and told members of my staff that the Friends of Addon wanted to erect a large statue of me here, on the White House grounds, I did have some reservations. But looking at this incredible piece of work now, well, I just cannot seem to recall what those reservations were!" The crowd started laughing and the applause started up once more, until Addon again motioned to the crowd to quiet down. "This incredible, wonderful statue, it is such an honor. I…"

A crackling sound suddenly reverberated through the crisp morning air, as a rifle cartridge struck Addon in the back of the skull, close to the Sagittal suture, before exiting from his forehead, leaving a large, unsightly, and gaping hole, in the middle of his forehead. Addon stood there briefly for several seconds, until his knees began to wobble and he collapsed out-of-sight behind the lectern. The crowd let out an almost simultaneous gasp. The Secret Service leapt into action, and like a colony of ants moving together in unison, they quickly identified and executed the assassin on the spot.

Some in the crowd began crying, others moaning, others screaming hysterically, creating a surreal landscape, until a man in the crowd yelled out, "Shhh… everyone quiet down! Listen!"

The crowd abruptly quieted to a whisper, as everyone listened intently for whatever it was that the man in the crowd was calling attention to. Suddenly, sounds of groaning and movement were heard coming from behind the podium. To everyone's shock and amazement, a hand unexpectedly appeared on the podium, followed by a second. Slowly, Addon's head appeared from behind the podium, as he lifted himself up from behind the fixture. In front of the international media, as well as the endless throngs of followers in attendance, Abe Addon slowly stood up, the wound still clearly visible, and a steady flow of blood streaming from his forehead and down his cheek. With the entire world watching, the blood flow slowed to a trickle before stopping altogether and drying up. I watched along with the rest of the world as the large gaping wound began to close, before disappearing completely. The crowd grew so quiet that one could nearly hear a pin drop.

Watching the scene unfold, I could not help but admire his acting prowess. There was no doubt about it; Hollywood had nothing on Abe Addon.

Simon Faust looked around at the assorted gathering of men, women, and children, many with their mouths still hanging open. The silence among the throng of people created an eerie atmosphere. Faust slowly turned towards Abe Addon, and smiled. Addon looked back at Faust and smiled thinly, before waving to the crowd. It was Faust's cue.

"Ladies and gentlemen, have you ever seen anything like this before? Have you? Did you see what just happened? The blood of this man is *still* splattered all over the stage, and yet, *he lives!* Not only does he live, he healed himself before your very eyes! Why, Abe Adon is not just a man! It's not possible for a man to live after being fatally wounded in the head as he was, in front of the entire world! Did you see the way the wound healed while we watched, did you? No man can do that! Why, to do something like that, he must be something *more* than a mere man. Perhaps he is a... dare I say it? I *do* dare. Is it possible, that Abe Addon is not just a man, but rather, *a god?*"

Faust stopped speaking for a moment as he looked around; assessing the temperature of the crowd, listening to the buzz in the crowd that started when he'd finished speaking. Incredibly, some in the crowd began nodding their heads in response to the question Faust had just put to the gathering, agreeing that maybe, just maybe, Abe Addon *was* indeed a god. Others voiced considerable skepticism, suggesting it was some kind of a trick. Faust looked over at Addon, who flashed a brief look of irritation at him. Faust, however, turned back to face the gathering and continued.

"Why, ladies and gentlemen, given what we have just seen, if someone were to do nothing more than to simply invoke his name, I believe that this statue of Abe Addon, this *image* of him, would soon come to life, in front of you and in front of the whole world! Even those of you that still have doubts must agree that if this did occur, it *must* be a sign that Abe Addon truly *is* a god, and should, therefore, be worshipped like one!"

A number of people began nodding their heads in agreement. Even a large burly man, one of the staunchest of the naysayers in the crowd, after looking at Addon, and then at the large statue, looked back at Faust.

"If President Addon can make that hunk of metal come to life, I would agree, he would have to be a deity."

"Very well then, sir, let's give it a try, and see what happens then, hmm?"

Just then, the camera did a close up and I caught what looked like Faust winking at Addon, who stood by with his arms crossed, looking magnanimous. Faust walked over to the statue, and making several grand gestures and sweeping motions, began speaking to the statue.

"Oh image of our most glorious and wonderful spiritual leader, image of him who suffered a fatal wound and yet lived, healed in front of the whole world. If Abe Addon is indeed something more than a man, if indeed he *is* a god, as I believe he must be, then I invoke his name, the name of Abe Addon, and I command you, Oh statue, though made of nothing more than metal, to take a breath, and to come to life this very moment."

Once more, an eerie silence fell over the crowd as they waited to see what, if anything would happen next. For some time (I believe it was merely for dramatic effect), nothing happened. Then, just as some in the crowd began shaking their heads, someone yelled out something.

"Hey, did you see that, I saw its eyes blink!"

A middle-aged woman in the crowd who was close to the statue cried out, "I just saw its hand move!"

Then, slowly, the statue began moving to face Addon, slowly raising its massive hands into the air, before kneeling down and bowing to Addon.

"Look at that everyone, he has made the impossible possible. Abe Addon has breathed life into this lifeless hunk of metal! Can there still be any doubt, any doubt at all, that you should follow this living statue's example, and bow down to worship Abe Addon, and serve him?"

The camera began panning the crowd, looking for a response to the challenge. A young college aged man in his twenties stepped forward.

"I believe Abe Addon *is* a god!" he yelled, before getting down on his knees facing Addon, who simply looked upon the young man and smiled, nodding in a pontificating, patronizing manner. Others began following suit, dropping to their knees before Addon, worshipping him. All the while, Addon looked into the camera and flashed a not-so-subtle smile.

I flicked off the television, and considered what I had seen. This was certain going to pose a challenge. Some had already been quietly proclaiming Addon to be something more than a man, but they had been confined to a small but growing minority. After what I had just witnessed however, I had no doubt that the minority was quickly going to become a vast majority. Recovering from a rifle shot to the head, and bringing an enormous metal statue to life, it was like something out of a bad Hollywood movie. The seemingly miraculous healing and the statue, coupled with his powerful supernatural influence, would exponentially increase his power and his hold on the people. Only those that faithfully followed the Lord Jesus Christ remained unmoved by the power displayed by Addon, though I suspected that even many of the faithful were frightened by it.

Lara and Samuel had gone out to run a few errands so I decided to walk next door to discuss what I had seen with Moe. I walked out into the fresh night air, hoping that they had not gone to bed. It was only ten o'clock but I knew that they sometimes went to bed early. I was about to knock on the door when I heard raised voices coming from inside the home. It sounded as if Moe and Doris were in the midst of some kind of an argument. I wheeled to turn around and leave when I suddenly heard my name mentioned. Embarrassed yet curious, I stopped for a moment to listen.

"I will not!" Moe insisted. "How could I ever say anything like that to him? John March is my friend, my brother, and my partner in this mission."

"Partner? I thought *you* were the one that just said that you felt like the redheaded stepchild in this relationship, that he had 'taken over', acting as if he were the 'boss'."

"I didn't say it like that, Doris, and you know it."

"Well, you might as well have, Moe. Listen, I'm your wife, I've known you for almost five decades. Did you think I couldn't tell that something has been wrong for a while now?"

"It's just that, well, he's so young Doris, young enough to be my son. Now it seems like he's the one in charge. He does most of the talking, and he makes most of the decisions. I feel like I should be doing more, that's all."

"Well if you ask me, Moe, I think you should walk right over to his place right now and tell him what's on your mind. Tell him that you didn't move all the way around the world to Israel just to follow him around like some puppy dog. I don't think you have it in you, Moe!"

"Alright then woman, I'll show you that I can..." Suddenly, the door flew open and I found myself staring at a suddenly confused, humiliated, and guilt-ridden Moe. He looked down for the longest time, and when he finally raised his eyes to meet mine, he spoke quietly.

"John, listen, I..." He stopped speaking as I turned around, stepped off his porch, and walked towards my house. I'm certain that he stood on his porch and watched me until I disappeared inside.

Chapter 26-Wormwood

A year had passed since the Earthquake shook Jerusalem during the eclipse. I had been soundly and blissfully asleep, when there came a loud and persistent knock on our front door. I looked over and noticed that Lara was still asleep. Looking down at my watch, I saw that it was still only seven o'clock, a bit early for a Saturday morning. The knocking was getting continually louder the longer I waited.

I grudgingly climbed out of my bed and put on my robe. If it was not important, I planned to give someone a bit of an earful for disturbing me so early in the morning. For some reason, I was not surprised to find the disturber of the peace to be none other than Moe. Reluctantly, I opened the door.

"What is it Moe, what in the world is so important?"

"Have you turned on the television yet?"

"No, I haven't. It's only seven o'clock in the morning, I was still in bed."

"I'm sorry to disturb you, John, but this is important." I just shook my head.

"Listen Moe, whatever Addon is saying, we can talk…"

"This isn't about Addon this time."

"Then   what…"
"May I please come in?" he asked sheepishly. I had left him standing out in the cold up until that point in our conversation.

"Of course, sure." I opened the door and Moe made a beeline for the television. He turned it on and sat down on my sofa.

"Moe, can't this wait? I…" I was going to tell him I wanted to go back to bed when what I saw on the television screen stopped my complaint in midsentence.

"Wow," was all I was able to muster. On the television screen was the picture of a massively large rock in outer space, an asteroid. On the bottom of the screen was a caption that read, "Planet Killer Asteroid

161

Named 'Wormwood' headed for Earth." I reached for the remote control and turned up the volume.

"The asteroid, named Wormwood by Christian astronomer Celeste Lewis, was discovered only yesterday, but appears to be on a rapid collision course with planet Earth. Here to speak with us at this late hour is reporter Vicki Reynolds, who is at the Near Earth Objects Observation Program at NASA headquarters in Washington, D.C. She is there with Dr. Steve Eagle, the current head of the program. Good evening Vicki. So what can Dr. Eagle tell us about the asteroid?"

"Good evening to you as well, Susan. As you stated, I am here this evening with Dr. Steve Eagle, the head of the Near Earth Objects Observation Program at NASA. Dr. Eagle, what can you tell us about this asteroid, and the threat it holds for our planet?"

"Well, it was spotted early yesterday morning by one of the large telescopes at our observatory just outside of Flagstaff, Arizona."

"You said it was just spotted yesterday morning? How is that possible? I thought something like this would have been easy for NASA to spot."

"Well you are correct, it should have been. The truth is that NASA has been too severely underfunded over the past few decades to be able to do everything that needs to be done, including searching for near Earth asteroids like this one."

"So you are saying that the reason that this thing wasn't spotted sooner was because NASA is underfunded?"

"That's exactly what I'm saying. Our telescopes just happened to be pointed in the general direction of this asteroid, and that's the only reason it was detected. It was pure chance that we saw it, but we *did* see it, and we alerted the proper authorities immediately after its discovery. The problem is, well, I don't know if I..."

"What is it, Dr. Eagle?"

"Well, this thing seemed to come out of nowhere. Dr. Celeste Lewis, the astronomer that first spotted it, told us that it was as if this thing appeared out of nothingness. One minute there was empty space, the next minute, there it was. Incredible, I know, but as you said earlier, Dr. Lewis *is* one of those Christians, so who knows what to believe?"

"Wait a minute. Dr. Lewis said that it just popped into existence, that one minute nothing was visible, and the next minute there it was?"

"That's what she says."

"But you don't believe that because she is a Christian?"

"No, that's not what I said. I said that it's hard to know what to believe from her because she is a Christian."

"I take it that you don't think much of Christians."

"Listen, if Christians want to believe in fairy tales about some fictitious God; they can, at least for now. But I'm a scientist, and I deal in facts, not fantasy."

"Like asteroids that appear out of nowhere?"

"Listen, I told you, that's what *she* said."

"If it didn't just *pop into existence*, why didn't you or someone else spot it sooner?"

"I told you, because we're underfunded."

"Dr. Eagle, please tell our audience, exactly what kind of danger is posed by this asteroid?"

"Well, we have estimated that this asteroid is approximately four thousand feet across. That means that if it remains intact, this asteroid could prove to be an E.L.E… an Extinction Level Event… and the end of life on Earth as we know it."

"You mean an event like the one that supposedly wiped out the dinosaurs."

"Not supposedly, Ms. Reynolds, remember, this is *science* we are talking about. It *definitely* wiped out the dinosaurs."

"Is there any possibility of it disintegrating in the Earth's atmosphere?"

"There is no possibility whatsoever that this asteroid will just disintegrate in the Earth's atmosphere, it's far too large."

"Is there any possibility of it missing the Earth?"

"No. It is close enough now that we can say with absolute certainty that it will, without question, strike the Earth."

"When do you expect it will hit?"

"We anticipate its impact sometime tomorrow night around nine o'clock Eastern Standard Time, somewhere in the Atlantic Ocean midway between the United States and Africa."

"Can you offer us any hope, any hope at all, Dr. Eagle?"

"I'm afraid not. If you are looking for hope, you might want to contact those so-called prophets that you interviewed a while back. Maybe *they* can offer you some hope." Susan gave him a cold and irritated look.

"Thank you, Dr. Eagle. Well there you have it Susan. According to Dr. Eagle, we are all going to die sometime around nine o'clock tomorrow night. Now I'll give it back to you, where I believe you have General Warren Easley from the Pentagon on the phone?"

"Thank you, Vicki. Yes, we have General Warren Easley, Chairman of the Joint Chiefs on the phone from the Pentagon. General Easley, are you there?"

"Yes I am, Ms. Smith, good evening to you."

"Good evening. General Easley, I understand that the Pentagon has been looking at options for destroying it ever since the Wormwood asteroid was discovered yesterday. How is that progressing?"

"We have been looking at options non-stop around the clock, and of course we will continue to do so. As your last guest, Dr. Eagle said, this thing could well be a planet killer. We have to find a way to destroy it."

"But General, if it *is* so close, is there really anything we can do?"

"Well, we don't know this for certain, but there is a chance that we can hit this overgrown rock with a number of nuclear missiles before it enters the Earth's atmosphere."

"But won't fragments of the asteroid still strike the Earth? There is no way of destroying it completely is there?"

"Well, we are certainly going to try, Ms. Smith. We have no choice, as I said."

"Are you able to tell us anything that will offer us any hope, General? It sounded as if Dr. Eagle was not."

"Well, I know it's not a popular thing to say these days, Ms. Smith, but I am certainly not afraid to say it. I am a Christian, so I always believe there is hope. If this thing is the same Wormwood that was prophesied in the Bible, this is all part of God's plan, so anything is possible, and I mean *anything*."

"And does President Addon know that you are a Christian, General? He's been aggressive about purging his administration of any Christian influence since he first entered office."

"I guess he does now, Ms. Smith."

"General, thank you for taking the time for this interview."

"You're welcome, Ms. Smith. I know there are many people out there who are frightened out of their minds about now. Let me just add that despite what anyone says, this is all in God's hands. Good night."

"Good night, General. We will be following this story, possibly the biggest story of all time, the end of the human race and possibly all life on Earth, throughout the day. Now, let's bring in our panel, who will discuss the likelihood that the Wormwood asteroid will end all life on Earth…"

I clicked off the television and fell back into my chair.

"Wormwood," I said quietly.

"Yes, Wormwood," echoed Moe.

"So many are going to die from this," I told him.

"I know," answered Moe. "What should we do?"

"Do? This is from the Lord; there is nothing much for us *to do*, except what we were called to do of course."

"You mean, warn the people."

"Yes, warn the people. Remember what I told you, if we do not warn them, their blood will be on our heads."

"But how?"

"Let's contact Vicki Reynolds, perhaps *she* can help us."

We found the information and dialed her number. She picked up right away.

"Hello, John March, is that you?"

"Yes, Ms. Reynolds, it is."

"You are calling about Wormwood, I take it?" she asked.

"Yes, I am." I answered matter-of-factly.

"It's going to strike the Earth, isn't it, and many are going to die, aren't they?"

"Yes, on both counts. But remember, Ms. Reynolds, just as General Easley said, this *is* from the Lord."

"This really is the end of days, isn't it?"

"Yes."

"What can we do, Mr. March?"

"Are you a Christian, Ms. Reynolds?"

"Well, yes, no, sort of. I mean, I go to church sometimes."

"Then I recommend you get on your knees, and accept the free gift that he has already given you. Reject him no longer, and he will not reject you. Turn your heart wholly to the Lord Jesus Christ, the only begotten Son of God, believe that he has died for your sins, and that he rose again, and you will have life."

The phone went quiet for a long time.

"Ms. Reynolds, are you still there?"

"Sorry, I'm back now. I did as you said, and I called on his name, acknowledged him as the son of God, and asked him to forgive me."

"Welcome into the family, Ms. Reynolds."

"Thank you, Mr. March, thank you so much. Now, what can I do for *you*?"

"We need to get in front of a camera, warn everyone about what is going to happen. Warn them to repent now, before it is too late."

"Will everyone die from Wormwood?"

"Not everyone, but many *will* die from it, and many more will die from the plagues that follow it."

"I don't know how I could make it to Jerusalem before Wormwood strikes."

"Do you know anyone here that would be willing to interview us?"

"Let me do some checking, and I will let you know."

"There is not much time, Ms. Reynolds."

"I know Mr. March, I know."

Chapter 27-The Warning

Michael Levy motioned to the cameraman. At six-foot-three, Levy was somewhat tall for an Israeli. He told me that he was a second-generation Israeli, his grandfather having emigrated from Poland some fifty years earlier. "Okay, Simon, are you ready?"

"Sure, Mike, I'm all set to go. We are live in three-two-one..."

"Good morning. My name is Michael Levy, with Israeli News One, an INC affiliate based in Jerusalem, Israel. I have the privilege this morning of interviewing the two prophets that recently pronounced warnings of disasters tied to the prophecy of the end times, as written in the Christian Bible's book of Revelation. They are here this morning to talk with us about the approaching Wormwood asteroid, so-named because of the prophecy about a star called Wormwood. Who are these prophets? Please let me introduce Mr. Moe Princeton and Mr. John March. Good morning, gentlemen."

"Good morning," we answered in unison.

"So, Mr. March, we'll start with you. What do you think is going to happen late tonight? Do you believe that this asteroid is the Wormwood mentioned in Revelation?"

"This asteroid *is* the Wormwood mentioned by St. John, and it *will* strike the Earth tonight."

"Which means that there is no way to stop it?"

"Correct."

"But gentlemen, every country on the planet with nuclear launch capability will be launching nuclear missiles at the asteroid later this afternoon. The United States, Russia, China, Great Britain, and France have all already announced launch plans. How is it possible that this thing will still have the capacity to wreak havoc on the planet?"

"It will happen, let there be no doubt about it."

"If they don't succeed, from what I am told this thing is a planet killer... no life on Earth will survive. How could this be the same celestial body mentioned in Revelation?"

"Perhaps the missiles will fail, perhaps they will only break the asteroid into smaller pieces, but this *is* the same Wormwood mentioned by St. John, and it will strike the Earth this evening. Our purpose for this interview is to warn people before it's too late."

"Too late for what, Mr. March?"

"Too late to turn back to God, of course!" answered Moe.

"What can we do to avoid being struck by Wormwood?" asked Levy.

"Absolutely nothing. If it does not strike the Earth this evening, then we are not prophets of the Lord, and He has not sent us."

"Well, if there is nothing we can do to deter it, what can we expect when it strikes?

I answered the reporter by quoting from the book of Revelation. "'The first angel sounded, and there followed hail and fire mingled with blood, and they were cast upon the Earth: and the third part of trees was burnt up, and all green grass was burnt up.

"And the second angel sounded, and as it were a great mountain burning with fire was cast into the sea: and the third part of the sea became blood; And the third part of the creatures which were in the sea, and had life, died; and the third part of the ships were destroyed.

"And the third angel sounded, and there fell a great star from heaven, burning as it were a lamp, and it fell upon the third part of the rivers, and upon the fountains of waters; And the name of the star is called Wormwood: and the third part of the waters became wormwood; and many men died of the waters, because they were made bitter.

"And the fourth angel sounded, and the third part of the sun was smitten, and the third part of the moon, and the third part of the stars; so as the third part of them was darkened, and the day shone not for a third part of it, and the night likewise.

"And I beheld, and heard an angel flying through the midst of heaven, saying with a loud voice, Woe, woe, woe, to the inhabitants of the Earth by reason of the other voices of the trumpet of the three angels, which are yet to sound!'"

"Mr. March, do you really believe that the end of the world will happen *now*, literally, as it is written in the book of Revelation? You must know that many scholars, perhaps even *most* scholars, believe Revelation is either mostly or altogether allegorical in nature."

"I understand."

"So you believe there will be mass destruction and death, beginning tonight?"

"That is correct."

"What will happen after that?"

"There will be more plagues, pestilence, and war on a global scale. Then, the Lord will come."

"You mean the return of Jesus Christ."

"Of course."

"Well Mr. March, as a secular Jew, I hope you are wrong on all counts."

"I assure you Mr. Levy, I am not. Perhaps you should consider that, given current events, perhaps Jesus Christ *is* the promised messiah, the Son of the Living God, and the Savior of all mankind."

"Again, as a secular Jew I..."

"Please reconsider your position after Wormwood strikes today, Mr. Levy, if not before."

"Perhaps I will. Is there anything else you would like to share, Mr. March?"

"Yes, there is. I do not know how many more opportunities we will have to reach as much of the world as we have now. Therefore, I would like to say something now to all that will listen: Please, I beg you, turn to the Lord *now*, before it is too late! Time *is* running out for this world, the time of the end has come; indeed, it is already at hand. There is nothing anyone else can do to stop this from happening, for this thing is from the Lord. This asteroid, and even more terrible disasters that have been ordained by him, *will* happen just as he has said they would. Many people will die tonight and many more will die later. Afterwards however, there will be eternal life and no more death, for all that love him and call on his name. Turn from the beast, and turn back to the Lord, and do it now. Acknowledge that the Lord Jesus Christ *is* the Son of God, that he died for your sins, and that he truly is your Lord and Savior."

"Mr. Princeton, is there anything you would like to add?"

"Just this; like all storms, this one will pass. For those whose names are written in the Lamb's Book of Life, the Lord says the following:

'Then I saw a new heaven and a new Earth, for the first heaven and the first Earth had passed away, and there was no longer any sea. I saw the Holy City, the New Jerusalem, coming down out of heaven from God, prepared as a bride beautifully dressed for her husband. And I heard a loud voice from the

throne saying, "Now the dwelling of God is with men, and he will live with them. They will be his people, and God himself will be with them and be their God. He will wipe every tear from their eyes. There will be no more death or mourning or crying or pain, for the old order of things has passed away.'

The Lord has marvelously promised an end to death and pain. He Himself will dwell with us forever! When the current tribulation is over, His people will all rejoice with great gladness and great joy! How glorious it will be! As it is written in the Psalms:

"For his anger endures but a moment; in his favor is life: weeping may endure for a night, but joy comes in the morning."

"Thank you, Mr. March and Mr. Princeton, two modern day prophets from the Lord."

He turned back to the camera and said, "So there you have it folks. If these two prophets are wrong, if the asteroid is destroyed, or if it misses the Earth entirely, then when we wake up in the morning, it will just be another day. If they are correct however, the Wormwood asteroid is just the beginning of a series of plagues. The good news then according to these two men is that a wonderful eternity with the Lord himself is ahead for those that trust Jesus of Nazareth as their savior. Either way, all of us will know something sometime this evening. Reporting for INC News, this is Michael Levy."

We had done what we could to get the message out to the world that the asteroid *was* going to strike, and that many people would die. We had also offered people hope; not that the disaster could be averted, but hope for what was to come when the plagues and wars were past. There was nothing we could do, of course, to force people to believe, because God allowed men to choose. All we could do was warn them as the Lord had instructed us to do, and try to open their eyes.

Moe and I returned to our homes, pausing at times to glance toward the heavens and try to imagine the giant that was speeding towards us. After spending hours praying and giving thanks after returning home, we turned on the television to follow the news.

I flipped from channel to channel until I found Vicki Reynolds reporting on the Wormwood asteroid.

"As you can see, the asteroid is now very close. There can be no question now that it is on a direct collision course. The Pentagon told us today they were successful in coordinating an assault on Wormwood between the major world powers. The plan is to launch missiles armed with nuclear-tipped warheads from each respective country in a coordinated attack in such a manner that the missiles will rendezvous with the asteroid at exactly the same time, before it enters the Earth's atmosphere, and far enough away that there will be no EMP damage to electronics on the ground. There will, of course, be several satellites that will be destroyed but at this point, they are considered collateral damage in this global fight to save the Earth. If successful, the combined strike will pulverize the asteroid into pieces so small that the remnants will all be burned up in the Earth's atmosphere. Dr. Eagle from NASA said today that...hold on. Did everyone else see that? There was just a brilliant flash in the night sky. The coordinated strike, however, was not scheduled to launch for another three hours yet. I feel certain that it must have been a nuclear explosion that we just witnessed. Nothing else could have...wait a minute...reports are just now coming in. Oh no... Ladies and Gentlemen, it appears that the country of North Korea, in an apparent attempt to upstage the coordinated effort by the world community from which it was excluded, launched a nuclear missile of its own a short while ago that was successful in intercepting the asteroid. Wait a minute...there are independent reports just now coming in from NASA and the Pentagon that, while the North Korean missile did intercept the Wormwood asteroid, the yield of the single warhead was far too low to destroy it. Instead, the blast merely broke the asteroid into smaller pieces. Hold on for just a second, we are getting some more information...it appears that there are now two large pieces, I repeat, two large pieces, and a number of smaller pieces, still headed for the Earth. The smaller pieces are expected to enter the Earth's atmosphere at various points all over the planet. The larger pieces will strike the Earth's oceans; one currently has a trajectory that will cause it to strike the Pacific, while the other will strike the Atlantic. We are trying to get with Dr. Eagle at NASA, we... hold on, Dr. Eagle, are you there?"

"Yes, I'm here Ms. Reynolds."

"Dr. Eagle, can you tell us what the impact of the North Korean missile will be?"

"Well, as you said, we have plotted the trajectory of the remaining pieces of the asteroid, and it appears that one of the two larger fragments of the asteroid will strike the Atlantic, one will strike the Pacific. The remaining fragments, while much smaller, are still expected to survive reentry into the Earth's atmosphere over land and most will remain intact."

"The anticipated result?"

"Tsunamis, coastlines destroyed, ships destroyed, tremendous loss of life across the globe resulting from destruction along the coastlines, all resulting from the strikes in the oceans. Massive destruction in large, populated areas, fires in both the urban as well as the rural areas. In short, the North Koreans have ruined any chance we had of destroying this thing and have instead created one heck of a mess."

"Dr. Eagle, do you realize that the scenarios you have just described fit the descriptions in the Book of Revelation to a tee?"

"Is that so?"

"It is."

"Well, how about that."

"Okay, well thank you for your time Dr. Eagle. I hope you will keep us updated as you learn more."

"Of course."

"Thank you Dr. Eagle. This is Vicki Reynolds, INC News."

Chapter 28-Bitter Waters

I awoke early the next morning and was surprised to find that the electricity was still on in our house and the other houses in our neighborhood, and from the looks of it, power was still on for all of the other homes in Jerusalem as well. After getting a shower and some breakfast, I turned on the computer and began surfing the Internet, hoping to find out what had taken place the evening before. As everyone expected, there was devastation all over the world from Wormwood's devastating assault on the Earth. The death toll, though the number had not yet been determined at the time, was expected to be enormous. The world was in chaos as New York, Hong Kong, and Tokyo, and other key financial centers around the world, lay destroyed, submerged underwater after being struck by the largest and most powerful tsunamis ever to strike the Earth, by a factor of ten. World leaders predicted doom and gloom while the financial infrastructure began to unravel. Around the world, governments struggled to maintain order.

As I continued surfing the Net, it soon became apparent that other parts of the world that had escaped the tsunamis had fared no better. I found a lot of information on the website of one of the large news networks.

"…wildfires began burning out of control all over the world as smaller fragments of the asteroid struck landlocked cities rupturing gas lines, igniting gas stations, and pulverizing buildings. Firefighters have been so busy putting out fires near populated areas that they had to let fires in the more rural areas burn out of control. Reports suggest that around a third of populated areas around the world are reporting major losses due to fires. In some places, the fires are burning so intensely that the resulting smoke is blocking the sun, which was barely visible on a clear day at noon.

Several reports regarding Wormwood's entry into the Earth's atmosphere indicate that fragments of the Wormwood asteroid began striking the Earth at 9:30 PM Eastern Standard Time. As predicted by NASA, one of the largest pieces made ocean-fall in the Eastern Pacific, near the North China Sea. The other struck in the Atlantic, approximately halfway between North America and Africa. As expected, the asteroid's impact generated powerful tsunamis in both oceans. The impact in the Pacific Ocean resulted in devastating tsunamis well over seventy-five feet in height that devastated all or large portions of Tokyo, Beijing, Hong Kong, Taiwan, and the Koreas. The asteroid that landed in the Atlantic Ocean created another mega-tsunami, whose devastation was felt all along the eastern seaboard of the United States. The loss of life was greatest in the coastal cities, with unbelievably heavy casualties, with reports of unparalleled devastation and massive flooding throughout New York City.

"Incredibly, the remnants of Wormwood that fell over land has created even more destruction than the mega-tsunamis. Fires have broken out all over the world, on every continent except for Antarctica. A particularly large fireball from the once massive asteroid struck just outside of Moscow in Russia, virtually erasing the capital city from the face of the Earth. Massive fires have consumed hundreds of millions of acres of grasslands and forests and besieged much of Africa, Australia, and the mid-western United States. Estimates predicted that the fires would affect a third of all inhabitable land mass…"

Despite the greatest number of fatalities and the greatest destruction in recorded history that was reported all over the planet, the worst news was still yet to come. I finished reading a story about the fires in the greater Chicago area and went to check the headlines. Just as I refreshed my browser, a new story broke across the top of my screen. "Enormous Fish Kills Reported in Atlantic and Pacific; Ocean Wildlife Found Dead in Catastrophic Numbers." I read the story and learned that something appeared to be poisoning marine life all across the planet. The article quoted a number of marine biologists as saying that the impact on the oceans was expected to be so devastating, the damage would very likely be irreparable.

The mainstream media outlets generally blamed the Wormwood Asteroid for all of the misery being inflicted on the planet, claiming that it was simply a random occurrence and that whatever had poisoned the waters must be something that was present on or inside of the asteroid. Others, particularly those in far left circles, took the position that if there was a God, *he* was certainly to blame for all of the suffering, giving them, they claimed, yet another reason for despising him, *if* he even existed.

Most reporters blamed the fanatical religious right for fanning the flames of paranoia with their claims that biblical prophecy was being fulfilled in front of their own eyes. One article went on to blame the religious right for the re-awakening of many to the Gospel, causing them to renew their commitments to Jesus Christ or in some cases, turning to him for the first time.

For the most part, however, people were just becoming increasingly callous, bitter, and angry, gnashing their teeth, and crying out against the God they blamed for their torment, rejecting him instead of turning towards him in humility. It was puzzling why, given the evidence before them, people would continue rejecting the very One that held in his hands the power to save them from the plagues. I figured that people denied Him for much the same reason people had denied Him for two millennia; they wanted to do what they wanted, and not what God wanted.

I continued monitoring the Internet and the television for the next several days, attempting to stay apprised of world events. I was also interested in how people around the world were reacting to the recent disaster. I had just walked into the kitchen to fix myself a fresh cup of coffee when the phone rang.

"Hello?"

"Hello, is this John March?"

"Yes it is. Who is this, please? "

"Heidi Hyatt, GNN news."

"Hello, Ms. Hyatt."

"Please, call me Heidi. Am I disturbing you?"

"No, of course not and please, call me John."

"Okay, John."

"So what can I do for you this morning, Heidi?"

"I was wondering whether you would consider doing an interview with me. I would like to get your comments on the recent Wormwood asteroid, and how it is affecting people around the world. Of course, I would also like to get your perspective on the relationship, if any, between the asteroid and biblical prophecy."

"Certainly, Ms... I mean Heidi. Would you like to do it now while we are on the phone?"

"No. I would rather do it in person, if that's okay with you."

"Okay, when will you be in Jerusalem again?"

"I've already booked my flight to Tel Aviv for next week."

"You're coming here just to interview me?"

"Of course."

"That was a little presumptuous of you wasn't it. How did you know I would agree to do it?" I asked, slightly irritated.

"Perhaps it was, if so I apologize," she replied. "As to how I knew that you would agree to an interview, I didn't know for certain, but I had a feeling… let's just call it women's intuition. How does one week from today look, say around two o'clock in the afternoon?"

"That should be just fine," I answered. "I'll give you my address…"

"No need to, I was hoping I could buy you lunch around noon, at Ben Daniels Restaurant, to give us a chance to talk before the interview. Have you been there before?" she asked.

"No, I haven't," I answered, somewhat surprised she had chosen such a lavish restaurant to meet. "But I understand that it is one of the nicest restaurants in Jerusalem."

"That's why I picked it for us. I am so looking forward to meeting you, *John*. I have seen your interviews on INC and of course, I have read all about you. You are a fascinating enigma, John, I look forward to getting to know you," she said softly.

Was she flirting?

"That sounds good, Heidi."

"It's a date then! I'll see *you* next week at noon, at Ben Daniel's Restaurant. Until then!"

"Until then…"

She was most definitely flirting. Despite myself, I couldn't help wondering what she looked like.

A few moments later, the phone rang again.

"Did you forget something, Heidi?" I asked.

"Who's Heidi? John, this is Ben."

"Oh, Ben, hi! Oh, um…Heidi Hyatt is a reporter with GNN. She wants to interview me."

"Of course. John, listen, something has come up here. Is Lara around?"

"She's out at the moment, Ben. She said she had some groceries to pick up. She should be back within an hour or so."

"Oh. Well, please have her call as soon as she gets in."

"Okay, I will be sure to do that. Is everything okay?"

"No, not really John. It's Madeleine, she had a stroke, and, well, it's pretty serious. The doctors aren't sure how much longer she has to live. I thought Lara should know just in case…"

"Of course, of course. Is there anything we can do here?"

"No, I don't think so. Just pray for her, John, that's all. I wasn't sure whether Lara would want to come home to see her mother before something…happens. As I said, the doctors doubt she has very long. In fact, they're not even sure she will be with us through the night."

"I *will* pray for her, of course. I'm sure Lara will want to get back to the states to be with her mother as soon as possible. So how are you holding up Ben?"

"I am…excuse me for just a moment…" I could hear the pain in my father-in-law's voice. His voice was breaking as he struggled to regain his composure. After a few moments, he came back to the phone. "I'm doing about as well as can be expected, Johnny. This all came on somewhat suddenly. She's all I have anymore, Madeline I mean."

"I know, Ben."

"Well, listen, I had better go. I need to get back to the room to sit with her. Give Lara the message for me, will you please?"

"Of course. You take care of yourself Ben, okay?"

"Thanks, John." As I hung up the phone, I looked at the clock as I tried to figure out how I was going to break the bad news to her once she returned.

***

"What do you mean you're not coming with us?" Lara asked me, half-yelling, after she returned home and I had told her about her mother. I had just broken the news to her that I would not be accompanying her back to the states to see her mother. She was not thrilled with my decision.

"John, you *must* come! Why don't you want to come with me? She's my *mother* John! I just don't believe this!" She continued pacing the room like a jungle cat waiting to pounce on its prey.

"Lara, I have to stay here for that interview next week. Besides, I have work to do here. I have responsibilities…"

"What about the responsibilities you have to your family, John? What about your responsibilities to me, and to Sam's grandmother? Don't you even care that my mother is dying?"

"Of course I care, Lara…I just …can't leave. My work here is too important."

I was saying the right things of course, but for the wrong reasons. The truth is that her parents had never liked me very much. Perhaps they had never forgiven me for taking their daughter away from them; in any case, I had always resented it. Nothing I had ever done, despite my many countless attempts, had ever been good enough for them. They

177

never stopped thinking of me a hooligan, as a troublemaker. As a result, our relationship had been fragile at the best of times. I had hoped that with the birth of our son Samuel, their opinion of me might change, but it did not. I had tried to forgive Lara's parents for the way they had treated me over the years, but I never had much to do with them, short of the obligatory holiday gatherings like Christmas, Thanksgiving, and Samuel's birthday. I had tried talking the matter over with Lara, but she always defended them, saying it was nothing more than my imagination. Now, with Madeline at death's door, I knew deep down that I should find a way to fix things with her and Ben, but the awkwardness had gone on for so long, I just didn't know how.

Lara walked over to where I had been sitting on the edge of the bed watching her pack her suitcase. She laid her head down on my shoulder and released a heavy sigh.

"Oh, John, I understand that you don't want to abandon your work, even for a few weeks. I understand honey, I do. You go ahead and stay here and take the interview, fulfill your mission here while you can. I should only be gone for a week or so. Samuel and I will be back in Jerusalem before you know it." She turned and looked at me before adding, "You will be okay, won't you?"

"Of course, I'll be fine. You have a safe trip to the States, and please say hello to your folks for me. I hope your mother recovers soon." Just then, we heard the cabbie honking his horn outside. She put her arms around me and held me so tightly and for so long that, it soon became difficult to breathe.

"Take care of yourself, John. I love you so much; I'm going to miss you!"

"I love you too honey, I'll see you next week." We walked into the living room where Sam was laying on the sofa, watching a re-run on television.

"Is it time to go, Mom?" he asked.

"It's time to go, Tiger. Listen, your father can't come with us, so it will just be you and me. Give your dad a hug and get your coat on. The cab is outside waiting on us."

"Yes, ma'am." He ran over to me and jumped into my arms, nearly knocking me down.

"Now, Sam, you take care of your mother while you're gone, you hear me?"

"Yes, sir. I'm going to miss you, Dad!" He grabbed my neck tightly and made one of the saddest faces I had ever seen.

"I'm going to miss you too, son."

"Let's go now Samuel, he's waiting for us."

After a final round of hugs and tears, they left and climbed into the cab. As I watched them pull away, I waved at them, and wondered whether I would ever stop feeling like such a heel.

The Last Prophet

Chapter 29-Unexpected Guests

The call had come in the middle of the night, so I had to shake myself awake to be certain it had not been merely a dream. Still sitting up in bed, I looked over at the clock and saw that it was still two o'clock in the morning. I was unable to hold back a long and powerful yawn as I climbed out of bed and stretched. Someone must really want to meet with me to call and wake me in the middle of the night. Whoever it was, and whatever the reason, it all sounded so cloak-and-dagger, I suspected it had to be for real. One thing I was certain of however; whoever was behind the call and the late night meeting, it was *not* Addon; this was not his style. When *he* came for me again, he would do so in a very public way, so he could gloat about it in front of all of his hapless followers, demonstrating his power and victory over me as he ended my life. Addon aside, I had not yet finished the work that I had been given to complete. I knew that the time for me to depart had not yet come, although I also knew that it would arrive soon enough.

If Addon was not behind the mysterious rendezvous, who else could it be? The man on the phone had said that it was important that *they* meet with me, whoever *they* were. It seemed that some important people wanted to meet with me, but given the level of attention currently focused on me, they had to be careful. They said I was constantly being watched, and that it was dangerous enough for them to meet with me at three o'clock in the morning, much less during the day. If the meeting were not handled discreetly, the lives of the men seeking the meeting would be forfeit. They were not afraid to die, the man told me, but they still had an important task that they felt it was extremely important for them to complete first. Whoever *they* were, they certainly had a flair for the dramatic; but then again, given the recent course of events, who was *I* to talk?

With Lara and Sam still in the states visiting her parents, I had the house all to myself, so the phone had awakened only me when it rang. I grabbed a quick shower and walked into the kitchen. I took out a couple of waffles and several slices of bacon, before starting a fresh pot of coffee brewing. At the request of the secretive caller, I did everything that I could to keep the lights and the noise to a bare minimum. I felt little concern for my own life, already knowing how it would end. If what they told me was true however, and I *was* being watched as they said I was, I did not want someone else to die because of my carelessness.

I grabbed the bacon, the waffles, and the coffee, before sitting down at the breakfast table to eat. After giving thanks, I glanced back at my watch; did a quick time check, and saw that it was now two-thirty. I had fifteen minutes to finish my breakfast and get out the door. The man on the phone said he believed there would be a shift change for my surveillance team around two-forty-five, and that my best chance to escape unnoticed would be to leave at precisely two-fifty, before the next team showed up at two-fifty-five. The voice said that I had been under surveillance for well over a year, and that my habits were now well known by the teams. Since I had not once left the house after settling in for the night, they had grown complacent and careless in handling the shift change. This small window would give me just the opening that I needed.

I took the piece of paper with my notes scribbled all over and looked over it as I enjoyed my waffles and my coffee.

"Exit through the back door at two-fifty. Walk briskly to the street behind the house, turn right, and walk down the street to the next intersection. Turn left at the intersection. Look for a white Crown Victoria parked on the right hand side of the street. Quickly walk to the car, open the back passenger side door, and get in."

I could not help chuckling as I thought to myself, *sounds like second-rate material from a B-movie.*

I finished my breakfast and my coffee and left the house promptly at two-fifty. I took in a deep breath of morning air as I began walking hurriedly to the street behind the house. I tried not to be excessively paranoid, but I could not resist the urge to glance around, wondering whether I was being watched, or followed. Perhaps whoever had arranged the meeting was not as thorough and prepared as they had thought they were. I was startled when a dog barked in a neighbor's yard. I looked around and as far as I was able to determine, I was not being watched, or followed. I turned right at the street and walked briskly towards the next street. As I walked along the deserted neighborhood, I was struck by my lack of fear. In fact, rather than fear I found myself somewhat amused by all of the clandestine activity. I suddenly felt more like James Bond than I did Moses or Elijah.

When I reached the next street, I turned left and found the white Crown Victoria parked about thirty yards ahead. I walked as quickly and quietly as possible to the car and as instructed, opened the rear passenger-side door and climbed in. Once inside I glanced over at my host, seated next to me in the rear of the back seat. The driver wasted no time quickly pulling away from the curb and driving off, taking pains to be drive as fast as possible, while also driving slow enough to avoid drawing any unwanted attention.

"Good Morning, Mr. March. I do hope you will forgive the excessive theatrics. Given the times we find ourselves in, we are unfortunately compelled to practice an abundance of caution." The man wore cassock sleeves and fascia made of fine scarlet watered silk, the distinctive wardrobe of a cardinal in the Roman Catholic Church. "Please, allow me to introduce myself. My name is Cardinal Pierre Amiere. I represent His Holiness Pope Phillip I. May I say what an honor, a privilege, it is to meet you at last, Mr. March."

"Thank you Cardinal Amiere. It is nice to see a friendly face for a change."

"Believe me, Mr. March; I feel exactly the same way."

"Pardon me if I seem in any way ill-mannered, Your Eminence, but may I ask what this is all about?"

"Of course, please forgive me. The Holy Father has asked that I brief you along the way." He paused for just a moment to study me. When he had finished, his face betrayed no evidence as to any conclusion he had come to. "His Holiness would like to meet with you, Mr. March. We have been monitoring your mission with great interest, listening to your recounting of the messages that you have given, and the incredible signs in the heavens and on the Earth that followed, with great interest," he stated with a neutral tone.

"And what conclusion have you come to?" I asked, slightly agitated.

"Well, that's just it, Mr. March. Many of us at the Holy See believe that you and Mr. Princeton *are* the two witnesses mentioned in the revelation our Lord Jesus Christ gave to St. John the apostle. Nevertheless, we must take great care to be *certain* of who you are, as we can leave nothing to chance. There is far too much at stake, I am afraid, for us to make haphazard, even dangerous conclusions as to who you are without first taking adequate steps to ensure that we have exercised the necessary due diligence. With your permission, I would like to begin by asking you to answer a single question for us, if you would be so kind."

"If I can, Your Eminence. What is your question?"

"Are you certain that these are *the* end of days, Mr. March? Are we truly watching the events written in the prophecy being fulfilled before our eyes? Are these truly the last days upon the Earth before the return of our Lord and Savior, Jesus Christ?"

"Why don't you tell me what you think, first, Your Eminence?"

"Well, as I have said, many..."

"I would like to know what *you* think, not what the others at the Holy See think."

Cardinal Amiere looked at me with a flash of irritation. I could tell he was not accustomed to being talked to in such a manner. His demeanor soon changed, however, as he struggled to answer the question.

"To be frank, Mr. March, I have had my doubts at times. I have had my fair share of skepticism over the last few years, given the many false prophets that have plagued the Church since our Lord's ascension. Nevertheless, we have seen the evil that has spread a vicious and merciless net over the Earth in as much time, entangling so many in its twisted web. We have seen the great suffering caused by the evil one. We have however, never seen the incredible signs and wonders that we have witnessed since you and Mr. Princeton began prophesying. I want to believe, I *need* to believe, Mr. March, but I must be certain. Can you help me?"

The sincerity in his voice was unmistakable. I felt obligated to share what I knew with him.

"I am a simple man, Cardinal, what you see is what you get. I never attended seminary and I have only a college education, which I consider myself extremely fortunate to have received. I come from a wonderful family but one of only limited means. Believe me when I tell you that I never sought out the road that I now find myself on, and neither did my friend, Moe. We were, for whatever reason, blessed with the great honor and singular privilege, of having been chosen by the Almighty himself, to be his witnesses, to carry his message to a broken and dying world. You ask me whether we are living in the last days... yes, Your Eminence, we most certainly *are* living in the last days, and they will soon be drawing to a close. The power of the beast will continue to grow, for a short while, until the Lord himself comes as prophesied, conquers him, and casts him into the lake of fire. Soon afterwards, as foretold in the book of Revelation, there will be a glorious new Heaven and a new Earth."

Cardinal Amiere turned and looked out the window for several minutes, saying nothing as we passed house after house, alone in the privacy of his own thoughts. Eventually, he turned back to me, the look of a broken and contrite man on his face instead of the stiff and formal appearance that greeted me when I first climbed into the car.

"Please forgive me, John March, for my doubts, for my misgivings. I believe now that you truly are a prophet sent from God. I see now that it is true, all of it."

"It is alright, Your..."

"Please, John, call me Pierre. We are brothers in Christ, after all, and the days of pretense and titles are behind us now, except of course for titles like King of Kings and Lord of Lords." Tears of joy streamed down his face, as he grappled with the reality of it all. "I have had doubts from time to time over the long course of my life, not often, just occasionally; doubts whether I did the right thing by becoming a priest, doubts whether I was making a difference. Now, that has all changed. Thank you, John, thank you." I was a bit surprised when he reached over and hugged me, like a brother he had longed to see for a very long time.

"You are truly welcome, Pierre. I must admit that I am still coming to grips with all of this myself. I have no idea why he chose me, but I am honored that he did. I simply try my best to do what he tells me."

While I was still talking, I saw the expression on Pierre Amiere's face suddenly change to a look of concern with a hint of sadness.

"If you are the two last prophets, then it means that...you, and Moe Princeton, you..."

"Yes, my brother, we will die soon, at the hands of the beast... we know. However, don't mourn for us when we are gone. The end of this world will soon come for all of us. It will be a time for great rejoicing, however, as our Lord will come again to live with us forever!"

About that time we slowed as we entered one of the more upscale areas in Tel Aviv, before the car came to a complete stop outside of a large hotel, one of the five-star luxury hotels that call Tel Aviv home. I could not help but notice it was the kind of hotel where it would not be at all unusual to see a limousine outside, a limousine like the one the Pope traveled in.

The driver pulled up to a gate in front of an underground rear entrance, an entrance reserved for the guests that preferred to make discreet entrances, and exits, from the hotel. The driver pulled close to the entrance into the hotel to let us out. We climbed out of the car and walked into the hotel. As we walked inside, the high ceilings, the beautiful and elaborate paintings, and the intricate, beautiful latticework that decorated the hallways amazed me. In the distance, in the foyer of the hotel, stood a large, exquisite fountain, with water pouring down the side of a large ship and at the bottom, a whale with its mouth opened wide, preparing to receive a frightened Jonah. Well before we made it to the foyer, Pierre stopped and knocked on one of the doors. The room must have been a large suite, for there were no other doors close to or across from it. A large, serious-looking man answered the door. Cardinal Pierre Amiere led me inside, for a meeting with the Pope.

Chapter 30-The Pope

The pontiff sat in a chair at the head of a large table. Around the table sat a number of other Cardinals, bishops, and priests. Other clergy sat around the table as well, some had faces I recognized, while others I did not. I was surprised to see that many, while Christian, were certainly not Roman Catholic. Some were dressed in clothing of various non-catholic denominations. One elderly man, seated next to Pope Phillip I, resembled a picture I had once seen of the Patriarch of Constantinople, James II, the leader of the Eastern Orthodox Church. Others around the room I recognized as Protestant clergy from several different denominations, along with other well-known Christian leaders. I assumed the remaining men were also leaders in their own respective denominations. Suddenly, despite my conversation with Pierre on the drive over, it dawned on me that I was still completely in the dark as to why I was there.

As we entered the room, I was startled when all of them, to a man, rose and began gently clapping their hands, led, interestingly enough, by the Pope and the Patriarch of Constantinople. The pontiff began walking towards me but I soon closed the distance, sparing a man that was many years my elder the long walk. As I approached, he held out his hand and with a surprisingly firm handshake, and thanked me for coming. After also shaking hands with the patriarch, as well as many others in the room, we all took our seats. The Pope was the first to speak.

"Welcome, Brother John March, to our modest gathering here this morning. We are deeply honored that you would join us." He then turned to Patriarch James II and said, "Your Holiness, would you please open our discussion with prayer?

"Of course. Most merciful and Almighty God, please Lord, lead and guide our hearts, the hearts of your people, as we try to discern your will for us in this incredibly important and significant time. Give us wisdom, grant us courage, and bless our efforts this morning, for we ask and pray in the holy and precious name of our Lord and Savior Jesus Christ, amen."

"Amen. Thank you, Your Holiness," the pontiff said, before turning back to me once more. "I would like to offer my sincere and heartfelt gratitude to you for joining us, and I would like to apologize for the inopportune time for this discussion, but as I feel certain Cardinal Amiere has already told you, you are a man under a microscope."

"I understand," I replied. Can you tell me please why you called me, and why my companion Moe Princeton is not with us?"

"It was not an oversight, I assure you. We felt that given your relative youth, and the fact that your wife and child are now in the United States, well...we felt that you had the better chance of escaping undetected," he answered. "We know that you have been under constant surveillance, at least since your arrival here in Jerusalem. We too have been coming under increasing scrutiny, but I doubt any of us share in the attention that you and Mr. Princeton seem to have elicited from President Addon"

"Forgive us, Mr. March, if this in any way makes you uncomfortable. We do not intend for this to be an interrogation, but we have little time before the window closes for us," the patriarch offered. "Is Addon the beast mentioned by St. John the Divine, and are you and Mr. Princeton, the two witnesses mentioned in Chapter Eleven of the Book of Revelation?"

"You would be accurate in calling Addon the beast, Your Holiness," I answered, "for I have personally seen him in his true form. He *is* Abbadon, the Destroyer. As for Moe Princeton and myself we are most certainly the last two prophets, or witnesses, mentioned in the book of Revelation. I did not choose this role, Your Holiness, but neither do I deny it. These are the last days, and the arrival of Our Lord Jesus Christ on this Earth is imminent."

The room suddenly erupted in a myriad of conversations. The Pope raised his hand and waived it to attract everyone's attention.

"Brothers, please, we must move quickly. We do not know for certain whether his absence has been discovered, or how much time we have." The room grew quiet as everyone nodded in agreement.

"What can I do for you gentlemen? What is so important that you left your homes, your families, risking torture and death, to meet with me?"

"Look around this room, Mr. March," said the Reverend Ben Greer, a well-respected preacher from the United States. "We represent most of what remains of the world's leading Christian leadership. Those of us that haven't been imprisoned, or murdered, that is. Despite the substantial persecution all over the world, perpetuated by this man, this Addon, there remain many in our flocks that have not yet gone after the beast. Some are wavering, others are not, but each of us in this room desperately wants to communicate with our people, to tell them something, to help them understand what has been happening. There has been much confusion, Mr. March, about who and what you are, and whether these really are the end of days."

"Some," began Patriarch James II, "believe that the recent events, the asteroid, the Earthquake, the waters turning to blood, can all be explained by science, that they are just a strange string of coincidences. Others have been convinced for some time that you and Mr. Princeton are indeed the two witnesses, the last two prophets, as foretold in the book of Revelation, that would appear in the end times, that would be slain by the beast…oh my, please forgive me."

"That's okay, Your Holiness, as I told Cardinal Amiere earlier; I have known what awaits me at the end of my road for some time."

"At the end of *our* road, brother," added Pierre.

"Indeed."

The pontiff cleared his throat once more before looking up at me.

"My friend and brother, John March, we desperately want to share with our brothers and sisters all over the world, our assessment of what is happening. We feel it is imperative, as much as it is possible, for us to speak with one voice, in order that we may provide direction, solace, and comfort, to those that the Lord has so graciously placed in our charge. Brother March, tell us please, how did you come to discover the plans that the Lord had for you? Please, we implore you; help us to understand you and your mission, so that we may tell our brothers and sisters."

I cleared my throat, clasped my hands, rested them on the table, and began.

"I welcome this opportunity, Your Holiness; for this is one of the reasons why the Lord has sent us. Well, where to begin …it all started when I was a boy…"

I went on to recount to them the dreams, the angel, how I came to meet Moe, about Addon, all of it. I spent hours summarizing for them everything that had happened, stressing to them that if they would only 'read the signs of the times,' they would see unequivocally that the end of days was upon them. Everyone listened intently, interrupting me on occasion, seeking clarification on some detail here or there. When I had finished, I took a deep breath, sighed, and sat back in my chair.

"Brothers, I will conclude by asking you to consider for a moment the words in Joel 2: 28-31.

'And it shall come to pass afterward, that I will pour out my spirit upon all flesh; and your sons and your daughters shall prophesy, your old men shall dream dreams, your young men shall see visions:

And also upon the servants and upon the handmaids in those days will I pour out my spirit. And I will show wonders in the heavens and in the Earth, blood, and fire, and pillars of smoke. The sun shall be turned into darkness, and the moon into blood, before the great and terrible day of the LORD come...'"

As they talked intently amongst themselves, it was my turn to study them. Each of the men sitting in front of me had risked the real possibility, perhaps even the likelihood, of being taken into custody, imprisoned, tortured, and killed. Each of them seemed sincere in their desire to take back what they had learned to those in their care. I found myself greatly impressed with their devotion, and their fervent desire to execute faithfully the responsibilities that the Lord had given to *them*. It occurred to me that while I had spent a few years serving the Lord, many of *them* had spent their entire lives in service to him. It was a humbling moment for me. I began to wonder what it was going to be like in Heaven, surrounded by Holiness, and I started to smile.

The discussions continued for another thirty minutes, with an occasional pause when one of them would ask me a question. Some of their questions I was unable to answer. Several times, I had to explain that I knew only what the Lord had revealed to me, nothing more. Finally, they all nodded in agreement, and the discussions ended.

"Brother John, we are all in agreement, perhaps for the first time in history!" Pope Phillip I said, smiling and nodding at others around the table, triggering a short outburst of laughter. "We believe that you are indeed one of the last two prophets, the two witnesses, the lamp stands, chosen by the Lord. We further believe that Addon, as you say, is indeed the beast, that these are the last days, and that the return of our Lord Jesus is imminent. We glorify and praise his Holy Name!"

The patriarch then picked up. "We will go back and share this blessed news with God's people, Mr. March, that you are the Lord's prophet, that they are *truly* living out the Revelation of Our Lord to St. John. We will tell them to prepare for the Lord's return. We will tell them that Addon is the beast mentioned in the prophecy and that above all, when the time comes, that they *must not* take his mark, because *it is indeed* the mark of the beast, lest they join him in his torment. We will encourage them to take comfort in the knowledge of their Lord's return, that He is in charge, and that he will overcome and vanquish the beast, which will then be cast into the Lake of Fire."

"It is a glorious time, Brother John, as we look for our Lord's return!" the pontiff said as he smiled, with tears welling in his eyes. He nodded towards one of the cardinals, who brought in some bread and wine.

"Brothers, will you please join me in celebrating the Holy Eucharist at this most wonderful, marvelous time!"

The Spirit of God seemed to fill the room as we were all filled with an indescribable joy, the likes of which I had never felt; the feeling of brotherhood, of fellowship, and of holiness. I believe it must have been one of the most fulfilling moments of my life.

Chapter 31-Baiting the Trap

It was another beautiful, sunny day in downtown Washington, D.C., as it had been for the past several days, not that Raul or any of his staff had noticed it of course. He had not seen anything outside of the bunker since the day before the asteroid struck. Raul and the others had been terrified upon learning that the Wormwood asteroid was going to strike the Earth. Then there was news that the asteroid had split into pieces, and that one of the fragments landed in the ocean, creating a massive tsunami that struck New York and Washington. Many people had died, while many others had escaped further inland. Raul still had no idea whether any of his own family had survived the disaster.

Until the asteroid, it had all seemed a bit surreal to him. The enigmatic Abe Addon, who had promoted so many of the same ideals that he treasured... equality for all, a centralized form of government, and taking from the rich and to give to the poor... the man who seemed to share so many of his values, had turned out to be something else, something *more* than just another politician. At first, he had embraced his master's true persona, thinking that he might somehow benefit from being close to him, and through his new position, somehow force his beliefs on the world. He had never cared much for the Christians so Addon's persecution of the same had never bothered him. He had started to question, however, whether he might have ended up on the losing side of the fight. It was becoming more and more evident to him that there was a God, and that Addon, despite his considerable power, was still subservient to him. In addition, if evil existed, as was evident in Abe Addon, there must be some force of good in the universe as well. He had read the Bible as a child, but he had always been taught that the prophecies in the book of Revelation were simply a lot of myths, a bunch of stories, purely symbolic in nature. There was nothing symbolic in what he was experiencing as of late.

Most of Washington was still under water, and was expected to remain so for at least a few more weeks. The Secret Service had rushed Addon, the Vice-President, and Congress down into the vast bunker the day before the asteroid struck.

Deep in the vast underground bunkers that lie directly underneath the White House, Raul Raymond knocked on the door where Addon lay resting.

"What news do you bring to me, Raul?"

"Good news, Master. She was successful in making contact with him. He believes that she is legitimate so everything is now in place. With the others out of the way now, the timing is perfect for her to make her appearance. He will not be able to resist her."

"Excellent. The bait is now in place and the trap is set, ready for him to fall into it. He has been a thorn in my side since all of this began. " Addon lay on his back with a smile from ear to ear. " As your people like to say, Raul, your words are music to my ears!"

"Yes, Sir. The plans of the Eternal will be foiled, and you will be victorious!"

"Raul, you simple fool!" Addon turned to his aide and allowed his natural form to re-appear. "Do you really think even for a moment that I, or that *any* of us for that matter, could possibly thwart the plans of the Eternal, much less *defeat* him? You idiot! None of us can defeat *him,* or else we would have done so long ago. However, while we cannot defeat him, we *can* certainly cause suffering for his human pets. It is only because he has bestowed these pathetic creatures with free will that we are able to make any progress at all in leading them away from his presence, and towards the same miserable fate that awaits us."

"Sir, do you still remember what it was like, before…"

"Before? Oh, you are referring to before we were cast out. Yes…I do…it is something he will never allow us to forget, what we gave up, what we lost. I'll tell you something, Raul. His appearance was so magnificent, so glorious, far beyond the realm of words. Did you know that *I* was once one of his favorites? Well, at least I used to think I was…"

"What happened?"

"We discovered what it was like to do what *we wanted to do.* We decided to use *our* free will to make a choice. We rebelled against the Eternal, but we were defeated and cast out. Now, there will be a price to pay. There is always a price to be paid for rebellion against the Eternal, for human beings as well as for us."

"So what will happen when the human falls into your trap, master?"

"His mission will fail."

"What will happen when his mission fails?"

"Many humans will never turn to the Eternal. As I said, we may not be able to thwart his plans, and we may face perpetual torment for what we did, but we will drag as many of them along with us as we can. Now then, on to other matters. Where are we regarding the next phase of the plan?"

"It is all set. We have been taking full advantage of the recent collapse of the banking system in order to usher in the next phase of your plan. We have already begun floating the idea of a new form of currency, a new means of providing for the buying and selling of goods, a new market economy."

"And what has been the response?"

"Well, at first people objected, saying that the public would never accept such a preposterous idea. However, when we told them that *your* name would be required on the stamp, just as presidents have had their image pictured on currency for hundreds of years, they bought it completely. We will need to hold a press conference within the next few weeks to announce it to the world."

"We will hold a press conference tomorrow, Raul. We will announce that soon, there will be no more buying, selling, trading, investing, no commerce of any kind conducted in or with the United States going forward, without the mark of my name or my number. My mark will be stamped on the forehead or on the right hand of any person wanting to buy or purchase anything in the United States. Any other country wanting to conduct business with the United States of America will have to follow this process as well. If any man, woman, or child wants to buy or sell anything… a product or service of any kind, they must have my name or my number stamped on their forehead or on their right hand. Anyone not bearing my mark that attempts to buy or sell anything at all, will be taken into custody to be *re-educated* by his or her benevolent government officials. Those refusing my mark a second time will be imprisoned; the third time put to death. It is after all, a matter of national security," he said smiling. "Now get that press conference scheduled for tomorrow. Do it now."

Chapter 32-Caught

Have you ever wondered what might have happened had things turned out differently? What would have happened had Eve refused when the serpent tempted her in the Garden of Eden? What if the French ships had been caught up in a storm and sunk in the Atlantic, leaving the Americans to the mercy of the British troops? What if Truman had refused to use the atomic bomb in World War II and the Japanese had invented one first, one they used to later bomb Washington, D.C.? It seems life is an intricate web, interconnecting people and events through what appears to be chance happenings.

In my case, a specific question sometimes crossed my mind. *What would happen had I decided not to become a prophet?* It was always my choice, of course, my free will, whether I would choose to obey God's calling, or to refuse him. I knew that God *could* always replace me at any time; I just never thought he would have to.

I arrived at Ben Daniels, in Old Jerusalem, late for our appointment, so I was concerned that I had missed her when I found myself standing outside the restaurant by myself for nearly half an hour. One of the most beautiful women I had ever seen sat alone at a table. Young, blonde, and attractive, she stood out in the crowd of Jews and Arabs that frequented the establishment. While I searched the restaurant looking for someone that matched the voice I had heard on the phone, I tried not to stare too long in her direction, something that she made even more difficult by smiling at me flirtatiously. As I had never met Heidi Hyatt before, I had no idea what she looked like. I stood waiting, regretting the fact that we had not made any specific arrangements for identifying one another in the crowd. All I could do was hope that since she had seen at least one of my interviews, she would recognize me.

After waiting a few more minutes, I grew exasperated and decided to leave, assuming that perhaps the woman on the phone had been less than sincere about who and what she was, or else she had grown impatient and left before I had arrived. With a parting glance over the crowd, my eyes fell once more on the beautiful young woman sitting alone. This time, she was laughing while looking straight at me. I must have had a puzzled look on my face, perhaps even anger, because she finally held up a press badge with her name in large bold letters at the bottom. Heidi had been laughing so hard she had tears streaming down her face. I walked over to the table and started to share a few choice words with her.

"Oh, no…please don't be angry. I was curious how long you were going to wait before giving up!"

"Didn't you recognize me?' I asked her as I sat at the table across from her.

"Oh yes, of course. I told you, I saw your interviews on television."

"Then why didn't you bother to introduce yourself?"

"Why would I do that?"

"So that I would know who you were, of course!" I said with some exasperation. I was uncertain what she was up to, but I didn't care much for it.

"Why, you didn't *know* who I was? But Mr. March, you *are* supposed to be a prophet, aren't you? Aren't you supposed to know these things?"

I had heard enough. I stood and prepared to leave.

"No, no, please don't leave. I'm sorry if I offended you. I promise you, that certainly wasn't my intention." I turned back toward her. The pleading look on her face convinced me that as ill conceived as her notion of fun had been, it had been in good fun and had not been intended as malicious.

"I agreed to meet with you in order to share an important message with the world. I…"

"Are you always so serious?"

"Wha…"

"No, really. Are you always so serious? Don't you ever have *any* fun?"

"Fun? I don't…"

"That's what I thought." She took a sip from her glass of wine before motioning to the waiter. We ordered our lunch and as the waiter left to turn in the order, she leaned over with both elbows on the table, placed her delicate chin in her hands, and peered deeply into my eyes, almost as if she was trying to find something.

"You need to lighten up a bit, John March, have a little fun. It wouldn't kill you to enjoy life just a little you know. Always Mr. Doom and Gloom, the world is going to end, always..." This time, it was my turn to interrupt.

"This is serious business, Mrs. Hyatt!"

"*Miss* Hyatt," she corrected, "or better yet, just Heidi." *Smiling again.* I sat there, trying to discern what she was up to. "You see what I mean? Always so *serious!*"

I threw my hands into the air as she started to giggle again. I tried to maintain a serious composure, which in turn, caused her to start laughing again, pointing at me as she did so. Finally, I could contain myself no longer. We sat there at the table, both of us laughing hysterically for several minutes.

"You are certainly not what I expected, Miss Hyatt."

"Why? Because I like to have a little fun? You should try it more often; you might find that you like it."

"No, it's not that I don't like to have fun, Miss Hyatt."

"*Heidi,*" she corrected again.

"Heidi. This is serious business, Heidi. The world as we know it is about to change forever. Just look what happened with the Wormwood asteroid."

"Yes, I know." She took on a more somber posture for a moment. Then the buoyant, mischievous, pixie-like smile returned, as she shook off the seriousness of the moment, just as a dog shakes off the water after a bath. "Still, life goes on, doesn't it? Just look how free love in the sixties came in after the stodginess of the fifties."

"This is different."

"Is it? So what if it is?" she added, shrugging her shoulders. "Can't we have some fun before the world ends?"

"Well, I don't see why no...,"

"I mean, is this the message that you want to share? That the fun is over, that from here on out it is all misery and suffering?"

"Well, there will be more suffering, *considerably* more suffering, before the end, which will be here soon."

The cheerful look on her face disappeared and she became despondent.

"How long do we have before the end, John?" Her question caught me off guard. It took me a while to respond.

"Well, I don't know exactly, maybe a few years."

"But I have so much life to live yet, John. For instance, I have never been married! I would like to bear children, raise a family."

"I don't know. I suppose that there is a possibility you could marry and have children, but the end is very close." Tears began streaming down her face. I felt compelled to get up and move over next to the chair where she was sitting. I put my arms around her, trying to offer her some comfort. She laid her head down on my shoulder.

"I'm sorry, John. You must think me such an unprofessional idiot! It's just that if what you say comes to pass, my dreams will never come true."

"Listen, it's going to be okay. There is something far better waiting for you, waiting for all of us, on the other side of this, I promise."

She then did something I never saw coming. She reached around the back of my head with her hand, leaned in, and kissed me. Her kiss was filled with more passion than I had ever experienced throughout my entire life. It happened so quickly, and so unexpectedly, that while I should have been able to break it off sooner, it was one of those things that are much easier said than done. It had been a long time since a woman as young and attractive as she was had kissed me. The whole thing seemed so surreal yet, regrettably, satisfying as well. Finally, the kiss ended and she sat back. I was struggling with what to say, because as much as I enjoyed the moment, I was a servant of the Most High, and I loved my wife. As I prepared to tell Heidi that, I saw her. There, standing no more than five yards behind Heidi stood Lara, tears pouring down her face. She said nothing, as she turned, sobbing and distraught, and disappeared into the crowd. I leapt from my seat and into the crowd, searching desperately for her in the throngs of locals and tourists in the crowd.

Had I looked behind me in the direction from which I came, back towards the restaurant, perhaps I would have seen Heidi Hyatt as she sat back down at the table and, wearing a Machiavellian grin, took a sip of her wine, clearly pleased with her performance.

Chapter 33-Waiting

I sat and stared out the window, watching the pastel colors paint the late afternoon sky as the sun set behind some buildings across the street. A large flock of Spanish sparrows flew high above the buildings, fleeing the approaching cold front that would signal the beginning of winter. Winter would arrive soon, marking the end of our first year of living in the Holy Land. As I sat watching the final moments of twilight, it occurred to me that I simply could not fathom living my remaining years without Lara by my side. We had been together for so long that we had become inseparable.

I watched the sun touch the ocean on the horizon, just as I heard a knock at the door. I felt my heart leap in my chest once more, daring to hope that maybe, just maybe, I might find Lara waiting there on the other side of the doorway. I mustered every ounce of self-control possible as I slowly stood and walked towards the door, fighting the urge to race to the door to find my beloved wife waiting for me.

"Lara, I…"

"Hello, Johnny!" Bryce stood in the doorway, grinning from ear to ear. My head dropped and my heart sank at the disappointment.

"Oh, Bryce. What are you doing here?"

"Okay then, it's great to see you too, old friend! May I come in?"

"Oh, yeah, I'm sorry, Bryce. Come on in."

Bryce walked in and looked around at the mess strewn all over the house.

"My goodness man, look at this place, look at *you*! Is everything okay? Are you all right? You look as if you haven't slept in weeks! What in the world is going on?"

"Lara's gone," I answered weakly.

"Gone? Gone where, to the store?"

"Back to the States."

"Wow, how long is she gone for, John? I'd hate if Lisa and I came all this way and we missed her! When will she be back?"

"I don't know, Bryce, she might be gone for good," I said, burying my face in my hands.

"You're kidding, you mean she left you?" Bryce asked.

"Yeah, I think so."

"Aw, man, I'm so sorry John, I had no idea. How long?"

"It's been two weeks," I told him poignantly.

"What happened, Johnny? Why don't we go in here and you tell me all about it, hmm?"

"Where's Lisa, isn't she with you," I asked him, still shaken by yet another disappointment.

"No, I left her at the hotel. She wasn't feeling well, so she said something about watching a movie in the room. She wanted me to tell you and…well, tell you that she'd come over tomorrow."

Bryce and I walked into the living room, sat down. We spent the next several hours talking, as I relayed the whole story to him, about Heidi, about Lara finding us together in the restaurant, about the doubts I was starting to have.

"…so after racing back to our home and finding our house empty, I roamed up and down the streets of Jerusalem for the rest of the day. From the Old City, to the Christian Quarter, down to the Armenian Quarter, down to Givat Ram, as far as Rassco, I searched up and down most of the city trying to find my wife, finally combing through the newer parts of the city as well as the old. It must have been sometime during the early morning hours of the following day before I finally gave up and made for home, exhausted.

"I've stayed here by the phone for the past two weeks, waiting for her to call me, to come home to me, something; waiting for a chance to explain to her what happened, to apologize to her, to beg her forgiveness."

"Listen to me, Johnny, you can't stay here by yourself, you're going to drive yourself mad. Why don't you come back with Lisa and me to the States? You can stay with us for a while until you find yourself another place to live and make a fresh start."

"I don't know, Bryce. I have work to do," I protested.

"John, take a look around you, take a look at yourself! Do you really think this is what God wants? Face it John, you did the best you could, now it's time to come home."

"I don't know, Bryce, I…"

"Listen, I tell you what. You come home with us, get back on your feet, and if after a few months you think you need to come back here, I'll come with you. How does that sound?"

I sat there in the living room, still in my bathrobe, having not bathed since the day before. Trash littered the house, and the not-so-faint odor of trash was becoming a stench. I thought about what had happened, about Bryce, about everything we had been through together. *Who am I kidding? I'm no prophet; I'm not some holy man from God!*

"That sounds like a good plan, Bryce, thank you."

"No need to thank me, Johnny, what are friends for? But first things first, we have to get your house cleaned up, *and you*."

We spent the next few hours picking up the trash and washing dishes. I had done very little since Lara had disappeared, and it showed. Once we had the house straightened up, Bryce left to make arrangements and to tell his wife what was happening, leaving me sitting alone, stewing in my own juices.

Thirty-minutes later, there was another knock at the door. I answered it to find Moe standing there.

"Hello, Moe."

"Good evening, John. May I come in?"

"Oh, sure, please do," I answered.

Moe came in and sat down in one of the chairs opposite where I sat on the sofa.

"So tell me, John, how are you holding up?" he asked.

I sat there for a moment, trying to determine how I would break the news to Moe. After a while, I decided to come out with it.

"I'm throwing in the towel, Moe. I'm going back to the States. I just can't do this without Lara." Moe sat there speechless for a couple of minutes while the news sank in, before finally speaking.

"Come to your senses, man. You can't do this! Surely you realize that this is Addon's doing? His fingerprints, if he had any, are all over this, and you are playing right into his hands. You *cannot* stop now!"

I just sighed and threw up my hands. "What am I supposed to do, Moe? My wife has left me and taken my son from me because of this *mission*. Besides, I failed the Lord just as surely as I failed my family."

"You haven't failed *anyone*, John. You know that's how this creature is, both he and his master; it's their method of operation! They tempt you to do evil, and as soon as you slip up and do something, then they turn around and immediately accuse you before the Father! You've been setup. Besides, nothing happened did it, besides the kiss?"

"No, but it easily could have." Moe came over and, sitting down next to me, he put his arm around my shoulder.

"Listen to me son; you haven't done anything that every other man hasn't done, or wanted to do, at some point during his marriage. Man is not perfect, none of us are."

"I should have stopped her, Moe."

"Just who do you think you are John, anyway? Only one man ever born of woman has ever been sinless, and he is sitting at the right hand of the Father. We all sin John, and you are no exception."

"But Lara…"

"All you know is that Lara saw some strange woman kissing you before she disappeared. You don't know that she's gone for good. For all you know she may have simply gone back to be with her mother."

"It's been two weeks now, Moe. If there was any possibility that she was coming back to me, she would have been back by now, or she would at least have called. No, I can't do this anymore. God will raise up someone to take my place."

"Now listen, John, I…"

"No, *you* listen, Moe…" I was angry, not so much at Moe but at myself, but I was allowing some unsettled, ugly business to surface, "…this is your chance. Aren't you the one that 'felt like a puppy following me around' some time ago, that felt like a 'redheaded stepchild', and that I was 'acting like I was in charge'? Well here is your chance, Moe, take it! Get out there and show the world who Moe Princeton is! Don't you want *your* moment in the sun?"

Moe must have still held considerable guilt over the episode, because he fell silent, turned, and walked out. Just before he walked out the door, however, he stopped, and without turning around, said to me "John, I'm so sorry about what I did, about what I said… I really and truly am. I was having a bad day and feeling a little low that night, so I indulged in a little self-pity. I have prayed about it many, many, times since then, believe me, and I have asked the Lord's forgiveness. I was wrong, and I was acting like a real jerk. Now I'm asking you for your forgiveness as well, John. I believe that the Lord has forgiven me; I just hope that you can do the same. They were rash words, John, that's all. I realize it might not make any difference to you now, I just thought you should know. Please…forgive me." And with that, he disappeared into the night.

As the door closed behind him, I was cut to the heart over the way I had treated Moe since that night. I felt particularly bad about what I had just said to him. I knew that Moe was a good man, as good as any sinful man can be, and I had never heard any other cross words from him since that night. Actually, Moe had acted completely to the contrary ever since. He had gone out of his way to more than make up for what he had said about me to his wife that night, when he had obviously been unaware that I was eavesdropping on his porch. If anything, I had wronged him just as much as he had wronged me that night by invading his privacy. I knew that I had shared many rash words to Lara in haste, knowing they would never be heard outside the privacy of our home.

It wasn't Moe's careless words that had caused me to unload on my dear friend. It was my own reckless behavior that had gotten me into the mess I was in with Lara, not Moe's. I could say that my outburst of anger was because I missed Lara so much, or I could blame the "mission" for what had happened, but neither were true. The truth was that I was just feeling a bit overwhelmed by everything, and I had for some time. Ever since the first dream I had about my father that later came true, it had always been a bit much. No, I just needed to stop long enough to let life catch up with me. I wanted to continue in the work God had set before me, but I was tired, and I felt I just could not go on. My wife and my child were gone. I walked back into the kitchen and turned on the television.

"…and in other news, the Pope in Rome joined with the Patriarch of Constantinople, and with many other evangelical leaders across the globe today, in affirming the words of the two prophets, John March and Moe Princeton, and proclaiming to their respective church bodies and parishioners, that these supposed prophets have indeed been sent by God. They encouraged those still adhering to the Christian faith to support these prophets and their mission in any way possible, even at the risk of imprisonment, and death. They claim that what we see unfolding is indeed the fulfillment of the Bible's book of Revelation, written down by the apostle John, a follower of the man Jesus of Nazareth over two thousand years ago. In addition, they echoed the words of the two prophets, encouraging non-Christians worldwide to consider opening their hearts to Jesus Christ, turning to him with their whole hearts. The Vatican also issued another warning to their members all over the world, regarding President Abe Addon's increasingly open assault against the worldwide Church, and his growing appeal to non-Christians, as an alternative to worshipping the God of the Bible…"

"Also in the news today, with the old financial infrastructure literally washed away and the world's major financial centers destroyed, it is widely believed that the move by the President today, announcing the new form of currency exchange is… well let's face it… unprecedented in the history of mankind. For the first time goods and services will be exchanged not by bartering or by currency, but through the use of an image that is permanently imprinted on a person's skin."

"On the skin, Connie?" another member of the news network asked her.

"That's right, Jim. Each person will have a unique image of the President, along with his name underneath. The new 3D-Format of the image, designed by a team of graphic artists, includes a design that some radical say can be interpreted as the number six-hundred and sixty-six, a number associated with the beast from the book of Revelation in the Bible."

"But Connie, the only people that are even claiming to see a number in the image are those crazy right-wing extremists. Of course they are going to make every kind of bizarre association with President Addon that they can."

"I could not agree more, Jim. This new method of commerce is just the prescription that the world needs now. Abe Addon certainly is someone that I worship, let me tell you!"

"I know what you mean Connie. I am becoming a true believer as well. Just when I was beginning to believe that the world was going to end, as financial markets began to tumble and the world began to slip into chaos, along comes Abe Addon with a plan to save our world."

"I saw a new poll that just came out today. The President has a staggering ninety-five percent approval rating, by far the highest in the history of our republic. In addition, when asked how they felt about Addon, nearly seventy-five percent of those polled claimed they worshipped him, and would follow him to the ends of the Earth…"

I turned the television off in disgust. I knew who he was, I knew what he was, and I had tried to tell them, to warn the world, but had they listened? Only a few seemed to heed our warnings. Now he was deceiving more and more people every day. I felt like a loser.

Chapter 34-Dinner

I scrounged through the empty refrigerator, looking for something to have for dinner. Eventually, I settled on warming up some microwave lasagna and garlic bread. I had just taken my first bite of lasagna when the phone rang. I had been planning to walk over to Moe's house to apologize after dinner anyway, but I was delighted that he had broken the ice first by calling me. Aside from my inappropriate words the night before, I knew he was going to stay on me until I either acquiesced, or until I left.

"Hello, Moe. Listen, I'm glad you called, I wanted to tell you…"

"John? It's me, Lara." It was as if my heart had stopped beating and suddenly restarted again, beating more vigorously, fiercer and faster than it ever had before.

"Lara! Listen, I have to tell you something. I…"

"I need to tell you something first, John. What I did was wrong, leaving you the way I did. You've been under a lot of pressure and I know and understand that. It's just that with my mother and all, well, I just couldn't deal with you and that, *woman*. I decided to go back to visit with my parents for a while longer."

"Lara, she was just some reporter, someone I had never even seen before the day you saw us together. She called me, said she wanted to interview me, and we met for lunch. We were just talking when she kissed me unexpectedly, just out of the blue."

"She just happened to be a beautiful, young, female reporter then?"

"Lara, it was just an interview, I promise!"

"Okay, John, okay. I still don't understand why you called me though, asking me to come home early and meet you there at the restaurant."

"I *didn't* call you, Lara."

"Are you sure? It was your voice, John."

"It had to be *him*, Lara, it must have been. It was a setup the entire time."

"But for what reason? What could he possibly hope to accomplish by driving us apart."

"Most likely exactly what happened, Lara. I decided to abandon the mission when I thought I had lost you and Samuel."

"Oh no, what are you saying John? As much as I wish it were so sometimes, you can't simply quit, your mission is much too important!"

"But I would be lost without you and Sam, Lara. How could I continue without you?"

"Oh John, my John. I should have talked with you about what was happening, instead of disappearing like that."

"Nothing happened, Lara, you have to believe me!"

"I do, John, I do believe you. Can you forgive me?"

"There is nothing to forgive, Lara. I miss you so much."

"And I miss you too, Johnny!"

"How is your mother doing?" I asked her.

"We are so blessed, John! She has been doing much better. She was already out of intensive care by the time I arrived the first time, and now she is out of the hospital and back home. I thought I would spend a couple of more days with her and Dad before coming back, if it's okay with you… and assuming of course, that you'll even take me back."

"Try to stop me! How soon can you be home?" I asked impatiently.

"I'll leave in a few days," she said.

"That sounds great. I can't wait to see you again, Lara."

"Same here, sweetheart. I love you so much John, I *really* do. I can't breathe without you in my life. You are my soul mate, you always have been."

"And you have always been mine, Lara. Please don't leave me again."

"I won't, I promise."

"Then I'll see you when you get back. Call me from the airport before you leave, and have a safe flight back, okay? And Lara?"

"Yes?"

"I'm sorry I didn't go with you in the first place. If I had none of this would have ever happened."

"It's okay, John, don't worry about it. I'll see you in a few days, honey."

"Okay, see you in a few days."

I hung up the phone, feeling like a giddy schoolboy who just found love for the first time. I spent the rest of my dinner alone, planning a romantic evening upon Lara's return. After spending some quality time with Samuel, I would ask Moe and Doris if they would keep an eye on him for a few hours, while Lara and I spent some much-needed time together. I felt sure that Moe would not object; assuming he was able to forgive me for the way I had treated him.

I finished dinner and called one of the most romantic restaurants in Jerusalem, The Jewel of Jerusalem, and made a reservation for the day following her return. Lara would be tired from the long flight, but I was sure the gesture would not be lost on her. After making the reservation, I went back into the living room and picked up *The Pilgrim's Progress*, determined that I would finish it in one sitting. It would seem, however, that the Lord had other ideas.

"John." It was the first time I had heard His voice in a while.

"Speak Lord, your servant hears you."

"It is time for you to carry another message to the people so that they will have ample opportunity to turn back to me, before the end comes…" When he had finished, I felt an urge to speak up.

"But Lord, I am such an unworthy servant. What can I, a poor miserable sinner, possibly accomplish for you, oh Lord, Most High? I am afraid that I will fail you!"

"What did I say to my servant Moses, when he resisted speaking to Pharaoh?

"As it says in the book of Exodus, 'And the LORD said unto him, Who has made man's mouth? or who makes the dumb, or deaf, or the seeing, or the blind? have not I the LORD? Now therefore go, and I will be with your mouth, and teach you what thou shall say.' *Exodus 4:11-12.*'

"Now go and do likewise, John. Do just as before, and I will put my words in your mouth, and you will be a mouthpiece for me before the nations.'"

"Yes, Lord…"

I sat there for a long time, considering all that the Lord had shared with me. I would take up the mission once more and this time, I would re-double my efforts. I would carry the message that the Lord had given me with a renewed vigor, as I now knew that the end was almost upon us, especially for Moe and me. We would be with the Lord soon enough, but not before carrying His light to the world, and not before doing battle once more with evil.

About that time there was another knock on the door, that all-too familiar knock, and the sense of urgency that it always seemed to convey. "Hold on, Moe." I opened the door and sure enough, Moe stood in the doorway. I simply stood there, smiling at him.

"John, it's true then?"

"What are you talking about, Moe?" I said, trying to conceal my amusement.

"What are you talking about, Moe?" he repeated. "You know *all too well* what I am talking about, young man!"

"Yes, Moe, it's true. The Lord visited me and wants us to carry a new message."

"So I heard. And Lara, you spoke with her?"

"I did. She is flying back in a few days." Moe grabbed me unexpectedly and gave me an old-fashioned bear hug.

"I'm so glad to hear that John, for you *and* for me." He looked at me and grinned. "You know, I'm not sure how much longer I would have been able to put up with you, 'Mr. Poor-me-I'm-too-pathetic-to-continue-March'. Praise God for the return of your wife, and your re-commitment to complete the work the Lord has set before you!"

"Thanks, Moe... I think. Listen; about what I said last night, I was wrong, *very* wrong. I'm so sorry about that, Moe. I hope that *you* will forgive me for being such a jerk." Moe just smiled and reached out to embrace me again.

"Think nothing of it, dear boy. So... what do we do now?"

"Well one thing's for certain, I would prefer not to meet any more strange, female reporters at any restaurants alone, at least not anytime soon."

"What about Vicki Reynolds?"

"Well, I don't know. Do you think she is still in Jerusalem?"

"I suspect she is, especially given everything that's been happening lately. Is there some way we can contact her?"

"Yes, there certainly is. She gave me her cell phone number a while back. Why don't we give her a call and see about setting up another interview. "

"John, are you sure that these interviews are the best way to deliver the Lord's message? I mean, none of the other prophets did it the way we have."

"That's true Moe, none ever have. But then again, they didn't have satellites and cable television back then either!"

Moe laughed and brought me the cordless phone. I found her cell phone number in my wallet and gave her a call.

"Hello?"

"Vicki, it's John. How about another interview?"

"John! You bet, I'd love to do another interview. Where have you been? I was wondering when you were going to call!"

"It's a long story. I have another message to deliver from the Lord. How soon can you be ready?" I answered.

"How about tomorrow afternoon?" she asked.

"Tomorrow afternoon works perfectly," I replied.

"Where would you like to meet?" she asked.

"How about at the Temple Mount?" I suggested.

"Great, it's a date."

"Please, don't say that Vicki."

"What?"

"Never mind, it's another long story." There was a long pause.

"John, have you been following the news?"

"Not really. I had the television on a little while ago and saw something about a new monetary system being implemented back home."

"You might want to turn the television on John, it's terrible."

"What's terrible, what are you talking about."

"You'll see. Listen John, I have to run. I'll see you and Moe tomorrow, around 4:00 in the afternoon at the Temple Mount. What say we meet at the Lion's Gate? We can do the interview in front of the Golden Gate, which is close by. How does that sound to you?"

"We'll be there. Thanks, Vicki."

"You bet, no problem. Good night, John."

"Good night."

Chapter 35-The Message

"It is official ladies and gentlemen. Yet another great accomplishment for this great man, this great, can I say it, this wonderful new messiah? It is yet another great first in the history of humanity. For the first time in the history of the world, the entire planet, at least as represented by all members of the United Nations, the world is under a single world leader. For those of you now joining, the President of the United States, President Abe Addon, has now been voted by the United Nations to become the first democratically elected world leader. The United Nations has awarded him the title of President of the United Nations of the Earth. Although most nations still have to have their respective legislative bodies confirm the decision to relinquish their authority to President Addon, there is no doubt whatsoever that these various bodies will confirm the vote. In addition to his election as the secular leader of the world, many are also now proclaiming that he also be proclaimed the Vicar of Humanity, a religious title, intended to recognize the billions of people, myself included, that already consider him a deity, or at the very least a demigod. Yes ladies and gentlemen, for those of you watching this evening across this great planet, it is a truly unforgettable and historic moment. President Abe Addon, who stepped forward to provide leadership after the recent devastation across the globe which left so much death in its wake, has been now recognized and voted as the first world leader ever. I...excuse me just a moment." The news anchor, who had been tearing up during the entire broadcast, now had tears streaming down her face. "Please excuse me, ladies and gentlemen, I was just so touched by this recent development, I was suddenly overcome with emotion. He is truly a great man, a worthy man, who deserves all of the recognition he has been getting, and more." The anchor paused for several moments before continuing. "In other news, reaction across the planet seems to be overwhelmingly an affirmation of the decision by the United Nations as directed by the member world leaders. As before, the only government to vote against his election was Vatican City, which of course, has always been against Abe Addon, even with his election to the Presidency of the United States. Some of the other fringe elements of the Religious Right, who have opposed nearly everything our beloved leader has done, have also voiced their criticism of the recent vote. Fortunately, their protests are being ignored, as they always are, by the world at large. In other news..." I clicked off the television and shook my head in disgust. *Unbelievable, how can they be so blind!*

"What do you think about this, John?"

"I don't know *what* to think, Moe. I mean, I know what the book of Revelation says, but who could have foreseen the way this is all unfolding?"

"The Lord?"

"Except for the Lord, of course."

"Well, one thing is certain, the timing for tomorrow couldn't be much better. What will we say?"

"*We?* We will not say anything, Moe. As always, we will simply serve as mouthpieces for the Lord. Whatever he puts into our mouths will be what we speak. After all, how could we possibly hold back the words that the Lord put in our mouths?"

Moe looked at me and grinned from ear to ear.

"What are you grinning about? You look like the Cheshire Cat."

"The what?"

"The Cheshire Cat, from *Alice in Wonderland.*"

"Oh, of course." He stared off into the night for a few moments, lost in thought.

"Well?" I asked, raising my voice, impatient to learn what he found so amusing.

"What...oh...I was just thinking how good it is to have you back."

"Thanks, Moe."

"Well, I guess I had better be getting back to Doris. She made me promise that I would not keep you up late tonight, what with Lara coming back tomorrow and all."

"Moe?"

"Yes, John."

"How did you know...about Lara?"

"The Lord told me, of course."

"Oh yes, of course." Moe got up from the sofa and walked to the door.

"Good night, John."

"Good night, Moe."

It was good that Moe and I had cleared the air, before the end.

***

We started out early the next afternoon for the Temple Mount. We drove to the parking lot below Jerusalem's Old City walls, before walking the rest of the way to the Temple Mount. We arrived at three-thirty, a full thirty minutes before our meeting. Nevertheless, we found Vicki Reynolds waiting there for us as we arrived at the designated meeting spot, the Lion's Gate. It would be a short walk to the Golden Gate, where we would do the interview. It seemed an appropriate location, given the fascinating history around the Golden gate, once called the Beautiful gate, sometimes called the Eastern Gate. The Golden Gate is the only gate that remains of the gates built by Nehemiah after he returned from the exile in Babylon. It appeared to me that Vicki had done her homework.

"John… Moe… hello again!" she said warmly as she walked over to us. "We have to stop meeting like this you know!" Moe and I just stared at one another and then back at her, smiling.

"Okay, if you're ready we'll start the interview," she said, turning and walking toward the temple.

We followed her as she approached the Golden gate, which had been closed for over five-hundred years. Ottoman Sultan Suleiman I, during the occupation by the Ottoman Empire, sealed off the Golden Gate in 1541, allegedly to prevent the Messiah's entrance. The Muslims also built a cemetery in front of the gate, supposedly in the belief that the precursor to the Messiah, Elijah, would not be able to pass through since he was a Kohen, though this belief was in error.

"So, John, did you have a chance to catch the news last night?" she asked, giving me a serious glance.

"As a matter of fact I did. Unbelievable," I answered. "It seems as if the whole world has been deceived," I said solemnly.

"It has," added Moe, "at least almost all of it. Keep in mind that the evil one's power of deception and distraction is powerful. He seeks to take as many human beings as possible with him into the Lake of Fire."

"You know, guys, when I first met the two of you, I believed you were just a couple of….*eccentric* fellows."

"You mean *mentally insane* fellows," I responded, smiling. "It's okay, Vicki. I would have thought that myself, not so many years ago."

"What do you think of us now, Vicki?" asked Moe.

215

"Oh, believe me, given what has been happening over the past year or two, I have no doubt that you two are exactly who and what you say you are. I mean, it really does seem like the end of the world to me. How does that go again? 'For then shall be great tribulation…'something."

"I believe I can help," answered Moe. 'For then shall be great tribulation, such as was not since the beginning of the world to this time, no, nor ever shall be. And except those days should be shortened, there should no flesh be saved: but for the elect's sake, those days shall be shortened. Then if any man shall say unto you, Lo, here is Christ, or there; believe it not. For there shall arise false Christs, and false prophets, and shall show great signs and wonders; insomuch that, if it were possible, they shall deceive the very elect. Behold, I have told you before. Wherefore if they shall say to you, Behold, he is in the desert; go not forth: behold, he is in the secret chambers; believe it not…'"

"Yeah, that," she answered.

"Well Vicki, you don't have to worry because as you said, John and I are the *real deal*. But more importantly by far is the fact that God himself is *the Real Deal*," Moe added.

"He's right, Vicki," I said. "This will all be over soon. First, however, as you can tell by watching what's happening in the world, many people will be deceived by Addon. Do you know who he really is?"

"You referred to him as, 'the beast'."

"That's right, Abaddon the Destroyer, the beast that came out of the Abyss."

"Wow."

"Don't be in awe of him, Vicki," said Moe. "He will be cast into the lake of fire, where he will be tormented day and night forever, as will all of those who follow him."

We hiked the next few minutes to where the Golden Gate, now closed to the public, stood with the gate itself blocked. It stood like a great, silent guardian of something important, something sacred. After a few minutes, Vicki and the cameraman, Mike Tanner, were setup and ready for the interview.

"Okay, we still have about an hour, maybe two, of sunlight left, you two. Are you ready?"

"We're ready," I answered.

"Okay, we're on in three, two, one…"

"Good evening. I'm Vicki Reynolds with INC Network News. We are here this evening with two familiar and distinguished individuals,

Mr. John March and Mr. Moe Princeton, also now widely known as the Last Prophets. Okay, Mr. March, I understand that you have a new message from God to share with us?"

"Yes, we do, Ms. Reynolds, thank you." I looked directly into the camera.

"Good evening. I have come before you today in order to bring you an incredibly important message; the dreaded Day of the Lord has come upon you. You have already seen the mighty hand of the Lord at work, as the seals of the Lamb's book have been opened, as the angels in Heaven have blown their trumpets, as the plagues have been poured out on the Earth.

"The evil one however, the dragon, seeks to deceive and corrupt you, so that you will turn from the Lord and consequently share in the dragon's eternal suffering. He has given power to the beast, so that he might turn you from seeking the Lord.

As it is written:

'Therefore rejoice, ye heavens, and ye that dwell in them. Woe to the inhabitants of the Earth and of the sea! For the devil has come down to you, having great wrath, because he knows that he has but a short time.' Revelation 12:12

'Be sober, be vigilant; because your adversary the devil, as a roaring lion, walks about, seeking whom he may devour: Whom resist steadfast in the faith, knowing that the same afflictions are accomplished in your brethren that are in the world.' 1 Peter 5: 8-9

Very soon now, the Lord will punish the beast, and a short while later, his master as well. It is written:

'And the devil, who deceived them, was thrown into the lake of burning sulfur, where the beast and the false prophet had been thrown. They will be tormented day and night for ever and ever.' Revelation 20:10

Listen to me now please, I implore you, and understand that the Lord Himself has provided a means for you to be reconciled to him. The Lord seeks for all men to come to him. As it is written:

'For this is good and acceptable in the sight of God our Savior; Who will have all men to be saved, and to come unto the knowledge of the truth. For there is one God, and one mediator between God and men, the man Christ Jesus; Who gave himself a ransom for all, to be testified in due time.' 1 Timothy 2: 3-6

I urge you to stop for a moment and consider that the Lord, the creator of the universe, who sent his Son, the Lord Jesus Christ, to provide for you a means of escape, even the Lord, seeks to reason with you:

'Come now, and let us reason together, says the LORD: though your sins be as scarlet, they shall be as white as snow; though they are red like crimson, they shall be as wool.' Isaiah 1:18

"Those that turn away from following after the beast, and turn to the Lord Jesus Christ, even that man, woman, or child, will find salvation. As it is written:

'For God so loved the world, thatworld that he gave his only begotten Son, that whosoever believeth in him should not perish, but have everlasting life. For God sent not his Son into the world to condemn the world; but that the world through him might be saved. He that believeth on him is not condemned: but he that believeth not is condemned already, because he hath not believed in the name of the only begotten Son of God. And this is the condemnation, that light is come into the world, and men loved darkness rather than light, because their deeds were evil. For every one that doeth evil hates the light, neither cometh to the light, lest his deeds should be reproved. But he that doeth truth cometh to the light, that his deeds may be made manifest, that they are wrought in God.' John 3:16-21

'Then shall he say also unto them on the left hand, Depart from me, ye cursed, into everlasting fire, prepared for the devil and his angels...' Matthew 25:41

And I saw a great white throne, and him that sat on it, from whose face the Earth and the heaven fled away; and there was found no place for them. And I saw the dead, small and great, stand before God; and the books were opened: and another book was opened, which is the book of life: and the dead were judged out of those things which were written in the books, according to their works. And the sea gave up the dead which were in it; and death and hell delivered up the dead which were in them: and they were judged every man according to their works. And death and hell were cast into the lake of fire. This is the second death. And whosoever was not found written in the book of life was cast into the lake of fire. Revelation 20: 11-15

For those that seek the Lord and do not reject his salvation through his only Son, the Lord Jesus Christ, unbelievable, marvelous, wonderful things await you when these days of wrath have passed:

'Then I saw a new heaven and a new Earth, for the first heaven and the first Earth had passed away, and there was no longer any sea. I saw the Holy City, the new Jerusalem, coming down out of heaven from God, prepared as a bride beautifully dressed for her husband. And I heard a loud voice from the throne saying, "Now the dwelling of God is with men, and he will live with them. They will be his people, and God himself will be with them and be their God. He will wipe every tear from their eyes. There will be no more death or

mourning or crying or pain, for the old order of things has passed away.'
Revelation 21: 1-4

'*I did not see a temple in the city, because the Lord God Almighty and the Lamb are its temple. The city does not need the sun or the moon to shine on it, for the glory of God gives it light, and the Lamb is its lamp. The nations will walk by its light, and the kings of the Earth will bring their splendor into it. On no day will its gates ever be shut, for there will be no night there. The glory and honor of the nations will be brought into it. Nothing impure will ever enter it, nor will anyone who does what is shameful or deceitful, but only those whose names are written in the Lamb's book of life.'* Revelation 22: 1-5

'*Then the angel showed me the river of the water of life, as clear as crystal, flowing from the throne of God and of the Lamb down the middle of the great street of the city. On each side of the river stood the tree of life, bearing twelve crops of fruit, yielding its fruit every month. And the leaves of the tree are for the healing of the nations. No longer will there be any curse. The throne of God and of the Lamb will be in the city, and his servants will serve him. They will see his face, and his name will be on their foreheads. There will be no more night. They will not need the light of a lamp or the light of the sun, for the Lord God will give them light. And they will reign for ever and ever.' Revelation 21: 22-27*

"Again, the Lord has sent us, as his messengers, to warn you of the wrath to come if you do not turn from following the beast. I bring you this warning: do not take the mark of the beast, or this wrath will come upon you.

'*And I heard a great voice out of the temple saying to the seven angels, Go your ways, and pour out the vials of the wrath of God upon the Earth.*

And the first went, and poured out his vial upon the Earth; and there fell a noisome and grievous sore upon the men which had the mark of the beast, and upon them which worshipped his image.'

Revelation 16: 1-2

When the Lord gave this Revelation to his apostle John, while he was in exile on the island of Patmos, he warned us of these end times. Nevertheless, you must remember and understand that the book of Revelation finds its culmination in Christ. Some may think that when we say Christ we are just talking about what happened 2000 years ago, but that's not it. Revelation doesn't make that distinction. It doesn't speak of Christ as the God who saved us long ago and now lets us tick away our days until we go to Heaven. No, Revelation talks about Christ as the one having been crucified, the Lamb having been slain, who is forever and dynamically with his church, in the midst of her difficulties. He sends a steady stream of witnesses to call mankind to himself. This is why, whenever the church passes through difficulty, people have often said 'this is what Revelation talks about', and whenever a faithful witness has arisen, the Church has said 'this is one of the ones that Revelation speaks of'. Yet the Lord Jesus Christ also said that during these end days, this current tribulation would get even worse. That is why it should not surprise you that the Lord has sent us, his last prophets, mentioned in the eleventh chapter of Revelation, to deliver one last, final message to the world, to you, to repent, before the end comes, and it is too late.

"Soon, very soon, the end will come. Please, choose carefully. Remember, if you take the mark of the beast, the wrath of God *will* come upon you."

Chapter 36-The Knesset

After the interview at the Golden Gate, I had no further word for some months. I took some of that time to spend with Lara and Samuel, to make certain that we enjoyed the time the Lord had given us; for I knew that soon, very soon, events would begin to unfold at a dramatic pace. The time remaining was now growing short.

I specifically tried to squeeze in as much father-son time with Samuel as I possibly could, while also preparing him for my inevitable departure. I took him and Lara to a park outside of Jerusalem, just after breakfast on one cool, Saturday morning. We brought a picnic lunch with us, so that we could enjoy a full day at the park, throwing a baseball, fishing, and an occasional walk around the lake. We were on the other side of the world, in the Holy Land, enjoying a picnic, throwing baseball, and fishing on a Saturday morning. What could be more American than that?

It was a surreal experience however, knowing that the world would soon end. Sure, many across the world had seen my interviews, but how many had actually believed the message I had carried? The Lord said once that narrow is the way that leads to eternal life, and few will find it, so I had to believe that the vast majority of humanity would reject the message as well as the messenger. I shook my head in discouragement, before trying to free my mind to focus on my family.

We spent the morning, lunch, and afternoon much as we had planned, taking in the fresh air, the beautiful lake and the woods of the park, thankful for the bright, sunny, day we were enjoying. Samuel seemed the happiest I had seen him in for years.

Late in the afternoon, we lay on a blanket in the park by the beautiful fabricated lake. We looked up at the beautiful clear blue sky, dotted here and there with a number of small clouds, creating the impression that we were looking at a field of blue grass dotted with dandelion seed heads. Samuel had been quiet for a while, so I looked over at him and noticed that something seemed to be bothering him.

"Is everything okay, Sam?" I asked.

"Dad?" He turned over on his side to look at me. I could tell he was upset because he was tearing up.

"Yes, Sam, what is it?" I asked.

"What will happen to Mom and me, I mean, once you are gone?"

"I don't know Sam, but I do know that the Lord will take care of both of you."

"I don't want you to go Dad, not without me anyway. Can I go with you when you leave?" At this, *I* began to tear up as well. I looked over at Lara and saw that her lips had tightened and that she already had tears streaming down her face.

"Listen, Sam, it's going to be a while, yet, before I have to go anywhere. There's no need to worry about that yet. Besides, you and your mother will be following me soon after, but at a time of the *Lord's* choosing, not ours." Sam tightened his lips, trying to hold back the onslaught of emotion that had already welled up from deep inside of him. Finally, it burst forth involuntarily.

"Dad, I love you!" he exclaimed, wrapping his arms tightly around my neck as he buried his head on my chest. I could feel him shaking slightly as all of the pent-up feelings poured out all at once. Lara also wrapped her arms around the two of us, sobbing as she did so. So many tears fell on me that I began to feel the dampness through my shirt.

After a while, I lifted up my head and said, "Hey now, what's all this about? Don't you know that I am doing God's work, just as so many men and women have done all over the world for thousands of years? I mean, how cool is that?"

"Pretty cool, Dad, I guess," said Sam, as the tears slowed and he regained his composure. A few minutes later, Sam lay back down on the blanket and resumed his assessment of God's handiwork.

"You know something, Dad?"

"What's that, Son?"

"God sure made a beautiful world. Look, he's still busy painting the sky!"

"I agree, Son."

We finished the day by stopping by the grocery store to buy a few groceries prior to heading home. It was a chain store, one based out of London, England. Fortunately, we only had to pick up a few staples, a gallon of milk, some bread, and some beef. After waiting in line, cutting up and talking the entire time we waited, we arrived at last at the register, where we placed the items we wanted to purchase on the counter.

"Good evening," I said to the clerk standing at the register.

"Good evening," she replied. She stood looking at me when I handed her some paper currency.

"I'm sorry, sir. We no longer accept paper currency. If you'll stretch out your arm and present your mark I will scan your hand." A shiver ran down my spine when I realized what she was talking about.

"I can't do that, because I refused to take the mark of the beast," I answered.

"Mark of the beast, what are you talking about? It is the mark of the President of the United Nations of the Earth, the President of the World, Abe Addon. *You* must be one of those fanatic Christians! You must leave now. We don't want *your* kind here," she said, pointing to a sign we had passed by without taking any notice of it. The sign read, *No Christians Allowed!*

"Leave now," she said, "or I will be forced to call the authorities."

We tried several stores before finding a smaller grocery store which still defied Addon's order regarding his mark. We picked up what we needed, along with a good bit more. I decided that at that point forward, we would begin stocking up on groceries, canned goods, and so forth, so that our family would have enough to last until the end. It appeared that while most stores enforced Addon's order, a number of others did not. There appeared to be enough resistance to Addon's edict around the world well that stores could still be found in most cities that continued selling with currency, or through bartering. It was clear however that their numbers were rapidly shrinking since the world's financial institutions were beginning to deny handling paper currency. Since they were unable to switch immediately to the new system where people would be scanned, the new system had to be implemented slowly, over an extended period, giving those refusing the mark of the beast the ability to continue buying, at least for a while, groceries, supplies, and so forth.

After picking up enough groceries to last for some time, I drove Lara and Samuel back home and dropped them off alone with the groceries. I had a late meeting with Judah Ben-Jacob, the current Speaker in the Knesset-the legislative branch of the Israeli government that enacts laws in Israel. An aide from his office had called me the day before, requesting that I come to the Knesset, to tell him more about my "mission." It remained unclear to me where he stood in relation to what was happening, but I was hopeful that he would be on the Lord's side.

I was only a mile or so from our home when he appeared to me. He appeared in the back seat of my car with no warning. It looked like the same angel I had seen before. My heart beat so rapidly I felt certain it would leap out of my chest at any moment.

"Greetings, John March," he said, with the same soothing, yet unearthly quality in his voice that I had heard before.

"Hello. You know, you scare me to death when you do that," I told him, afraid of offending the angel, yet telling the truth at the same time.

"I apologize for frightening you, John March. I have come to tell you that the seven bowls of God's wrath are about to be poured out upon the Earth, beginning this night. Mark the time, John March, for soon it will be time for you to confront the beast, where you will be overcome, but only after first overcoming those that seek to harm you. Be of good cheer, for the Lord God *is* with you, John March!"

"But, I…" Once again, he vanished as suddenly as he had appeared.

Still pondering the words of the angel, I pulled into the underground parking garage beneath the Knesset Square. It was built in 1999 to replace the parking lots scattered in and outside of the Knesset domain. A young man that I assumed to be an aide to Judah Ben-Jacob met me as I reached the entrance.

"Are you Mr. March?" he asked me, looking a bit nervous.

"I am John March."

"Shalom, Mr. March. I am Benjamin Levi, aide to Speaker Ben-Jacob. It is a great pleasure to meet you at last, sir. I have only the deepest respect for you and your mission."

"Shalom, Benjamin Levi. It is a pleasure to meet you as well."

"If you would please come with me, Mr. March, I believe that Speaker Ben-Jacob is waiting for you in the Kedma wing."

"Of course," I answered, "please lead the way."

The polite young man led me through the passageways and the corridors of the Knesset, until we arrived at the Kedma wing, where he stopped just outside a chamber. He opened the door and said to me, "I will be waiting out here for you, Mr. March. When you are ready, I will escort you back to your car."

"Thank you." He nodded and closed the door behind me.

An older man was standing at the farthest end of the chamber. He appeared to be taking his time looking me over, obviously attempting to size me up in order to assess my worth.

"Mr. March, it is a great pleasure to make your acquaintance," he said, never taking his eyes off me. He extended his hand to me, gripping mine with considerably more strength than I would ever have imagined him capable of possessing.

"It is my pleasure to meet *you*, Mr. Speaker," I said to him, hoping that the title used for the American Speaker of the House applied to the Israeli Knesset Speaker as well. If it wasn't correct, he either didn't care or had something much weightier than titles on his mind.

"You know something, Mr. March, my father always taught me that you can size up a man by the look in his eye and the grip of his hand."

"So what do you think, Mr. Ben-Jacob?"

He looked at me once more with that same intense stare until finally he began smiling.

"I have been in politics for most of my life, Mr. March. I loved my father dearly, but I have learned that judging a man by a handshake and the look in his eyes is about as accurate means of assessing his character as using tea leaves." He smiled at me and chuckled, before inviting me to sit. "So tell me, Mr. March, what kind of man are you?"

"Well, I guess I'm like most other people," I answered. 'I'm a fallible, weak, and sinful man, I suppose, that for some reason has been chosen by God to be a messenger, at least for a short time."

"So you really *do* believe you are God's messenger?"

"Of course I do."

"Do you think you are the Messiah, Mr. March?" he asked, with that intense stare that seemed to peer into my innermost being.

"Of course not," I replied sharply. "I am a Christian, Mr. Speaker, so I believe the Messiah, the Lord Jesus Christ, has already come, remember?"

"Oh, yes, of course," he answered.

"Why did you want to meet with me, Mr. Ben-Jacob?"

"Right to the point, I like that, Mr. March." He began pacing around the room for a moment, gathering his thoughts.

"I know something of your past, of your experiences when you were still a child, and again as a young man."

"How…why…"

"I am a very powerful man in my country, Mr. March. I have been looking into your background because Mr. March, you and your associate are magnets for great controversy, claiming to be modern-day prophets, stirring up fears about the end of the world, your accusations about President Addon, the Wormwood asteroid. Because you chose to live here, Mr. March, in Israel. Because you scare people, Mr. March, and because you scare me."

"You have nothing to fear from me, Mr. Speaker. It is not I but God that performs these great works, YAWEH, the Lord, he who created the universe."

Judah Ben-Jacob continued pacing around the small council chamber staring at the floor.

"Are you truly a prophet from the Lord, Mr. March? Is Abe Addon truly the beast from the abyss? Is this truly the end?"

"Yes to all three questions, Mr. Speaker." I looked on the older man and discerned that he seemed to be a good man, a man that desperately sought to know the truth.

"I have never been a good, orthodox Jew, Mr. March. I have attended the synagogue intermittently over the years. Please don't misunderstand me; I have been devout, only I have had many questions about God, about Christianity, about the Bible. If the Messiah we have been waiting for truly came two-thousand years ago, in the form of Jesus of Nazareth, and these are the end days, I must decide now, is that not so?"

"That is so, Mr. Speaker."

He walked away from me and over to the table that sat in the middle of the room. After pushing a couple of chairs out of his way, he knelt down at the table and began to pray.

"Oh, God of my Fathers, Lord Almighty, he who appeared to our father Abraham so long ago, and brought us up out of Egypt. I confess now the Lord Jesus Christ, that he is your son, that you sent him to save me from my sins. Please Lord, forgive me for my stubborn and rebellious pride, and accept me into your kingdom. I pray in the name of the Lord Jesus Christ, amen."

"Welcome into the family, Judah Ben-Jacob," I said to him, reaching out with one hand to shake his, and placing my other hand on his shoulder. "I am happy for you, and for your family."

"Thank you, Mr. March, I am truly grateful for your coming to meet me this evening." He walked over to the door for a moment, looking to his left, then to his right, then back to his left again. After concluding that we were alone, with the exception of Benjamin, he closed the doors back and walked back over to where I was standing.

"He has many followers here, as he does all over the world, Mr. March, and he desperately wants to destroy you, or at the very least, do you harm."

"Addon?"

"Yes, Addon."

"I know, we have already met, he and I."

"There are many vile men that seek to destroy you and your families, on his behalf, hoping to win favor with President Addon. They think only of power, and of the political advantages of winning favor with one such as Addon. I believe they will come for you, soon, Mr. March. Be on your guard."

"I will, Mr. Speaker, thank you. I…"

A loud and piercing yell erupted suddenly from somewhere in the building, followed by another and another. We could also hear screams coming from outside the Knesset building as well.

"What is going on, Mr. March, do you know?"

"I don't know, I…" I then recalled what the angel had told me about the seven bowls of God's wrath being poured out upon the Earth, starting *tonight*.

"How many people do you know that have taken the mark of the beast?" I asked him.

"Almost everyone I know, with the exception of a few. It is about the only way to buy or sell anything now that Addon has changed out the currency."

"I believe what you hear is God's wrath being poured out upon the Earth, because men have chosen to follow the beast rather than the Lord. Ugly and painful sores have broken out on the people who have the mark of the beast, and have worshiped his image."

"Oh, my. You must go, John March. They will come for you tonight. Get your family and go out into the countryside, far away from Jerusalem. You must save your family and yourself."

"I must obey the Lord, Mr. Speaker. If you will excuse me however, I would like to take my leave, so that I can go to be with my family. Shalom, Judah Ben-Jacob."

"Shalom, John March, prophet of the Most High. Let's stay in touch."

I nodded before leaving the chamber. After following Benjamin back to my car, I made my way home with more than a little sense of urgency. Trouble was coming and I would have to face it, perhaps that same night. Nevertheless, I would not be facing it alone…

Chapter 37-Surrounded

The phone rang early the next morning, waking me from a deep and restful sleep. The morning sun shone on our bed through the curtains in our bedroom. We had all been up late the night before, unable to drown out the wailing we heard all around us from those that had developed the painful sores all over their bodies. The wailing had been clear evidence that the wrath of God was indeed being poured out upon the Earth, retribution for worshipping the beast.

Whoever was calling must have been determined to talk with us. I had been dreaming of bells, so the phone had apparently been ringing for some time before eventually waking me up. I struggled mightily just to climb out of bed, nearly tripping over our shoes as I tried to get to the phone, which I finally picked up and answered.

"Hello," I said with a trace of annoyance in my voice.

"John? Is this John March?"

"Yes it is. Who is this?"

"John, it's Vicki."

"Oh. Good morning, Vicki. Is everything okay?"

"John, listen, you have to get your family and leave your home, *right now.*"

"Why, what are you talking about, Vicki, what's wrong?" I asked, suddenly jolted awake by the urgency I detected in her voice.

"I just heard about it a few minutes ago or I would have called earlier. People have been talking about it all over Jerusalem this morning. I think something is going to happen, soon."

"Talking about what?"

"They are coming for you, John. I'm not sure that they will limit themselves to just taking you to jail this time either."

"You mean Addon? He knows he can't do anything, at least not yet."

"No, it's not Addon, John, but some of his followers. I can't be certain of course, but I suspect that they are acting on their own, taking matters into their own hands. Wait a minute John...hold on for a minute." There was a pause for a few seconds before she returned to the phone. "I was just informed there is a large mob, possibly led by police, on their way to your house this very minute. They have been threatening to kill all of you, your wife, your son, Moe, all of you."

"Well, I'm not going to let that happen."

"John, there must be hundreds of them, maybe even thousands, or more, and they are armed to the teeth. You *must* leave, now!"

"Oh, well now, that *could* be a problem."

"John, please, you need to leave!"

I walked into the living room, peered out the window, and stared down the street. I saw an endless throng of men carrying shotguns, handguns, knives, and clubs, walking down the street and towards our house. A smaller group of men had already started to gather outside in front of our home. I watched as two men came out of Moe and Doris' house next door with the couple in tow.

"Vicki, thank you for warning me, but I have to go." Even before I hung up the phone, however, the front door burst open and slammed against the wall. Two men, a younger man in his twenties, and another man that looked to be around forty or fifty, entered our home, each man was armed with a 9mm Glock. I dropped the phone and rushed towards the bedrooms for Lara and Samuel. The younger man moved much faster however, and jumped in front of me, blocking my way as the other came up from behind me and tied my hands with large tie-wraps.

"Take him out into the street, Simon. Remember, we want to make this a *public* execution."

"Okay then. Don't forget the wife and kid."

"Don't worry, I won't. I'm going to get them now."

"No!" I screamed out at them. Then, I felt a blow to the back of my head and watched as the floor suddenly raced towards my face, and everything went black.

When I came to my head was throbbing like a jackhammer. I found Lara and Samuel standing next to me in the middle of the street. Moe and Doris stood next to Samuel with their hands tied behind their backs, just as mine were. Surrounding us was an angry mob of men and women, all with sores broken out all over their bodies from the plague. Television cameras also surrounded us, along with accompanying television crews from all around the world. I heard one of the men standing in front of me yell to another man some distance away.

"He's waking up now, Saul."

"Oh, is he now?" the man said as he walked towards me. He pulled out an intimidating knife with a large bone handle, and an even larger blade. It looked like a variant of the bowie knife, named after one of the best American knife-fighters that ever lived, Jim Bowie.

"Well now, isn't that nice. The would-be prophet has finally come around. Well now, Mr. Prophet, who's going to save you now?"

The sight of the knife coming towards me once more roused me to consciousness. The man came over to me and stood behind me, holding the knife to my neck. Though I could not see it, I could feel something warm trickling down my neck, which I correctly assumed was blood. I looked over at Lara, Samuel, and the others, and saw that men held knives to their throats as well.

Panic filled me as my heart began to race, as the pounding in my chest seemed to keep time with the throbbing in my head. *What could I do?* We were clearly outnumbered, and there seemed to be no clear path for retreat. *How could this happen?* We were supposed to have more time; it was not time for us to go yet.

Then, like a warm breeze it came to me what I must do. I calmly bowed my head and prayed quietly to the Lord, asking him to save us from the wicked followers of the beast. I felt strengthened and refreshed as the Holy Spirit filled me. Then, unexpectedly, I felt a new boldness as words flowed out of my mouth on their own accord.

"*Who* is going to save me, you ask, you wicked and deluded man? You trust in your knives and in your guns to protect you. I however, trust in the Lord, who is mighty and true in word and deed. It is the Lord that fights for us!"

No sooner had the words left my mouth then suddenly, and without warning, fire came down from heaven, devouring the wicked crowd that surrounded and sought to destroy us. So bright was the light and so hot the flames that I instinctively closed my eyes. Once I had the courage to open them again, I took an anxious look around, knowing that how long we lived depended on what I saw. Miraculously, standing beside me was Lara and Samuel, and beside him Moe and Lara. Other than the five of us, the street was empty, save a few, mostly neighbors, who had been fearfully watching the unexpected events as they unfolded. I noticed that none of those remaining had moved a muscle. They stood motionless, dumbfounded, along with a lone reporter, who had been doubling as his own cameraman, and had been filming the entire incident, though he had neither been a part of nor condoned what had been happening. Based on the absence of sores on his body, it was obvious he had not taken the mark of the beast.

"Why do you stand in awe of us men and women of Jerusalem, as if by our own power we called down fire from Heaven? Do you not know that God answered our prayer, just as God heard Elijah's prayer for assistance when he called down fire from heaven to consume the king's men? Glorify God, and give thanks to him that made you, and to his son, Jesus Christ, who bought you for a price!"

I gathered Lara and the others together and walked back into the house with them. Once inside, I found a knife that I then used to cut my own bonds first, and then the bonds of the others. None of us said anything for quite some time, trying to take in the danger that had come upon us so unexpectedly, and the subsequent miracle from God that had rescued us from the hands of our enemies. I was the first to speak.

"Breakfast anyone?"

Chapter 38-Mission Accomplished

As I sat down at the table to enjoy the strips of bacon, fried eggs, and the fresh cup of coffee Lara had prepared, I began reflecting upon recent events. It would soon be all over for Moe and me; it was time for us to prepare our families for what was to come. It was not going to be easy… for any of us. Since Moe and Doris had joined us for breakfast, it seemed as good a time as any. By the time we had finished our breakfast, I pretty much knew what I wanted to say.

"Listen, everyone. The time has probably come for us to talk about something. I believe that it's only a matter of months now before Addon comes for us…our work here is nearly finished. We have warned the world, we have done what we could to prepare everyone, and God has worked through us to demonstrate to the world that he is alive and well, despite everything that men like Friedrich Nietchze have said to the contrary." Lara looked at me as her eyes narrowed.

"What are you trying to say, John?" she asked, fearing she already knew the answer.

"We have always known what was going to happen, Lara, ever since we started out on this mission over three years ago. We will have to face Addon again, and this time, *he* will win."

"But, John, it's too soon. No, it's not time yet." Tears had already started to flow before I could say anything to comfort her.

"I'm sorry, Lara, but it's only a matter of months now. There is nothing any of us can do about it, nor should we want to even if we could. After all, this is the *Lord's* doing, not man's. Besides, we can and should take great comfort knowing that he is in control, and that he has prepared something far better than anything we have ever known."

"Of course, we still have several months before the end," Moe added, "so we still have a *little* time."

"That's right," I confirmed.

Lara and Doris looked at one another and then back at us.

"What should *we* do? What do you *want* us to do?" asked Doris.

Moe and I looked at each other. "Well, that's part of what we're trying to figure out, honey," Moe answered. "We're thinking that it would probably be best for the two of you to go home, back to the States," I said. "As bad as things are likely to be everywhere, we expect them to be worse here."

"I... don't know how Doris feels, John, but I can tell you what *I'm* going to do," Lara stated with resolve.

"You don't really want to put yourself through this do you Lara, or Samuel?" I asked.

"I...don't know John. I guess I don't want to put Sam through anything more than necessary. He's my son after all, and it's my job to protect him..." she began.

"There you go. Now I suggest that you take Sam and..."

"...but I believe that our place is here, with you John, to the very end," Lara continued.

"Listen to me Lara, you have to go, there is no other way."

"John, what is this all about? Why are you saying all of this anyway?" she asked me, exasperated, almost angry.

"Because God chose *me*, Lara, and Moe. I can't ask you and Sam to face what you'd have to endure if you are here when the end comes."

"You don't have to ask, John. When God chose you to do this, then he chose all of us... we're *family*. Why should Sam or I be afraid?"

I looked at her and I grew flush with anger.

"Lara, you know what's going to happen to me...hold on a minute." I turned to Sam, who was still sitting at the table with us. I had forgotten he was still there as the conversation had begun to heat up. "Sam, why don't you go into the living room, see what's on television?"

"Sure thing, Dad," he said, tightening his lips as he did so. Samuel was getting older, and I could tell that he understood far more than we ever gave him credit for. Once he was in the living room at the other end of the house, and was engrossed in the television, I continued.

"Now Lara, I don't want to get into an argument about this. You know we *are* going to die, you know *how* we are going to die, and you know what's going to happen afterwards. Why in the world would you want to be here when that happens, and to have Sam here to see it?"

"It's simple, John... because I love you, and so does Samuel. We want to spend every moment that we can here with you, can't you understand that? We all die eventually... are we all supposed to abandon the ones we love, just when they need us the most? Now you listen to me Jonathan Elijah March, if you want me to leave here before the Lord calls me home, well... good luck with that!"

"I'm with Mom on this Dad, I'm not going anywhere either. I want to be with you as long as I can be; you're the best Dad in the world." Once again, I had completely missed Sam's rejoining us at the table.

"Son, things are going to get ugly soon. I don't want you here when..."

"...when he kills you, and then refuses to allow anyone to bury your body for three and a half days? I know all about that Dad, and you want to know something? I am so proud of you; I couldn't be more proud to be called your son." I looked over at Moe, who had already teared up, looking for some assistance, hoping that he would be able to help me dissuade my family from staying on until the end. Instead, he just shook his head and shrugged his shoulders.

Doris, who had been quiet for the longest time, tapped her husband on the shoulder. Moe looked at her and asked, "What about you sweetheart, would you like to go stay with your mother, or with your sister?"

"You just try to get rid of me, lover! Wild horses couldn't drive me away. I'm with Lara, there is no way that I am going to abandon my husband when he needs me the most," she said. Moe and I just looked at each other and shrugged.

"What did we ever do to deserve such families, John" Moe asked me, before giving his wife a kiss and a hug.

"I don't know, Moe, I just don't know," I said, before doing the same with my wife and son.

Chapter 39-Rivers of Blood

As I gazed up into the fading night sky, I could still make out the constellation Orion. The belt of Orion was the most prominent feature that was still visible in the lingering darkness. The light of the moon also waned as the light of day began to peek over the horizon. We walked in the direction of the rising sun as it came up in the east.

We walked together along the beach, listening to the sound of the ocean waves lapping against the shore, and the sound of seagulls as they took turns diving for breakfast into the cold waters of the ocean. The fresh smell of a new day filled the air as the rays of the sun found us enjoying the beautiful, deep blue waters of the Mediterranean.

Lara and I had decided to try to do something special for the weekend, and Moe and Doris had been kind enough to allow Samuel to stay with them for a couple of days. We had heard of a Yacht Race off the coast of Herzliya that was taking place starting Saturday morning. We drove down on Friday night to the coast and stayed at a condominium we rented for the weekend. It seemed the perfect opportunity to spend some quality time alone with Lara.

I glanced at my watch and noticed it was almost seven o'clock. The yacht race was not scheduled to start until ten, so we decided to walk back to the condominium to grab some breakfast and return to the marina afterwards. A number of locals had informed us that large crowds often gathered for the annual race, so we wanted to find a good place to watch. As we neared the condominium, we saw camera crews from local as well as international press organizations unloading equipment, preparing for a planned live broadcast of the nationally televised event.

When we arrived back at the condominium, Lara walked on inside, while I sat out on the patio. I intermittently listened to the sound of Lara preparing breakfast, the sound of the ocean, and the sound of seagulls as they flew overhead, looking for a handout from tourists like us. I had always relished vacations to the beach, having grown up near the Atlantic Ocean. I looked down at the beach and watched as the camera crews started setting up their equipment. Up and down the coastline, I could see people here and there slowly starting to make their way to the water, preparing for a fun and relaxing day at the beach.

Lara walked out on the patio with a hot cup of freshly brewed coffee in her hand.

"Penny for your thoughts," she said, as she handed me the cup of steaming coffee, wrapped her arms around me, and gave me an affectionate kiss. *What a fortunate man I am to have had a wife like her!*

"Oh, I was just watching the television crews as they setup to broadcast the races. I wonder how many of the spectators really come to watch the races."

"What do you mean, silly?" she asked as she sat in my lap and smiled. "Why else would they be here?"

"Oh, I don't know. Maybe for the same reason we are, trying to spend some quality time together, maybe just hoping to escape the constant, unrelenting stress of life."

"You have a good point, Johnny. Who in their right mind would come to the beach just to have fun and enjoy themselves?"

"You know what I mean," I said, playfully feigning irritation. I looked up at the beautiful blue sky with no cloud in sight and marveled at the beautiful world that the Lord had made.

"What do you think it will be like, John?" she asked as she sat in my lap.

"What do I think *what* will be like, dear?"

"*Heaven*," she answered. I looked back in the sky again and thought about it for a moment.

"Well, I don't think we really *can* know, this side of eternity at least, exactly what it's going to be like," I answered. "There is one thing that I do know however, it's going to be considerably better than anything we have ever imagined. So very much has been lost, ever since the fall in the Garden of Eden," I said sadly.

"I know Jesus said that in Heaven, people will neither marry nor are they given in marriage. What do you think it will be like for *us*, John? Will we still be as close as we are now?"

"I don't know, honey, I'd like to think that we'll be even closer than we are today." Lara smiled for a moment before starting to frown.

"It just doesn't seem fair, John, that our time here is cut so short."

"*Fair*?" I asked. "What is *fair*, Lara? Is it fair that a little boy dies of leukemia? Is it fair that his parents have to watch him die? Is it fair when poor families die for lack of bread, when the scraps of food that most people throw away after a meal would be considered a feast to them? It all comes back to sin, honey. Life isn't fair, Lara, but God is. We have to trust him, we must have faith." As I finished talking, a scent in the air caught my attention. "Is something burning?"

"Oh no, the biscuits!" She leapt out of my lap and ran towards the kitchen. While she dealt with the crispy critters in the oven, I walked into the living room and turned on the television.

"This morning's remarkable achievement marked the largest number of arrests on a single day yet, as a large sting operation lead by the President's Monetary Enforcement Task Force this morning discovered literally thousands of fugitives, men, women, and children, being hidden, protected by members of a large protestant church, located in New York City. They were immediately taken into police custody, arrested for trying to obtain goods under false pretenses after refusing to take the mark, which has been the cornerstone of the president's economic recovery plan. In addition to these charges, all of the suspects were charged with violating the Freedom from Religion law passed last year, which made it a crime punishable by life in prison and in some cases, even death, for worshipping any deity other than President Addon. Police charged the men and women arrested with aiding and abetting known criminals. The conspirators are to be tried and sentenced to death for their crimes against humanity.

President Addon had these words to say in a press conference earlier today, 'These criminals are perfect examples of those that want to wreck havoc on our society, destroy our successful economic system, and destroy the fabric of what it means to be free. We will continue to aggressively hunt down and prosecute each and every rebel, whether here in the United States or abroad. We simply *will not* tolerate this kind of criminal behavior any longer. In regards to the Freedom from Religion law they violated, I'm not saying that they cannot worship, I'm just saying that they cannot worship anyone except me...'"

"Turn that thing off, honey," said Lara. "Today, mister, you belong to me!"

After breakfast, we grabbed our chairs and our umbrella and left for the beach. There were already large crowds gathering all around the marina by the time we arrived, though most were on the beach north of the marina. As we slowly made our way in the direction of the race, I suddenly realized that no matter what happened next, the world would never be the same again. Events like this race would soon be a thing of the past. Everything was going to change in a little while, for the better.

"*John.*" The voice came as a quiet whisper as we were walking in the sand. "Go and say the words that I shall put into your mouth..."

As we approached the marina, I wondered how I could get the attention of those gathered for the races, much less those living abroad, long enough for them to hear the words I had to tell them. It seemed impossible, but I was resolved to trust in the Lord to provide. As we drew closer, I saw where a large platform had been erected that I had not seen earlier, but that had to have been setup long before we arrived. It appeared that all of the reporters were gathered around the platform. When we were finally close enough, I discovered why. Judah Ben-Jacob, the current Speaker in the Knesset, was preparing to climb the platform to speak. When he recognized me and saw me walking towards him however, he stopped, apparently waiting to see what I would do. Several security guards grabbed me as I neared the platform. Speaker Ben-Jacob rushed over and told them to allow me through to the platform.

I climbed the stairs of the platform and made my way towards the center of the stage, where the microphones were. Some of the cameramen, recognizing who I was, swung their cameras around and pointed them at me. As I approached the microphones, the words of the Lord weighed heavy in my heart, though I was thankful to be counted worthy to utter them.

"Listen children of Israel and Gentiles alike. You have sinned grievously against the Lord. You have altogether rejected him and spurned him, even *after* he gave you his only Son. Instead of the Lord, you follow after demons and idols. Addon is not a god, nor is he a man; he is a demon. He is not a savior; he is the destroyer. He does not seek to save you, but destroy you.

"Turn to the Lord Jesus Christ now, with all of your heart. Accept the precious gift of salvation that the Lord offers you, or *you will* join the beast, and his master, in the lake of fire that burns for all eternity.

"Consider now Oh Israel, and all mankind, the words of the Lord!

'*And the second angel poured out his vial upon the sea; and it became as the blood of a dead man: and every living soul died in the sea.*

And the third angel poured out his vial upon the rivers and fountains of waters; and they became blood. And I heard the angel of the waters say, You art righteous, O Lord, which art, and was, and shall be, because you have judged thus. For they have shed the blood of saints and prophets, and thou hast given them blood to drink; for they are worthy. And I heard another out of the altar say, Even so, Lord God Almighty, true and righteous are thy judgments.'

And the fourth angel poured out his vial upon the sun; and power was given unto him to scorch men with fire. And men were scorched with great heat, and blasphemed the name of God, which had power over these plagues: and they repented not to give him glory.'

"After today, I will speak to you no more. The beast will come against us, and he will overcome us, but remember, *he cannot* overcome the Lord. For those that believe do not lose hope, and do not mourn us. Rather be patient, for after three days, the Lord will call for us to join him where he is. Remember, 'Greater is he that is in you, than he that is in the world.'"

Then, turning towards the ocean, I pointed toward the water and said to them, "Behold, the judgment of the Lord!" I let out a heavy sigh as I walked down the platform. Someone in the crowd yelled out, "What a fruitcake!" and someone else "Another crazy Christian! Who does he think he is?"

After that however, another pointed towards the ocean and yelled out in a loud voice, "Look at the sea! It's turning red, like the color of blood!"

A red patch that had suddenly appeared in the middle of the sea had started growing rapidly, growing larger and larger. It looked as if it would never stop. Soon, the entire Mediterranean was the color of blood.

This would be the most devastating plague yet, greater even than Wormwood. I must have been visibly shaken, because Lara ran over to me, grabbed me by the arm, and started pulling me towards the house.

"Look, the fish are dying!" someone yelled out, pointing to the dead fish that had begun floating to the surface.

We walked on back towards the house, and with all eyes focused on the ocean, no one even noticed.

Chapter 40-Scorched

Panic ripped throughout societies all over the world, as the oceans and the rivers turned into blood one by one. World leaders across the planet, led by Addon, cursed God, and uttered greater and greater blasphemies against him. The persecution of those that continued to worship the Lord grew more and more severe. The faithful, however, continued looking to the Lord for their strength, thankful to be counted worthy to suffer on behalf of the Lord. Many sang hymns or quoted scripture, as their persecutors led them away to prison, or to their execution.

Moe and Doris joined us for dinner the following day, as we prepared ourselves for what was still to come.

"So what happens next?" asked Lara, after Moe finished giving thanks to the Almighty for our meal.

"We should look to the sky," answered Moe.

"What does that mean?" asked Doris.

"It means that the second and third angels have poured out their vials upon the Earth. When the fourth angel pours out his vial upon the Earth, we can expect the sun to begin scorching men with fire," he answered his wife. Doris made a squeamish look.

"When should we expect this to occur?" she asked.

"There is no way to know, Doris, unless the Lord reveals his plan to us," I answered. "The Lord has not told us, and we have already carried our last message to the world. "

"We believe it will happen soon, however; perhaps as early as tomorrow."

We had barely finished dinner when we had our answer. It was already well past dusk when we finished eating, yet when I looked out the window; I noticed there was still light in the night sky, despite the absence of moonlight due to a new moon. Moe was sitting next to the window.

"Moe, would you mind taking a look out the window and tell me what you see?"

"What?" Moe looked out and noticed what I had, the light in the night sky. "Certainly, John." He pulled the curtain and gasped at what he saw.

"What is it, Moe?"

"It looks like we won't have to wait until tomorrow, John. The fire is already here."

Moe pulled back the curtain so we could all see what he did. There were lights in the night sky, similar to an aurora borealis, only much more intense. The lights could only have been caused by one or more solar flares, but these flares behaved unlike any other. The night sky grew steadily brighter as the lights from the flares came closer. A few minutes later, it looked more like daytime than night as one of the flares struck the waters of the Mediterranean. Enough water was instantly vaporized that a thick fog immediately formed, even as the sky returned to a darkness more typical of the evening. We all got up from the table and walked into the living room. Lara turned on the television, something that had become a common practice over recent days. The intermittent images that appeared then disappeared on the television both shocked us and served to confirm what we had suspected. On the screen were images of massive fires burning, and of men and women who were marked with the sign of the beast, running frantically as their clothes burst into flame.

"In Atlanta, a massive flare struck, knocking out electricity across the entire Atlanta metro area, and setting fires to homes and businesses across much of the viewing area. A particularly large flare struck California near the city of Los Angeles, setting fire to much of the state, ranging as far north as Hollywood and as far south as San Diego. Early reports indicate there has been massive property damage and significant loss of life. There are also reports coming in that a flare has struck Washington, DC. According to some reports, President Addon was still at the White House when power went off for several minutes after the flare struck. While the President is reported to be okay, he is said to be frustrated by the recent natural disasters that have plagued the Earth, something he attributes to the God of the Christians. He is expected to hold a press conference in just a few minutes about the recent string of disasters, and how he plans to address them. Wait a minute...okay, we now go live to the President of the United Nations of the Earth, President Addon..."

"Good evening. As all of you know, we have been plagued recently by a series of so-called natural disasters. First, there was the drought when no rain fell for a long time. Then, there was the Wormwood Asteroid that struck, causing so much devastation all over the world. Today, one of the greatest disasters yet occurred; we watched as the oceans and the rivers turned red like blood, causing marine life to die, and wreaking incalculable damage to the world's food supply. Now, we are faced with another great disaster. There was a massive coronal mass ejection from the sun at approximately five-thirty, Eastern Standard Time this morning. It took just thirty minutes for the resulting solar flares to begin reaching the Earth. There have been many, many, casualties reported among my followers, something that disturbs me greatly, not to mention the massive property damage. Power was also knocked out all across the United States as the power grid failed, as it has in countries worldwide.

I have come to believe that each and every one of these disasters is not natural at all, but is in fact, *supernatural*. I believe they have been caused by the God of the Christians, the God of those two prophets, who have been doing nothing but prophesying doom and gloom. You can blame them and their God for the great calamities that have come upon us as of late. I therefore order that all remaining Christians are to be arrested immediately, and sentenced to prison or put to death. Any found aiding or abetting any of these Christians, will suffer the same fate. As for the two prophets of the Lord, however I have only this to say to them…" Addon then leaned into the camera, looked directly into the lens, smiled, and said, "time's up. I'll see the two of you soon, real soon."

"Well, it looks like it won't be long now," I said aloud. "He's coming for us, and this time, it will be over."

"Have faith John; remember what happens to us afterwards. Remember what happens to *him* afterwards. He doesn't win the war, just a battle, and only a skirmish at that. We must not forget that no matter how powerful he may seem to be, he is, like all of us, only a created being, completely subject to the Father's will. He will be cast into the Lake of Fire, where he will be tormented forever, while we will be living blissfully forever with the Lord."

"I know, I know. It's all about faith, isn't it?"

"Indeed, it is," Moe answered.

I turned and looked at Sam and the women. "How about the rest of you, how are you doing?"

"I'm scared, John," Lara answered. "I believe we all are." Everyone nodded in agreement. Sam came over and hugged me.

"Hey, are you doing alright, Champ?" I asked him.

"Yeah Dad, I'm okay. I'm just glad that we know what happens, afterwards I mean."

About that time, the phone rang, and Lara walked over to the phone in the kitchen and answered it while we continued our discussion in the living room. Lara walked back into the living room a short while later.

"John, it's for you."

"Hello?"

"Mr. March? It's Judah Ben-Jacob. How are you this evening?"

"Oh, I'm doing okay, Mr. Ben-Jacob, thanks. How are you?"

"I'm doing well, Mr. March, thank you."

"Well, what can I do for you this evening, Mr. Speaker?"

"Well, I believe it may be what I can do for you, Mr. March, with your permission, of course."

"What do you mean?"

"Well, Mr. March, I know you are aware that someone very powerful doesn't like you very much and is out to get you. From what I am told, he will be making a move against you soon, very soon."

"Yes, I know."

"Mr. March, I believe that I might be in a position to help. As you know, I am the Speaker of the Knesset, and I have some powerful allies throughout the government. I believe I have convinced some of them to help."

"Help, how?" I asked, interested to find out where this was going.

"We believe that he will start small, by sending someone from the CIA, or perhaps someone from the Special Forces. This is where we can help. We can protect you, up to a point. We can take you somewhere, and keep you safe, assuming of course that he doesn't want you so badly that he sends in the Marines!" He laughed, expecting me to laugh as well. After a few moments, he added…"He doesn't want you *that* badly, does he?"

"Well, let's just say that he might lead with the Air Force, followed by the Marines."

"Why is that?" he asked me.

"Because it's faster," I answered.

"I see. Well then, I guess we will have to find you someplace deep underground then!"

"No, we cannot allow you to do this. He will eventually kill us, no matter what you or anyone else does."

"True enough; but then, we all die eventually, do we not? Look, many in my government feel as I do, if we are going to go down, it's best to go down fighting on the right side! It's clear that Addon is either a demon, completely insane, or both."

"Which do you believe?"

"Me? I'm with you. I expect to see him suffer eternally for his rebellion against God." He paused for a moment before asking, "Will you accept our help, John?"

"I guess so. I cannot thank you enough Mr. Speaker."

"We will send a car then. How soon can you be ready?"

"Um, how about tomorrow?"

"Mr. March, John, you will be lucky to survive another hour if you do not leave immediately!"

"Really? Okay, how soon can you have a car here?"

"He is already outside of your house waiting for you, your family, and your companions."

Chapter 41-Under Attack

"It looks as if we got you out of there just in time," the Mossad agent told us as we continued driving down the quiet, deserted roads in Jerusalem.

"Why, did something happen?" Moe asked him.

"Both houses were blown completely apart a short while ago. It was probably predator drones, or smart bombs. It may be a while before they discover that none of you were inside. We've tightened up security around the site."

"How long do you think it will be before they figure it out?"

"It's hard to say. A day, maybe two."

"Where are we going?" asked Lara.

"One of our safe houses in the Christian Quarter. We think it will be one of the last places he would ever look, given the way the area has been ravaged."

"Do you think they will suspect anything, that you helped us I mean?"

"I don't know, it is hard to say."

"What do you think, Mr. Speaker?"

"Please, call me Judah. After all, we are *brothers* now!"

"Indeed, we are," I said smiling, "and please, call me John." He just nodded at me and smiled.

"Well, I think that were it just another country, it would be months, perhaps years, before they could find you. Given the current environment, with every government on the planet at his disposal, and *who* it is that we are dealing with, I would say we have days, a week at the most before they learn that we have helped you. Perhaps another week, probably less, before they learn your exact location. Once they find us, well, let's just say that we will do what we can."

"Let me thank you once again, Judah, for what you are doing for me and my family. May God richly bless you, and everyone else that has a hand in helping us," Lara told him.

"Thank you, dear lady," he answered. "We will do what we can."

Once they were confident that we had not been followed and that it was safe, the car carried us to an unmarked building, disguised to look like a house inside and out, with a hidden, underground parking deck. We parked, got out of the car, and entered the house. Inside, I saw furniture, a television, and a kitchen, everything needed to make it look like someone's home. We walked to the rear of the house, where our escorts opened a door to an exceptionally large closet where there was a concealed elevator, which carried us down several floors beneath the surface. The elevator came to a stop at a floor identified as SB4, which I took to be sub-basement four. The elevator doors opened to reveal several large rooms, the largest of which appeared to serve as a kind of living room area, complete with a large screen television, two sofas, and several paintings that served to make the dwelling a little cozier and more like a home. There was also a kitchen with a refrigerator, a stove, a microwave, and a dishwasher. Lara, who made a beeline for the kitchen, found that it already been fully stocked with groceries.

"It is the best we were able to do on short notice," said Judah. "I hope you will accept my apologies for anything we may have overlooked. There are four bedrooms as well as a smaller apartment located across through the other door you saw when you came in here. Several Mossad agents will stay in the adjoining room, to help ensure that you have everything you need, and of course, to help provide for your safety."

I walked over to Judah Ben-Jacob and said to him, "Judah, I..."

"There is no need, John March. It truly is my pleasure. Now then, if you will please excuse me, I need to see what that crazy-man, that *thing*, is up to. You are safe here, at least for the moment. I hope you rest well tonight." Lara walked over to the older man, and straining slightly on her tip-toes so that she could reach the taller man, she kissed him on the cheek."

"Thank you Mr. Ben-Jacob."

"Really, Ms. March, I am a married man," he said, smiling warmly at her first, then at me."

"Now then, I will say good night."

"Good night, Judah." He left and one of the remaining Mossad agents said to me, "We will be just outside, in the adjoining room, Mr.

March. That phone there on the table, if you dial "8" will come directly to us."

"Thank you," I replied, shaking his hand.

It was getting late by this time, so we settled down in our new home for the evening. There was still considerable fear amongst all of us at this point, the fear of dying, fear of the unknown, and fear of the suffering that was to come. I asked Moe to say a prayer before we all retired for the evening.

"Oh most Sovereign Lord, we give thanks to you for all of the many blessings that you have bestowed upon us, your most humble servants. We ask, oh Lord, that you will comfort us, and take away from us the sinful despair that we are now experiencing. After all Lord, you have protected us this far, and you have demonstrated your mighty power to us, working extraordinary miracles in recent days, as you have in times long past, when you led your people Israel out of the land of Egypt, out of the land of their captivity. Be merciful to us now, oh Lord and thank you for your great goodness. Strengthen us oh Lord for the difficult time ahead, and comfort us with the knowledge of the wonderful things you have planned for us when we come into your kingdom. We thank you, and we praise you, in the most blessed name of your son, the Lord Jesus Christ, in whose name we pray, amen."

"Thank you, Moe," I told him.

We all found our rooms, said good night, and lay down for a restful night's sleep.

Sometime during the course of the night, the Lord came to us in a dream.

"John."

"I am here, Lord."

"The Lord is with you, John March! Just as you and Moe have each been faithful to him to the end, so he will also be faithful to you. Have faith and great courage John March, for the Lord *will* be with you. He will work yet one more sign amongst the people of this age before the end comes. As for you and Moe Princeton, tomorrow, as it is written, the beast will come to you, he will fight against you, and he will overcome you. This is from the Lord, John March, so do not fear the beast, for the Lord will be with you to strengthen you. Then, after three days, you will be called up, and you will come into the presence of the Almighty, where you will dwell with him for all eternity."

I awoke after the dream and sat up in the bed. *They have already found us.* I had no idea how it was possible the beast had already found us, but I knew it was so. As I looked down at Lara, there was still so much that I wanted to say to her, things I had left unsaid. I considered waking her, so we could spend what remained of our time together talking, and enjoying each other's company. After considering it for a couple of minutes, I realized how selfish it would be for me to do that. I would be leaving the world, but Lara would need to continue, to go on for a short while at least. She would need her rest and her strength for the days ahead, so I let her sleep. I walked over to the large picture hanging in our dining room and studied it for a moment. It was a serene painting, depicting a beautiful waterfall, set deep in the woods, with the sun rising in the distance. The sunrise in the painting prompted me to check the time. Looking down at my watch I saw it was already six o'clock. I debated for a moment about going back to sleep before realizing how pointless the endeavor would be.

I walked into the kitchen and started the coffee maker, so I could brew a pot of coffee for myself and everyone else. I had just poured my first cup of coffee when the knock on the door came. *It is time, John.* I answered the door and found a shaken Mossad agent standing there.

"Sir, I don't know how to tell you this..."

"I already know. They have found us."

"But how could you possibly know that when we only just found out ourselves?" I just smiled at him in response. "Oh, of course, you're a prophet."

"Yes, the Lord told me. Don't worry about it, Special Agent Levi. Everything will be okay."

We were interrupted when the phone began ringing.

"Hello?"

"Good morning, Mr. March? I hope that I did not wake you?"

"Good Morning, Judah. No, I was already awake."

"Good. I am calling o let you know that..."

"...that Addon has already found us. Yes, I know."

"Of course. Well, we have men stationed all around you. We will hold them off as long as we can. Would you like for us to try to move you somewhere else?"

"No, but thank you. It has become clear to me that our time has come, and that this is God's will. We will face him here, now."

"Are you certain? We could..."

"No, I am certain, but thank you."

"Very well. I would like to tell you, Mr. March, John, how much I respect you for everything you have done. You are a brave and courageous man."

"No, I'm not, but thank you for saying so. I should hang up now, Judah. I need to wake everyone and let them know what is happening."

"Of course, as you wish. Is there anything I can do?"

"No, I don't think so."

"It has been my great privilege knowing you, John. I look forward to seeing you again."

"As do I, Judah, thank you."

"*L'hitraot* (see you soon), my brother," he told me.

"*L'hitraot*," I replied, before breaking the connection.

I walked into the bedroom to wake Lara, who was still sleeping peacefully. I felt guilty about waking her but she and Sam would want the chance to say goodbye. As it turned out, I did not have to do either. A series of explosions overhead took care of that for me. Despite being four stories underground, I was able to hear the explosions clearly, as well as some gunfire exchanges. Just then, the phone rang again. I walked over and picked up the phone.

"Hello?"

"Good morning, Mr. March." It was Addon.

"What do you want, demon?"

"I want your miserable life of course; I would have thought that a prophet like yourself would already know that."

"You may win the battle but you will lose the war, demon," I said.

"I know that you hairless ape. Your friends are putting up a fight to protect you, Mr. March, but it is a lost cause of course; you will be in my hands within a day, no matter what happens. I wanted to give you the opportunity to surrender yourself to me. If you do so, I will spare the rest of your family from a slow and painful death."

"How do I know that you will keep your word?"

"It is simple, Mr. March, I don't care about them, I only care about *you*, and your partner in crime."

I thought about it for a few minutes before giving him an answer. "I'll have to talk it over with Moe."

"Of course. I would hurry, however, if I were you. I have several more battalions of men and several squadrons of planes already on the way."

"I understand. How do I reach you."

"I'll call you, in about fifteen minutes. I expect your decision at that time."

"I understand."

By the time I hung up, Moe and Doris, awakened by the explosions, had joined me in the living room. Lara and Samuel came in a short while later.

"What's going on, John, was that him?" Moe asked.

"Yes."

"The explosions we heard, that was him as well?" he asked. I nodded.

"Hmmm. What does he want?"

"He wants us to surrender, Moe. He says he will spare the others if we do so."

"Well, that's it then. Let's do it."

"No, you can't do that, no! I'm not ready!" Doris shouted, wrapping her arms around Moe as if she were protecting him from harm.

"It's time Doris, we have to go."

"No, Moe, please...don't go!" Doris burst into tears, clinging desperately to Moe.

"Please, Doris, don't do this," he said to her gently. "I love you Doris, I always have, and I always will. Besides, we will be together soon, remember? This will all be over soon, for all of us."

I looked over at Lara and Sam. Lara had tears streaming down her cheeks, as did Samuel. In a sense, I felt better for Lara and Sam than I did for Doris. When I was gone, at least Lara and Sam would have each other. Doris, on the other hand, would be all alone, except for Lara and Sam of course.

"Do you have to go, John? Is there no other way?"

"We have to go, Lara. The Lord told me in a dream that this would happen today. It is *his* will... Listen, Lara, I could never in a thousand years, even in a thousand times ten thousand, have found a better companion, a better friend, than I found in you."

"Nor could I have ever found a more noble man, a finer husband, a better father for Sam, than I found in you. I'm going to miss you John, I'm going to miss you so much!" Lara looked at me with an expression of love mixed with confusion, and sorrow.

"We will see each other soon, Lara, I promise."

She walked over to me and wrapped her arms around me. Samuel came over and followed suit.

"I love you, Dad," he said. "I'm going to miss you so much."

"Samuel, you have no idea how much I adore you, or how proud I am of the young man you have become." We all sat there for several minutes, saying our goodbyes to one another through tears. After a few minutes, the dreaded sound came. I held a secret hope that maybe, just maybe, it would be Ben-Jacob, calling to tell us that the coast was clear.

"Hello?"

"Time's up, what's your decision?"

"We're coming up." I hung up the phone and faced Special Agent Levi. I turned briefly to look at Moe, who nodded to me in response.

"We're ready."

Chapter 42-Facing the Enemy

Moe and I walked into the elevator in silence. As the doors closed, Moe began singing the hymn, "Amazing Grace." I joined in as well, while Special Agent Levi watched, marveling at us as the elevator finally opened on the top floor and into the presumed closet.

We exited the elevator and walked back toward the front of the house. Looking out of a window to assess the situation, we found a number of Israeli troops and tanks stationed outside of the building. A hundred yards from the house, several tanks had already been destroyed, and bodies of several fallen soldiers lay all around them. As I looked up and surveyed the landscape, in the distance I could see thousands of enemy troops and hundreds of enemy tanks, even as enemy aircraft flew overhead.

"Who is in charge, Agent Levi?" I asked.

"General Simon," he answered, pointing toward a soldier standing outside, dressed in desert fatigues.

"Thank you." I walked out of the front door and to where the general stood standing.

"General Simon?" The general, who had been talking on his radio as he continued exploring various military options at his disposal, turned to face me.

"Who are you?" he asked gruffly.

"My name is John March." The man's countenance changed dramatically as I shook his hand.

"Mr. March, It is a great pleasure to meet you. We're a little busy at the moment, sir. Is there something I can help you with?"

"Please tell your men to stand down, General."

"But Mr. March, we are the only thing standing between you and the enemy!"

"I understand that General, but there is no need for any additional loss of life on our account. This thing is from the Lord. We have carried the message that the he has given us; our time here is over. I would like to say thank you to you and your men, for the brave stand you made here today; you are all very brave and courageous men."

The general looked at me for several moments before finally letting out a heavy sigh and saying, "No, Mr. March, I believe you and Mr. Princeton are the brave and courageous ones here. May God go with you, gentlemen."

"Thank you, General. May God go with you as well," I replied.

Moe and I walked back into the house that made up the first floor of the building, and sat down in the living room.

I sat there on the sofa waiting, staring intermittently at the clock, the one with the minute hand that seemed to be racing around its circular course faster than any timepiece should. I looked out the living room window, where I could see nothing but gray skies and stillness. I knew he was coming for me, and that he would arrive within the hour. He would come and this time, kill me. Addon and his followers would undoubtedly rejoice once I was gone. I was the one that they feared and despised, the one they held responsible for the many plagues they had endured.

Having long ago said our goodbyes to our families and the believers we had met since arriving in Jerusalem--the wonderful, glorious, holy city-- Moe and I were ready. We had done all that we could to comfort our brothers and sisters, to assure them that we would see them again very soon. While all of them rejoiced with us that we were about to go be with the Father, some had left only when we told them that it would be easier for us if they did so. Even then, they left in tears for our sakes.

We knew that our waiting was almost over when far off in the distance we heard a low, faint, rumbling noise which seemed to be getting closer. The reverberating sound grew louder and more distinct as the source of the roar drew near. It soon became apparent that the noise was coming from the rolling tracks of a column of tanks. The house began vibrating with an ever-increasing intensity as the tanks drew closer to our home. Several paintings hanging on the walls in the living room began to rattle. They leapt from the walls and crashed onto the hardwood floor, shattering and sending shards of glass in all directions. Judging by the considerable contingent Addon had sent for us, we assumed that he knew what happened to our would-be executioners the last time someone had attempted to silence us before our time had come.

Moe and I looked at one another before rising unsteadily from our seats. We both nodded in unspoken agreement as we began walking towards the door. We were scared, but we refused to stay and cower inside, just waiting for our enemy to arrive. We would meet him outside and face him as the faithful soldiers we were. Each of us took comfort from the words, "greater is he that is in you than he that is in the world." We would not give the enemy the satisfaction of finding fear in our eyes when he arrived.

Our work was finally finished after traveling a long and difficult road wrought with trials and tribulations. We had dutifully accomplished our mission by delivering the message that the Lord had sent us to bring, and we had warned the peoples of the Earth about the coming destruction. Our work was over; it was time for us to go home…

General Simon had radioed his men to stand down and to begin withdrawing. The tanks rolled out and the men fell in behind them, marching out of the city in the opposite direction from where the enemy troops were positioned. As they moved out, the enemy troops moved in. Within fifteen minutes, all we could see around us were enemy troops and tanks. Soon after, we heard the whirring sound of a helicopter approaching overhead. Looking upwards, towards the approaching sound, I could see that it was Marine One, the Marine Corps helicopter known for carrying the President of the United States and more recently, for carrying the President of the United Nations of the Earth. The helicopter circled overhead several times before landing on the street in front of us. The pilot switched off the helicopter, and just as the blades stopped moving, Abe Addon exited the aircraft, an evil smile stretching from ear to ear.

"Mr. March, how nice it is to see you again. Oh how I have longed for this meeting!" He walked over to where we were standing, even as men raised their M16A4 rifles. Positioned atop the buildings all around were snipers with their M82A3 sniper rifles, all pointed at two unarmed, civilian men. They must have considered us dangerous men indeed.

"Too bad I can't say the same, demon!" I said defiantly.

"Please, Mr. March, come closer. I want to really *savor* this moment, get it, savor! Oh, that was a good one, I'm such a jokester!" The three of us stood there on a street, in the middle of Jerusalem, with tanks and soldiers all around us. Next to the massive army gathered all around us, we felt small indeed.

"Look Mr. March and Mr. Princeton, look around you and behold the power at my command. You too could have held such power, if only you had chosen to join with me, instead of *him*!"

Moe stepped forward and said boldly to the beast,

"*And the beast was taken, and with him the false prophet that wrought miracles before him, with which he deceived them that had received the mark of the beast, and them that worshipped his image. These both were cast alive into a lake of fire burning with brimstone. And the remnant were slain with the sword of him that sat upon the horse, which sword proceeded out of his mouth: and all the birds were filled with their flesh.*"

"Yes, yes, I know all of that," he said, "we've been here before, remember? I know what my end will be; but for now, I will just savor yours. Goodbye, Mr. March." He reached out and placed one hand on my shoulder and his other hand on Moe's shoulder. His hand felt as cold as ice. I suddenly felt myself collapsing to the ground as everything went black.

Chapter 43-The Vigil

I stood and watched as events unfolded outside of the house. I wanted to turn away, to go back down the elevator to be with Sam, to do anything but stand there and watch. But stand there and watch is exactly what I ended up doing. I knew what was going to happen, that he was going to die, but what else could I do; He was, after all, my husband, the last prophet, John March.

I stood and watched through a window as the beast touched John and Moe on the shoulders, and I watched on in horror as they both fell to the ground, dead. Several onlookers tried to collect the bodies for burial but Addon, who stood there for the longest time staring at their lifeless corpses, would not permit anyone to get anywhere near them.

"No, you *may not* bury these men. You *will* leave them here. General Miller!" A man dressed in a military uniform with several stars on his helmet came forward.

"Yes, sir?"

"Post a twenty-four hour guard here, General Miller. I want at least a dozen men, armed to the teeth, and two tanks, standing guard here at all times, where they will remain twenty-four hours a day, seven days a week, until I personally give orders to the contrary. No one is permitted to move or bury these men. Let their dead bodies lie here and decay, until nothing remains but dried bones. I will permit only camera crews from the major news networks to setup cameras, which they may leave here day and night if they wish." He then approached the general. "General Miller, if anything, and I mean anything, happens to the bodies of these two men, I assure you that you will wish that you had never been born."

"Yes, sir!" he answered, shaking a bit as he did so.

Film crews from all of the major television networks and reporters from all of the major news organizations surrounded the bodies of the men we cared so deeply about. Addon had no problem allowing them to get as close as they wanted to film or take pictures of our husbands' bodies.

Let their dead bodies lie here and decay until nothing remains but dried bones.

I could hardly believe my own ears. What purpose could it possibly serve, leaving their bodies to decay for all to see? I started to run out the door, but someone grabbed me from behind by the arm. Doris had somehow come up to join me without me noticing.

"Lara, what are you trying to do?" she asked me forcefully.

"I'm not going to allow them to desecrate my husband's body by leaving it exposed to the elements, and to the vermin!"

"Lara!" she yelled. "You *have* to get a grip. Now get a hold of yourself. Think of Samuel! What will happen to poor Samuel if something happens to you? Now take a deep breath and think about what I am telling you."

After giving it some thought, I knew she was right. All I could do was to stand there quietly and watch. The monster must have known we were watching, because though I was standing in the shadows with the sun behind me, he looked in our direction, stared straight at me, and smiled. I was nervous, but I was even more angry. I found solace only in the thought that I knew that John and Moe would go to be with my Lord and savior Jesus Christ, while the demon Abaddon would be thrown into the Lake of Fire. I had to bite my tongue and just stand there, no matter what happened.

A few moments later, he stared back down at them and started laughing. He began walking away, laughing all of the way to Marine One, where he waved goodbye in our direction. I was happy to see him go.

After waiting for another hour or so, we took the elevator back down to the apartment, where we tried to comfort one another. For the most part however, we just cried. Sam and I adored John, and Doris felt the same way about Moe.

"Doris, I wanted to thank you for what you did up there when I wanted to race out the door to Addon. You saved my life."

"Think nothing of it, dear, and for the record, I felt like doing exactly the same thing."

"I'm sure you did. What a monster!"

"Yes, but remember, dear, he will get his come-uppance."

There was a knock on the door and since whomever it was had to pass through the Mossad agents, I suspected I knew who it must be.

"Hello, Mr. Ben-Jacob."

"Hello, Mrs. March. Ladies, my most sincere condolences to you both, and to *you* young man," he said, pointing to Sam, who was still on the sofa, watching us. "How are you two dear ladies holding up?"

"As well as can be expected, I suppose. I wanted to thank you again for the kindness you've shown us, especially to my husband."

"It was my great pleasure, Mrs. March. I only wish there had been more that I could have done for your husbands."

"There was nothing more you could have done, Mr. Speaker," said Doris, joining the two of us by the door. This is all part of God's plan. The Lord Jesus Christ will be coming again soon, and all of this has helped to prepare the world for it. Our husbands' deaths were certainly not in vain."

"Amen. I suppose you are right, of course, Mrs. Princeton."

"Mr. Ben-Jacob, is there any way that we could possibly stay here for a while?" I asked. "We will, of course, try a find another place to live as soon as possible..."

"Mrs. March, you and Mrs. Princeton may stay here for as long as you like. Please take no thought for it whatsoever. In fact, I would be insulted if you did not take your time looking," he said smiling at us. I had always liked Judah Ben-Jacob. He had been among the nicest, most decent people that I had ever met, anywhere. I had been excited to hear that he had become a Christian and that he would be with us after all of this was over.

"Thank you, Mr. Speaker," Doris answered.

"You are most welcome, dear lady. Well, I am afraid that I must be on my way now. There is much governmental business to discuss. If there is anything you need, or even if there is not, please feel free to call me anytime." He handed us each a business card. "Here is my phone number. You can call me directly or ask for me through one of the Mossad agents, who will continue staying in the apartment next door, with your permission of course. We would be more comfortable leaving someone with you for a while, until we know that you ladies will be safe."

"Thank you, Mr. Ben-Jacob," I replied, closing the door as he walked away.

We heard the television suddenly turn on in the living room. Doris and I must have had the same thought at the same time, as we both rushed into the living room. It was too late however, as images of our dead husbands, lying motionless there in the middle of the street, were already being splattered all over the television screen.

"...so here they are. The two men, the two supposed prophets, that tormented so many all around the world for so long, are finally dead. Our wonderful leader, our hero, President Abe Addon, is the brave man that finally ended our suffering. Already, well wishes and gifts for the President have started to appear at the White House. We are told that President Addon has been receiving calls from governmental leaders all over the world, thanking him for ridding the world of these two men. The two so-called prophets were widely believed to be somehow responsible for the plagues that have taken so many lives and destroyed so much property all over the globe for the last several years. If President Addon was not hailed as an anointed messiah before, he certainly will be now. This is perhaps one of his most remarkable achievements. You may or may not be aware of it, but a large crowd of men had tried taking matters into their own hands recently, kicking in the door of one of the prophet's houses. They came close to destroying the infidels, but through some kind of bizarre, turn of events, the poor men were themselves destroyed. Thankfully, the miserable lives of these prophets were cut short by our marvelous savior, whom all of the world worships, President of the United Nations of the Earth, Abe Addon..."

As I pressed a button on the remote control and the television clicked off, I began to understand, to *finally* understand, something that John had been trying to tell me for the longest time, that the prophecies in the book of Revelation in the Bible were *real*. Something had happened that I never would have thought possible. The world itself had been turned upside down. It was bad before, but it was getting even worse. The world was now truly bent, twisted into a misshapen form, an evil that caused good to seem evil and evil to seem good...

I had often tried to see the world, at least a little, through John's eyes, but it was not easy. The Lord had appeared to John, but not to me. While I loved my husband dearly, I was alternately either jealous of him, or a little dubious of everything he was telling me. The stories he told me had always seemed so fantastic, ever since he was a little boy. I wanted to believe him, but at times, I had my doubts. After everything I had witnessed over the past few weeks, there was no longer any doubt. The end was fast approaching and the Lord would be coming soon. I also took great comfort knowing that Addon would soon be gone, cast into the Lake of Fire, along with his master. It also meant that I would be seeing John again, soon.

I spent most of the rest of the day making sure that Samuel either watched recorded movies or left the television off altogether. Doris and I reminisced about our husbands, and what we thought would happen next with us, and with the world. We both longed for home, and for relatives that we hadn't seen since moving to Israel. But for now, , according to the prophecy, the Lord was going to raise our husbands, and call them into Heaven in just three days. Looking for solace, I picked up our Bible and turned to the eleventh chapter of Revelation.

'And after three and a half days the spirit of life from God entered into them, and they stood upon their feet; and great fear fell upon them which saw them. And they heard a great voice from heaven saying unto them, Come up here. And they ascended up to heaven in a cloud; and their enemies beheld them.' Revelation 11:11

There was no way either of us would go anywhere until after the three days had passed. It was what we should do *afterwards* that we could not agree upon. According to the prophecy, the fifth angel would pour out his vial on the seat of the beast.

'And the fifth angel poured out his vial upon the seat of the beast; and his kingdom was full of darkness; and they gnawed their tongues for pain, and blasphemed the God of heaven because of their pains and their sores, and repented not of their deeds.' Revelation 16:10

After what the beast had done to my husband, to our family, and to our *world*, if I had the chance to see this happen, and the opportunity to see him cast into the Lake of Fire, I wanted to be there. I knew however, that while he would be punished, I thought it unlikely that I would see it.

The next two days passed by painfully slow, each hour seeming to progress slower than the one before. Both days we woke up to live pictures on the television of our husbands' bodies lying just four stories above us on the street. It seemed every world leader on the planet had called Addon to congratulate him on his victory, and to thank him for finally ending the prophets' 'reign of terror'. Doris and I felt like the wives of convicted felons. Had *we* been in the public eye we would certainly have been shunned, perhaps even arrested as co-conspirators, or killed. Celebrations were being held all over the world, in large cities and small towns alike. The networks ran stories twenty-four hours a day about people out in the streets, celebrating. It looked like one giant Mardi Gras, or a worldwide Carnival festival, as Addon, along with businesses and governments around the world, declared the day our husbands died to be an international holiday, adding fuel to the celebrations already being held.

On the third and final day of our vigil, Doris and I felt as if we were being tortured as time slowed to a crawl. If the prophecy was precise, we surmised that since our husbands had been murdered in the morning, it seemed logical that they would be called up to be resurrected by the Lord Jesus on the evening of the third day.

As it turned out, we were in store for more than just one surprise that day.

Chapter 44-Come up Here

Finally, the hour came that we had been waiting so long to see. We left the apartment about thirty minutes before the time that would mark three and a half days since Addon had murdered our husbands. The crowds had begun to dissipate, and all but one of the television networks and a handful of local stations had already packed up and left. While many people knew of the prophecy that told about the Lord calling the two prophets up to Heaven after three and a half days, few actually believed anything would happen. Most believed it would just be another day of the corpses lying in the street. Had they believed in the prophecy, then of course they would never have taken the mark of the beast, because they would know the eternal suffering they would face, the penalty for all who reject the Lord God Almighty. Had they even believed just enough to take a closer look at the dead bodies of the two prophets, perhaps they would have noticed that the two bodies had not started decomposing, although they should have. Indeed, they had not decomposed whatsoever, although our husbands were quite dead.

It had been getting colder during the evening hours after the sun had set, so by the time we got off the elevator, everyone had left with the exception of the soldiers responsible for guarding the bodies, the sole network camera crew that remained along with the handful of local stations, and a group of believers. The group had been gathering at night, when they felt it safe enough to come out. The soldiers guarding the body were not believers to be sure, but neither did they care about whether people coming to see the dead prophets lying in the middle of the street were followers of the Nazarene or not. They only cared about ensuring that nothing happened to the bodies of the two men, as they had been given a warning passed down to them from President Addon, that that if anything *did* happen to the two men, they would suffer the same fate as the two prophets.

None of us gathering around John and Moe's lifeless bodies knew exactly what to expect, we only believed that something miraculous would happen. We had fifteen minutes to go until it would be exactly eighty-four hours since their untimely demise. That is when I first spotted saw them coming down the street. At first, there seemed to be only a few but as they drew closer, we could see that there was a large crowd of people coming towards us. Among the large gathering were a number of cameramen from the major news networks, as well as some world leaders. I later learned that here had been a large anti-Christian rally being held nearby in Jerusalem, and a reporter had asked one of the speakers, the Prime Minister of a European country, whether *he* believed anything was going to happen with the two dead prophets. Once the reporter explained the question, (apparently the Prime Minister had been wholly ignorant of the fact that anything was *supposed* to happen), he suggested that everyone follow him down to the site of their happy demise to see if anything had happened, since it was only a couple of blocks away.

When I first saw the group and recognized by the signs they were carrying who they were and what they stood for, I was angry. I started to ask God to send down his fire from Heaven just once more, so that they would not be permitted to desecrate the ground that the two men of God had sanctified by their blood. Upon reflecting on it for several minutes however, as I watched them approaching, laughing and yelling, more like weekend college kids enjoying a night on the town than like civilized adults, coming towards where we were standing, it dawned on me. God had sent these wicked men to come and to bear witness to the wonder he was about to perform. If only a few of his people had been gathered around to see the miracle occur, it would not have been as readily believed by those the Lord still wanted to reach. It was most proper and most fitting I realized, that these men, who denied the very existence of God, would bear witness to his power.

The crowd of unbelievers reached the site with only five minutes remaining. With their arrival, I was more certain than ever that God was going to do something great. Some of the pagan crowd began laughing and carrying on. Many were clearly quite pleased to find the prophets still dead, lying in the same spot where they had collapsed after Addon touched them. Others in their group expressed disgust, claiming they had defiled themselves by coming into the presence of Christians.

"Hey, wow, look at that, it looks like the only place these men have been is to rigor mortis! Ha, ha..." The man had apparently been drinking, because the stench of cheap whiskey filled the area around me when he laughed.

"No, no, I've got it. They're only taking a nap! Ha, ha, ha…whoa ha, ha, ha…"

The group carried on in similar fashion for several minutes. I found myself completely appalled that none of them seemed to have any respect whatsoever for the dead, until at last, one of them yelled out something.

"Hey, quiet everyone, quiet down, it's time. This is it, it's show time!"

The crowd erupted in laughter, as I and the other believers with me tightened our jaws, repulsed and incensed by their crude and hateful behavior. The laughter soon died down and subsided however, as everyone grew quiet and watched. Some of the louder-mouthed men took on fearful expressions, wondering perhaps what it would mean for them if the Christian God raised the two men from the dead and subsequently called them up into Heaven. The crowd stood there for several minutes, waiting patiently, growing increasingly confident that nothing would happen. A number of men in the crowd once more grew belligerent, before turning and walking away. The rest of the crowd was preparing to leave when one of the younger men among their number cried out.

"Wait! I think I see something!"

The crowd turned around, trying to discern what the young man had seen, not wanting to miss anything. Everyone watched as a glow suddenly appeared around John and Moe's bodies. It was very faint at first, but it gradually grew brighter and brighter, until it took on the appearance of a blue flame, similar to that of a gas stove or fireplace. The glow engulfed their bodies as an orange flame appeared inside the blue, wrapping itself around their bodies like a tight bodysuit, yet not consuming them. We watched as a gentle white mist or smoke entered their bodies through their nostrils. God was breathing life back into our husbands' bodies!

About that time one of our number, a believer that had come out to see the resurrection, yelled out, "Look, I can see them breathing, come and see how their chests are moving up and down. "

"No way," yelled another, "that's impossible, I was here when they died. They haven't moved in over three days. It's your imagination, I'm telling you!"

Just then, John opened his eyes, followed by Moe, and they both looked around. The crowd of wicked unbelievers gasped in horror, as Moe and my husband stood up on their feet and looked around at the crowd with an interested but not surprised look. Both men looked very serene, more at peace than I had ever seen them.

I watched as the magnificent scene began to unfold. The blaspheming men, who had only moments earlier been laughing and carrying on like crass hooligans, were now terrified out of their minds. Several of them screamed out, others were so paralyzed with fear that they couldn't move. Surprisingly, the experience so moved a few of the men that they fell to their knees and glorified God. My husband John then turned to me, and Moe turned to Doris. John said nothing with his mouth, but he said everything with the look in his eyes, and the warm smile that he had on his face, as he looked first at me, and then at Samuel. He had a glow on his face, as if he had stood in the presence of God himself. Serenity and joy radiated off of him like light from the sun. I glanced over at Moe, and found the same glow about him as well. He looked back and smiled at me, with the same tranquility I saw on John's face. I turned back to John and our eyes met, instantly locked in an indescribable expression of love. Samuel broke free from me, and ran to his father.

"Dad! Dad! I love you so much! I love you so much!"

Samuel was the first of us to reach his father. Sam wrapped his arms around him and hugged him tight. John embraced his son and smiled back at him with the same expression of love, the kind of bond that only a father and son can share.

After a few minutes, which seemed more like hours to Sam and me, it was time for them to go. It had been so good to see John alive again, and to know for certain that the prophecy was true, to see it unfold before our eyes.

We then heard a voice call down from Heaven to the two witnesses, the last two prophets, the men that Doris and I called *husband*, the ones that had faithfully carried the last message of the Lord to a dark and sinful world. The voice called out, "Come up Here!"

Immediately a cloud began to envelop John and Moe, and as they smiled and waved at us, the cloud began to lift them up towards heaven. So great was the love and the pride that I held for my husband at that moment, that it surely surpassed all others. Only the Lord himself exceeded the love I felt for John.

The men ascended ever higher towards Heaven, to the fear and consternation of those watching below. Fear overpowered the wicked men in the crowd, fear of the wrath of God, the Lord of all the Earth, my God, Sam's God, and John's God. Soon the last two prophets of God disappeared, as rivers of tears flowed freely down the cheeks of those that loved the Lord. I knew at that moment that I would not see my husband again until I was with him and Sam, in our Father's Heavenly Kingdom.

Within minutes after they had disappeared, we began to hear dogs barking all across Jerusalem. Other animals were also growing increasingly jittery. Then, suddenly, it started--a foreign and inarticulate noise that began as a deep, guttural sound, before progressing to something akin to large Japanese Taiko drums. The ground began to shake so violently and so severely that we all fell to the ground. All around us, we saw buildings weaving back and forth, *bending* to the point that they began to crack and fall apart all around us. A number of the profane men in the group, who had come to laugh and ridicule our husbands, died during the massive Earthquake, which lasted for ten minutes before finally subsiding, leaving over seven thousand people dead. Some of the wicked men who had seen what happened to the two prophets, and who had seen and felt the terrible Earthquake that followed, joined with the believers across Jerusalem that had witnessed these things either in-person or on television, and gave glory to the God of Heaven and Earth.

I looked at Doris, who wore the warmest smile that I had seen on her face for the entire time I had known her. We shared the same warm expressions of overwhelming joy that we had seen on the faces of our husbands. I then glanced over at Samuel, whose wide-eyed expression and astonishment, amazement, and joy.

As the three of us began walking back towards the house, it seemed to me that things were finally beginning to take a turn for the better.

Chapter 45-The Fifth Angel

"Raul! Get in here, now!"

He always hated it when Addon was worked up about something and this time, he was the worst Raul had ever seen him. He had done everything he could to avoid Addon's office. He had heard what had happened so he knew what was coming. He had been having those nagging doubts again, ever since he had seen a recording of the event. It was too late for him, however. Despite finally coming to the realization that he had hooked his wagon to the wrong side, he was trapped. It probably did not matter anyway; the way he had it figured, he had taken too long, and the point of no return for him had long since come and gone.

"Yes, master."

"Is it true?"

"Is what true, sir?"

There was no coming through this unscathed. Raul had concluded that at this point, all he could hope for was to survive his master's rage, no matter how painful it may be. He trembled as he saw Addon's form begin to shimmer, as his true form emerged for a moment, before once more fading and allowing his human appearance to reemerge.

"Did he resurrect his prophets? Tell me they didn't ascend up into Heaven on international television, in front of my followers! Answer me now, Raul!"

"Yes sir, it is true." This time, Addon cast aside his human vesture as his true form emerged in all its potency, alternating from the deepest black to a deep dark red. He had never seen Addon this angry before, and concluded the strange occurrence meant he was angry, *really* angry.

"How dare he? How dare the Eternal perform such a miracle in front of my followers, my followers! They worship *me*, not him!"

"They do worship you, sir." The red began to fade as Addon slowly began to regain his composure.

"Your supporters sir, they follow *you*, they are completely in your power now, and your hold on them is absolute. Nothing that he can do now will change that." Raul wondered how he was doing. It appeared that his master was calming, but in his true form, there were no features visible, so it was impossible to read any reaction whatsoever. He soon had his answer.

"You know something, Raul?" he asked, as he began to slowly resume his human clothing once more. "This is precisely why I kept you alive after you learned my true nature, my true identity. You are the only hairless ape that I can count on to help me focus on the positives, to remind me of everything I have accomplished, to help me keep things in perspective."

"Thank you, sir…"

Raul suddenly stopped talking as he noticed a strange orange glow that seemed to emanate from outside of the White House. He looked out of the window and stared in awe at the wondrous site that lit up what had been a darkening sky. Addon turned and looked out the window as well, having noticed that something had suddenly captured Raul's attention. Addon found himself staring at an enormous fire in the sky. It was another flare, a monstrous flare, and this time it had been directed at Washington, D.C..

The enormous flare was unlike any before or after it, however. This one burned only the men and women that had turned their backs on the Most High, the ones that had taken the mark of the beast, following *him* instead of the Lord. All over the city, men and women cursed God because of the destructive flare. They cursed the only one that had the power to stop the plagues and to heal them; the sores they carried on their bodies, and the pain they endured because of the flare.

As if the suffering from the previous plagues had not been enough, all across Washington, D.C., power was knocked out as the enormous flare wreaked havoc on the city's electrical grid, causing cars, planes, anything running on electricity to suddenly fall silent before stopping altogether. Washington, D.C., the city which had for hundreds of years been a beacon of light for the entire world, the city that had fallen under the shadow of the beast, was now darkened completely as power went out all across the city. Not a single light powered by electricity remained on after the fifth angel poured out his bowl on the throne of the beast. Yet, despite the punishment inflicted upon the men and women of the great city, those afflicted by the plague still refused to repent for what they had done.

Addon sat back on his throne, sitting in the darkness, pondering the meaning of the most recent plague sent by the Eternal, along with the recent resurrection in Jerusalem. For the first time in a long time, Addon felt fear, concerned about what this meant. He would have to consult with his master as to how to proceed. For the first time he was beginning to feel his grip on the world loosening instead of tightening. He *was* losing control, and he could feel it. With the untimely appearance of the solar flare, and the subsequent loss of communications, he had also lost his ability to coordinate with governmental leaders all across the planet. As Raul returned with candles, Abe Addon sat staring out the window into the darkness. He was not looking forward to having the next discussion with his master. He knew how angry and uncontrollable he could get...

Addon's fear intensified as he came to grips with what was happening; the Eternal was bringing the reign of his master to an end. Nevertheless, he and his master would not go quietly into the night.

Chapter 46-The Sixth Angel

'The sixth angel poured out his bowl on the great river Euphrates, and its water was dried up to prepare the way for the kings from the East. Then I saw three evil spirits that looked like frogs; they came out of the mouth of the dragon, out of the mouth of the beast and out of the mouth of the false prophet. They are spirits of demons performing miraculous signs, and they go out to the kings of the whole world, to gather them for the battle on the great day of God Almighty.'
Revelations 19:12-14

I finished reading chapter nineteen in the book of Revelation and closed the Bible. I had been looking for clues as to what was going to happen. I kept asking myself why I should even try to guess what was coming next. After all, wasn't my role in the drama over? Besides, God had chosen *John* to be the last prophet, not me. As I considered it, I wondered whether after spending so much time with John, and living through the fulfillment of prophecy with him, I was probably just having a hard time letting go. Or maybe I continued to follow the prophecies because in some strange way, by continuing to follow the course of events, by continuing to watch as the prophecies in the book of Revelation were fulfilled, Sam and I were able to feel closer to his father, to stay more connected to him somehow. Perhaps it was also because I was curious, fascinated with what I had seen, and even more fascinated with what I expected yet to see.

Regardless, seeing John resurrected the way we did had affected Sam and I on a deep and profound level. I had anticipated seeing something miraculous, but what I ended up seeing had far exceeded any expectations I had. I had always been a believer, but seeing what happened to John, on top of all of the other signs and wonders, caused all of it to suddenly become profoundly real to me, in a way it hadn't been before.

I turned my attention back to the chapter with the sixth angel, pondering its meaning, and wondering whether or not it was indeed the next sign to watch for. It seemed to me that for the most part, the prophecy that the Lord had given to the apostle John was being fulfilled in roughly the same chronological order in which they appeared in the book. If that were the case, I would have to watch for anything relating to the Euphrates River, as well as anything relating to Abe Addon. If I understood the prophecy correctly, Addon would soon reveal *his* true identity to the world, along with the strange man, Faust, who seemed to fit the description of the false prophet to the tee, before the great battle that was to come.

About that time, Sam came into the room, shouting and hollering for me.

"Mom, you have to turn on the television, hurry!"

"What's going on, Sam?" I asked him as I reached for the remote control."

"You're not going to believe this, turn it on, quick!"

"What channel?" I asked.

"Any channel, Mom, now hurry!"

I turned on the television, curious as to what I would see. My jaw must have dropped as I watched; Sam looked at me and smiled.

"Wow, Sam, this is incredible."

"You're telling me! I was planning to watch the pre-game show for the playoff games. When I first saw it, I didn't expect it to amount to anything. But once I started channel surfing, I couldn't find anything else on any other channel!"

"Well look at that..."

We sat and stared at the television screen. I had never seen anything like it except in history books and even then, it was nothing like this. The aerial shot, taken from a helicopter, zoomed in and out to show the spectacle in as much detail as possible, while also preserving the sense of scope.

"Scientists are still speculating about what could have caused this incredible catastrophe to occur. The river, the entire Euphrates River, has suddenly and mysteriously disappeared, apparently drying up overnight. The dry riverbed was discovered early this morning, but it has only recently been made public knowledge. There has been considerable speculation whether what happened to the river could have been caused by a massive solar flare, like the one that just days ago knocked out electricity across Washington, D.C.

"The disappearance of the Euphrates River is only the most recent in a series of strange and bizarre events that have taken place all across the planet. More and more people are blaming the Christian God for these strange occurrences, suggesting that acts like these are the reason why we should all follow our beloved Abe Addon. Some of the wicked Christians that we spoke with, under the condition of anonymity of course due to the threat of execution, admit that the mysterious and supernatural disasters are the fulfillment of prophecies written in their holy book, the Bible.

"Whether this incredible occurrence is the result of their God, or some kind of unusual natural phenomenon that we still do not understand, it is the first time anything like this has ever been seen, much less recorded.

"On another note, we have just received word that President Addon will be holding an unscheduled press conference within the next hour or so, to address this and some of the other bizarre events that have taken place recently. For GNN news, this is Beth Kelly reporting."

Sam and I sat and looked at one another.

"Now what do you suppose *he's* up to?" I asked Sam.

"I don't know, Mom. Maybe he wants to address what happened with the Euphrates?" he answered.

"Not likely," I answered. "Caring for humanity is not one of his strong suits."

"Then what do you suppose the press conference will be about?"

"I don't know Sam, but I have a few ideas. I've been reading up on the prophecies in the book of Revelation. I suspect that from here on out, things are going to heat up a bit. I believe that what happened with your father is only the beginning, Sam. Whereas the Lord used him and Moe to help get the ball rolling, according to the prophecies in the book of Revelation, things are about to come to a head. If what I believe is true, soon, very soon, we will be face to face with the Lord Jesus Christ himself." I looked over at Sam, who I expected would be excited about the news. Instead, he was somewhat withdrawn, and sullen.

"Sam, what's wrong?" I asked, sitting down next to him and placing my arm around his neck.

"Mom, I'm only thirteen now. If the Lord Jesus comes back tomorrow, doesn't that mean that I will never grow up, and get married, and have children of my own?"

The question that came out of the mouth of my teenage son floored me. It was something that I had considered from time to time, ever since John first learned of his destiny. Nevertheless, I had never once considered the possibility that *Sam* would ask me that question. Having been a mother for thirteen years, I had learned that when your child asks a powerful question like this one, the last thing in the world that you want to do is answer it hastily. With John gone, Sam was all that I had left. The answer I gave him could affect him deeply. I made the decision that I would answer truthfully yet deliberately, and delicately.

I yearned to talk with another, more experienced adult, preferably someone considerably older and wiser than me. I considered reaching out to Doris, but after giving it some more thought, I decided to give her some space. She had not had the same reaction as Sam and I to the recent events concerning our husbands. Moe had been the only person that Doris had been close to for many years. She would come out of it, but it was going to take her some time.

I bowed my head for a moment, whispered a short prayer for support and guidance from the Lord, and looked up at Sam.

"Sam, honey, you're right. If the Lord does come again soon, and frankly I believe he will, then you will not grow up, get married, and have children of your own, at least I don't believe you will. But think of it this way, honey, neither will you have to worry about losing your job, making house payments, about getting sick, or seeing someone you love suffer, of any other of the endless list of unpleasant things that you would likely experience as an adult. In addition, what is an adult anyway but just an older kid? I don't think you will be missing out on as much as you might think. Besides all of this, you will know the joy of spending all eternity with the Lord himself, and with all of those you love and care about, and the endless others that you will meet in Heaven. Does that make sense?"

Does that make sense? It is one of those questions that a parent or most any leader will ask when someone is trying to get a point across or teach something but he or she is not sure how well they have done. This described exactly how I felt. I looked at Sam and I could tell that he was processing what I had just shared with him, tasting it, and swirling it around much like a wine connoisseur when tasting a new vintage.

"Yeah, Mom, I think it does. You're saying that while I might miss out on some of the neat stuff, like having my own family, the bad things I will also miss out on helps make up for it."

"Yes, that's right, Sam. Moreover, the joys that God has in mind for you are certain to be far, far, better than anything that you could even remotely hope for in this life, which has been corrupted, and twisted by sin for so long." I held my breath, hoping that my last response would be enough to give him the comfort and the peace that I wanted so badly for him to have.

"Thank you, Mom. You know what?"

"What, Honey?"

"You're the most awesome Mom in the whole world!"

"Thank you, Sam." I cupped his chin in the palms of my hands as I added, "Do you have any idea how much I love you, little man?"

"I love you too, Mom,"

Even as I began to relax, realizing that I had just dodged a bullet, I glanced at the television and saw Addon preparing to give his press conference. I turned up the volume.

"Good evening," he began. "As all of you know, there has been considerable discussion recently about the many disastrous events that have taken place around the world over the course of the last few years. There have indeed been many plagues that have come upon us, afflicting so many of those that worship me. There was the Wormwood asteroid that came from space and wrecked havoc on my people. Soon after the asteroid came the rivers of blood, the droughts, the solar flares, and so forth. In addition to all of this, I am told that there have also been some outlandish claims, particularly by the Christians, that I am some kind of evil character… I believe they refer to me as *the beast*. They claim I am some kind of monster, the demon Abaddon, mentioned in the book of Revelation.

"The truth is, there is a war coming soon, a war against a large and extremely powerful army, led by someone more powerful than you can imagine, that seeks my destruction, and the destruction of those of you that have followed me and taken the mark. Soon, very soon, I will be going out with my brethren, and with *my* master, to go out to all nations, recruiting as many as I can in our fight against our great and powerful common enemy. In order to accomplish this great task, I will need your help. I have come to help you prepare. It is time for me to tell you who I really am…"

Chapter 47-The Seventh Angel

They came from all over the world. Military experts, world leaders, and civilians from all walks of life. It was shocking to see how many nations which had at one time been the most bitter of enemies, had come together, all of them answering the call from Addon to begin assembling in Israel. We had begun seeing the men dressed in the military uniforms of countries from all around the world with growing frequency during the week following Addon's startling revelation. It was not just the men and women in uniform that we were seeing either. We saw endless numbers of planes, jets, tanks, trains, and missiles, continuing to pour into Jerusalem from all over the world. It soon became apparent that they were not staying in Jerusalem in large numbers... most of them were making their way to some location north of Jerusalem. The constant noise made day and night by the endless convoys made it nearly next to impossible to sleep, and we couldn't go more than five or ten minutes without feeling the ground shake underneath us as large columns of tanks passed through the neighborhood. Once again, several large pictures fell from the wall and crashed on the floor as a large column of tanks rumbled down the street in front of our house, shattering the pictures into hundreds of glass shards, all over our hardwood floor of the safe house. Having yearned for sunshine, Sam and I had moved upstairs, leaving the relative safety of the bunker below.

We tried to watch a movie on television, doing everything we could to ignore what was happening outside our home. We knew how the story would end so as difficult as it was, we just had to be patient. During one occasion, when the commotion was particularly noisy, I found myself turning the volume louder and louder in a no-win competition, as we attempted to drown out the noise of the war-machines outside. Even over our considerably loud home theater system, we listened as squadron after squadron of jets flew overhead, presumably running exercises in preparation for the great battle to come.

From my perspective, it all seemed so insane; watching the world's militaries mobilizing their most advanced technologies to fight alongside a demon in a vain and futile war against God Almighty, the creator of the universe himself.

Although there were no news reports covering it, I had heard rumors through friends, both in Jerusalem and back home, that there had been mass defections in the military and several attempted coups meant to topple Addon from his position of power. Since Addon had publicly acknowledged who and what he, his master, and his awful false prophet Faust, really were, there had surprisingly been far fewer defections than I had expected. Indeed, once there were no more pretenses about who and what Addon was, everyone had been forced to get off the fence and pick a side. Many had decided to fight against Addon once the truth became known, and had decided to follow Jesus Christ instead. Far more followed the beast, however. In retrospect I noted that the Lord himself had warned us, even while he still walked the Earth as a man, that the way that leads to destruction is wide and many would go there, while the way that leads to eternal life is narrow and that relatively few would find it. Once more, I witnessed the prophecies of the scriptures being fulfilled before my eyes.

The seventh angel poured out his bowl into the air, and out of the temple came a loud voice from the throne, saying, "It is done!" Then there came flashes of lightning, rumblings, peals of thunder and a severe earthquake. No earthquake like it has ever occurred since man has been on Earth, so tremendous was the quake. The great city split into three parts, and the cities of the nations collapsed. God remembered Babylon the Great and gave her the cup filled with the wine of the fury of his wrath. Every island fled away and the mountains could not be found. From the sky huge hailstones of about a hundred pounds each fell upon men. And they cursed God on account of the plague of hail, because the plague was so terrible. Revelation 16:17-21

The noise of war outside our front door grew louder and louder with each passing minute, as tanks, planes, and armies marched within earshot of our home. We were scared, and I longed for John's presence. I found I was missing him more and more as the situation deteriorated.

Suddenly, we heard a sound much louder than anything we had heard before. The noise sounded similar to the rumblings of the many tanks we had heard, but this was somehow much different. It sounded more like the crackling and rumbling of thunder, only much, much, louder. My first thought was that the war had somehow already started but as I looked outside and saw the incredible site in the skies, I knew it was something else.

Growing up I had seen a number of severe thunderstorms, called super cells, make their way from the western states into ours. I had experienced the countless tornado watches and warnings that came with the darkened skies, sometimes pitch black, that create the powerful twisters that cause such damage. Now, the skies I remembered from my youth paled in comparison with what I saw as I looked out of our front window. The clouds had turned the day into night, and for the first time I saw ferocious lightning lighting up the darkened skies. If there was such a darkness that could be *felt*, like the one that the Lord had sent upon Egypt during the time of Moses, than it must be something similar to what I was witnessing. I grew increasingly nervous as I witnessed the supernatural spectacle taking place outside of my window. Once more I took comfort in the knowledge that it was my Lord who was in charge of these great plagues and wonders, and that I was his child.

I watched on while yet another column of tanks passed in front of our house, and once again, the house began to shake. I could see by the expressions of the young men that poked their heads out of their tanks from time to time to have a look around, that they were terrified by the strange and unusual lightning that flashed with fury all around them. One tank passed by our home with a young man inside, clearly wearing the mark of the beast. He couldn't have been more than twenty-five. I noticed something flash in front of my eyes, just before something the size of a cannonball struck the front of the tank, leaving a huge dent and nearly crushing the tank itself. The terrified young man, who had just missed being struck by the object, scurried back inside of the tank. As I continued to watch, I began to see many more of the objects striking the tanks in rapid succession. They were beginning to fall rapidly and after only a few moments, one landed nearby and I was able to get a glimpse at what was assailing the column of tanks. They were by far the largest, most enormous hailstones I had ever seen or heard of. While I had heard of hailstones the size of softballs falling from particularly nasty storm systems in Texas and Oklahoma, these were closer to the size of basketballs. I estimated that each of the colossal hailstones must weigh at least one-hundred pounds. The veracity of the hailstones' assault on the tank column grew in intensity. On several of the tanks, the turrets were badly bent, or knocked completely off the tanks. Massive dents began to appear, and soon all of the tanks were, in one way or another, completely incapacitated.

A number of jets also raced to the ground, either with wings missing, engines dangling or gone, or with large, gaping holes in the wings or fuselage.

By the time the hailstones stopped falling from the sky, there was decimation everywhere, with tanks, jets, and buildings either in pieces or on fire. I turned on the television only to find that the assault I had witnessed in Jerusalem had been repeated all over the world. I watched for another hour as the sun set in the distance, and soon, Addon appeared at a news conference. I could not help but notice that although he had revealed his true identity to the world, he *had not* revealed his true *appearance*. He was holding out his hand, shaking it as he looked towards the sky.

"...so if that's the best that the Christian God can do, then..." Addon stopped talking because he was interrupted by the sudden and violent shaking that had started mid-sentence. The camera was shaking violently, the screen was full of frantically moving feet and legs, as the cameraman had either dropped the camera or been knocked unconscious. I was surprised to find that my own home was shaking as well, though nowhere near as violently as what I had seen elsewhere on television. After several minutes, the violent shaking began to subside. The television screen went black for several minutes, and I noticed for the first time that there was screaming and wailing coming from outside. I heard police cars and fire trucks with sirens whirring all over Jerusalem. I got up from the sofa and walked with Sam over to the window. We saw flames rising from buildings all across Jerusalem. It was difficult to see much of the city from our vantage point.

We ran back to the television and changed over to a local station. The anchor was trying desperately to remain calm, and keep everyone around her calm.

"We are now going live, to Joel, who is airborne even as we speak, flying in a helicopter somewhere over the city. Joel, are you there?"

"We're here, Wendy. We are just now flying over the city of Jerusalem for the first time, even as we speak. We see houses burning and collapsed buildings. Much of the city wall in the old city itself has been shaken into rubble. We... oh no! This is just too much, it is truly unbelievable...it is the most incredible, impossible thing that I have ever seen. The city, our city, Jerusalem, has been...divided...for lack of a better word, by this powerful earthquake, into pieces...into sections. This is horrible, horrible. Jerusalem has been burned, destroyed, and broken to pieces countless times throughout it's over one-thousand year history,

Wendy…but nothing, and I mean nothing like this has ever happened throughout the history of our beloved city…we…" <click>. The picture went momentarily blank, before once more a picture with the news anchors reappeared.

"It appears that we have lost Joel for the moment. Well, you heard it. As incredible as it sounds, Jerusalem has seen massive devastation from one of the most powerful and most bizarre earthquakes that we have even seen. In addition to the incredible devastation here in Jerusalem, however, we have reports coming in from all over the world about damage caused by similar earthquakes. It appears this is a worldwide event.

"The quake here in Israel has physically divided our beloved city into three geographical sections. Hold on…wow. I have just been told that we now have some footage being made available to us by our parent company. Ladies and gentlemen, the worldwide damage has been catastrophic. These appear to be the most powerful earthquakes to have struck the planet in recorded human history. The cataclysmic damage is said to be off the scale, with cost estimates starting in the tens of trillions of dollars, more than what most nations take in annually. The loss of life has also been reported to be horrendous, as cities all over the world have been reduced to nothing but piles of debris. Okay, we're ready…here is some of the recent footage taken across the world…'"

Images of the widespread destruction began to appear on the screen. "In London iconic structures like Big Ben, London Bridge, and Buckingham Palace, have been destroyed. Across Russia, famous structures like St. Basil's Cathedral and the Kremlin have been decimated, and in the United States, the Golden Gate Bridge in San Francisco, and the Washington Monument in Washington, D.C. have both collapsed.

"All across the planet people everywhere, men, women, and children, those of us that have taken the mark of the beast, curse the Eternal on account of the awful pain and suffering that we have all endured…'" <click>

I had seen and heard enough. I now knew with certainty that Sam and I would soon be reunited with the man that I had known and loved for most of my life, and I knew that we would experience the joy of living with our Heavenly Father in his kingdom.

I looked down at my son, Samuel March, as we sat quietly together, and smiled.

"I'm scared, Mom," he said. "What's going to happen? Is everything going to be okay?" he asked.

"Oh yes, Sam, there is no need to be frightened. You saw what happened with your father; how the Lord miraculously raised him from the dead, and then called him up into Heaven. We will be with him before long, and we will meet our Lord Jesus Christ face-to-face! I'd say everything will soon be far more than just fine, Sam, it will be wonderful!"

Chapter 48- Rider on the White Horse

I now saw the Earth from a perspective I had never seen it from before. I saw images of the Earth as if I were standing on a cloud looking down.

The beast had assembled his armies to do battle with the armies of the Lord. I could see the armed forces of the Earth gathering together for a great and terrible battle. Terrible plagues struck the Earth while I watched. I saw the fire, the hailstones, and the earthquake that eventually split Jerusalem into sections.

Then, I saw the Lord himself, arrayed for battle, sitting atop a great white horse, his eyes like a flame of fire. He led enormous armies, which followed him riding upon white horses, all of whom were clothed in white linen. The beast and the vast armies gathered together from around the world went to war against the Lamb, and his army, in a fierce battle. To their eternal loss and shame, much of humanity had chosen to follow the beast, his false prophet, and the dragon that gave him power, rather than the Lord, even until the end.

The beast. It seemed incredible that he had dared to openly challenge the Lamb of God. Taking the lives of two prophets was one thing, but warring with the Lord of Hosts?

Having successfully deceived humanity until his hold on them was complete, Addon had rallied the nations of the world in a hopeless battle that he knew he they could not possibly win. He knew his days were growing short; indeed, they were nearly over, and he was determined to take as much of humanity as he was able to with him, into his everlasting punishment.

The battle began as the armies of the Lord engaged the armies of the beast, and the dragon, but it was short-lived, as the Lord and his armies quickly and easily overcame the beast and his followers. I watched on with no small satisfaction as I saw the power of Addon and his armies crumble before the Rider on the White Horse, and I rejoiced greatly in the victory of the Lamb over the beast.

Abe Addon, the beast, Abaddon the destroyer, the one who deceived humanity, leading throngs of men and women to worship *him* instead of God, was forever defeated. The beast, one of the fallen angels who had rebelled against the Lord, the one who had murdered us, the Lord's two witnesses, along with many others, was cast into the lake of fire as his eternal punishment. His companion, the one that had helped him deceive the nations, the one known as Simon Faust, the false prophet, was thrown in with him, along with all who worshipped the beast and took his mark, where together they would be tormented day and night for all eternity.

Having taken care of the beast and his armies, the Lord then turned his attention towards the beast's master, the dragon. He sent an angel with a key to the bottomless pit and a great chain, which he used to bind the dragon and imprison him for a thousand years.

Those who died for the witness of Jesus, for the word of God, and all who refused the mark of the beast, lived and reigned with the Lord during that time. After the thousand years were over, however, the dragon was released one final time from his prison, and set out to trouble the nations. This time however, God sent fire from Heaven to devour his armies, achieving the final victory over the one whose very name means "the Accuser," the one who had troubled humanity from the very beginning. His time was over and his punishment at hand. The devil was cast into the Lake of Fire where the beast and the false prophet are, to be tormented day and night forever.

***

At last, the saga of man's time on the Earth, along with all of his suffering and his pain, was over. The great day of final judgment of the Lord had arrived. Every human being would now stand before the Lord of all the Earth to face the Creator. Those with their names written in the Lamb's Book of Life would live with the Lord for all eternity, while those whose names were not written there, would be cast into the lake of fire, where the beast, the false prophet, and the dragon are.

"And I saw a new heaven and a new Earth: for the first heaven and the first Earth were passed away; and there was no more sea. And I John saw the holy city, new Jerusalem, coming down from God out of heaven, prepared as a bride adorned for her husband. And I heard a great voice out of heaven saying, Behold, the tabernacle of God is with men, and he will dwell with them, and they shall be his people, and God himself shall be with them, and be their God. And

God shall wipe away all tears from their eyes; and there shall be no more death, neither sorrow, nor crying, neither shall there be any more pain: for the former things are passed away…" Revelation 21: 1-8

Epilogue

"Eye has not seen, nor ear heard, neither have entered into the heart of man, the things which God has prepared for them that love him." 1 Corinthians: 2-9

The struggle with sin, death, and the devil is over now, for all of humanity. The old world has passed away; it's now time for the new.

Lara and Sam are here with me now, along with Moe and Doris. Our reunion was a time of tremendous rejoicing.

I don't know exactly how I will spend eternity with an all-knowing, all-powerful, Omni-present, loving, and merciful God, but I certainly am going to enjoy leaving the old life behind, and finding out.

Life on Earth is, after all, only a brief stop on the road to eternity.

 Jeff Horton was born in North Dakota, the youngest son of a career Air Force Master sergeant, where he spent the first four years of his life before moving to North Carolina. A somewhat voracious reader growing up, he read everything from comic books to The Bible, including stories by many popular authors such as Sir Arthur Conan Doyle, H. G. Wells, Jules Verne, Edgar Rice Burroughs, Michael Crichton, Tom Clancy, C. S. Lewis, and J. R. R. Tolkien.

Jeff Horton's novel, The Great Collapse, a story about the coming of the pulse and the end of civilization, was published in 2010. He is a member of the North Carolina Writers Network.

His next novel, The Dark Age, the sequel to The Great Collapse was published in July 2011.

When he's not penning his next novel, he enjoys reading, going to church, and spending time with his family.